Unholy Murder

Felicity Pulman

momentum

First published by Random House Australia in 2006
This edition published in 2015 by Momentum
Pan Macmillan Australia Pty Ltd
1 Market Street, Sydney 2000

A CIP record for this book is available at the National Library of Australia

Unholy Murder: The Janna Chronicles 3

EPUB format: 9781760300050
Mobi format: 9781760300135
Print on Demand format: 9781760300142

Cover design by Raewyn Brack
Edited by Kylie Mason
Proofread by Laurie Ormond

Macmillan Digital Australia: www.macmillandigital.com.au

To report a typographical error, please visit momentumbooks.com.au/contact/

Visit www.momentumbooks.com.au to read more about all our books and to buy
books online. You will also find features, author interviews and news of any
author events.

Felicity Pulman is the award-winning author of numerous novels for children and teenagers, including *A Ring Through Time*, the Shalott trilogy, and *Ghost Boy*, which is now in pre-production for a movie. *I, Morgana* was her first novel for adults, inspired by her early research into Arthurian legend and her journey to the UK and France to 'walk in the footsteps of her characters' before writing the Shalott trilogy— something she loves to do. Her interest in crime and history inspired her medieval crime series, The Janna Mysteries, now repackaged as The Janna Chronicles.

Recently awarded the inaugural Di Yerbury writer's fellowship, Felicity will spend several months in the UK in 2015 researching and writing the sequel to *I, Morgana*. She has many years experience talking about researching and writing her novels both in schools and to adults, as well as conducting creative writing workshops in a wide variety of genres. Felicity is married, with two children and five grandchildren, all of whom help to keep her young and technosavvy—sort of! You can find out more about Felicity on her website and blog: www.felicitypulman.com.au or on Facebook.

Also by Felicity Pulman

Chapter 1

The abbey's great gate clanged shut, its metal bars vibrating with the impact. The sound held an awful finality. Janna shuddered as she realized what she had done. True, she'd found sanctuary from those who wished her harm—most especially the lord whose secret she held close to her heart—but in doing so, she had cut herself off from the world, and from all those whom she'd come to love. But Janna knew she had no choice. While she lived, her knowledge, her very presence, threatened the lord's status and the comfort to which he had become accustomed. There was no place other than Wiltune Abbey for her to hide in safety.

She looked through the darkness to where Godric still lingered beyond the gate. In the light of the flares that lit the gatehouse, she could read the misery on his face, a misery she was sure was reflected in her own expression. More than anything, she wished she was free to follow her chosen path: her quest to find her unknown father and seek justice for the death of her mother. Instead, she was trapped within a convent of women who had given their hearts and minds to the Lord Jesus Christ. Janna couldn't understand why they'd want to do that, how they could bear to shut themselves away, just as she herself was about to be shut away.

"Janna!" Godric was beckoning her to come back to him.

She turned away, knowing that if she went back to Godric now she might not have the will to leave him again. But she couldn't change her mind; she could not return to the outside world until her mission was accomplished and she was safe. Her only source of comfort was that she'd taken time along the journey to tell Godric, in confidence, everything that had led up to the death of her mother and the real reason she'd run away rather than let anyone know she was still alive. He, more than anyone, deserved an explanation for her behavior. Although her revelations had so shocked him that, at first, he could hardly speak, the fact that he'd drawn her close, and given her a lingering kiss, told her that she was truly forgiven. More, he understood her decision now, even though he wasn't happy about it.

"Janna!" he called again.

Despite her resolve, she couldn't resist one last look over her shoulder.

"I forgot to give you these." He held out his hand and she saw the glint of silver in the hollow of his palm. "Take the coins!" he said. "Take them all. Thanks to my lord Hugh's gift of land and my new service to him, I have no need of any further reward, but you still have your way to make in the world."

Tempted, Janna hesitated. She could not afford to be proud. Apart from the few objects secreted in her purse, which held value only for her, she had nothing to offer the abbey in return for food and shelter. The coins would help to buy her a way in, and smooth her path when, later, she took to the road in search of her father.

Turning her back on the ill-tempered and sleepy nun who had admitted her and was now waiting to lead her to an audience with the abbess, Janna hurried to Godric. "Are you quite sure you want me to take it all?" she asked, as she opened the drawstring of her purse.

"Of course." He carefully poured in the coins. Janna beamed her gratitude.

"Ahem." The sound of a throat being ostentatiously cleared warned her that the porteress had retraced her steps, and that they were being watched.

"God be with you." She touched Godric's hand one last time. "And good luck. Take care of yourself, and thank you for everything." She had so many reasons to be grateful to Godric; he had come to her aid on so many different occasions. "Mayhap we'll meet again one day?" She tried to sound hopeful but knew she was not succeeding.

"*Ahem!*" This time the throat-clearing was an ultimatum.

Godric ignored the vigilant nun. "Be sure that I will come to you if ever you call, wherever you may be!" He seized hold of Janna's hand through the bars, raised it to his lips and kissed it. "You know I would not leave you, Janna, not by choice. Not ever!"

"I know." Reluctantly, Janna disengaged her hand from his. "I know." She swallowed hard over the lump of misery that had lodged in her throat, and hastily turned away. If only they could wed, if she could trust in his protection, she might have begged the porteress to unlock the gate and let her free to go to him. But she knew that even Godric, who would give his life for her, could not protect her at this time, nor could he help her to fulfil her quest. This was something she must do, and do alone. In truth, she preferred it this way, for she was not ready yet to commit her life, or her heart, to anyone's keeping save her own. All the same, she felt a great dread for the future. Following her chosen path would take all her courage and strength. With reluctant steps, she returned to the porteress, who scowled at her. "I can't think why you've come here," the nun muttered, "dressed up in men's clothes, and carrying on with that young man right here at the abbey gate. Who do you think you are?" She clucked her disapproval. "If you had not come from Dame Alice's nephew and with a message for the abbess, be sure I would never have admitted you."

"I am grateful that you did, mistress," Janna murmured.

"Sister!" the nun snapped. "My name is Sister Brigid."

"And my name is Johanna." Silence met Janna's offer of friendship. With lips clamped into a disapproving line, the nun led Janna across an open yard to a building set on one side of the entrance to the church. She walked through a small parlor and rapped on a door. Together, she and Janna waited for an invitation to enter.

"Come in." The voice sounded weary, and rather impatient. Curious in spite of her low spirits, Janna followed Sister Brigid into the private quarters of the abbess.

The receiving room was large and lit by torches held in sconces on the walls. Richly embroidered tapestries hung between them, their bright colors glowing in the light. A fat wax candle sat in a silver candlestick on a table illuminating a scroll of parchment. Janna stared in puzzlement, for the symbols inscribed on it looked different from those in the letter written by her father. These were set in long columns and divided by lines. She could not make sense of them at all. Her gaze moved on around the room. A gold cross hung above a small altar, exquisitely chased and decorated with colored gemstones. Stairs to one side led perhaps to quarters for the nobility, even royalty, who were rumored to stay here from time to time. There were several stools with fat cushions to soften hard wooden seats, while the box bed Janna glimpsed through an open door contained a thick mattress and was piled with more cushions plumped down on a warm, woolen covering. For certes, the abbess was living in great comfort and style. She wondered if the sisters of the abbey lived in the same comfort as their abbess.

Fascinated, Janna dragged her gaze back to one of the wealthiest and most powerful women in the land. Her mother had once told her that Wiltune was one of the largest abbeys in England, with vast estates, mills and other resources spread over several shires. *"The abbess is the king's tenant-in-chief. She holds the entire barony in return for the service of five knights, should the king call for them in times of war,"* Eadgyth had said. Janna wished she'd thought to question how the abbess managed to provide five knights, living as she did in a house full of women.

At their entry, the abbess had risen from her work. She scowled suspiciously at Janna. "Who is this ruffian, and what do you mean by disturbing my peace so late at night?" She spoke in Norman French, addressing the question to Sister Brigid. It was clear she didn't expect Janna to understand her. Janna bent her head, thinking it wise to pretend that the abbess was right.

"She says she's really a young woman, and she bears a message from the lord Hugh, nephew to Dame Alice of Babestoche Manor. I would not have admitted her else." Sister Brigid's face pinched into a disapproving frown. "She was accompanied by a youth, and he kissed her hand!" There couldn't have been more venom in the nun's voice if she'd accused Janna of dancing on the altar of Christ. She handed over the brief message signed with Hugh's seal to the abbess, who perused it silently.

"Johanna?" she said then, reverting to the Saxon language. She sat down once more, leaving Janna standing in front of her. "Daughter of the *wortwyf*, Eadgyth?"

Janna knew a moment's panic before she managed a reluctant reply. "Yes, Sister, uh…um…"

"Mother Abbess. We were told you were dead, Johanna. The lord Hugh begged us to say a Mass for your soul." The abbess's expression had darkened into a thunderous frown. A sinking feeling told Janna what was coming next. She wished she'd thought to ask Hugh not to mention her name so that she could, once again, invent for herself a new identity. Now it was too late. She braced herself.

"Out of the goodness of my heart, in Christ's holy name, and in spite of your mother's disgrace, I gave her the piece of land and the cot that was your home—and you repaid my generosity by burning it to the ground!" The abbess was practically spitting with rage.

"No! No, I did not." But Janna's protest went unheeded.

"You might not have cared to stay on there after your mother died, but there are many others who would have been grateful for that land and cot. How dare you destroy what I gave you so generously!"

Generously? Janna opened her mouth to defend herself, then closed it again. It was useless to point out to this self-righteous, miserly old dragon that when Eadgyth had first moved in, the land had been rough and untilled and the cottage a tumbledown wreck. The midwife Aldith had told Janna how hard her mother had worked to repair the cot, and to turn the surrounding wilderness into the garden that had sustained them both. She and her mother had always worked hard, and had often gone hungry in order to pay the rent demanded by this greedy abbess, handing over silver coins and produce from their garden that they could ill-afford. The unsaid words almost choked Janna, yet she knew the abbess would not believe that it was the villagers who'd burned down her cot and who'd almost succeeded in burning her alive at the same time; not unless Janna told her all of the story, and perhaps not even then. But she could not speak up, she could not tell the truth, for there was far too much at stake, and so she stayed silent.

"Not only that, but you led everyone to believe you had died in the fire! You have even disguised yourself as a youth."

The abbess's tone was full of contempt. "Was that so you did not have to pay for the destruction of my property, and heriot for your mother's death?"

"I—No! No, that's not true."

"The girl has coins to pay, Mother," Sister Brigid piped up unexpectedly. "I saw her *companion* pour silver into her purse." She flashed a spiteful glance at Janna. It was clear she thought the worst of her relationship with Godric. The abbess stopped abruptly. She ran her tongue over her top lip as she considered the possibilities. "The lord Hugh has asked me to give you shelter, and so I will," she conceded, "but in turn I demand recompense for the cot and garden you have destroyed by your wanton action. And as your overlord, I also claim heriot for the death of your mother."

"That's not f—" Janna's outrage was stifled as Sister Brigid's hand clamped hard on her arm.

"It is the custom," the nun reminded her.

With an effort, Janna smoothed her face into calm acceptance, but inside she raged at the injustice. No wonder Wiltune was such a wealthy abbey! The midwife's account of the abbess's treatment of her mother should have warned her how avaricious and grasping she was. Janna was quite sure that Dame Alice had stayed true to her word that she herself would pay the heriot due, but it seemed the abbess did not scruple to be paid twice. Angrily, Janna untied her purse, pulled out a handful of silver and dropped it on the table in front of her. The abbess reached for it with eager hands.

"There is also the matter of your food and shelter," she said, not taking her eyes from Janna's purse.

Seething, Janna pulled out the last of the coins. "This is all I have, Mother Abbess," she said. "The mementos I have left are for my own comfort, and are of value only to me." She patted her purse, hearing the comforting crump of her father's letter, feeling the lumpy trinkets, tokens of his affection for her mother; feeling, too, the small figurine she had found in the forest. On no account would she hand over any of her treasures. She would rather leave the abbey and face an uncertain and dangerous future than part with any one of them. She folded her fingers around the small figurine, taking comfort from the carved shape of the mother and her child. It gave her the strength to face the abbess and wait for her future to be spelled out.

"Very well," the abbess said grudgingly. She considered a moment and then said, "Harvest is about to begin, and extra hands are needed. You may stay so long as you are prepared to help in the fields, and do not disrupt the life of the abbey. We lead a simple life here, a life of contemplation of God and his mysteries. There is no place for those who do not believe in Him. Do you love the Lord God and His Son, Jesus Christ?"

Faced with such an unexpected demand, Janna hesitated. She could lie and say yes. It would smooth her path and make her life a whole lot easier. Or she could be honest and say no. The one and only time she'd ever been into a church, Eadgyth had dragged her out in a rage against the priest's preaching. She'd railed against him, calling him a narrow-minded bigot, an opinion Janna had shared, although in the end her mother's actions had helped persuade the villagers to turn against them. She could not tell the abbess "Yes," for it was not true. But nor could she say "No," for then she would be thrown out of the abbey, left to the mercy of those who wished her harm. Even worse, she would lose her only chance of finding out more about her mother and, more importantly, learning how to read and to write so that she could make sense of her father's letter. In that lay her salvation, the answer to all her hopes: the secret of her father, of her own heritage, and the chance of bringing to justice the man responsible for the murder of her mother.

"Well?" the abbess demanded impatiently.

"I am here because I don't know Him," Janna said slowly, sticking to the truth as closely as she could. "I am here to learn."

"Hmph." The abbess gave her a narrow look full of suspicion. "You may stay here as a lay sister, for the moment. I am not prepared to accept you as a postulant in our convent. For one thing, you have no dowry." Her eyes rested on the pile of silver coins on the table in front of her. She looked up then and had the grace to look slightly ashamed. "I will not accept you into our community until you have proved yourself fit to serve the Lord," she amended. "You may live and work with our lay sisters. They tend the garden, do the cooking, keep the abbey clean and help out in the fields when necessary, leaving my sisters free to say their prayers, to worship the Lord, engage in contemplation, or keep busy with more important tasks on the Lord's behalf. Be sure that I will keep close watch on you to ascertain if you are worthy of my trust."

"Thank you, Mother Abbess." The words stuck in Janna's throat. She bowed her head so that the abbess could not see her anger and dismay. *I don't have to stay here forever, just until my mission is complete*, she reminded herself silently, taking some comfort from the fact that being locked within the walls of the abbey was not a life sentence.

"That will be all. It is very late, almost time for the midnight office, and I still have my accounts to reckon." The abbess turned to the porteress. "Take Johanna to the lay sisters' dorter, Sister Brigid." She fixed Janna with a steely gaze. "You will attend the Harvest Mass tomorrow morning with the lay sisters and our visitors. Sister Grace will speak to you afterward about your duties while you are here. I expect you to work hard and earn your keep." She turned back to her papers, dismissing Janna and Sister Brigid with a flick of her hand.

Janna bobbed a curtsy and followed Sister Brigid back out across the courtyard toward the gatehouse. Her eyes were drawn to the flare lighting the gate, but there was no sign, now, of Godric. She felt abandoned, bereft, as she stared at the empty place where once he had stood.

"This is where you will sleep, above the undercroft." Sister Brigid mounted a flight of steps and flung open a door. Janna squinted into the long, dark room, barely able to make out the humped shapes of the sleepers on their pallets. "Tonight you may sleep in the clothes you wear." She paused to give an outraged sniff. "We shall find you more appropriate apparel tomorrow." She waved Janna into the room and shut the door behind her, cutting off what little light had shone through from the starry night outside.

Left alone, Janna stood still for a few moments until her eyes became accustomed to the darkness. Now she could make out the sleeping figures once more. She moved cautiously as she looked about for a spare pallet on which to sleep. There was none. Nor had she been offered any refreshment. It seemed that Wiltune's famed hospitality was reserved only for those with the coins to pay for it. The thought came to Janna that she'd just handed over silver enough to the abbess to pay for a banquet every night for the month to come. No matter. She was thirsty after her journey, but not hungry; she was too distressed for that.

She was just settling into a space, resigning herself to sleeping the night on the rushes covering the wooden floor, when she heard a quiet hiss. Startled, she looked around for the source of the sound, and saw a pale hand beckoning her. Curious, she rose and walked toward it. The hand was attached to a young woman. Janna could just make out the pale moon shape of her face and the gleam of her eyes in the darkness.

"My name's Agnes," the hisser whispered. "Come, sleep beside me. My pallet is thin and has many lumps in it, but it is large enough for both of us if we lie very still." She shifted across to make room for Janna, who subsided gratefully.

"My name is Johanna, but I'm usually called Janna," she whispered in return. "Do not let these men's clothes trouble you," she added hastily, as she saw her companion peer more closely at her. "I really am a maid, but it's a long story. I'll tell it to you in the morning."

"Be quiet over there," a sharp voice commanded. "Some of us are trying to get some sleep."

Agnes patted Janna's arm. "Don't mind her," she whispered. "She's like a gnat. Always whining."

Janna grinned in the darkness, her spirits lifted by the young woman's show of friendship. "Thank you," she whispered, and lay down to compose herself for sleep. She felt a little awkward lying in such close proximity to a stranger. Sharing a pallet reminded her of her life with her mother, when they had shared everything. Janna felt a shaft of pain at the memory of Eadgyth. It was quickly followed by hot annoyance; she'd been so intimidated by the abbess that she'd neglected to ask for information about her mother. Eadgyth might well have had to give an account of her misfortune to the abbess in order to win even such a derelict cottage as had been given to her. What might the abbess have told her, if only she'd had the wit to ask? *Your mother's disgrace.* The abbess's words echoed in Janna's mind. A sinking feeling told her that she'd missed a golden opportunity to find out what she wished to know. It was unlikely she'd be granted another audience, and even if she was, the abbess obviously held Eadgyth in such contempt it was doubtful she'd willingly pass on any information at all. Nevertheless, Janna determined to question her if another opportunity arose. The more she could find out about her mother's circumstances, and in particular where her mother had come from, the more it might help her find her father.

"Why have you come to the abbey? Where's your home?" Agnes's whisper broke into her thoughts.

Home! Janna's heart twisted with grief. Fighting the urge to confide her misery to Agnes, she said only, "My mother and I lived not far from here, in a small cot beside Gravelinges forest. But—but she died and I was forced to flee." That much was already known by the abbess, so there was no point in telling lies about it.

"But why come here? Do you have a calling?"

"No." Janna hoped it was safe to tell this truth at least. "I know little of the Christian faith, and even less about life in an abbey," she admitted. "Will you help me, please? What am I supposed to do?"

"Observe the Rule of St Benedict. You have to take a vow of poverty, chastity and, most important of all, obedience," Agnes said promptly. "And you have to confess if you're not. Obedient, that is. Or if you do anything else wrong."

"Like what?"

Agnes gave a small huff of sour amusement. "Just about everything! Even if you don't know whether you've done a wrong thing, you can be sure someone will have seen you and they'll report you at chapter. Then you'll be punished. The punishment's even worse if you haven't admitted your fault, because it means you've shown the Sin of Pride, or the Sin of Forgetfulness, or the Sin of Something or Other. The prioress and the priest can always find faults and sins to be punished."

"And then what happens?" Janna was beginning to feel more and more depressed by the minute.

"You have to do penance. You get to say a whole lot of *Aves* and *Paternosters,* or you go without meals or lose privileges, or you have to work extra hard and put in extra-long hours. But we do that anyway. They call us 'lay sisters,' but we're actually servants here. We do all the hard, dirty jobs that the nuns won't do for themselves because they're too busy with what they call the 'work of God,' *opus Dei*. But the lay sisters work for God too, not just the nuns."

As the dreadful future she'd chosen was laid out before her, Janna fell into a dismayed silence. Then a thought revived her flagging spirits somewhat. "It can't be that bad," she said. "Being a nun is a chosen profession for many women, surely?"

"For those who can't get husbands," Agnes said gloomily.

"Then why are you here?"

"Because of this." Agnes reached out into the darkness for Janna's hand. She grasped it and held it to her face, smoothing Janna's palm and fingers across her right cheek. Janna's first instinct was to pull her hand away as she felt the rough scar tissue, but she forced herself to keep tracing the terrible wound that ran from Agnes's eye right down to her chin. "What happened to you?" she whispered, appalled.

"Fire. I crawled too close to our hearth as a child, and my hair caught alight. My shoulder was burned as well as my face." Agnes's voice sounded unbearably sad. "I was like to die, so my mother brought me here and begged the infirmarian to take care of me, and so she has. I am fortunate to be alive. And I have made my life here. Sometimes I think I would like to wed, and to bear children, but who would have me as I am?"

Janna hesitated, unsure how to answer, then said, "Burns leave terrible scars, I know. But there are salves to relieve their pain. If you wish, I can make you such a one."

"That's kind of you, Janna." Agnes sounded surprised. "But there is no need for your trouble. Sister Anne still takes care of me. She is our infirmarian and she has given me an ointment to rub on my skin every night, to soothe it and keep it soft. She's very kind to me, and she's a very skillful healer. Her medicaments have helped us all."

Sister Anne. Janna made a note of the name. If she could impress the nun with her knowledge of the herbal lore that

Eadgyth had taught her, she might well improve her lot while she was here; ease the burden of living in an abbey, the burden that had been spelled out so clearly by Agnes.

"God be with you tonight, Janna. Sleep well." Agnes turned over with a sigh, and settled onto her half of the straw pallet. Janna stared up into the darkness. Her eyes pricked and burned with tiredness, but her brain buzzed with voices, conversations and images from the day. So much had happened, from making up her quarrel with Godric, to finding the lost child and then being recognized by the lord of the manor and having to flee for her life. The abbess's stern face and harsh words came into Janna's mind. They were partly tempered by the friendliness of Agnes, and the news of a kind infirmarian.

Janna turned on her side and tried to get comfortable on the lumpy pallet. It scratched and tickled, but it was still much better than sleeping on rushes and a wooden floor, she told herself as she wriggled and squirmed in an effort to smooth out some of the bumps. Agnes stirred and murmured something unintelligible. Not wanting to disturb her, Janna forced herself to lie still. This, then, was to be her life: obedience or punishment. It wasn't much to look forward to. It wasn't much at all.

Chapter 2

Janna awoke with a start, heart pounding as she listened to the insistent tolling of a bell. For a moment she thought she was back at the manor farm, listening to the bell that had tolled repeatedly after Hamo disappeared, calling the lost child home.

Then she remembered where she was, and her spirits sank even lower. She sat up and looked across at Agnes. Even though her touch had warned her what to expect, still the sight of the girl's disfigurement in the daylight made her catch her breath with startled pity. Agnes's right eye was half-closed from the injury, the skin above and below a crisscrossed mass of rough red scars. The whole side of her face was affected. Too late, Janna tried to conceal her shock, but Agnes's eyes had opened, and she had seen.

"It's really bad, isn't it?" she whispered.

Janna bit her lip. Of course there would be no looking glass here in the abbey, no way for Agnes to see the extent of the damage unless she caught a glimpse of herself in some piece of polished metal, or the still surface of a pond. But her own touch must tell her the worst of it. Yet the proud tilt of Agnes's head warned Janna that her pity would not be welcome.

"I think anyone coming to know you would soon see only your kindness and your sense of humor," she said awkwardly.

Agnes flashed a grateful grin. "It's a Sin of Pride even to be asking!" she muttered. "Don't tell on me, will you?"

"Only if you promise not to tell on me—and I'll wager there'll be far more to tell about me than I could ever tell about you."

"That's another sin to be confessed," Agnes said promptly. "We never, ever make wagers in the house of God."

Janna pulled a face, and Agnes's grin grew broader. "Sister Grace is the novice mistress," she said. "She's also in charge of discipline among the lay sisters. She's quite fair, really, and a good teacher, but I'm sure her brain is crammed tight with all that learning and so I try not to bother her with things she doesn't need to know."

"Like sins, you mean?"

"Exactly. But we'll have something else to confess unless we hurry." Agnes jumped up and pulled a black gown over the tunic in which she'd slept. "It's time for the special Mass to mark the beginning of the harvest," she said, as she picked up the wimple laid neatly beside her pallet. "Lateness is one of the great sins, along with running, so we can't hasten to the church either. Nor can we shout, skip or sing. Oh, and there's also anger, bearing a grudge, causing friction, telling lies, being greedy, breaking silence, impure thoughts and desires, deceit, stubbornness—"

"Stop!" Janna clapped her hands over her ears.

The lay sister's mouth curved up in a wide smile. "I'll take you first to the reredorter," she said, and hastily tucked a stray lock of hair into the concealing folds of her wimple.

Reredorter? Janna followed her guide. Her question was soon answered, and she was glad of the chance to relieve herself, and also to visit the lavatorium to wash away the dust and grime from her journey.

"Hurry!" Agnes urged, as Janna dried her face and hands on one of the rough napkins beside the long basin. The lay sister led the way across the open yard. Janna noticed that she carried herself straight, and that she favored her right arm. Agnes had drawn her veil down low over her forehead and had draped the soft folds of the wimple about her cheeks so that they were almost covered. To make doubly sure no-one had a chance to stare at her scars, she walked with her head bent, risking only swift glances up to check for obstacles.

It had been too dark to see a great deal the night before, and now Janna looked about with interest, noting the pilgrims in their wide-brimmed hats, the wealthy travelers and their wives, and the beggars, the blind and the lame emerging from their various quarters set about the courtyard. Lay servants streamed through the gate; all were approaching a pair of carved wooden doors that opened into the great stone church. Janna looked about for the abbess and her nuns, but they were nowhere to be seen. She frowned as she tried to puzzle it all out.

The abbess had worn a black veil with a silver cross embroidered at its center, and a long black habit with wide sleeves, and bound at her waist with a girdle. Underneath her veil was a white wimple, which sat in folds around her face and neck. The porteress had been dressed in similar fashion, although her garments were not of the same fine quality. Here, the lay sisters like Agnes wore white wimples and veils of rough homespun, while the lay servants coming through the gates wore the same smocks and breeches as the villeins on the manor farm from which Janna had come. She tugged on Agnes's sleeve to get her attention.

"Where is everybody?"

"Who?"

"The abbess, and the other nuns…" Janna waved her hand around the courtyard to indicate their absence.

"We're in the public part of the abbey grounds, and we'll stay in the nave for the mass. The convent is through there." Agnes indicated a narrow passage. "The nuns enter the church from their own part of the convent and sit together in the choir stalls."

"Don't we see them or have anything to do with them?" Janna felt a vast disappointment at having her plans thus shattered just when the next step had seemed so close.

"Yes, we do. Shh." Agnes laid a cautionary finger across her lips as she went through the door of the church. She stopped to dip a finger into a dish of holy water, and made the sign of the cross. At once, Janna copied her, then followed her new friend into the nave where a group of lay sisters, servants and guests were already waiting for the Mass to begin. Full of amazement and awe, she looked about her, studying her surroundings.

The roof of the church towered high above her head, supported by thick columns down each side of the nave, joined together with rounded arches. Some of the windows in the church were set with glass, which let in shafts of sunlight. Most of the glass was clear, but there was colored glass in a couple of the windows, forming pictures of people with gold rings around their heads. The light that shone through them cast bright lozenges of red, blue and green onto the stone flagging. Janna had never seen anything so wonderful. Fine, fat beeswax candles stood on an altar at the end of the nave, illuminating the gold crucifix in the center. A fainter light came from burning wicks that floated in shallow stone bowls filled with animal fat. The church was redolent with their rank, smoky smell, overlaid with a spicy scent that mingled with the odor of sweat and unwashed bodies.

The walls of the church were plastered and painted with scenes of people, each one different from the last. The same figures appeared in several of the scenes, a man with golden hair and long white robes who was also crowned with a golden ring. There was a woman in blue, seated and nursing a small child on her lap. Janna recognized the figures from various shrines she'd encountered while journeying between Berford, Babestoche and Wiltune. They were Christ and His mother, Mary. The same Christ figure hung from the cross on the altar. There He wore a crown of thorns and an expression of agony. Janna shuddered. She knew something of His birth, His crucifixion and resurrection, and when they were celebrated. Her gaze moved on to a picture of His crucifixion that was painted on a wall. She wondered about the other pictures; perhaps they all told stories from the life of Christ?

She was about to ask Agnes when a line of black-clad nuns filed in from a side entrance and settled into the choir stalls. Following close behind came a man in a long white robe, carrying a stoup of water. Janna craned to see what was happening. The bearer headed a procession to the high altar at the farthest end of the church, where the water was blessed by a priest. The man then set off once more, moving down into the nave at the head of the procession. Behind him came someone else carrying a large cross, flanked by two more men, each with a lighted candle. A man bearing a large bound book followed them. Next came the priest, who wore a glorious embroidered vestment over his white robe. He seemed to be in charge of the proceedings. Several young boys brought up the rear, one of them swinging a censer. Janna caught another strong whiff of the spicy fragrance. In a wave of rustling movement, the congregation knelt as they passed by. The procession moved along the back of the church, the bearer sprinkling the holy water as he passed. They came back up the nave toward the altar, passing by on the other side.

Janna nudged Agnes, leaning over to speak in her friend's ear. "Who are all these people?"

"That's Father Mark, the priest. He comes from St Mary's in Wiltune to celebrate the Mass. The deacon and subdeacons are in front of him, and there are some acolytes as well."

"Why can't the abbess celebrate the Mass?"

"She's not allowed. Shh." Agnes closed her eyes and listened with a rapt expression as the priest came to a halt beside the altar. He stood with his back to everyone as he made the sign of the cross, "*In nomine Patris, et Filii, et Spiritus Sancti. Amen.*"

Janna listened intently to the Mass, anxious to understand what was going on. But the priest wasn't speaking in the Saxon tongue, nor were the words Norman French. She remembered again the first and only time she'd been into a church. It was new, and not nearly so grand as this one. It had been built to replace the old preaching cross at Berford, and a new priest had been appointed in place of the elderly priest who used to visit their community once a month. The new priest had prayed in what sounded exactly like this gibble-gabble. Eadgyth had called it Latin, the ancient language spoken by the Romans. Janna had asked her mother if she understood what the priest was saying, and Eadgyth had said she did not. Janna had formed the impression at the time that her mother might have understood more than she'd admitted. She'd certainly seemed to know when to kneel and when to stand. As they were doing now, Janna realized, and scrambled to her feet.

There was a moment's silence, and then the nuns in the choir stalls began to chant. The church was filled with the sound of their voices. It wasn't a bawdy song such as Janna had heard occasionally in the marketplace, but it was a sound she recognized. She froze into stillness. As she listened, the whole world seemed to tilt and grow dark, so that she was no longer aware of what was happening around her. Everything she knew from the past, everything she'd taken for granted, now had a different shape and a different meaning. She felt as if she'd been cast adrift on a vast ocean where nothing made sense any more, for she no longer knew who she was, nor who her mother had been.

The thread of music filled Janna's mind and left her heart overflowing. Eadgyth had sung like this sometimes when she thought she was alone. Perhaps she was hardly conscious that she was doing it. Certainly she had not expected Janna to hear her, and had been confused, embarrassed and—yes—angry, when Janna had once questioned her about it. From Eadgyth, Janna had learned that there was something wrong with music, with singing, something shameful. Why? And where and when had Eadgyth learned to sing like this?

Janna bowed her head as the answer flooded her mind. Her mother must once have been a nun! It was the only thing that made sense—and nonsense, for if Janna was sure of anything, it was that Eadgyth had no time for the church or for those who served in it. Janna remembered the embarrassment of that service in Berford. After praying for a time, the priest had launched into a tirade against women, and against Eadgyth in particular, speaking this time in the Saxon language so that all would understand the import of his words. And in the middle of it all, right in front of everyone, Eadgyth had grabbed Janna's arm and dragged her outside. Although she understood her mother's anger, Janna still blushed when she recalled the scene.

Could her mother once have been a nun? If so, it wasn't at Wiltune, for the abbess had claimed that her mother had come to seek her help. Janna knew that her mother was already close to giving birth by then, for Aldith the midwife had told her much the same thing. If not Wiltune, then which abbey had Eadgyth come from? More importantly: why had she turned against her faith, and her life in the convent; why had she never mentioned it even once to her only daughter? Had she been expelled when her pregnancy became apparent?

Janna was struck by another thought. If her mother was once a nun, how on earth had she managed to become pregnant in the first place? What was she thinking? And what about Janna's father? What was *he* thinking, seducing a nun and leaving her with child? Had he, perhaps, been a priest himself, forbidden by the church to have an intimate relationship with a woman? That might well explain her mother's shame, and also the need for secrecy.

Overwhelmed by her discovery, by the questions that hammered insistently in her mind and clamored to be answered, Janna sagged down onto the hard, stone floor. It was too much to take in all at once.

A strong hand under her arm jerked Janna to her feet. Agnes. Everyone had risen, and her friend was making sure she followed suit. Janna smiled her thanks, but her thoughts were wholly preoccupied as the psalms, lessons and prayers continued. Whether standing or kneeling, she was blind to her surroundings as she tried to puzzle out this mystery of her mother's life. Never, at any time, had Eadgyth even hinted at the fact that she'd once spent time in an abbey.

Janna's thoughts turned briefly to Agnes as, once again, her friend yanked her upright. Agnes was a lay sister at the abbey, really a servant. Could her mother also have been a lay sister rather than a nun?

Janna peered along the crowded nave, past the lay sisters and servants of the abbey, the guests, pilgrims and beggars attending the Mass, trying to see the nuns more clearly. She caught glimpses of black veils and white wimples framing pale faces. She wondered which one of them was the kindly Sister Anne, the infirmarian. According to Agnes, an infirmarian was someone skilled in the art of healing, and with knowledge of herbs. Someone like Eadgyth! Was that where she had learned her healing arts—in an abbey? That made sense. But if her mother was an infirmarian, it meant she had taken her vows; it meant she was definitely a nun. How, then, had she met Janna's father and, even worse, come to know him well enough to be seduced by him?

Janna was no fool and besides, Eadgyth had told her exactly how women became pregnant and bore children. She'd used their own goats and fowls as living examples, so that Janna could witness for herself how such things came about. So she knew what her mother and father must have done in order to bear a child. Janna shook her head in wonder. Truly, they must have loved each other dearly to defy the church in such a way. But they had been well and truly punished for it. Bitterness against her father welled up in Janna's mind. Perhaps he thought his duty to God more important than his duty to the woman he loved, and to his own child? Or was her father someone important outside the church, wealthy enough to do as he pleased and with no thought for the consequences of his actions? Janna became more determined to seek him out, so that she could accuse him to his face and in front of his family, if he had one. He must be told Eadgyth's fate. Even though Janna's knowledge of the church was limited, she knew that nuns and priests were required to lead celibate lives in the worship of God, though it had not always been thus. Janna was coming to realize just how unforgiving both her father and the Church must be to have turned Eadgyth away and abandoned her at a time of such great need. Small wonder then that Eadgyth, in turn, had forsaken the church and all that it had once meant to her.

Blindly, numbly, Janna knelt once more, pushed down by the ever-vigilant Agnes. She was oblivious of the rough stone flagging pressing against her knees, oblivious of her surroundings. Her thoughts were consumed by the plight of her mother, and how wretched and frightened she must have felt when she realized she was with child and that her lover had abandoned her. With knowledge came some understanding. Janna had known her mother to be cold and proud. It had been a source of some resentment that Eadgyth had seldom spoken a kind or loving word to her, or given her any praise while she was growing up. But Janna could understand now that this was how Eadgyth had protected herself when, disgraced and abandoned, she had been forced to beg the abbess for charity and had thereafter struggled to survive, to make a life for them both. Janna's resentment gave way to admiration as she contemplated Eadgyth's courage, the iron will that had not allowed her to give up, to be beaten or condemned in the eyes of the world. Her father might be a man of God, or even someone wealthy and important, but in Janna's eyes he was a coward, a nothing and a nobody, compared to her heroic mother.

"Come." Agnes tugged on Janna's arm, and Janna followed her obediently out of the church and into the sunlight. "Are you all right?" the lay sister questioned. "What happened in there? You're as white as my veil!"

Dazed by the bright light, by the questions still whirling through her mind, Janna shook her head. "I-I just had a revelation," she said slowly.

"A revelation? You saw Our Holy Mother? Or even Christ Himself?" Agnes's eyes grew wide with wonder.

"No! No, I mean I—"

"Johanna!" Sister Brigid swooped down like a great blackbird. "You're a disgrace to our order, dressed the way you are. Come with me." Without waiting for a reply, she set off at a fast pace toward the small parlor they'd passed through on their visit to the abbess's quarters the night before.

Janna wrinkled her nose at Agnes, and got a shrug and a grin in reply. "I'll see you later," she called, and earned a frown of disapproval from her guide. She followed the black-habited figure into the parlor, which now was guarded by a nun, engaged in haggling with a chapman who was determined to pull the wares out of his heavy packs and display them to her. Sister Brigid ignored the pair, choosing this time a different door from the one they'd used the night before. It led out into a sunlit grassy square, bound by the stone church on one side and wooden buildings on the others. A vaulted walkway ran around its four sides, supported by graceful arches that framed the garth. A fountain splashed at the center, a gentle murmuring that echoed the tranquil scene. A sparrow hopped about, poking an inquisitive beak into the grass, which was drying and browning in the summer sun. Janna hoped it might find a worm, for there was no-one about to spread any crumbs for its succor. She wondered where everyone was.

"This is the cloister, where we may read, chant, sew or spin, study the Rule, or take our rest," the nun said, and waved an encompassing arm at the peaceful, sunny scene as she turned right and walked briskly along the corridor.

Read? Janna pricked up her ears.

"Along here is the refectory where we take our meals." Sister Brigid gestured ahead as she turned left into another arm of the walkway. Janna licked her lips at the mention of food. The nun noticed, and said hastily, "Those who have taken their vows, as well as the oblates, postulants and novices, eat here. The lay sisters have their own refectory in the outer courtyard." She turned left once more, then swooped to the right and into a small parlor adjoining a larger storeroom. "You may wait here for Sister Grace," she said, and hurried off.

Janna wondered if Sister Brigid was as curt and gruff with all the visitors who came to the abbey. Still, the porteress had told her a little about the abbey's buildings, and Janna was grateful for that. She was finding it difficult to get her bearings, while she was sure she would never become accustomed to the new life she had chosen, which seemed so hard and so joyless.

Sister Grace was aptly named, she thought, as a nun glided through from the storeroom, a large bundle clasped in her arms. She stood, head on one side, studying Janna. A small twitch of her mouth spoke of her amusement, which was confirmed as she said, "We're not often called on to give a sister's apparel to a youth! Are you sure you want these?" Sister Grace's voice was low and musical, her gestures graceful as she set her burden down upon a table.

"I'm dressed as a youth, but I am a maid, mistress—Sister." Janna felt self-conscious under the nun's careful scrutiny.

"Then once you have changed, you may bring your old clothes back here to our wardrober. I am sure one of the workers at the home farm will be glad of them. But tell me, if you are a maid, why do you wear such unbecoming garments?"

The question sounded kind, as if Sister Grace genuinely wanted to know. Janna sighed. "It—it is my disguise."

"And why should you need a disguise?"

"I believe my life is in danger." For all that it sounded dramatic, it was no more than the truth. Yet, noticing how Sister Grace's expression stiffened somewhat at her words, Janna understood that the nun wasn't sure whether or not to believe her. Nevertheless, she pushed the bundle of clothes toward Janna, along with a pair of rough leather sandals.

"You're safe here. Besides, no-one will recognize you among so many others when we all look so alike."

Safe. Janna saw the truth of the sister's words, and felt a slight easing of tension. She would become just another black crow, indistinguishable among the flock.

Sister Grace patted a rolled bundle set to one side. "Here is also a pallet for you to sleep on, and a blanket to keep you warm," she said. "You may take these to the lay sisters' dorter, and you can change into your habit while you are there. The scapular is for outside work only."

Scapular? "Thank you, Sister." This largesse was more than Janna had expected. She smiled her relief at Sister Grace. The nun looked steadily at her, all trace of amusement now vanished.

"If you have come here for sanctuary, you may be sure you will find it here," she said. "What is your name?"

"Johanna."

"Well, Johanna, I am in charge of the postulants, novices and lay sisters, and I am answerable to our abbess for your behavior. I understand you are not yet familiar with our ways but I'm not prepared to be lax on that account. If you have any questions or troubles, bring them to me and I shall certainly do all in my power to help you if I can. Is that understood?"

"Yes, thank you, Sister."

"Good." The nun nodded briskly. "We follow St Benedict's Rule of Silence, so you will not indulge in idle chitchat with the lay sisters. Speak only if there is a need to know." She paused for a moment, and Janna tried to keep her dismay from showing on her face. "After you have taken your bedding to the dorter, you will find the lay sisters in their refectory, breaking their fast," Sister Grace said. "Go and join them there and, when you have finished, come to the chapter house, where your duties for the day will be told to you." Giving Janna no time to say anything in reply, the nun glided out of the small room.

"I don't know where the refectory is!" Janna called after her. The nun stopped and, with an impatient click of her tongue, beckoned Janna to follow her. Once more they traversed the walkway that fringed the cloister, then through the small parlor and out into the large courtyard. To Janna, it felt almost as though she'd escaped from a dungeon, for all that she was still within the walls of the abbey. She looked longingly at the gatehouse on the far side of the courtyard, where pilgrims and guests of the abbey still milled about, talking after the Mass. It took all her willpower not to run off and join them, and escape into the freedom of the marketplace beyond.

"The lay sisters' refectory is over there." Sister Grace indicated its position across from the dorter. "You may break your fast once you are properly attired."

Conscious of the nun's gaze on her, Janna trudged toward the building in which she'd slept the night before, wondering if Sister Grace understood her longing to escape. Perhaps she'd read it in Janna's expression, and was lingering to make sure that if Janna fled the abbey, the garments and bedding did not go with her.

In the daylight, Janna could see that the lay sisters' dorter was built over a storeroom. The door of the undercroft stood half open and she could make out barrels and chests in the dimness beyond. No doubt they were all stuffed to bursting point, given the wealth of the abbey. Reminded of food, Janna's stomach growled with hunger and she hastened up the stairs to the empty dorter. She dropped her new bedding onto the pile of thin pallets and possessions set tidily on one side of the room, then stripped off the breeches and smock she'd worn, and bundled them up. After a moment's thought, she refastened her girdle and precious purse against her skin, then donned an under-tunic followed by a black habit, which she secured with a cord that had been tucked within its folds. There was a sleeveless tunic, rough and stained. The scapular for outside work? Janna put it aside, and turned to the wimple. She draped it carefully over her head and neck, trying to recall how it had looked on Agnes. She took pains to tuck her hair out of sight, just as Agnes had done. The white homespun veil came last, different in every way from the silky black veil worn by the abbess. What did she look like now? Janna wished she had a looking glass in which to see herself! No matter that she hated looking like a nun, these clothes must surely suit her better than the peasant's garb she'd worn before, and they would certainly prove an effective disguise. She wondered what her mother would say, if only she could see her daughter now.

Eadgyth! Questions about her mother's past filled Janna's mind once more, banishing any vain thoughts about her appearance. They continued to occupy her as she handed in the bundle of discarded clothing to the cellaress, who was now busy dealing with a prosperous-looking merchant in the parlor. A bell began to ring, and the sister looked up. "Chapter's about to start," she said. "You'd better hurry."

Conscious of her empty, rumbling stomach, Janna raced to the refectory for a snatched portion of bread and ale before hurrying after the lay sisters, who were fast disappearing into the parlor at the far end of the courtyard.

Chapter 3

The cloister seemed to be the hub around which the wheel of the abbey revolved. Janna followed the lay sisters in a different direction from the one she'd taken earlier with Sister Grace. This time they walked along the side of the stone church, turned right and then left into a large room. Black-robed nuns occupied the benches in front; the lay sisters were expected to sit behind them. Janna spied Agnes and slipped past a few of the lay sisters so that she could reach her friend. The abbess stood in front of everyone to read the prayers and lesson of the day, after which she consulted the martyrology and asked the community to mention those saints listed for that day in their prayers, along with some of the abbey's benefactors and several deceased sisters. The weekly duty list was read out, and the abbess's place was then taken by a nun with a long face and a hairy mole on her cheek. She seemed to have a number of complaints to get off her chest.

"I had to reprimand her again for gluttony at meal times, and for breaking the silence to ask Sister Maria to pass her a platter of fish instead of signing her need, and that's not the worst of her faults. Only yesterday I had cause to witness..."

"Who's that?" Janna whispered.

"The prioress. Shh." Agnes cast a nervous glance around the assembled company.

None the wiser, Janna sat back to listen to the catalogue of faults attributed to the hapless nun in question, a slight young woman who kept her head bent as she knelt in front of everyone, and who constantly wiped her nose on the back of her hand. Janna wondered if she was crying. None of the nun's faults sounded so very bad, but it seemed the abbess had a different opinion. She beckoned the young nun forward to listen to her judgment.

"A diet of bread and water for the next three days might help to concentrate your mind on the Rule of this house as set out by our revered St Benedict," she said. She waited a moment, but the nun didn't raise her head or speak. "In addition, and as punishment for your pride in not confessing your own faults, I bid you lie down at the door of the church for the rest of today's offices so that all may step over you on their way in. Pride has no place in our community."

Janna looked at the abbess's costly robes, her carefully draped wimple, and the gold cross that hung down the front of her habit. She wondered who called the abbess to account for any infringements of the Rule. The priest? The bishop? Remembering her interview with the formidable abbess the night before, she suspected neither of them would dare to reprimand her. They wouldn't have the courage.

A pair of bright eyes caught Janna's attention, and she watched in disbelief as a mouse crept out from under the wimple of a nun sitting nearby. It perched on the nun's shoulder and began to groom its whiskers. A hand snaked up and fondled it surreptitiously.

"That's Chester," Agnes muttered out of the side of her mouth. "He belongs to Sister Ursel. She's the—" Her words were drowned by a sudden furious barking. A small dog shot off the lap of a nun sitting a few seats along and jumped onto the bench, pawing at Sister Ursel's chest in a desperate bid to reach the mouse on her shoulder. The nun's hand closed protectively around her pet while she pushed the dog away with a panicky gesture. She quickly secreted the mouse safely within the folds of her habit, and sat with bent head while the abbess turned on the dog's owner.

"I've warned you before—I've warned all of you—not to bring your animals into the chapter house," she hissed furiously.

"But—"

"Silence!" the abbess thundered. "Do not make matters worse with feeble excuses, Sister Catherine. Remove yourself, and your dog, at once! And, as penance for disobeying the Rule, you may go to your bed hungry for the rest of the week. You will sit at the table with your sisters, but you will content yourself with a diet comprised only of bread and water while you contemplate the Sin of Disobedience."

The hapless nun jerked to her feet. Flushed with anger, she pushed past her sisters on her way to the door. As she passed, Janna caught a glimpse of her baleful glance at the downcast face of the mouse's owner, who stayed seated on the bench. Even here, in the company of good women, it seemed that spite and rage still flourished. And fear too, Janna thought, as she surveyed the quaking Sister Ursel.

"Sister Anne!" The name caught Janna's attention and she leaned forward, eager to identify the infirmarian who looked after Agnes. She hoped the good nun wasn't in trouble, but it seemed she was only being called to give an account of those in her care who were too ill to attend this inquisition.

Sister Anne was a small, round nun in her later years, with rosy wrinkled cheeks and a cheerful smile. Just looking at her warmed Janna's heart, and quashed some of her trepidation. If such a woman, obviously kind and obviously knowledgeable, could live here by choice and so cheerfully, there must be some good things about the abbey. She listened to the infirmarian's clear voice discussing the progress of her patients and then, to Janna's relief, the meeting in the chapter house seemed to be over, for everyone stood up. The nuns in front filed out in orderly fashion, but the lay sisters sat down again.

The abbess had led the nuns out, but Sister Grace and the prioress remained. Her gaze fastened on Janna, and Janna immediately lowered her eyes, not wanting to draw attention to herself.

One of the lay sisters leaped to her feet. "I have a fault to report." Janna recognized the sharp whine from the night before. "We have a new lay sister and, I regret to say, I saw her *running* toward our refectory this morning."

Janna's heart sank. She'd forgotten about the Sin of Running. From the way this lay sister spoke of it, it was obviously a grievous sin, right up there with…Janna was hard put to think of anything bad enough. Murder? Adultery? Sister Grace stepped forward. "The lay sister is indeed new to our abbey and unfamiliar with our ways. I am also to blame, for I kept her in the storeroom and so she was late going to the refectory to break her fast. I crave the convent's indulgence for this infraction of the Rule. I undertake to reprimand our new sister, and I will make sure to set her on the right path. This will not happen again."

Janna was grateful that Sister Grace had spoken up for her. Her glance flicked to the complainer, who met her eyes with a vindictive smirk.

"*And* she broke the Great Silence. She talked after we'd all retired to bed last night," the gnat said virtuously.

"That was my doing," Agnes spoke up quickly. "Our new sister came late in the night and had nowhere to sleep. I offered to share my pallet with her, and I also explained to her some of our Rule for she knows nothing about how we live here in the abbey."

"That was kindly done, Sister Agnes," Sister Grace said briskly, before the prioress could open her mouth.

"*And* her hair is showing under her veil," the gnat continued.

Janna raised a hand and quickly tucked away an offending curl. She'd kept her hair cut short while masquerading as a youth. It was now just long enough to be untidy, but not long enough to be tied back and brought under control.

Sister Grace frowned at the gnat. "I thank you, Sister Martha, for sharing your concerns with us," she said, forestalling any further complaints. "You are always very quick to point out our faults and give us the chance to rectify them, and we are grateful, but in this case you should know that our new Sister Johanna has not lived within a religious community before, and therefore has much to learn. My hope is that we will all go out of our way to make her transition into our community as smooth and as pleasant as possible."

Effectively silenced, a frustrated Sister Martha sat down.

"*Laborare est orare*," the prioress said briskly, drawing all eyes in her direction once more.

"To work is to pray." Agnes's lips hardly moved as she obligingly translated St Benedict's injunction for Janna.

"Silence!" The prioress glared at them both. "Today you will all join the lay servants at the home farm, for harvest is about to begin and your labor is needed there. The bailiff will meet you beside the barns. He will give you the implements you need, and explain which tasks he wants you to do. I'm sure I have no need to tell you that I expect your greatest care in harvesting our grain, for our livelihood, the very bread we eat, depends on you. A poor harvest means we all go hungry."

"Go with God and with a cheerful heart, in the knowledge that God cares for us and will provide for all our needs," Sister Grace added with a cheerful smile. Janna wondered if she took pleasure in deliberately contradicting the prioress.

She was about to rise and do as she'd been told when she realized that the prioress was now uttering a prayer, presumably entreating God for success in their endeavors. She settled back and waited for the prayer to be over.

"Harvest!" Agnes sounded gleeful as the lay sisters poured out of the chapter house and once more threaded their way around the corridors of the cloister. "It's hard work, cutting and binding the wheat, and tying it into sheaves. I'm often in great pain—" Agnes touched her scarred shoulder, "—but it's worth it just to escape from the confines of the abbey for a time." She skipped aside to avoid several children and young nuns, all of whom sat on the stone flagging on the south side of the arcade. They had wax tablets upon their laps, and were laboriously forming letters on the surface with a pointed metal stylus. Janna immediately stepped closer to watch. One of the sisters had settled herself at a small table at their head. She, too, had a tablet and she held it up for all to see while she demonstrated the letters she wanted them to copy. Sister Grace came to stand beside her, keeping an eye on her young charges. On noticing Janna, she smiled. Janna wanted to thank her for intervening on her behalf. She hadn't expected such kindness from anyone. But Agnes had caught hold of her sleeve and was urging her on.

"Can all of us learn our letters with Sister Grace and that other sister?" Janna asked eagerly.

"Oh, no!" Agnes sounded shocked at the very idea. "Rich merchants pay to have their children taught their letters by our chantress, Sister Maria. That's her sitting with Sister Grace over there. And some of those children are oblates. They're given by their families to the church. It's Sister Grace's task to look after them, that's why she's there."

"What about those nuns?" Janna gestured at the black-clad older students, who seemed to be about her own age.

"They're not nuns, they're postulants or novices. They've paid a dowry to the abbey just to be here. So have the families of the oblates. You can't just come in here without payment, Janna, not if you want to become a full member of the convent."

Depressed at having her hopes of learning to read and write crushed so quickly, Janna wondered what would happen if she cast herself on Sister Grace's mercy, and begged to join the students. The nun had already shown that she was kind; perhaps she might agree. But the brief flare of hope was extinguished as she remembered the abbess's command to work hard and earn her keep.

"What about you? Are you going to become a nun?" Janna asked Agnes as they left the abbey precinct and walked on toward the fields rising in the distance.

Agnes shrugged. "I have no dowry."

"Yet you've lived here since you were a child." A thought occurred to Janna. "The abbess seems so greedy for money, I'm surprised she agreed to take you in. Or..." She was suddenly confused. "I beg your pardon, I mean no disrespect. Perhaps your parents paid for the infirmarian to take care of you?"

"Not they." Agnes gave a quiet chuckle. "They are poor peasants, tenants of the abbey. I believe I came with nothing more than a plump fowl as a gift. Fortunately for me, the old abbess was here then, although she died shortly after my arrival. I don't remember her very well, but she is spoken of as if she were a saint. Everyone loved her, not like Abbess Hawise. Sister Anne once told me that as soon as our new abbess was elected, she tried everything to get my parents to take me back. But our dear infirmarian spoke up for me, and so did the other nuns, and for once, the abbess didn't get her way."

"And are you glad about that? Do you like living here?" Looking at her new friend, Janna surmised Agnes to be some years older than herself. For certes she was of an age to be wed had she lived in a village and not an abbey. For once, the talkative Agnes was silenced. "Actually, I've never really thought about it," she said finally, sounding surprised. "I've always taken my life here for granted." She was silent a few moments more. "I know I said I'd like to marry and have children, but in truth I am content to stay here. This is my home; the nuns who live here are my family. Besides, I-I don't wish to show my face outside the abbey. I prefer to stay where I'm known, where people are used to my appearance."

Janna nodded in understanding, but Agnes was not yet finished.

"I'm used to the life here," she said. "I work hard but I love the Lord so it is no burden. Indeed, my work gives meaning and purpose to my days. And it is a joy to hear the chants and singing of the nuns, and to join in with their worship." She turned to Janna with a sudden smile. "Thank you," she said simply.

"For what?"

"For making me realize I accept what has happened to me, and to know that, given the way I am, I'm happy to be here."

Happy? With all the sins that could be committed so unknowingly, and the confession and punishment that must follow thereafter? Janna shook her head in wonder.

"But I still love harvest time, and the freedom of being out in the fields—and not having to observe the Great Silence," Agnes confessed as they forded the river and crossed water meadows toward a number of roughly built wattle-and-daub barns.

Freedom? Janna kicked out at her habit, irritated by its clinging folds when she'd become used to striding about in a man's breeches. Yet Agnes spoke what was in her mind for she, too, relished being in the open space of the fields even after such a short time within the confines of the abbey.

"Who lives over there?" She pointed to a cluster of small cots set around a pond.

"The lay servants. They live here at the home farm with their families and they tend the abbey's beasts and fields. Our work usually lies within the walls of the abbey itself but, as you see, our labor is called upon at busy times like haymaking and harvest. It's always such a pleasure to be out in the open!" With a broad smile, Agnes pushed her way through the crowd gathering around a heavyset man in his middle years.

"Good day to you, Master Will. God be with you," she called cheerfully.

"Sister Agnes. Welcome!" He smiled down at her, his countenance reflecting the pleasure of their re-acquaintance rather than registering her disfigurement. Janna thought he must be the bailiff, and his words confirmed it.

"Those on my right will split into groups and walk in front to cut the wheat." The sweep of his hand encompassed Janna, Agnes and several other lay sisters and laborers. Some of the laborers already carried sickles, which Janna thought they must own for their personal use. She followed Agnes to one of the sheds, where the bailiff's underling handed her a small, curved blade and a pair of heavy gloves. She moved back and made an experimental stroke to slice through an imaginary plant. She and her mother had grown some wheat in their small patch, but it had never been enough for their needs and they'd been obliged to trade precious honey in return for bags of coarse flour from the miller. Still, she knew how to cut wheat, even if she'd never had a full field to practice on before.

The bailiff indicated those remaining in front of him. "You will follow behind, to pick up the wheat and bind it into sheaves. Tomorrow you will alternate your tasks, taking it turn and turn about to either cut or bind. The stooks will then be piled into the wagon and carted to the barn." He scanned the villeins in front of him, then beckoned to a couple of brawny youths. "I want you two to get out and cut gorse. Bring it to the barn. We'll stack the wheat on a bed of it so that the prickles will keep out the rats."

The two chosen groaned loudly, obviously not relishing their task. The bailiff grinned briefly, then hailed a group of youngsters who were playing catch around the sheds. "Children! Listen to me. You are to follow behind everyone and glean the fallen grain. Make sure you get to it before the crows! I won't have them getting fat while we go hungry!"

A gust of laughter followed this injunction, and the bailiff beamed.

"Before you go!" His words stopped the flow of workers toward the fields. "While harvesting takes place you will work until dinner time, after which you will be free to go to your own fields. As is the custom, you will receive your dinner from the abbey, and there will be a great feast when at last the harvest is safely in."

A hearty cheer went up. The hayward sounded his horn, and the bailiff held up his hand for silence. Janna noticed that he clasped a small straw doll. "The horn will sound at the start of each day of harvest," he said, and solemnly handed the straw doll to the hayward.

Janna listened, intrigued, as the hayward uttered a prayer. This prayer she could understand, for the man spoke in the Saxon language, asking God to bless the harvest and make it bountiful, and to keep the rain away until all the wheat was safely reaped and stored.

"Amen," the workers uttered with great fervor. They moved to the edge of the first field. There the hayward knelt and intoned another prayer while burying the straw doll. "Go to work, everyone," he shouted and, in accordance with the bailiff's instructions, Janna's group began to cut the wheat.

Janna had been toughened during the time she'd spent working the fields at the manor farm. Along with Edwin, the outlaw whom she'd first encountered in the forest, she had been expected to do a man's labor every day. Although her muscles had initially almost seized up in protest, over time she'd become accustomed to the labor. Now she worked with a will, moving along in a line with the others, while the second group followed.

Beside her, Agnes toiled without complaint, but there were beads of sweat on her pale forehead. She switched the sickle from her right hand to her left, and made an awkward attempt to keep on cutting the wheat. After a short time, she switched back again. She did this several times, and her movements became slower and her gestures more feeble. She winced each time she swung the sickle.

"Why don't you take a rest?" Janna urged.

Agnes paused and straightened up with a groan. "No. If the hayward believes I'm not fit to do the work, I'll be sent back to the abbey." She flung her hand out to the sky, which arced blue and blazing above them. "I love to be out here. Smell the air! And the flowers! They're so pretty!" She picked up a red deadnettle from among the cut wheat and sniffed its fragrance.

"They're weeds. They may be pretty, but they're a nuisance—and some are poisonous." Janna remembered her backbreaking weeks at the manor farm wrestling with just such weeds as these. Scratchy purple thistles, yellow flowering charlock, the white daisies of corn chamomile, bright blue cornflowers and pink corncockle. They lent color to the wheat fields but some were poisonous enough to kill.

"How can you say they're a nuisance when even our Lord loved wild flowers?" Agnes closed her eyes the better to remember. "'Consider the lilies of the field, how they grow; they toil not, neither do they spin: And yet I say unto you, that even Solomon in all his glory was not arrayed like one of these,'" she quoted triumphantly.

"Who was Solomon?"

"A famous king. It doesn't matter. What matters is what the priest told us about the lilies of the field, and all that. Do you know that the big white ones are sometimes called Madonna lilies, after our blessed Virgin Mary? We have them in our church for feast days; they're very beautiful. But they don't smell as sweet as little wild violets."

"So you're interested in plants?"

"I don't know much about them, but I always volunteer to work in the abbey gardens when I can. I love to look at the flowers. They're so—so perfect." Agnes's tone was wistful.

Janna wondered if she was reflecting on her own damaged face. "Just as well we're not all lilies," she commented briskly, anxious to distract her friend. "Who'd do all the toiling and spinning at the abbey then? Who'd bring in the harvest?"

"The nuns are lilies, or at least some of them are," Agnes answered promptly, with a giggle. "That's why they need us!" Good humor restored, she switched the sickle to her right hand and bent to cut the wheat once more.

The long, hot morning dragged on. Janna felt hampered by the scapular she wore over her habit, which was making her sweat profusely. She had a raging thirst, so she was glad to stop working when the hayward blew on his horn for dinner. There was a goodly spread of bread and cheese, meat pies and fruit, with jugs of ale and mead to wash it all down. She was hungry after her efforts, as well as thirsty. As soon as the prayer was over, she wasted no time in tucking into the feast. After a while, she became aware that Agnes had eaten hardly anything. She held a meat pasty out to her friend. "Here. You must eat, keep up your strength."

Agnes groaned. "In truth, I am in too much pain to have an appetite," she said, and touched her shoulder.

Looking at the strain on the lay sister's face, Janna understood what an effort of will it must have cost Agnes to continue working in the field for so long. Yet she understood, too, her friend's reluctance to speak out about her injury. "Rest, and try to eat something," she urged. "Tonight, if you'll show me where it hurts, I'll see if I know of anything that may help to bring ease, something that Sister Anne may not already have tried."

"That's kind of you. Thank you, Janna." Agnes frowned, puzzled. "But how do you know of such things?"

"My mother was a *wortwyf*—a herb wife and healer. She taught me all she knew before she died." That wasn't quite true; her mother had let her prepare potions, but hadn't trusted her to actually treat the sick, or take care of their various complaints. It had been a bone of contention between them, an argument that had lasted until Eadgyth died. Janna sighed. Her mother hadn't trusted her with the truth either. "I still have much to learn," she confessed, and took a bite from the pasty.

Belly full, she was just licking her fingers clean when she noticed that one of the laborers was staring at her. As soon as his glance met hers he looked away and, with an air of unconcern, began to scan the other workers of the abbey, although his gaze didn't linger long on any one of them. Curious now, for she thought he might have been staring at her for some time before she became aware of it, Janna continued to watch him.

He sat slightly apart from the others. She noticed that he spoke to no-one, and that no-one spoke to him. Was he perhaps newly come to the abbey, like her? She frowned. She had come to a house full of women, begging sanctuary. What was his excuse? He was dressed in a villein's garments, tunic and breeches, but they were cleaner and of better quality than those worn by the abbey's lay servants. A man not used, perhaps, to manual labor? She narrowed her eyes, the better to study him. Was his face familiar? Had she seen him before?

She couldn't be sure, but his interest in her caused a twinge of unease.

She nudged Agnes, and pointed at the villein. "Who's that?" He stood up abruptly, and turned his back on them to survey the burgeoning golden fields ahead.

"I don't know. I saw him staring at you before." Agnes gave a sudden giggle. "I think he likes the look of you. If you value your virtue, perhaps you'd better make sure he doesn't get you alone somewhere to have his way with you!"

"Agnes!" Janna was a little shocked by the young woman's prurient imagination. Nevertheless, she felt somewhat reassured by her friend's words.

"He might be a bit old for you, do you think?" Agnes was still looking him over. "But his clothes are quite fine. He could be a good catch as a husband."

"You go catch him then," Janna answered without thinking, and then wished with all her heart that she could take back her words.

"He wouldn't want me, and besides, I've already taken a vow." Agnes sounded light-hearted enough. "You should think hard before you commit yourself to life here, Janna. You're not used to being confined, like I am, and you don't seem to have a vocation, if I may say so. Besides, you're so comely, you could wed anyone you want."

"I assure you, I have no interest in men, at least not at present." As she spoke, Godric's face came into her mind. How forlorn he'd looked when he'd said goodbye; almost as sad as she'd felt when the gate had clanged shut behind her and closed her off from the world. Godric was lost to her—and so was Hugh, she thought, as the Norman nobleman's handsome face superimposed itself over Godric's.

Janna sighed. The lord Hugh was not for her. Although he managed a manor farm for his aunt, Dame Alice, he would lose everything once his nephew, Hamo, came of age.

Hugh would have to marry, and marry well, if he wanted to maintain his status. And although he'd been kind to her, and had even kissed her once, he was so far above her in station it was foolish to entertain any notion of love, no matter how tender his kiss and how admiring his gaze. Besides, Janna reminded herself, she was not the only one enamored with the lord Hugh; there was also the beautiful Gytha, daughter of the cook. If Hugh decided on a dalliance with anyone, Gytha would be there right under his nose. Unlike Janna, who was now trapped behind the gates of an abbey. Janna shook her head, trying to dislodge all thoughts of love and marriage. She was here for two reasons: the first, to learn to read and write; the second, to keep out of the way of the man who saw her as a threat and who wanted her dead.

Inadvertently, her glance shifted to the stranger in their midst. He had turned around and, once again, was staring at her.

Chapter 4

Sleepy after their dinner and a hard morning's work, the lay servants left to toil in their own fields.

"It's time for us to go, Janna," Agnes said, judging the time from the position of the sun. She cast a regretful glance at the stubbled fields, and at the long strips of wheat still waiting to be cut. "Come on," she said, and reluctantly heaved herself to her feet. She set off for the abbey, pausing only to leave her sickle and gloves in the shed.

Janna followed her, anxious to reach the safety of the abbey once more. She looked about for the stranger, but he had left with the other lay servants, perhaps to cut his own wheat and bring it safe to the barn.

"Is it customary for strangers to join in with the lay servants at harvest time?" she asked.

"Oh yes," Agnes answered . Our abbey will give alms and shelter to any who need it, be they beggar, pilgrim or even the richest merchant in the land—although the wealthy have their own guest quarters, of course," she added. "And they're expected to work for their keep?" Janna slowed down to keep pace with Agnes, who walked with careful steps, her right elbow cradled in her left hand as if to keep her shoulder safe from any further movement.

"We don't ask guests to work for us, but some seem happy enough to help. The bailiff also hires extra hands if he thinks there are not enough workers to bring in the harvest." Agnes shot a shrewd glance at Janna. "Why? Are you worried about the staring stranger?"

"Yes. No." Janna gave an uneasy laugh. "I don't know."

"I saw him looking at you, and I also heard him ask the bailiff who you were."

"Why?" Janna's unease deepened. "Did the bailiff tell him?"

"How could he? He's never seen you before today, and you didn't give him your name, did you?"

"No." The bailiff might not know her, but others did. It was only a matter of time before the stranger found out who she was. And then?

"Don't let him upset you, he'll be moving on soon enough." Agnes looked wistful. "Isn't it nice to have an admirer?"

"If that's what he is." They forded the river and came back within the abbey precinct once more. "What now?" Janna asked.

"Now we do our work about the abbey." Agnes was back to talking out of the side of her mouth again. Janna remembered why and, nodding in understanding, followed her to the kitchen. "This is a good place to work, especially if you're hungry," Agnes muttered. She marched over to one of the sisters, who was busy stirring something savory in a huge iron pot. Its aromatic steam flavored the air. "This is Sister Johanna. She's new," she told the cook.

"Welcome, Johanna. I am Sister Euphemia." The nun's face was flushed from the heat of the fire, but her smile was friendly as she said, "I need some extra onions, some carrots and a cabbage, if you'd like to take our new sister out to the kitchen garden to gather them?"

A garden! Janna's face brightened. She looked forward to seeing which herbs were grown by the infirmarian, and how she tended her plants. She looked about her with interest as Agnes led her out of the kitchen, along the side of the abbey and into a well-tended garden. It was ringed with fruit trees, ripening apples burnishing bright in the sunshine. This was the largest garden Janna had ever seen. She gasped with pleasure at the array of plants and flowers spread before her. Forgetting their task, she walked along the rows of vegetables, marveling at their variety and abundance. The beds of herbs in a separate garden enticed her, and she moved to them. Fragrant agrimony, spicy sweet marjoram and creeping bugle, pungent pennyroyal and brilliant yellow toadflax, so-named because of the shape of its flowers. She recognized some but not all of them, and greeted those she knew like an old friend as she passed each bedding.

"Sweet woodruff, wormwood and woundwort, valerian and—"

"You know your herbs, I see."

Janna jumped in fright. She turned to the voice, and found herself staring into the bright eyes of the elderly infirmarian.

"Sister Anne," said Agnes. "This is our new lay sister, Johanna."

"And where is your home? Where do you come from, Johanna, that you are so familiar with the herbs in my physic garden?" the nun asked.

"I...uh..." Janna was at a loss how to answer. The nun's face creased in bewilderment.

"You have no home?" she asked gently.

Janna felt her throat suddenly constrict at this unexpected reminder of the past. Hot tears welled behind her eyes. She swallowed hard, unable to speak. The nun continued to watch her with a sympathetic gaze. Hating her weakness, Janna struggled to find her voice.

"My—my mother was a *wortwyf*, Sister. She taught me all she knew."

"A herb wife?" The nun's gaze sharpened. "Do you have her knowledge of healing?"

"Yes." Janna kept her fingers crossed behind her back to excuse the partial lie, telling herself it was worth it if it would gain her entry into the abbey itself.

"She offered to make me a salve for my scars," Agnes broke in. "I told her that you have looked after me and physicked me since I was a child."

"Yet I am always willing to learn new recipes. Tell me, Johanna, what would you or your mother have used to heal such serious burns as our poor Sister Agnes has suffered?"

Janna thought back to what Eadgyth had told her, and the salves she had made up to soothe the burns of a little boy who had spilled a pot of boiling water over himself, and who still bore the scars of it.

"If the burn is from liquid, you should boil elm bark and lily roots in milk and smear it on three times a day, but if the burn is from fire, you should boil dog rose, lily and speedwell in butter and smear it on the burn."

"The roots of the white lily?"

Janna nodded. "A dressing made from whole boiled linseeds will relieve pain and heat, prevent infection and help the wound to heal. The mucilage of marshmallow roots, with linseed and fenugreek also makes up an effective ointment."

"And afterwards, for scars?"

"Linseeds too. And burdock leaves for shrinking of sinews, or an ointment of boiled hog's lard and the roots of white lilies or hound's tongue. My mother told me that the juice of violets mixed with olive oil and goat fat is also very soothing."

"We sometimes use the flowers of the Madonna to adorn the shrine of St Edith and decorate the Lady Chapel on feast days," Sister Anne said slowly. "I haven't used lilies in medicaments before."

"The roots may be used for any number of skin ailments as well as to soften the scars of burns. Mixed with honey or hog's grease, they may also join cut sinews." Janna wondered if she was talking her way into further trouble, or even unknowingly committing some sort of sin. To her relief, Sister Anne smiled at her.

"I am grateful for your information, and I will certainly try out your recommendation," she said. "In fact, I'll make up a new salve straightaway. Pray visit me in the infirmary after supper tonight, Sister Agnes, and I'll give you the preparation to try." She nodded and moved briskly away. Janna noted that she was heading in the direction of a large clump of lilies, and hoped that both the infirmarian and Agnes would find the new recipe effective.

"I think you've impressed Sister Anne with your knowledge," Agnes said. "Will you teach me something about the medicinal use of plants? It's such a good excuse to visit the garden, and I do so love to work out here." She extended a hand to encompass the plants in all their showy summer brilliance, and the brightly colored butterflies that flitted among them.

"Gladly," Janna said, eager to repay Agnes in some measure for her kindness. She indicated the physic garden. "Let's start here and work our way through, just a few at a time, so that you'll remember what I've told you. You know flax?"

"Of course. We soak the stems and strip the fibers to weave into the cloth we wear." Agnes touched her habit, which, unlike the abbess's costly woolen robe, was made of rough homespun.

"It is also called linseed," Janna continued. "Oil from the seeds may be used to ease coughs, as well as taking the heat from burns. Perhaps Sister Anne made up a linseed poultice when you were first brought to her?"

"I don't remember."

"No matter. Remember it now, for flax is one of our most useful plants, and so is hemp." Janna pointed to a row of plants growing close to the flax. "This, too, can be woven into homespun, but it can also be used to alleviate pain and promote sleep. Boiled in milk, the seeds will soothe a cough. The juice mixed with butter is also good for burns." She moved on to indicate some long spikes of greyish leaves with small white flowers. "White horehound," she said. "In a syrup with fennel and dill, it will suppress coughing, soothe the throat and help expel phlegm from the chest." She encouraged Agnes to bruise the downy leaves and smell their fragrance.

"Flax, hemp, white horehound," Agnes murmured.

"This one I don't know." Janna paused beside a bed of white flowers. "They look a bit like poppies, but…"

"They are poppies." Sister Anne paused beside them, bearing a lily root and several other plants. "They come from the east, and I use them in preparations for calming the nerves, for pain, and to induce sleep."

"Oh?" Janna looked at the flowers with new interest.

"Their juice must be used with discretion, for it is a powerful sedative and painkiller. It is much stronger than preparations made from the common red poppies that grow in the fields." She walked around them and up the path between the beds of herbs.

"Thank you, Sister," Janna called after her. She turned to Agnes. "My mother told me about the opium poppy, but I've never seen one before. So we've both learned something new. But that's enough for now, I don't want to confuse you."

"And Sister Euphemia is probably getting very impatient," Agnes reminded Janna with a grin. They hurriedly picked the cabbage, carrots and onions, and returned indoors with their bounty. Thereafter, they were kept too busy to talk, being occupied with scrubbing, peeling and chopping the vegetables to be served in a pottage with beans in the refectory that night.

Their task completed, Sister Euphemia told them to scour the cooking pots and generally make themselves useful in the kitchen. But Janna overheard Agnes murmuring the names of the herbs and reciting their properties when she had occasion to pass by. She smiled to herself, so well pleased with the day's work that even the memory of the inquisitive stranger couldn't disturb her composure. Let him admire her from a distance, if that was his will. Soon enough he would move on, but in the meantime she would not allow him to deflect her from her purpose here in the abbey. She had made a good start, she thought, remembering her conversation with the infirmarian. If Sister Grace or the chantress weren't prepared to teach her, perhaps she could prevail on Sister Anne instead?

*

Once again, Janna woke with a start at the sound of the bell. She remembered where she was and arose from her pallet with alacrity, ready for Prime, the first service of the morning. After a break for bread and ale, and a brief hearing in the chapter house, they filed into the church for Mass. Janna knew what to expect now, and she listened carefully to the music of the nuns' voices. Their chants and prayers intertwined with her thoughts as, once again, she tried to fathom the secrets of her mother's early life. Finally, she gave up and let the nuns' quiet reverence soothe her troubled spirit and bring peace and a new strength of purpose to her cause.

"*Gloria Patri, et Filio, et Spiritui Sancto.*" The priest's voice rang out, commanding their response.

"*Sicut erat in principio, et nunc, et semper, et in saecula saeculorum,*" sang the nuns, their words followed by a hearty "Amen" from everyone standing in the nave. The chant went on, the lay sisters sometimes joining in. The visitors were mostly silent, although occasionally they said "Amen." Janna knew that signified the ending of a prayer, but she wished she could understand what else the priest and nuns were saying. Surveying those gathered in the nave around her, Janna surmised that they might not understand him either. Some of the abbey's more wealthy guests looked bored, and fidgeted or scratched themselves. Their ladies glanced about, perhaps comparing the stuff of their gowns and veils, and the precious stones on their rings, belts and head bands, with those of their rivals. Janna suppressed a grin as she judged their expressions: one looked smug; another slightly anxious; while a third wasn't paying any attention at all to the envious glances coming her way. With closed eyes and upturned countenance, she seemed to be listening to the voice of God Himself.

"Amen," came the chorus once more. Janna hoped it was all over at last, but the priest continued to chant and the nuns to respond, joined occasionally by the rest of the congregation. The gold crosses on the altars glimmered and reflected the candlelight. One of the servers swung the censer and the sweet spiciness of incense scented the cold air.

"*Amen*," sang the nuns.

"*Dominus vobiscum*," said the priest, after their voices died away.

"*Et cum spiritu tuo.*"

"What are you saying?" Janna whispered, as the priest began to pray.

"The priest said, 'May the Lord be with you,' and we said, 'And with thy spirit.' Shh," said Agnes.

"*Ite, missa est.*"

"Go, the Mass is finished. At last!" Agnes flashed a wide grin as the congregation said a final and heartfelt, "Amen."

Janna joined the crowd now pressing toward the door. Out in the bright sunlight once more, she felt her spirits rise as she and Agnes set off to the fields. Janna glanced at her friend. "Do you get tired of going to church so often and having to sit through that long mass?" she asked.

"No. It gives me the chance to rest, and to think."

"Do you understand what the priest is saying?"

"Some of it. The lay sisters are supposed to know the *Paternoster*, *Ave* and *Gloria*, as well as the *Credo*." Seeing Janna's confusion, Agnes continued her explanation. "The *Paternoster* is a prayer to God, Our Father, and the *Ave Maria* is a prayer to our blessed Mother. It's lovely, very comforting. Listen." She began to translate it for Janna. "Hail Mary, full of grace, the Lord is with thee, Blessed art thou amongst women and blessed is the fruit of thy womb."

Moved by the simple words, Janna touched the small figurine secreted in her purse, the mother and child. She would show it to Agnes one day. "And the *Credo* and *Gloria*?" she asked. "What are they?"

"The Creed is where we say we believe in one God, and the *Gloria* is where we praise Him. I can teach them to you, if you like? Then at least you can say some of the Mass with us."

"What about the rest of it? Why don't they teach you that too?"

Agnes shrugged. "It doesn't matter. If I don't understand what's going on, I just talk to God instead, quietly inside my mind."

Talk to God? Janna thought about it. There seemed something oddly comforting about the notion of having someone all-powerful to confide in. "Does He ever answer you?"

"Not really. But I know He listens to me, as well as to the nuns, and that brings me comfort and peace of mind. I know that He will help me, He will answer my prayers."

Janna wondered if Agnes had ever prayed to be made whole again. "And if He doesn't do what you ask?"

"Then it is His will, and I accept that."

Janna didn't know whether to envy Agnes for her faith, or pity her for having such blind belief in it. Had Eadgyth once felt like this too? The thought stopped her from questioning Agnes further.

"I used your salve last night, Janna. At least, the salve Sister Anne made up to your recipe. I felt so sore yesterday after our work in the fields, but my scar feels easier today. I think it's really helped me."

"I'm glad of that. Keep massaging it into your skin." Janna could imagine how painful the scarring must feel, for the skin would be stretched tight over muscle and sinew, having not grown properly since Agnes was a child. She wondered if there was anything else she could suggest, and wished she was able to consult her mother. Eadgyth had always had an answer for everything.

The sun blazed down. Janna was hot and sweating in her long habit and scapular as she took up her position beside the farm servants, who were already hard at work. Today it was Janna's and Agnes's turn to walk behind the harvesters, picking up the cut stalks and binding them with cords of twisted straw before stacking the sheaves together to dry in the sun. She looked around her as she worked, recognizing several men and women who had been physicked by her mother in the past, or who had bought creams and potions in the marketplace. Most of the land along the Nadder and Wylye Rivers was owned by Wiltune Abbey, and these villeins owed the abbess boonwork at this time. She envied the women their freedom to kilt up their gowns while they worked. How the whining gnat would complain in chapter if a lay sister bared her legs for all to see!

"Mistress Johanna?"

Janna's heart jumped as she saw who had spoken to her. The stranger. The slight upward inflexion made his words sound like a question rather than a greeting. She wondered if she could look blank and pretend she didn't know to whom he was referring. As she hesitated, she saw his slight smile and knew that he was sure of her.

"Do I know you?" she asked instead.

"Not yet." His smile grew broader, turned into a leer. "I was told a pretty new lay sister had joined the abbey. I wanted to see you for myself. I'm glad to say that the report does not do you justice."

"And who are you, *my lord*, to pass judgment upon me?" Fear banished by his over-familiarity, Janna's tone was tart with annoyance.

The stranger seemed a little disconcerted by her fiery spirit. Recollecting himself, he swept a low bow. "My name is Alan, but my friends call me *Mus*." Mouse? He was surely joking. "Your friends have a sense of humor," she observed.

"Not at all," he rejoined swiftly. "They know me very well." He grinned at her and stooped to gather the cut sheaves, brushing a nest of plaited grass belonging to a family of harvest mice out of the way. Janna moved to rescue them but was too late. His large boot came down and crushed them. To hide her distress, she bent and joined Mus in his labor, and worried about how she could move away without being too obvious about it.

The hot, heavy day wore on. Only the children's spirits seemed undiminished. They swooped about the field like little birds, calling and cooing to each other as they collected the fallen grain and stored it in the pouches slung around their waists. The screeches of greedy crows punctuated their playful chatter, while their sudden loud shouts and shrill whistles prompted noisy flappings of wings as the glossy black birds were frightened into flight.

The stranger stayed close to Janna whenever she moved, and smiled when he caught her eye. His presence made her deeply uneasy. She could not forgive him for the wanton killing of the mice. She was quite sure that Mus was not who he claimed to be, while his nickname certainly did not fit his temperament. No mouse, Alan. This man was bold, forward, and Janna was sure his intentions toward her were not honorable.

With a sinking feeling, she came to the conclusion that there was nothing she could do to have him removed from the band of workers. She resolved instead to be careful, very careful, and to keep a close watch. No matter if he misread her intentions, just so long as she never turned her back or gave him any opportunity to do her harm. Covertly, she studied him. She was sure, now, that she'd seen him somewhere before, and not all that long ago either. And then a possibility came to her, and she almost blurted it out. Instead, she decided to test him.

"Have I seen you somewhere before?" she asked.

"No, I don't think that's possible." He gave a merry laugh, although his eyes stayed cold and watchful. "I am a servant of the abbey. You mistake me for someone else, mistress, I assure you."

Janna nodded, and smiled as if she believed him, relieved that she'd kept her suspicions to herself. In spite of his denial, she well recalled that sad procession out of the forest as Dame Alice and her husband had hurried to the manor farm after receiving news that their only son had gone missing. Janna had been standing close by, desperate to conceal her identity once she'd recognized them. She'd kept her head bent as they rode past, but she remembered that they'd been accompanied by several servants. And Mus was one of them.

She shuddered. Robert of Babestoche had killed once to hide a secret and keep safe his position as the husband of the wealthy Dame Alice. As soon as he realized Janna knew what he'd done, he'd acted against her too. But he hadn't succeeded in silencing her forever, and he knew that now. If Mus was Robert's manservant, his reason for being here had nothing to do with helping to gather the harvest.

Agnes was working on her other side, and Janna took the first opportunity she could to draw her friend apart. Before she could say anything, Agnes dug her in the ribs and said, loud enough for Mus to hear, "I see your new beau isn't wasting any time getting to know you better, Janna."

Cursing inwardly, Janna gave a merry peal of laughter and tried to look coy. "Don't leave me alone with him, not even for a moment," she hissed out of the side of her mouth.

"Do you think he means to seduce you?" Fortunately her years of training in how to speak unobserved prompted Agnes to discretion now. Janna could only just hear her words.

"No, not that! I believe he means me harm. I'll tell you all about it later," she whispered, her words accompanied by another peal of laughter as she resumed her position. If Mus was an emissary from Robert, he could have only one thing in mind: her destruction. It must happen soon, for Robert would be desperate to silence her and would have instructed Mus accordingly.

Mus? Rat, more like! She glanced sideways, this time responding to his smile with a quick toss of her head. Under no circumstances must he think her afraid of him, nor must she let down her guard. Her muscles tightened, her heart sped to a gallop in response to the threat he posed. She felt as if she was sitting on a pile of dry tinder just waiting for a spark, for the conflagration to begin. "Let him do his worst," she muttered under her breath. "Just let him *try*!"

As if he'd read her thoughts, or even heard what she'd said, Mus sidled even closer to her. Just as Janna braced herself to foil his next move, Agnes gave a sudden groan. She dropped the heavy sheaf of cut wheat, and sat down abruptly. She bent over, clutching her stomach with one hand and massaging her sore shoulder with the other.

"What's wrong?" Janna asked urgently, stepping out of Mus's reach as she bent to help her friend.

"Nothing. Nothing." Agnes tried to struggle to her feet. Before Janna could lift her, the bailiff was there with his hand outstretched and his face creased with concern.

"You must rest a while in the shade, Sister Agnes," he said firmly. Not giving Agnes any chance to disagree, he picked her up and carried her off. Startled, Janna watched them, smothering a grin as she noticed Sister Martha. The lay sister had straightened and was staring after the odd couple with an outraged expression. The gnat would have a wonderful time in chapter for certes, but Janna determined she would speak up for her friend and make it clear to the prioress that the bailiff's action had been kindly meant and that Agnes had had no choice in the matter.

The bailiff settled Agnes under the shade of a tree and handed her a leather bottle. Janna's mouth became suddenly dry as she watched Agnes take a long drink and hand the bottle back to the bailiff. She said something to him, and they both laughed. Janna hoped her friend would be all right, that she wouldn't be sent back to the abbey, but she didn't like to break her own labor to enquire. Besides, watching the bailiff hover solicitously, she felt sure Agnes was in good hands.

She stooped over the fallen wheat dropped by Agnes, gathered the sheaf together, then deftly twisted several straws into a long tie to bind it up before hefting the bundle to one side. Uneasily aware that she was vulnerable without her friend's protection, Janna moved forward to rejoin the group, taking care to ensure that she was as far from Mus as possible.

As the morning wore on, Janna looked up periodically to check on Agnes's welfare. On one occasion the lay sister seemed to be rising, ready to return to the fields. The bailiff stooped and spoke seriously to her, and she sank back onto her grassy cushion. He sat down beside her. Curious, Janna watched them and wondered what they were saying. Agnes looked solemn. She bent forward, and seemed to be listening carefully. Once she appeared to be patting the bailiff's arm although, even as Janna suppressed a smile at the sight of it, she snatched her hand away and covered the scar on her cheek instead. Janna wished that she was a fly, so that she could buzz around them and listen in.

"You're not really a lay sister, are you?" Mus's voice made Janna jump. She tossed her head and didn't reply. "So why are you hiding in the abbey?"

"I'm not hiding!" Janna glared at him.

"A young beauty like you? You must have some admirers, surely?"

"No," Janna said firmly.

"I can do something about that." Mus stepped closer and slipped an arm around her waist.

Outraged, Janna gave him a hard push and retreated further out of his way.

"Playing hard to get?" he murmured. "I like your spirit."

Not deigning to answer, Janna turned her back on him.

"I know a quiet place we could go, where we could have fun together without being seen. I'll introduce you to the ways men and women may pleasure each other, for that's something you'll never learn in an abbey."

"Try anything, and I'll cripple you," Janna warned.

His eyes gleamed. "We'll see about that," he said, "for I warrant you're going to enjoy what I have to teach you." Whistling cheerfully, he bent to tie up a sheaf of wheat.

The hayward's horn was a welcome reprieve for Janna. Even though the wheat field was crowded and she was sure Mus wouldn't risk any move that might be observed, she felt uneasy. She left the field and hurried over to Agnes, who was still sitting under the tree.

"Are you all right to walk back to the abbey?" she asked anxiously.

"Of course. I would have come back to work, but Master Will won't hear of it." Agnes's eyes lit up with mischief. "I'm tempted to ask him to carry me all the way home, just to see Sister Martha's face!"

Janna laughed, relieved to see her friend in such good spirits. "Stay where you are. I'll fetch us some dinner," she said, and went to collect some meat pasties, fruit and a jug of ale. She sat down beside Agnes, and began to eat with enthusiasm.

It was some time before she realized that Agnes wasn't really listening to her chatter.

"I saw the devil last night." Janna licked the last crumbs of the pasty from her fingers. "He had fangs for teeth and snakes for hair."

"Good. Glad to hear it." Agnes continued to watch the bailiff, who had not yet sat down to eat, so busy was he with supervising the bundles of sheaves now being loaded onto a wagon.

Janna followed her glance, and nudged Agnes to get her full attention. "He seems like a very kind man," she said.

"Indeed he is. I've known him ever since I was old enough to come out and work in the fields. Poor man." Agnes's face softened in sympathy. "His wife died last year. He was telling me that his youngest child still calls for her mother in the night. There are times when he cannot console her."

"Does he have no other family to help him?"

"A sister, he says, but he doesn't often see her. His oldest child is but ten. Wat, he's called. That's him over there." Agnes pointed at a young lad, one of several who had quickly stuffed themselves with food and were now kicking around a pig's bladder filled with straw, scuffling each other to gain possession of the ball. It wasn't often that the children had time free to play. She looked up then as the bailiff approached.

"Thank you for your care of me, Master Will. I-I regret the trouble I have caused you. As I am of no use to you, I will not come out tomorrow. I don't want to be a burden."

Janna knew how much Agnes's sacrifice meant to her and felt deeply sorry, yet she could think of no way out of the problem.

"Never think you are a burden, Sister Agnes," the bailiff protested firmly. "I would not have you toil in the fields any longer, for I have seen how difficult it is for you, but..." He looked around, seeming momentarily at a loss for words. His face suddenly brightened. "But I have just the task for you," he said cheerfully, and beckoned one of the children forward. "As you know, the abbey takes a tithe of all the wheat we'll reap here." He took the cloth bag from the child and held it out in front of them. "See?" he said, indicating the gleaned wheat that the child had gathered. "Instead of keeping one of the mothers back to supervise the children, perhaps you might do it instead? The young ones especially need watching."

Agnes's smile stretched from ear to ear. "Oh, I would like that," she breathed.

"Then I'll see you both tomorrow." The bailiff's glance rested on Agnes for a moment longer before he walked away to deal with a question from a waiting villein. Janna took Agnes's left arm to help her up and together they strolled back to the abbey. While Agnes babbled happily about the bailiff's kindness, and what a good man he was, Janna wondered if kindness was his only motivation, and where it all might end.

Chapter 5

It was Janna's turn to cut the wheat on the following day. She and Agnes were late coming to the fields for, as expected, there'd been a complaint from Sister Martha at chapter. "He picked her up in his arms. He *carried* her over to a tree!" From her awed, horrified tone, Janna was quite sure the gnat's imagination had turned an act of kindness into a scene of utter debauchery. She hurried to intervene.

"The bailiff was merely trying to help," she said. "Sister Agnes was…" She hesitated, suddenly aware that it was not up to her, as a newcomer, to explain Agnes to her sisters.

"I was in great pain from having to lift the heavy bundles of wheat in order to tie them," Agnes said, with dignity. "Master Will carried me over to a tree so that I might sit under it in comfort to recover my strength." She glared at Martha. "You cannot make any more of it than that!"

"You had better stay within the abbey today, Sister Agnes," the abbess decided.

"But Master Will has a very important task for her to do today!" Janna protested, knowing how much Agnes looked forward to escaping from the confines of the abbey.

"You will allow Sister Agnes to speak for herself!" The abbess turned a fiery glance on Janna. "I know you are new to our community, but you will remember St Benedict's Rule of Silence, and you will only speak when you are spoken to." She turned back to Agnes. "What is your task?" she snapped.

"To...to look after the children who follow the reapers and glean the fallen wheat, thus allowing a more able worker than I to take my place." Agnes waited, with bent head, for the abbess's decision.

"Very well." But Abbess Hawise sounded somewhat reluctant. "You may go out to the fields today, to see how well you acquit yourself in your new task. But if you feel you could use your time to better purpose in the abbey, then I expect you to make a proper choice thereafter. Be sure I shall ask you for your decision at chapter tomorrow."

Janna admired the abbess's tactics, though was still afraid her friend would listen to her conscience and put duty before pleasure. But Agnes's care of the children would be genuinely useful; she must urge her friend to say so on the following morn.

The villeins were already hard at work in the fields by the time they came out of chapter, and leaving Agnes to go in search of the children, Janna entered the shed in search of a sickle and a pair of gloves. It was dark after the brightness outside and she waited a moment for her eyes to become accustomed to the gloom. The door banged shut behind her, cutting off what light there was. Janna jumped at the sound, but before she could hurry to open it, she found herself enveloped in a pair of strong arms.

"I knew if I waited long enough, I'd catch you alone," Mus murmured.

Janna was about to lash out but realized she was powerless in his grip. Fighting panic, she forced herself to relax. "What do you want?" she asked, her voice made husky with fear.

His grip tightened. He gave a short laugh. "You know what I want," he said, and kissed her, pulling her close so that she could feel his hard arousal.

Janna was sure his goal wasn't seduction, not if he was Robert's man. But it seemed he wasn't averse to satisfying his lust before he carried out Robert's instructions. As he clamped one hand on her breast, she noticed the gleam of a scythe over his shoulder, one of several stacked close to the door. If she could only maneuver him a little closer, it would make a good weapon. She softened into his embrace and forced herself to give him an exploratory feel. "Perhaps I've misjudged you," she said, as his grip tightened on her breast. She tried to shift toward the door, but he held his ground, keeping her close, pressing himself against her. She closed her eyes to think, to make a plan. His tongue pushed into her mouth. Janna tried not to gag, tried even harder not to bite down. Deliberately, she pushed herself against him, and rubbed her hips against his. She heard the hiss of his breath. He clamped his mouth more firmly on hers, while his hand moved down to loosen his breeches.

Shaking with fear, Janna managed to give a small giggle. "I can't breathe properly, Mus," she protested, and pulled away from him. Not giving him a chance to respond, she forked two fingers and jabbed forward, throwing all her weight into the action, aiming straight for his eyes. As he howled in protest, she flattened her hand into a blade and slammed it against his neck. For good measure, she hitched up her habit and gave him a hard kick in the bollocks. Leaving him doubled over in pain, she flung open the door and raced across to the bailiff.

"Help!" she shouted. "Help! I've been attacked!"

Everyone came running, the bailiff leading the charge. He marched into the shed, grabbed Mus and yanked him upright. A big, thickset man, he was more than a match for Mus and he shook him as a dog shakes a rat. "Is this the man, Sister?" he asked, while Mus fumbled with the tie of his breeches. Janna nodded.

"Do you know him? Have you met this man before?"

Janna hesitated. "The first time I ever spoke to him was here, out in the field," she said truthfully.

"Who are you?" This time the bailiff addressed Mus, who stayed silent.

"He told me his name is Alan, but he's called Mus," Janna said helpfully.

Mus glared at her. "She enticed me here. She begged me to come. I thought I'd oblige her, that's all."

"Liar!" Janna's fists clenched; she was white hot with rage. "I believe this man to be in the employ of Dame Alice's husband, Robert of Babestoche. He has come here under false pretenses," she said. If she couldn't make Robert pay for his crimes, she'd make sure she brought his servant to account.

Mus's scowl was so venomous, it spurred Janna on. "May I suggest you search his scrip, Master Will," she said, her suggestion not wholly motivated by spite. She was genuinely curious to know the full extent of Mus's intentions toward her. She noticed the flash of fear on his face, and her suspicion was confirmed as the bailiff extracted a long, thin cord from the scrip. Janna pictured it circling her neck, strangling tighter and tighter, and shuddered.

"What is this for?" the bailiff asked sternly, dangling the cord in front of Mus.

"It's to catch...animals."

"With two or four legs?" The bailiff looked from Mus to Janna. "I believe you've had a very lucky escape," he told her.

Janna felt a slight easing of tension. So he understood Mus's true purpose.

The bailiff switched his attention back to Mus. "I am sending you back, under guard, to your master. He can deal with you."

"No!" Janna protested, for Robert would surely let Mus go free to come back and try again. She thought quickly. "Master Will, as I am under the protection of the abbey, should not the abbess be called upon to pass judgment on this matter?"

"You are right." The bailiff nodded in agreement. "The abbess must certainly be told what has occurred this day—and also apprised of the full extent of the harm that was intended."

Janna felt cold to her soul. She began to shake. But she knew also a great sense of triumph for, whatever happened now, the abbess would not allow Mus to go unpunished, no matter what Robert might say in his defense. After today, the abbess might also understand her own desire for protection, even if she was unable to spell out the reasons behind it.

She watched as the bailiff tied Mus's hands together, using his own strangling cord to do so. Two sturdy villeins marched Mus off in the direction of the abbey. Janna lingered by the shed to watch them go. Great shivers still racked her body. She crossed her arms over her breast and held on tight, fighting for control.

"Janna! Are you all right?" Agnes hurried up, pushing through the crowd to reach Janna's side. "What's happened?"

"The rest of you—go back to work," the bailiff shouted, nodding to let Janna and Agnes know they might stay for some moments of privacy. As Janna recounted what had taken place, although not the main reason behind Mus's actions, she felt some relief: putting what had happened into words took away some of its horror.

"But how did you manage to escape?" Agnes's mouth was open in wonder.

"My friend Edwin taught me how to defend myself." Janna felt a flood of gratitude as she recalled how the outlaw had insisted she learn the moves that would keep her safe while she was living disguised as a youth. "I was hiding in the forest," she said, and went on to tell Agnes how she'd had to flee when her home was burnt to the ground, and how she'd met Edwin. "He showed me what to do."

"And I thank God and all His angels for it," Agnes said devoutly. "Truly He was looking after you today, Janna."

Or I was looking after myself? But Janna didn't put her thought into words.

"Do you want to go back to the abbey now, to rest?" Agnes asked.

"And miss our wonderful dinner and the chance to talk without being bound by the vow of silence?" Janna managed a shaky smile. "The danger has passed, and I have work to do. But what about you? Surely you don't want to go back?"

"No, I don't." Agnes sounded troubled as they walked toward the workers busy laboring in the field. "But the abbess is right. I cannot, in all conscience, believe that my work here is more important than God's work in the abbey."

"Surely all work is equally important in God's eyes?" Janna knew how badly Agnes wanted to continue taking part in the harvest activities. "*Laborare est orare*, isn't that what you said?"

"To work is to pray. Yes, I know, but this—" Agnes threw out a hand to encompass the golden wheat and the chalk downs beyond, "—this feels like an indulgence. The children are an indulgence. I so enjoy their company, looking after them, seeing to their hurts, their scraped knees, their small squabbles and rivalry..."

"Aren't you allowed to enjoy the work you're doing?" Janna wasn't being mischievous, she was genuinely curious. To her surprise, Agnes's face flushed a guilty red.

"Tomorrow I will stay in the abbey," she said firmly, and rushed to pick up a toddler who, determined to keep up with her older sibling, had run too fast and come tumbling down.

She was squalling loudly, but Agnes sat down with her, took her onto her knee and told her a story. The child's cries quietened; she listened intently. And Janna watched them, and wondered if this was the bailiff's youngest, who still cried for her mother in the night.

*

As it turned out, they were both told to stay in the abbey the following day. The attack on Janna had caused a great stir and the abbey buzzed like a hive of bees as everyone discussed what had happened in whispers and out of the corners of their mouths. From the glances that came her way, Janna surmised that some suspected she'd brought her troubles upon herself.

With Sister Grace and Sister Anne in attendance, the prioress summoned her to give a detailed account of what had happened. While Janna felt shame as she described how she'd gulled Mus into believing she welcomed his attention, she felt no regret over what she'd done next. She knew, only too well, why he'd carried the plaited cord, and she told the nuns that too.

"But why do you think he planned to murder you after he'd ravished you?" Sister Anne asked.

Janna couldn't answer, for the answer wasn't hers to give. It would mean betraying a secret that went right back to the death of her mother. So she stayed silent.

"You came to the abbey seeking sanctuary. Did you fear something like this might happen?" the prioress questioned.

"Yes."

The prioress waited for further explanation. When none was forthcoming she rose, indicating that the interview was over. "We shall do our best to keep you safe," she said. "Whatever the man's motive, you have no more reason to fear him. We have him locked away and have sent word to his master of his misdeeds." Janna was about to protest in dismay, but the prioress forestalled her. "I have ensured that the message is handed to Dame Alice, for she is the man's liege lord and must take responsibility for his actions."

Her words eased Janna's concern. Dame Alice was no fool. She would not allow Robert to be lenient on Mus, not when she realized whom Mus had attacked. Perhaps Hugh would be there too, to lend his weight to the argument? Janna felt great warmth and comfort as she thought of Hugh.

The matter was also aired at chapter, after Sister Martha complained that the new lay sister had behaved in an unseemly fashion.

"Could you explain what you mean?" the prioress asked, with barely concealed impatience.

Janna listened, open-mouthed, as the gnat tried to justify her complaint with the observation that, although an attack had been attempted, the attacker appeared to have come off worst in the encounter. "I am not sure what measures our new lay sister adopted to get the better of him," Sister Martha said virtuously, "but I wonder that someone with such...knowledge...should be made welcome in our abbey."

Janna was about to launch into a fiery defense of her actions, but the prioress got in first. "We may all be thankful that our new lay sister was able, so courageously, to defend herself and her *honor*." She stressed the last word, and paused so that all might ponder its meaning. "Should you ever find yourself in like situation, Sister Martha, and I pray to God that none of us ever do, you would do well to defend yourself just as vigorously as Sister Johanna has done." Not giving Sister Martha any further opportunity to complain, she said a final prayer and swept out of the room.

*

"*To keep you safe.*" The prioress's words echoed in Janna's mind through the long days that followed. "To keep you prisoner" was what the words really meant, even if that wasn't the prioress's intention. Janna was becoming used to living her life by the bells that summoned the sisters to church and the rules that governed when to eat, to sleep, and to work. She was becoming used to the life, but not enjoying it, confined as she was within the abbey walls. Even the usually cheerful Agnes moped about, doing her chores with grim determination coupled with a virtuous expression. Janna knew her friend hankered to be out of doors with the children, just as she herself yearned for the same freedom.

Whenever they could, the pair volunteered to help care for the garden. There was always digging, weeding or watering of plants to keep them occupied, so that at least some of their time could be spent outdoors. Janna continued to instruct Agnes about the plants in the physic garden: their appearance and their various properties, both culinary and medicinal. Sometimes they encountered the infirmarian, picking leaves and flowers or digging roots for medicaments. As she always greeted them and seemed willing to talk and ask questions, Janna took the opportunity to ask questions of her own about those plants she hadn't seen before. Acquiring information and passing on her knowledge to Agnes helped ease the frustration of knowing that she was no nearer to accomplishing her main reason for coming to the abbey: to learn to read and write. She would willingly have put up with everything else if only that came within her grasp.

By a stroke of ill-luck for Sister Anne, and the best of luck for Janna, the infirmarian sliced her finger open one morning while sawing at a tough root. The finger became infected, the infection spread and Sister Anne was suffering real discomfort and disability by the time she finally spoke out in chapter.

"I am unable to care properly for my patients," she said, and held up her bandaged hand for all to see. "I need help in the infirmary. But there's an added burden, for as you know we are about to celebrate the life of our patron saint, Edith, at our annual fair. It is our custom to sell some of our goods there, including our own special salves and medicaments. While I still have sufficient for our own needs, I need help to prepare an extra supply for sale at the fair." She looked about the assembled convent, and her gaze rested thoughtfully on Janna. "It has come to my notice that we have a new lay sister who is skilled in the use of herbs, knows well their healing properties, and knows also how to prepare them. I crave the abbey's indulgence for my weakness, and ask that Sister Johanna may be given permission to live within the convent for a time. She can sleep in the infirmary and help me look after those who are sick, while also helping me prepare for the fair."

All eyes swiveled to Janna. It took a moment or two for her to comprehend what she was being offered, and then her heart swelled with joy at the opportunity being handed to her. Yet, from the abbess, there was silence. She seemed to be deep in thought. Janna's hands clenched. She couldn't bear it if, having been offered the chance to put her plan into action, permission was now to be denied.

"Our new lay sister's mother was the *wortwyf*, Eadgyth," the abbess said finally. There was a collective indrawing of breath. Many of the nuns remembered that a Mass had been said for her soul—and for the soul of her daughter. Janna wondered how many of her secrets the abbess would divulge, and chafed under the knowledge that she was powerless to stop her.

"It became known to me that Mistress Eadgyth did not always follow the teaching of our Lord, Jesus Christ—but I am told she was a skillful healer. Has she taught you all she knew, Sister Johanna?"

Unsure how to answer, Janna was silent. Part of her mother's estrangement from the Church came from the help she had sometimes given to those women who, for compelling reasons, begged her to provoke their courses and prevent a baby coming to term. If she said yes, the abbess would know Janna possessed such knowledge, and might change her mind about allowing her to live within the convent. If she said no, the abbess would think her unskilled and deny her this chance. She cast a glance of mute appeal at Sister Anne.

"I see modesty prevents Sister Johanna from answering your question, Mother," the infirmarian said smoothly. "However, I have questioned her in the past, and also answered her questions. I am sure that she knows enough to be of great help to me, and that she has the sort of lively and enquiring mind that will enable me to teach her anything she yet needs to know."

The abbess nodded. "Very well."

Janna released a silent breath of relief. She was filled with exultation: to use the knowledge her mother had taught her, to have the freedom of the garden and, best of all, to have time with the infirmarian to learn to read and write—it seemed all her prayers had been answered at once. Excited, she turned to Agnes to share her good fortune, and read the desolation on her friend's face. Janna's exhilaration died as quickly as it had been born. She'd got what she wanted—but it had come at a price.

"We'll still be able to see each other," she whispered, as soon as attention had moved elsewhere and it was safe to talk.

"Of course we will." Janna could see Agnes was making a huge effort to look happy, to be glad for her. "But I shall really miss you," she added honestly.

"I'll miss you too." Janna brightened. "If I told Sister Anne how much you already know, maybe she can ask for you to come in and help us?" Agnes's smile flashed bright as the sun after a storm cloud had passed. "I'll do my best, anyway," Janna promised.

"The new lay sister is *talking* in chapter." The familiar whine came from behind them. The abbess pretended she hadn't heard, but her frown encompassed Janna and Agnes as well as Sister Martha.

As soon as chapter was over, Sister Anne beckoned Janna to her side. Janna felt a real sense of loss as she watched Agnes move away to stand with the other lay sisters, who were waiting to be told their orders for the day by Sister Grace. She'd never felt so close to anyone before. She realized how much she'd miss Agnes's company as the lay sister waggled her fingers behind her back in a gesture of farewell. It made her all the more determined to speak out on Agnes's behalf.

"Go and fetch your belongings from the lay sisters' dorter," Sister Anne instructed. "I'll wait for you here and take you to the infirmary."

"Yes, Sister. And thank you." Janna looked at the elderly nun. "I won't let you down, I promise."

"I know that." Sister Anne's eyes twinkled. "I've been asking questions about you, and about your mother. Some of the villagers I spoke to confirmed her skill, and said that they believe you've inherited her gift. While we won't have cause to use *all* of your mother's remedies here, I believe there is much we can teach each other."

Janna winced as she understood the nun's meaning, but she couldn't help feeling flattered when the nun continued, "But even before I made my enquiries, I had my eye on you. And this injury has made me even more aware that I must begin training others to take my place in the infirmary."

"Do you need more than one pair of hands to help you, Sister? For I know Sister Agnes is anxious to learn about herbs and their healing properties; I've already taught her much of what I know."

Sister Anne nodded thoughtfully. "I will bear that in mind, but I've already been granted a boon in gaining your help and I can't ask for any more at present. Let's just see how we get on for the moment, shall we?"

Satisfied she'd done her best to honor her promise to Agnes, and eager to get started, Janna turned and began to run toward the lay sisters' dorter. Her heavy habit constricted her movements. Recollecting where she was, she slowed at once to a rapid, but decorous, walk. Her heart sang with excitement. She was about to learn to live as she believed her mother had once lived, in a community of nuns. She would have the opportunity to question them all, just in case Eadgyth had spoken to any of them about her past. Best of all, at last she might have the chance to learn to read and to write. The secrets of her father's letter to her mother were finally within her grasp.

*

The first of Janna's disappointments came after dinner in the refectory. She'd washed her hands in one of the basins in the lavatorium, then filed in along with the nuns, half excited, half fearful as she contemplated the tasks that lay ahead. She'd been placed beside the door, and understood she was among the lowest of the low as she looked to the high table at the furthest end of the room where the abbess was seated under a great cross, flanked by several obedientiaries.

She was about to start eating when the abbess's voice stayed her hand. Janna bowed her head and waited impatiently for grace to be said. She helped herself from a platter of vegetables and began to eat, picking up the food from her trencher of bread with her fingers. Almost at once she was interrupted by a novice on her right, who waved a spoon at her. As Janna hastily picked up her spoon, the novice on her left tapped her arm to gain her attention and began to weave her hand through the air. Unsure what she was meant to do, she frowned in bewilderment. The novice repeated the action. Janna shrugged. Finally, with a smothered "Tsk" of impatience, the novice reached across and grabbed hold of a platter of mackerel. She placed it in front of her, and swam her hand through the air once more, then pointed at the fish. Janna nodded. It was all very confusing.

The novice helped herself to some fish and Janna took some too. It was delicious, but she hardly had time to take more than a few mouthfuls before a young oblate sitting opposite began shaking her hand, holding two fingers against her thumb. At a loss, Janna threw up her hands. The oblate reached across the table and took hold of a heavy salt cellar. Janna watched how sparingly she helped herself to the precious substance. As soon as she set it down, Janna took some for herself, keen to try what had always been too costly for her mother to afford. She dipped a portion of fish into the white crystals and cautiously tasted it, savoring the extra piquancy and flavor. Bemused, she watched the silent pantomime continue around her as the nuns signed their needs to each other, and passed dishes accordingly. She was beginning to understand how seriously the community took the Rule of Silence, and how much she would miss Agnes's irreverent whispering.

Worse was to come. One of the nuns walked up to the lectern. Janna had the impression that she came reluctantly, for her footsteps slowed as she came closer. Her face was downcast so that she looked only at her feet and not where she was going. Consequently, she tripped and almost fell as she encountered the steps that led up to the lectern. Instinctively, she clutched the book she carried closer to her chest, much as a mother might hold a child after a safe rescue. She climbed the stairs and carefully opened the book.

"H-h-h-hence…Hence th-the L-Lord s-says…in the …the G-Gospel, 'Who…whoever l-listens …'"

Janna looked down at the trencher of bread in front of her, no longer able to watch. She couldn't bear to hear the tortured sounds, and tried to close her ears to them, and her mind to the nun's humiliation. She'd read the shame and desperation in the nun's eyes as her mouth strained to utter whole words and managed only the smallest part of them. She remembered that this was Sister Ursel, owner of the mouse called Chester. She wondered if the mouse was keeping company with the nun up at the lectern, and risked a glance.

"'I…will l-liken him to a w-w-wise m-m—'"

Janna stuffed a piece of fish into her mouth and chewed vigorously, trying to take her mind off what was happening. The other nuns seemed unconcerned, obviously quite used to this appalling travesty of speech. They waggled or shook their fingers, stroked their wrists and noses, or their stomach, squeezed their ear lobes and knocked their index fingers together. Janna watched, and tried to make sense of it all.

The meal, and the reading, progressed. Janna couldn't wait to leave the refectory, and restrained herself with impatience while the abbess recited a last prayer before they were all free to go. She went at once to the infirmary, and found Sister Anne awaiting her there. The nun had already introduced her to the patients, one with severe toothache and another with a stomach ache, plus several ancient nuns who were now permanent residents in the infirmary, being too crippled or infirm to manage the stairs to the dorter or attend services in the church through the day and night.

"Here's a soothing balm," the infirmarian told Janna. "I'd like you to give Sister Angelica's back a good rub, for it troubles her greatly."

Janna looked at the greasy substance. She took a deep breath, knowing she must speak the truth for the infirmarian would find out soon enough. "I—my task was to make up the salves and decoctions. It was my mother who always ministered to the sick." Try as she would, Janna could not keep resentment from souring her voice. She had begged Eadgyth to give her more responsibility, but her mother had always refused, saying that there would be time enough for that later. But later had never come, and Janna was well aware of the vast gap in her experience that would have stood her in such good stead now.

"Did your mother teach you about the humors of the body, how they comprise blood, phlegm, red and black bile? Did she tell you what to do if the humors are not in balance?" Sister Anne queried.

"No, she did not," Janna admitted. She'd believed her mother had known everything, was startled to find that it was not so.

"She did not tell you that the body may be warm and dry, warm and moist, cold and dry or cold and moist?"

Mute with shame, Janna shook her head.

"Did she mention the body's relationship to the four elements: earth, air, fire and water?"

"No." Janna's confidence had evaporated. She felt extremely stupid.

"The art of healing does not rest only on knowing about herbs and their properties. Our knowledge is based also on medical practice passed down to us by the ancient Greeks, Romans and Persians."

"Oh." Janna waited, in distress, for Sister Anne to banish her from the infirmary now that she had learned the full extent of her ignorance.

"I believe that your mother was a skilled healer, and that she practiced the leechcraft of the Saxons," Sister Anne observed. "It could be that she was aware of the gaps in her knowledge, and feared them, and that was why she took upon herself the responsibilities of her healing practice and did not share them with you, lest you were made to take the blame for her lack of understanding should something go wrong."

Janna was silent. Sister Anne's words made sense. They certainly helped to explain Eadgyth's continued resistance to Janna's pleas. The last shreds of her resentment toward her mother slipped away.

"I feel sure there is much you can teach me, Johanna, for I know little of leechcraft but you obviously watched your mother carefully and learned from her all that you could."

"Yes, Sister, I did." Janna's hopes began to rise once more.

"Then massage Sister Angelica's back. I shall watch what you do, and instruct you as you go." Sister Anne gave a wry smile. "Besides, I have no choice in the matter." She held up her bandaged hand.

Janna helped the ancient nun disrobe and picked up the pot of ointment, thrilled to be given the opportunity for which she had always longed. She wondered if conversation was allowed during treatment, and decided to risk it. Her quest was too urgent for delay. "May I speak, Sister Anne?"

The nun nodded. "Talking is allowed in the infirmary, although I don't encourage idle chatter," she added severely. "What do you wish to know?"

"I am most grateful for your trust in me, Sister Anne." Janna thought it best to flatter before asking for a favor. "You'll find me a willing worker and a keen student, for I wish to know everything I may about healing the sick. Everything!"

"I shall do all I can to help you, Johanna." Sister Anne leaned forward. "A little higher," she said. "Use your thumbs, and move your hands in circles."

"My greatest wish is to learn my letters," Janna continued, following the nun's instructions as she spoke. "I shall willingly tell you all that I've learned from my mother, and help you in every way I can, but in return will you teach me how to read and write?" She held her breath, her hands moving in a slow rotation over the elderly nun's back.

Sister Anne frowned. "I didn't realize we were going to bargain over this, Johanna. When I asked for your help I expected a free exchange of information, for the joy of doing the Lord's work, as well as helping the sick and needy."

"Yes! Yes, of course!" Janna was horrified her words had been misunderstood. "I beg your pardon, Sister. Of course I will tell you all I know. I-I was just speaking what was in my heart, telling you my dearest wish in the hope that you may help me."

"I would if I could." Sister Anne gave a rueful laugh. "But I am not as skilled in letters as I would wish. What I know of medicine and healing was told to me by my predecessor, just as I will now pass on that knowledge to you. Those sisters who can read and write have duties elsewhere to occupy their time. The chantress and Sister Grace are our teachers, but they teach the oblates, postulants and novices, those who have come to the abbey with a dowry. And the greatest part of their instruction is in the forms of the offices and the rules and customs of our house. They also give lessons to those children whose parents wish them to learn their numbers and letters, but the abbey is paid a fee for that instruction, of course."

Sister Anne's meaning was plain, and Janna's high hopes evaporated like dew in the summer sun. "Besides, I have need of you here," Sister Anne continued. "St Edith's fair is less than three weeks away, and there is much to prepare before then."

It was a bitter blow to Janna's hopes. She knew of nowhere else, other than the abbey, where she might learn to read and write, yet it seemed those skills would be denied her. But there was one more thing that she might learn. "Did you find out anything else about my mother while you were asking questions, Sister Anne?" she asked eagerly.

"No, I did not. I heard how she had come to the abbey asking for help. That was shortly after our beloved abbess died and Sister Hawise was elevated to take her place." Janna noticed how tart the infirmarian's voice became at the mention of the abbess. She continued to massage industriously. Beneath her supple fingers, muscles eased and softened, and the old nun gave a murmuring sigh of relief.

"Do you know of anyone in the abbey who might have spoken to my mother or who knows anything of her circumstances?" Janna persisted, unwilling to accept defeat.

"No, I do not." Sister Anne looked in puzzlement at Janna. "Why do you ask? Is it important?"

"It's very important! You see, I know nothing about my mother, where she came from or what she did before she came here. She told me nothing about her past, but I...I have reason to believe she may once have been a nun, perhaps even an infirmarian like you?"

"Why did you not question her?"

"I did! She would not answer me, at least not until just before she died. She was going to tell me, she said, who my father is, for I don't even know that!" Janna's face flushed hot with shame at the admission. She pressed too hard, and the old nun groaned in protest.

"Be more gentle!" Sister Anne remonstrated. "Old skin is thin and old bones brittle, remember that."

"I'm sorry. I'm sorry I hurt you, Sister Angelica."

"It's all right, child. Your touch gives me relief and I am grateful for it." The sharp, clear tone reminded Janna that there was another witness to her shameful admission. She blushed anew.

Sister Anne stayed silent for a few moments. "I can think of no-one who knew your mother, or who spoke to her when she came here, but that need not stop you asking questions when talking is permitted, Johanna."

"Thank you, Sister. I'll do that." The conversation was over, all opportunities closed. Janna knew a bleak despair as she continued to carefully massage the old nun's back.

Chapter 6

The days rushed by, crammed with activities. If Janna wasn't ministering to the sick under the watchful eye of Sister Anne, she was out gathering plants and preparing healing salves and decoctions for sale at the fair. In spite of her disappointment over her failure to learn to read, she was happy to be busy and greatly looking forward to the fair, for she was hoping she might get leave to attend with Sister Anne. People were traveling to Wiltune from all around the country, and the guest houses of the abbey, both for pilgrims and poor travelers as well as for the well-to-do, were already full, as were the stables. Every day there was a hustle and bustle in the courtyard as traders came in to pay their respects to the abbess, and their tolls and fees to her steward.

Whenever she was outside in the cloister or in the garden, Janna could hear the faint sound of hammering from the marketmede as booths and stalls were constructed for merchants to display their wares. Master Siward and his manservant, the travelers who had so frightened her outlaw companion, Edwin, might be there to buy and to sell. Janna hoped, with all her heart, that Edwin had managed to stay hidden from their sight. He would have had help from his sweetheart, Bertha, and probably from Hugh too, for Hugh understood Edwin's situation and his need to stay safely out of their sight. A sudden thought set Janna's heart racing. It was quite possible, nay, even probable, that Hugh, and maybe Godric too, would also attend the fair. Now that Hugh's cheating reeve was dead and his hoard of purloined goods discovered, there would be an abundance of produce from the manor farm to sell. The thought made Janna more determined than ever to seek leave to attend the fair.

She remembered the attempt on her life and felt a shiver run down her spine. She might feel trapped inside the abbey, but its walls kept her safe. Her spirits revived somewhat as she began to rationalize the aftermath of the attack. After what had happened, surely Dame Alice would be keeping a watchful eye over Robert and his servants, while Robert should understand by now that she was keeping silent about his role in her mother's death, and therefore was no threat to him. Not yet, Janna amended grimly, conscious of the quest that still lay before her. She began to count back the days on her fingers, and finally gave up. The attack had happened some weeks ago; by now Dame Alice and her husband were probably safely home on their own manor. Their steward might well attend the fair, to buy and sell on their behalf, but it was most unlikely that they themselves would come.

*

The day celebrated in memory of St Edith's death dawned sunny and clear. Inside the abbey, all had been made clean and sparkling in honor of their patron saint. The church was resplendent, decorated with flowers and produce as thanksgiving for a harvest safely in and as a benediction to St Edith. Half asleep as she was, Janna's nostrils were overwhelmed with the scent of the flowers, fruit, nuts, herbs and spices heaped at the altar and around St Edith's shrine in its own side chapel. She took her place at the back of the choir stalls, and peered down the nave, searching for Agnes. She'd hardly had a chance to talk to her friend in the intervening weeks; making up creams and potions for the fair had kept her fully occupied. The only time they could snatch a few words was when Agnes came in for a new supply of ointment. Janna had taken over its preparation, adding lavender and sunturners to Sister Anne's usual mix in the hope that they might help to ease the tight scars.

Janna hadn't forgotten her promise to Agnes, but her entreaties to Sister Anne had not met with any success. She determined that, if she was given leave to go to the fair, she would try to ensure that Agnes came too. Meanwhile, she half listened as the Mass continued. Agnes had taught her all she knew, so Janna could follow some of the chants, but she still did not join in, although she loved to listen to the sound of the nuns' voices and the music they made. She was coming to know them now, and it amused her to watch them sing, for she thought their characters could be read in their faces and in the language of their bodies.

The sister who leaned forward, almost bouncing on her toes as she threw her heart and soul into glorious song, was just as enthusiastic and whole-hearted over everything else she did about the abbey. The nun who sang with hands folded and mouth pursed small, as if begrudging her time and the use to which it was being put, made sure that her disapproval touched everything to which she set her hand. A large nun sitting in the front row of the choir always opened her mouth just a little too early and finished with an extra trill that kept her singing on after the others were silent. As she had the loudest voice, the disharmony was often painful, just as her insistence on always coming first and being the best caused some heartache and muttering among her sisters in their daily lives. There were nuns who sang with serenity and joy, secure in the knowledge that God listened and was pleased. Others sang with unclear words and uncertain notes, reflecting perhaps their own lack of vocation and certainty. Janna, to her intense chagrin, had found she was unable to sing at all, producing only a dry croak as the sum of her efforts.

She had also come to know those nuns who broke the rules of the abbey in the keeping of pets. Sister Ursel was the only one who kept a mouse, and Janna had yet to make the acquaintance of Chester, for the nun kept him well hidden. But several nuns sheltered small dogs, docile for the most part, with the exception of the bad-tempered brute that had barked at Sister Ursel's mouse and was universally disliked, except by its owner. Rabbits were quite popular, being simple to feed, silent and easily concealed, but there were also a couple of cats, and one nun kept a squirrel and another a rook with a broken wing. Sister Anne had tended it after being sworn to secrecy, and had made its owner promise to release it into the wild as soon as it was able to fly and fend for itself.

Janna was sure the abbess knew of the pets but turned a blind eye if she could, as did the prioress and Sister Grace, under whose special care the young oblates and novices came. They were the worst offenders. Janna watched the love and attention they lavished on their animals, and felt sorry that they seemed to know so little of human love and warmth.

She looked down the nave, where the lay sisters and guests of the abbey stood. It was as well, she thought, that Sister Martha was not part of the nuns' lives within the confines of the abbey. Janna was sure that hard, self-righteous heart would have no room for furry pets given that there was so little room in it for her companion sisters. She would find much to whine about, should she ever take her final vows and be admitted to the community. Janna doubted even St Edith, with all the miracles she'd performed over the years, would be able to turn that annoying little gnat into a compassionate and glorious butterfly.

She took a breath of the sweet, scented air, while her thoughts turned to the saint whose life was being celebrated this day. Sister Anne had told Janna the story of St Edith, child of a handfast union between Edgar, King of England, and a woman called Wulfrid. "She may have been a nun, for it is said the lady wore a wimple and veil," Sister Anne had said, sparking Janna's interest as she recalled the fate of her own mother. "For certes, she would not consent to live with Edgar. Instead, she retired here to Wiltune with her baby daughter, Edith, who grew up devout and learned. Edith received the veil from the Bishop of Winchestre when still only a child, and she built the church of St Denis here at Wiltune, which was consecrated by St Dunstan. She died shortly afterwards, aged only twenty-three. But miracles were already happening in her name, and they continue still."

Miracles. Janna resolved to say a prayer to St Edith to help her find her father. But Sister Anne was still talking. "This is not the original church. That was built of wood, like the rest of the abbey, but both town and abbey were destroyed by the Danes. Our church was rebuilt in stone by another Edith. She was the wife of the Saxon king, Edward the Confessor. Pilgrims still come to pray to St Edith in the hope of a miracle, but we do have other saints' relics here too."

"Here? Where?" Janna had looked around the infirmary, while Sister Anne smiled at her innocence.

"Our precious relics are all kept safely in their own small chapels in the church," she said, and had gone on to tell Janna of a group of weary pilgrims from Brittany who had once visited the abbey, bearing the bones of a saint called Ywi. "They laid the bones on the altar before retiring to bed," she said. "In the morning, when they came to continue their journey, the casket bearing the bones was so heavy they could not lift it; it seemed stuck fast to the altar. Try as they might to shift the saint, he could not be budged." Janna was about to laugh, until she realized that the nun was in deadly earnest and that the story was not yet over.

"Our abbess expressed her regret, and did all she could to assist the pilgrims to lift the casket bearing the saint's bones, but he would not move. At last, accepting that the saint had decided to make his home here at Wiltune, the abbess had to give a large offering to compensate the pilgrims for their loss, and the saint stayed with us."

"Was that Abbess Hawise?" Janna asked, with an innocent expression.

Sister Anne gave a sly smile. "No, fortunately it was not, or the pilgrims might have been forced to take both casket *and* altar with them on their journey. Our abbess does not give away money lightly, not even for the relics of saints."

Janna looked now toward the small chapel where the bones of their saint reposed in her reliquary. The altar was usually illuminated by cresset candles, hollowed stone bowls, each filled with mutton fat and a floating wick. Under the care of the sacristan, they burned day and night and were never allowed to splutter out and leave the saint in darkness. There were extra candles today, and the shrine looked magnificent. The golden casket was decorated with flowers; the colors glowed in the soft candlelight. Propped against the walls were a multitude of discarded crutches, testimony to the healing powers of the saint. The chapel was opened daily to the pilgrims who came to kneel in devout prayer, asking for the saint's intercession in their lives. It would be crammed later with a press of eager bodies, all willing to make a donation for the privilege. But for now the space in front of the saint's altar was empty for everyone was in church, giving thanks for the day and for the saint's life and, no doubt, also eagerly anticipating the delights of the fair.

The priest concluded the Mass and the nuns began to file out. Janna, as befitting her humble status, came last after the novices and oblates. In the few minutes it took to walk into chapter, she put her request to Sister Anne. "May I come with you to the fair?" she asked.

When Sister Anne did not immediately reply, she pressed further. "I know, as well as you, what is in our lotions and ointments so I can help you tell people what is in them and give advice as to their use. Besides, my mother and I used to make up goods for sale so I have experience in the market-mede. I will get the best price for everything, I promise you!"

Sister Anne's expression turned from doubtful to extremely wary. "We do not haggle," she said severely. "Remember, we are about God's work here."

Janna was sure that she had won. She could not hide her delighted smile. "Wouldn't Mother Abbess be delighted to know that God's work doesn't come cheap?"

"Be careful you don't let your tongue run away with you lest I change my mind," Sister Anne warned, but her tone was more indulgent than her words. "Could our good Sister Agnes come too?" Janna pleaded, knowing she was testing the infirmarian, who might think she hadn't heeded her warning. But this was something that must be settled before chapter. "Sister Agnes knows something of our work and, besides, she'll provide an extra pair of hands when we're rushed off our feet with eager customers."

Sister Anne gave a chuckle deep in her throat. "Your enthusiasm does you credit, Johanna. Just take care that it does not carry you away altogether." Janna was so delighted she could have hugged the nun. She took a few dancing steps instead, then hurriedly straightened her face along with her habit as they walked side by side into chapter.

*

Both Agnes and Janna were hard put to hide their excitement as they stepped sedately beside Sister Anne past the porteress's lodge, out through the abbey gates and on to the marketmede, where trading had already begun. Janna looked around, happy beyond measure to be outside the confines of the abbey. "I expect we'll see Master Will supervising the abbey's business here at the fair," she commented. She chided herself for mentioning something that was none of her affair, but she was curious to know how things stood between her friend and the bailiff.

"Do you think he'll be here?" Agnes's ready smile flashed. Her eyes sparkled with joy.

"I do believe you care for him!" Janna instantly regretted her words when the look of surprise on Agnes's face turned to a hostile wariness.

"No, you're wrong. I don't care for him at all! My life is here at the abbey. I already told you that." Agnes quickened her pace to catch up with Sister Anne. Janna hurried after them, silently berating herself for her insensitive meddling. She could find no excuse for it at all.

Crowds swirled around them as they reached the heart of the fair. Janna glanced about, hoping she might see Hugh or Godric. She became aware that Agnes had dropped back to walk beside her. Agnes had pulled down the front of her veil and was busy rearranging the folds of her wimple to cover most of her face. She felt a pang of pity as Agnes whispered, 'Did you see how that merchant and his family turned their eyes from me when they saw my disfigurement?"

"Who? Where?" Janna had noticed no such thing.

"There." Agnes pointed at a small group of people clustered around a young man who was busy juggling balls, keeping five of them in the air at once.

"Perhaps they turned their eyes to watch the juggler?"

"I saw the look of horror on their faces before they turned away," Agnes insisted. Her steps had slowed. There was an expression of sorrowful bewilderment on her face. "I can't see how I look, and so I forget," she said. "Inside I feel whole, and joyful."

"And that happiness and serenity is reflected on your face," Janna reassured her. "Yes, people might stare, but only for a moment, and certainly not after they come to know you, Agnes."

"Look over there! That woman's pointing at me, and her little girl is laughing."

"The woman is pointing at the juggler, Agnes, and her little girl is laughing with excitement."

"No, you are mistaken. They're looking at me," Agnes insisted. Janna shrugged. She was sure Agnes was being too sensitive to people's stares and too quick to attribute them to her disfigurement, but she didn't know how to change her friend's perception of the situation.

"I'm known in the abbey. I'm not known here. It frightens me to see people staring so." Agnes hurried to catch up with Sister Anne who was striding ahead of them.

"May I have your permission to return to the abbey, Sister? I'm not feeling well." Agnes spoke before Janna could say anything. The infirmarian turned to them, an expression of concern on her face. Janna hoped she'd insist that Agnes stay, for she was sure part of the girl's insecurity stemmed from the fact that she'd never been beyond the abbey's protection since she'd been burnt as a small child. Perhaps the time to break those bounds was badly chosen, Janna acknowledged now. After the quiet and ordered calm of the abbey, this must look like bedlam. She surveyed the crowded fairground. The hustle and bustle of merchants, traders and chapmen calling out their wares and customers bargaining over goods was punctuated by screaming children, barking dogs and the bellows, neighs, grunts, cackles and cluckings from the animal and poultry markets set in their own portion of the meadow. All these sights, sounds and smells excited Janna. The fragrance of hot pies, the sharp tang of fish and the sweet aromas from the spice merchants set her head reeling with delighted anticipation. She glanced at Agnes and wished she'd considered this outing more carefully, and that she'd never spoken of the bailiff. If Agnes was frightened away now, it would take a lot of coaxing to entice her ever to leave the abbey again.

"Stay!" Janna begged. "Please."

Agnes flashed her a look of hopeless longing, then turned to Sister Anne to await her verdict. "It is your decision," Sister Anne said quietly. "Only you can know which is the right path for you to take."

In those words, Janna realized that the infirmarian shared her doubts about the real reason for Agnes's request but knew also that, for the infirmarian, a lifetime spent inside the abbey walls was not a penance but a preferred way of living. Having given Agnes an opportunity to glimpse the world outside, she was now making Agnes choose, and take responsibility for her choice.

Agnes hesitated, while Janna held her breath. Also at stake was the probability that she would be ordered to escort Agnes back to the abbey. Her day at the fair was at risk.

The moment was broken by the bailiff. He strode up to them, stuffing a handful of coins into a bulging leather satchel. "I give you good day, Sisters," he said. "God be with you." Janna noticed his gaze fall on Agnes, who flushed and turned away, pulling her wimple higher to hide her face.

"God be with you too, Master Will," Sister Anne returned his greeting. "The abbey is doing well out of the fees and tolls, I see," she said, indicating the satchel at his waist.

"Indeed. We have a record number of booths and stalls set up this year," the bailiff said with satisfaction. "'Tis fortunate that the troubles 'tween the king and his cousin have not come near enough to interfere with the harvest this year, or with those who are willing to chance the roads to sell their goods."

He smiled at Agnes before turning to address Sister Anne. "Let me escort you to the stalls where the abbey's goods are on display. Of course the steward will be on hand to oversee everything, while I and my deputy are available to trade on your behalf, should you wish it. But I know you take pride in your salves and medicaments, Sister, and I am sure those buying them will want to consult you regarding their properties."

It was only as they followed the bailiff through the crowded fair that Janna missed Agnes, and realized that she had made her choice and slipped away. Relief that she was still free to enjoy the day mingled with shame as she blamed herself for not choosing a more propitious moment to introduce Agnes to the world outside, and also for calling attention to her friendship with the bailiff. She could not shake off the feeling that something important had been lost. She'd witnessed Agnes's fear and disappointment, seen the light of joy die in her eyes, and she knew it was all her fault.

She wished she had a coin to buy Agnes some little trinket from the fair by way of reparation. The brightness and glamor had gone from the day. Subdued, she took her place beside Sister Anne at the stall, and looked out upon the fair with none of her former relish.

Her interest was pricked as she espied a youth whistling nonchalantly as he jostled through the throng. Something about him seemed ajar, and Janna watched as he brushed against a richly dressed merchant. A knife flashed and, just as Janna imagined the worst and opened her mouth to sound the alarm, the youth turned away and the merchant sauntered on. No quarrels and no blood shed then. Janna relaxed once more, only to prick with alarm as the merchant held up the cut cord of his purse and gave a loud shout: "Help! I've been robbed! Stop! Thief!"

At once she looked about for the young cutpurse but he had gone, melted into the crowd just as snow becomes water in a swiftly flowing river. Although the steward had appointed guards to patrol the fairground and keep a constant lookout for wrongdoers, Janna suspected the youth was probably one of many pickpockets and thieves who would try to turn a dishonest profit this day. She touched the slight bulge of her purse underneath her habit, glad it was hidden from prying eyes. More precious than anything were these few relics from her mother, and her father's letter. She would do all in her power to keep them safe.

Her thoughts were interrupted by a haughty request for information. Sister Anne was busy with another customer, and so Janna answered the dame's questions about the cream she was holding. "It's perfumed with violets," she said. "You may rub some on your skin every evening. It will do wonders for your complexion." Janna lowered her voice so that the nun couldn't hear. "And the perfume will encourage your husband's attention."

The woman gave her a startled glance and Janna grinned until, recollecting her new status, she settled her face into a more decorous expression. Judging the dame's worth from the rich fabric of her clothes and the gold band that kept her veil in place, she set a high fee on the cream and the woman paid for two jars of it. "And may I interest you in my special hair powders and rinses?" Janna continued, made bold by her success. She looked at the greasy locks of hair escaping from the confines of the woman's veil. "They're made from lemons and sunturners to add freshness and sunlight to your hair," she said persuasively.

"Sunturners?"

"Marigolds." Sister Anne had told Janna their real name, but Janna preferred the old name that described the way the flowers always turned their golden faces toward the sun.

"Remember, no haggling, Johanna," Sister Anne muttered as she reached across her to pick up a jar..

Janna bobbed her head obediently, and this time set a slightly lower price.

"I'll take one," the dame agreed, and unlaced her purse once more.

"And I'll take two," said a merchant's wife standing beside her. Janna felt a sense of satisfaction. This was honest trade, not haggling. She knew the worth of her preparations. The women would benefit from their use; they would not feel cheated.

Well pleased with her venture into business on the abbey's behalf, for she'd had to do some fast talking to persuade Sister Anne to allow her to prepare those creams and rinses that had no medicinal purpose, she handed over the coins to the infirmarian.

"You've done well, Johanna," Sister Anne murmured. "I see your years of experience in the marketplace are paying off!" Janna was especially pleased when the nun added, "Perhaps we shall add more of your special preparations to our stock at next year's fair." She turned to another customer, this time an elderly whiskered gentleman who wanted something for a gouty leg and an aching back.

Janna and Sister Anne were kept busy for some time thereafter, selling medicaments as well as Janna's preparations for skin and hair, teeth and bad breath, tired limbs and aching feet. As the coins clinked in, Janna's spirits rose. Although she didn't like the abbess, she was happy to think she was contributing something useful toward her new home. It took her another moment or two to recognize the true source of her growing contentment. Dressed as she was, everyone thought she was part of the abbey and treated her with respect. Respect was not something Janna was used to and she relished it, even though she recognized that nothing had changed: inside, she was just the same as she'd always been. But her smile was brighter, her face more cheerful as she undertook to be the best representative the abbey had ever had.

"You've worked hard, Johanna," Sister Anne told her, after a lingering customer had been served and there was no-one new in sight. She took a coin from the heavy purse, and held it out. "Would you like to buy yourself a pie and some ale for your dinner, and enjoy the fair for a little while?"

"Thank you, Sister!" Janna took the coin with alacrity. "Shall I buy you a pie too?"

"No." The nun smiled at her. "Don't worry about me, I'll eat my dinner later."

Afraid that the infirmarian might change her mind if she tarried, Janna hurried away. She avoided the fenced enclosure where traders bid for livestock, keeping instead to the rows of booths and stalls where myriad goods were on display: cheeses, wine, honey, fruit and vegetables were all set out in glowing fragrant piles. Janna's stomach rumbled. She sauntered onward, stopping to admire colored gems and baubles, knives and needles, swords and daggers, fancy leather gloves and shoes with pointed toes, and bolts of fine wool and linen cloth in every hue: light blue, red, yellow, black, grey and green. Only the nobility would be able to afford such luxury; the villeins had to make do with plain homespun.

Janna imagined herself wearing a fine green gown, with embroidered edges and fashionably wide sleeves, attending a ball at the castle at Sarisberie. She would be the most beautiful of all the ladies there, and all the nobility would line up to dance with her. Especially Hugh! A mirror of polished metal caught her eye. She picked it up, and promptly burst out laughing. Not a beautiful lady in a green gown but a lay sister! She was about to put it down when curiosity got the better of her, and she studied herself more closely. The veil and wimple were supposed to cover her hair, but some locks always managed to escape their confines. But she knew its color. It was her eyes that interested her, and she stared at them. *"You have your father's eyes,"* the midwife had once told her, although that was a guess. Janna wondered if she'd be able to find him through recognizing her own dark brown eyes. She searched for signs of her mother in her face, but could find only a fleeting resemblance when she frowned. Feeling slightly disappointed, she put down the mirror and walked on.

Precious silks from across the water, decorative objects chased in costly gold and silver, perfumes and assorted spices ensured that she made slow progress. Her habit gave her protection, she found. She could stop, sniff and finger articles for sale, and no-one harassed her or tried to make her buy anything. A tray of bright ribbons caught her eye and she stopped to choose one for Agnes. Janna was sure such a pretty thing would give her friend pleasure. She could tie it under her habit, and no-one would ever know it was there. But which to choose? Bright pink, or sky blue? The green of trees or the scarlet of poppies? She picked up first one and then another; each seemed more beautiful and more exciting than the last. A splash of golden yellow caught her eye and she dropped the handful of ribbons she'd collected and picked it up instead. The ribbon lay like sunshine in her hand.

"I'll take this one," Janna told the chapman, and he held out his hand for her coin. She waited for some wooden tokens in exchange, but none came. She realized then that she'd not asked about the price, and she was the loser for it. "This comes very dear," she said. The chapman shrugged, and turned to another customer. Janna pulled a wry face, and looped the ribbon around her wrist under the sleeve of her habit, tying it with a clumsy knot. There was no money left now for a pie, but she was well-pleased with her purchase and hoped it would give Agnes pleasure and comfort, in some part, for missing the fair. Realizing that her purchase probably didn't befit her apparent calling, Janna continued on her way.

"Hssst." A sibilant whisper attracted her attention, as did the grimy hand that plucked at her habit. "I have something that might interest you, Reverend Sister." Not troubling to correct his error in naming her, Janna looked down as a linen sheath was unrolled to reveal a grubby object. She stared at it, and then at the pedlar displaying his treasure so proudly.

"What is it?" she asked.

"'Tis a fingerbone from St John the Baptist himself." Wearing a devout expression, he crossed himself. "If you only owned such a precious relic, Reverend Sister, you'd be pardoned from all your sins and look forward to life everlasting with our Savior in Heaven." He crossed himself again.

Awed and impressed, Janna peered more closely at the small bone. She wished she had coin enough to offer for such a wonderful relic, and wondered where it had come from and how the pedlar had been so fortunate as to come by it. She noticed then that he was becoming somewhat agitated, and realized why as she saw one of the steward's guards striding toward them, made distinctive by the abbey's badge worn on his breast. Before she could blink, the linen sheath was deftly rolled, hiding the finger bone from view. Whistling innocently, the pedlar wandered off into the crowd, leaving Janna feeling rather foolish. But she couldn't help admiring the rogue's brazen audacity. She was sure he'd have many more such "relics" secreted about his person. She wouldn't be the only innocent fairgoer he'd trap with his colorful inventions.

She walked on. Her stomach rumbled as she smelt the enticing aroma of hot pies. All shops were forced to close during the three-day fair, but most enterprising traders in the town had removed their goods to the fairground for sale. The cookshop, although officially closed, was doing a roaring trade from a nearby stall. Janna hurried past, feeling saliva seep into her mouth as she watched a young man bite into a savory pasty.

Duty told her she should return to Sister Anne, but the delights of the fair drew her on. She continued her perambulation between the lines of makeshift stalls, listening to the cries of pedlars and stall keepers alike, all shouting their wares with the promise that their own goods were far superior to anything else on display.

Suddenly she caught sight of a familiar face. Her heart lurched sideways. Hugh! He was pushing through the crowd, followed closely by Godric. Before she could hail them, a young woman rushed up to Hugh, seeming delighted to see him. Just as Hugh was delighted to see her, Janna noticed, as he kissed the woman's hand, and held on to it for a few moments afterward. She, however, seemed to have no courtly inhibitions. Instead, she threw her arms around his neck and planted a hearty kiss on his cheek, holding on to him as she leaned back to survey him. They laughed together, and the woman said something. At once Hugh's expression changed, became serious. He launched into speech, and the young woman listened, shaking her head and trying to protest, but he would not be interrupted. Arms akimbo, and looking indignant, he finished what he had to say. The girl smiled up into his face and said something, apparently trying to coax him into good humor. In this she seemed to succeed, for Hugh eventually gave her a grudging smile in return, and then made a courtly bow in farewell.

The young woman moved into the crowd and Janna's envious gaze followed after her. She was extremely attractive, with a rosy complexion and sparkling eyes. Her long dark hair was bound in a gauzy veil and secured with a silken band. She wore a dark blue kirtle embroidered with flowers, her ensemble marking her as a cut above the commonplace. Who was she and, more importantly, what was she to Hugh?

Chapter 7

Anxious to escape Hugh's notice after what she'd witnessed, Janna turned and hurried off, at the same time reassuring herself that her habit would render her invisible to both Hugh and Godric. She could not face the lord now, not dressed as she was, and not so soon after his encounter with that beautiful, bright young woman who so obviously cared for him and knew him well enough to have earned both his respect and his affection.

Children ran about, laughing, shouting, playing tag and pushing each other, enjoying every moment of their freedom from toil. Janna saw a trainer with his bear in the distance, and felt a pang of pity for the huge creature that stood upon its hind legs and was being goaded to dance. She heard a sudden roar from a crowd nearby and, anxious for distraction, followed the sound to investigate its cause. She caught a glimpse of bloodied feathers and a torn coxcomb, and realized she was looking into a cockfighting pit. Half attracted, half repelled, she pushed through the crush of bodies to get closer, for she'd never watched a cockfight before, and was interested to see what it was all about.

A barrier of woven wattle surrounded the pit to prevent the cocks from escaping. The pit was already stained with blood and gore from previous fights. Those who had made wagers pressed closest, their expressions intent. The two birds leaped at each other with talons outstretched, engaging in deadly combat amid a welter of blood and flying feathers. As they watched the two birds attack each other, raking downward with their sharpened spurs, the crowd shouted encouragement or groaned in despair. The larger cock seemed to be the favorite, but its smaller opponent seized the advantage when it jumped high and slashed out. Blood spurted, and the larger bird fell to the ground, mortally wounded.

The crowd gave a collective groan – the favorite had let them down. The owners jumped into the pit to pick up their birds, while a few lucky winners jostled through the crowd to get to a man holding a satchel full of coins and wooden tokens. There would be money to put ale in their mugs this night, and Janna wished them good fortune with their winnings. But for herself, she'd seen enough.

Several of the spectators had wicker cages by their sides containing colorful cocks with glossy feathers. These birds were no longer proud and crowing for their beaks were bound, and their feet too. They must suspect, by now, what fate awaited them. As Janna began to push through the crowd, two new fighters were placed in the pit, ready to be released when the word was given. The men who were clustered around surveyed them carefully, and swapped judgments with their neighbors, pulling coins out of their purses, ready to make a new wager. Janna wondered how many of them could afford to lose on what was, at best, a contest based on guesswork and chance. To win or lose on the throw of the dice, or the prowess of two fighting cocks—she shook her head, marveling at the crazy optimism that urged men to such madness.

One such was surveying the bloody pit with an intent expression. He turned his head as she passed him by, and she was struck by the wild exhilaration in his dark eyes, a sort of crazed desperation that told her he would continue to wager until his last coin was spent, that he would wager even his soul if he could. She wondered if that point had already been reached, but was distracted by a young woman hurrying toward her. Hugh's beautiful friend. Sick at heart, Janna turned away.

The noise of the fair increased as her steps took her closer to the enclosure where all manner of livestock were for sale. Geese gobbled and hissed, horses neighed and oxen bellowed, a cacophony that was matched by the roar of human voices as prices were argued and agreed upon. Seeking somewhere quieter, Janna came upon the juggler once more. He was now throwing knives into the air and catching them, to the hopeful gasps of the onlookers who waited for him to miss and blood to flow. Among the crowd were several shifty-eyed beggars, as well as a woman with bold eyes and a seductive stance. Her lips and cheeks were scarlet patches on her white, powdered face. She gazed upon the scene with a haughty stare, but Janna was sure she was fully aware of the hungry glance of every man who passed by. Not everyone was about an honest trade this day, but Janna had no doubt these other enterprises would prove at least as profitable if not more so, provided the miscreants weren't apprehended.

A man stepped from the crowd into her path, blocking her way. Instinctively Janna flinched, but then relaxed when she saw who it was: Master Will, the bailiff. Curious, she waited for an explanation.

"I beg your pardon if I startled you, Sister," he said. He looked anxious, rather nervous, Janna thought. She brushed away his apology with a quick gesture and waited, intrigued, to hear why he had stopped her. "I-I wish to enquire after Sister Agnes," he said awkwardly. "I know, for she has told me, that you two have become close friends—not that such a thing is allowed in the abbey, of course," he added hurriedly.

"Yes, we are friends." Janna hid a grin, hearing the echo of Agnes's voice in his disclaimer, and seeking to reassure him.

Master Will passed a hand over his mouth, as if unsure whether or not it was safe to speak further. Finally he said, "Think you that Agnes is happy where she is, at the abbey?"

"She has told me she is content to be there." Janna had a suspicion she knew where this strange conversation was heading.

"I know she has lived there since she was a child. She knows no other life, and yet—" Master Will looked down at the ground. "There are other ways to live," he mumbled. "She could find a good husband, someone who would be kind to her, who would give her children of her own to love."

"But..." Janna had no doubt now that the bailiff had already cast himself in the role of "good husband." Nevertheless, there were several seemingly insurmountable hurdles he must face if such a thing was to come to pass.

"She has not taken the vow that binds her to stay there," the bailiff interrupted. "I know, because she told me, that she was given to the abbey after she was badly burned as a child. She had no choice in the matter! While I understand she has taken some vows of obedience and so forth, she has not yet taken the final vow that will dedicate her life to God." He raised his eyes to face Janna, looking defiant. "I've known her since she was a child, and I realize now that I love her," he said. "I know she feels ugly in the sight of God, but when I look at her, I see only her kindness, her sense of humor, and her courage."

"As do I," said Janna, feeling greatly encouraged by his words.

"Then will you speak for me?" In his urgency, Will caught Janna by her arm.

"And say what?" Conscious of the habit she wore, Janna gently disengaged herself.

"That I love her, and would take her for my wife. But that if her love of God is greater, then I shall try to understand her vocation, and will pledge not to annoy her with my continuing attention."

"You must know she is afraid of the world outside the abbey," Janna warned.

"Because of her scars, she fears the pity and scorn of others."

"I will shield her, I will protect her."

"It is Agnes you have to convince, not me."

"But how can I do that? I saw how she ran off today rather than face the fair-goers. How can I reach her if she takes refuge in the abbey and will not come out?"

The bailiff's words sank Janna's spirits even lower as she realized the full extent of the harm she had done.

"Say you'll speak for me," Master Will begged. "Reassure Agnes that my intentions toward her are honorable, and that I care deeply for her. Please, Sister, will you do that for me?"

"I will. But you must be patient. Having spent so many years under the influence of the nuns, Agnes needs to become used to the idea of living outside the abbey. She is innocent of the ways of the world—and of men."

"Could she think of me as a husband?" the bailiff asked eagerly. "Has she said aught of her feelings for me?"

Janna hesitated. She remembered the joy on Agnes's face at the mention of Will's name. She remembered too, her first conversation with Agnes and the lay sister's admission that she would like to wed and bear children but that no-one would have her, scarred as she was. Would the bailiff's love be enough to offset her fear? Janna had no way of knowing. "She called you kind, and good," she said slowly. "I saw you laughing together during harvest, and I know she was grateful for your care of her, and for giving her an excuse to escape the abbey walls for the freedom of the fields."

The bailiff smiled his relief. "That seems like a good start!"

"I will do what I can for you," Janna said, and his smile grew wider. He left her then, with a promise to look out for her on the morrow. Janna continued to wander along between the lines of makeshift stalls, enjoying the sight of so many luxuries and the opportunity to look at them all.

Lost in thought, she didn't notice Hugh until he was almost upon her. She was about to bob a curtsy when she remembered how she was dressed. Instead, she drew aside to let him pass, turning her face from Godric, who followed him.

Hugh gave her an impersonal nod and continued through the crowd until his companion stalled him with a delighted cry: "Janna!"

Hugh came to an abrupt stop. "Johanna?" His wondering gaze encompassed her black habit before moving up to her face and the veil and wimple that covered her hair and neck. "Jesu!" he exclaimed in amazement as he hurried back to her. "You look so different, I didn't recognize you."

"My lord." Janna felt her face turn pink under his gaze, and hastily turned to his companion. "Godric!" She smiled at the villein, openly showing her joy at seeing him again.

"You look so well—and so happy!" Godric reached for Janna's hand. His glance fell on her habit. He snatched his hand away and, in some confusion, hid it behind his back.

"This is a fortunate meeting," said Hugh. "I have thought of you often, and wondered how things are with you at the abbey, Johanna. Or must I call you 'Sister Johanna' now?"

"I will answer to Johanna, sire. Or Janna. And I am well. Content."

"But you are not safe!" Godric's expression reflected his concern.

"Indeed, we heard that Robert's man had attacked you." Hugh's face darkened in anger. "And I thank Christ and all

His saints that he was unsuccessful. But I wish you would tell me the real purpose of his attack, because I cannot believe it was happenstance, as Robert claims, or even a sudden fit of lust, as Robert's servant claims. The cord in his possession gives him away, even if his tongue will not. Nor could he give us any good reason for being at the abbey and pretending to work there."

Janna sighed. It was so hard not being able to tell Hugh the truth, but to do so would be to betray Dame Alice's tiring woman, and she could not do that. Godric, however, had no such qualms. "You'd do better to ask Mistress Cecily that question," he muttered. Janna gave Godric a sharp nudge. She hoped that Hugh hadn't heard him, for although she'd told Godric of the circumstances that had led to the murder of her mother, she'd told him in confidence.

"Have no fear. I'll say no more," Godric reassured her.

Hugh considered Janna with a quizzical expression. "Mus has been sent back to Babestoche Manor under guard. But he will have to answer for his actions to the abbess when next she holds court here."

"Mus will be coming back?" Janna felt a cold sweat break out at the thought of coming face to face with Robert's manservant.

"He'll be well guarded." Hugh hesitated for a moment, understanding that his news could be unwelcome. "As his overlords, Dame Alice and Robert will also be required to attend."

Janna swallowed hard, fighting panic at the thought of seeing them all again. Yet she could not flee, for if she did, Mus would go unpunished. Worse, he would be set free to come after her once more. "But I shall be here at his trial to support you, and so will my aunt," Hugh promised.

"And so will I," said Godric. "I shall do everything in my power to protect you, Janna. You know that."

"I shall also make sure that Mus's true intentions toward you will come out at the hearing. He must be punished for the crime he planned as well as for his actions," said Hugh.

Janna nodded in heartfelt agreement. She wouldn't feel safe until Mus was locked away for a very, very long time. "So the man's name really is Mus?"

"It's not his real name. It came about, so I am told, as a joke, because he is such a sly fox with the ladies. I must apologize to you on behalf of my family, Johanna. I am sure Mus's attentions were most unwelcome. But I can't say I was surprised to learn that, even though you are smaller and attired in a nun's garb, you yet managed to get the better of him."

Janna looked into his dancing eyes, and wondered if he was laughing at her. She decided to give him the benefit of the doubt. "I did warn him," she murmured. "I told him if he tried anything, I'd cripple him."

"And what did he say?"

"That he likes a challenge."

"I'll make sure to pay attention if ever you give me like warning," Hugh said with a smile. Janna remembered that they had once shared a kiss, and that she'd enjoyed every moment of it. Her face began to burn at the memory. Godric, too, had kissed her, kissed her until her bones had melted with wanting. She dared not look at either of them. "I have missed you all so much," she said hurriedly. "Please tell me, my lord, do your aunt and the lord Robert still reside at your manor?" She cast a quick glance around, suddenly fearful.

"No, no. They went back to Babestoche with Mus."

"And the young lord? Hamo?"

"He's still staying with me, and is thriving under the care of Cecily and Godric. He is learning how to ride, and fight with a sword, and how to be a good squire."

If Hamo was learning all those things, so Godric would also be learning them, and Cecily too, Janna thought, trying to stifle a pang of envy. Then she remembered the young woman she'd seen earlier with Hugh. Who was she, and what was their relationship? She was afraid to ask. There was, however, yet another rival for Hugh's affections, and this time curiosity got the better of discretion. "And how fares the cook's daughter?" Somewhat dreading the answer, she waited for Hugh's reply. Gytha badly wanted to marry Hugh, and had high hopes that her dream would come true—a dream made more urgent perhaps by the death and disgrace of the reeve who had risked all for her love.

"She fares well enough, I think." Hugh gave an indifferent shrug. "All is quiet about the manor now that my thieving reeve is dead."

"And Edwin? What of him, my lord?" Janna was anxious for news of the outlaw who had stolen her purse while she was lost in the forest, but who had later taught her the skills that had enabled her to protect herself from Mus's attack.

Hugh smiled. "He stayed under cover until the men from his manor departed for Winchestre. But I have spoken to him. He asked for permission to become betrothed to Bertha, which I have given, and he is living now with her family. He does week work for me at present, but I believe Bertha's father intends to take him on as an apprentice once they are wed. In time he will become a carpenter."

"He told me that was his dream: to become an apprentice and make his own way in the world. I'm so pleased he's found a safe haven with you, my lord, and that he's also found love and a livelihood with Bertha and her family."

"And what about you, *Sister* Johanna? Have you found what you wanted in the abbey or do you also look for love and a livelihood?"

Hugh's slightly mocking tone put Janna on the defensive. "I already have what I desire, sire," she said, and watched Godric's face fall. She longed to reassure him, but could not speak in front of Hugh, for she knew Robert would redouble his efforts to silence her if he found out that she planned to return one day and hold him to account for the death of her mother.

"What brings you to the fair, my lord?" she asked, to bridge what was becoming an awkward silence.

"To oversee the new reeve. With Godric's help I now have a full accounting of all the bounty from my manor: everything that Serlo had hidden in his cellar, plus the new fleeces and the surplus from our harvest. Godric has become my eyes as well as my right-hand man. I shall ensure that this will be a profitable year for my manor."

Janna nodded, understanding Hugh's relief in having good news to tell his aunt, for his living depended on his good husbandry of her property.

A group of musicians approached them. They were accompanied by a throng of laughing villeins and their children, who danced about and jostled all in their path. Janna took a step out of their way, spied a puddle of dirty water just in time and tried to step around it, but stumbled. As she fell against Hugh she heard him give a shocked gasp. She launched into a hasty apology, but realized he wasn't paying any attention. He was doubled over, hands pushed into his side, with an expression of disbelief on his face as he watched blood seeping between his fingers.

"My lord!" Janna was horrified. She looked about for the culprit as she scrambled to her feet, but the jostling throng had walked on and the three of them stood alone. Without asking permission, she pulled Hugh's hands from the wound and looked with dismay at the slash in his tunic and the blood now flowing freely from the wound. She snatched off her veil and used the fabric to staunch the blood, pushing it hard against his torn tunic and the wound beneath. "Hold this in place," she instructed, before unwinding her wimple and tying it around his waist to secure the makeshift dressing. There was no telling how deep the blade had gone, or what damage it might have done. She glanced up at Godric.

"He needs treatment, fast," she said breathlessly. "Get someone to help you take him to the abbey gate. Beg admission from the porteress. I'll run to fetch the infirmarian, and we'll meet you there." She whirled, all thoughts of propriety and the Sin of Running flown from her head as she raced back to the abbey's stall to fetch Sister Anne.

The infirmarian's words of censure regarding Janna's bare head and disheveled demeanor died on her lips as she listened to Janna's hurried explanation. Pausing only to snatch up the purse of coins and give it into the bailiff's hands for safe keeping, she hastened with Janna to the abbey. "Do you know how to treat wounds of this nature?" she asked breathlessly as she tried to keep up with Janna's urgent strides.

"Bugle, selfheal and sanicle to cleanse the wound, and the roots of white lilies mixed with hog's grease to help knit sinews. Yarrow, dog rose, sunturners and parsnips boiled in butter will make a good salve."

"Good," Sister Anne said. "You gather what we'll need and see about making up a cleansing lotion and a plater, while I find a bed for the lord Hugh and assess the extent of his wounds. I can't look after him properly in the guesthouse so I'll have to find a place for him in the infirmary."

As soon as they reached the abbey, Janna wasted no time in rushing to the physic garden, leaving Sister Anne to talk her way past Sister Brigid and into the convent with Hugh.

Godric was hovering, looking worried and getting in everyone's way, when Janna finally found them all in a curtained cubicle off the main dorter of the infirmary. She'd made up a paste of green herbs in the infirmary kitchen, and this she held out to Sister Anne along with a pot of hot water in which floated the cleansing herbs to which she'd also added leaves of soapwort to wash the wound. "I've left a decoction simmering; it's a tonic for the lord," she told the nun as she proffered a strip of linen to go with the paste.

"You've done well, Sister Johanna." Sister Anne took the pot of hot liquid, thought better of it and handed it back to Janna. "Let me see you wash and bind the wound," she suggested.

Janna took one look at the pale, still figure lying on the low truckle bed, and her courage fled. She held the pot out to Sister Anne once more. "Go on," the infirmarian encouraged her. "You'll never learn if you don't do it yourself. Be sure I'll tell you if I see you do aught wrong."

Janna had to take a deep breath to summon up enough nerve to approach Hugh. Sister Anne had stripped off his blood-soaked tunic and he now lay, hairy and bare-chested—and utterly defenseless—in front of her. She had to take a few more deep breaths before she found the courage to touch him.

He groaned and opened one eye. "What happened?" he asked warily. "How did I come to be wounded?"

"I don't know." Conscious of Sister Anne's watchful eyes, Janna had to force herself not to gag as she gently swabbed away the blood to cleanse the wound. Hugh's breaths came short and shallow; there was a sheen of sweat on his pale face, but he kept silent under her touch.

"Tell me what you see," Sister Anne instructed.

Aware that her heart was pounding hard with fear and excitement, Janna peered into the deep cut as best she might. "It seems to be a flesh wound only. It's deep, but it's not wide. I don't think it has touched anything vital," she told Sister Anne, and received a grunt of confirmation in reply.

"That sounds like good news." Hugh smiled faintly, but kept his eyes closed. Janna spread the healing paste over the wound then set about binding the torn flesh together with the linen strip, pausing every now and then to wipe away the beads of perspiration from Hugh's face. Careful and conscientious as she was, her mind was not wholly on her task. Hugh's question had set up questions in her own mind, questions that concerned her greatly. The attack had seemed to come from nowhere. It had happened so fast she couldn't be sure if she had been the intended target, or Hugh. Or had he, in fact, fallen on his own dagger when she'd stumbled against him?

A moment's reflection brought some ease to her troubled mind. Hugh's belt, plus a sheathed knife and dagger, all lay on a small chest beside his bed. They were stained with his blood, but the stains might well have resulted from the wound rather than being its cause. Janna tried to recall the scene. "Did you notice any fallen knife, or dagger, after the lord Hugh was attacked?" she asked Godric.

He frowned in concentration. "No," he said, after a few moments. "Whoever stabbed my lord must have hidden himself among the crowd around the musicians, and taken the dagger with him when he moved on."

"There were mostly women and children around the musicians," Janna said.

"Did you recognize anyone in the crowd?"

"I wasn't looking at them." Godric shrugged. "I was looking at you."

Janna blushed a deep, dark red. She dared not look at Sister Anne or Hugh, who must surely also have heard. "Could it have been an accident? Could the lord's own knife have pierced his side when he fell?" she asked.

"It may be so." Hugh spoke so faintly, Janna could hardly hear him. "Is the sheath cut? Is there blood on my dagger?"

"Yes, my lord." Godric pulled the dagger from its sheath and held them both up so that they could see for themselves the blood on the weapon as well as the cut marking the stained leather of the sheath.

"How stupid of me." Hugh's eyes closed once more.

"No, not so my lord," Godric contradicted. "Your knife was still contained within its sheath, but it was a naked blade that caused such harm."

Janna took the sheath from Godric and inspected it carefully, seeing that he had the truth of the matter. But that brought her back to her original question: who was the blade meant for? Her or Hugh? A blade aimed at her back might well have missed its mark when she stumbled and fell against him. In which case, it seemed that Robert had not given up his murderous intentions toward her and she must be more careful than ever.

*

Her thoughts were in turmoil as she joined the nuns in the refectory for supper that night. She'd missed dinner and was hungry, and so she ignored the questions filling her mind and concentrated on filling her belly instead.

She was further distracted when a small voice broke the silence. "Wh-whenever any im-imp-important b-business…" Janna wondered why Sister Ursel put herself and everyone else through the torture of her reading, then recalled what the infirmarian had told her.

"She's much better at lettering than reading," Sister Anne had said. "She spends all her time either in the scriptorium, or out in one of the carrels off the cloister. She is writing and illuminating the story of St Edith's life. I have seen some of her work and, although I cannot read the pages, her writing is neat and the illuminated letters and pictures are absolutely exquisite. It is a sublime work of art, and it will count as one of the abbey's great treasures once it is complete."

Janna looked up at the nun stammering over the text of the day. She seemed even more distressed than usual. Her eyes were red, and her nose too. As Janna watched, she surreptitiously wiped her nose on the sleeve of her gown. "L-let the Ab-Abbess c-c-call…"

Janna couldn't bear it. She stopped listening, but found that questions over the events of the day flooded into her mind instead. The novice on her left stroked three fingers on the inside of her hand, and Janna passed her a pat of butter. She placed some pieces of fowl onto her own trencher, and put the fattest piece into her mouth. Her arm brushed against her swelling breast through the fabric of her gown. She was eating well here in the abbey, she acknowledged, momentarily distracted from her whirling thoughts by the realization that she was filling out, gaining a woman's comely shape. Her breath quickened as she thought of Hugh lying in the infirmary, half naked and helpless under her touch. A sweet heat suffused her body. She dragged her thoughts back to the present with an effort as she tried to remember the gestures of the young novice sitting opposite who was pulling on her little finger. Milk. She pushed the jug across, and the novice smiled her thanks.

The tortured reading came to an end. Janna knew she hadn't imagined the sigh of relief that ran around the room. But Sister Ursel did not resume her seat. She jerked her head up so that, for once, she faced everyone, but her attention was wholly on the abbess as she stammered, "I-I have a-a fault to report, M-Mother. I h-have mislaid two p-pages of…of my m-manuscript."

A hush fell over the room. Thinking of the work that must have gone into the missing sheets, Janna felt intensely sorry for the nun.

"We will deal with this in chapter tomorrow morning. That is the proper place to raise faults and accept punishment," the abbess said severely. She rose from her chair for the final benediction, indicating that the meal was over and cutting off a faint bleat of protest from Sister Ursel. Janna was sure that the nun had been about to beg everyone to search for the missing pages. She hoped they all would and resolved to keep her own eyes wide open in case she should chance upon them. But all thought of the nun's loss was swept aside when Sister Anne materialized at her side and told her that Hugh was asking for her.

"I shall accompany you to the infirmary to attend him," the nun added severely, clearly not comfortable with the situation but powerless to do anything about it, for the lord was asking and Janna had taken no vows to prevent her from seeing whomsoever she wished.

There was no sign of Godric when they entered the infirmary. "The lord's manservant has taken the news back to his manor," Sister Anne told her, anticipating Janna's enquiry. "I've told him that the lord will need further treatment and that he is in no fit state to travel. I suspect we shall have to keep him here for several days at least." She sighed. "The abbess isn't happy about it, and I am sure the matter will be raised at chapter." She brightened, and darted Janna a mischievous glance. "I managed to allay some of our mother's fears when I suggested that the lord might well make a generous donation to the abbey if he is well treated here."

Janna gave a snort of laughter, but her mirth quickly died as she brushed aside the curtain and approached Hugh's bed. He was lying quietly, seemingly asleep, but looking so pale it seemed more like the sleep of death to Janna. With a cry of alarm, she bounded forward and laid her ear on his bare chest to listen for the reassuring thump of his heartbeat.

"Johanna," he murmured, and she felt his fingers, light as a bird's feather, stroke her cheek. She drew breath in an audible gasp and hastily straightened, meeting Sister Anne's frown of censure.

"I was just checking to make sure he still lived." She looked down at her patient. His smiling eyes showed that he was relishing the scene in spite of his discomfort.

"As you see, I live," he said helpfully, adding, "but the pain is such that death almost seems desirable."

"I can give you something for the pain that will also help you to sleep," Janna said, automatically repeating what her mother might have said. Recollecting where she was, she turned to the nun. "I beg your pardon, Sister Anne. I forgot myself."

"What, then, would you give him?" In spite of her misgivings over the situation, the infirmarian was more interested in an exchange of knowledge.

"I can brew up a decoction of primrose, wild lettuce and valerian, or hemp."

The infirmarian nodded thoughtfully. "I have a syrup of white poppies already prepared. You may give our patient just a few drops to help ease his pain. Meanwhile I have another patient awaiting my attention, but I need to make up a healing paste before I see her." She looked from Janna to Hugh. "I trust there will be no disruption or unseemly behavior while the lord is here under our roof," she said, her warning clear to both of them.

"On my honor," said Hugh. Janna nodded in agreement, although her lively imagination immediately provided a tantalizing range of possibilities. She hardly dared look at Hugh once they were alone.

"Don't look so miserable." Hugh's voice was determinedly bright. "The thought of a dalliance with me isn't so utterly dreadful, is it?"

Janna swallowed hard as she remembered their shared kiss. "Our infirmarian is right. It's not seemly even to think of it," she murmured.

"What with you being almost a nun and all?"

"With me being who I am, and you a lord," Janna returned swiftly.

Hugh was silent for a moment. "I must say, you look far more appealing in your habit than you did in those dreadful garments that you—" He hesitated. "That I stole from your aunt's barn before setting fire to it." Janna knew she was safe to admit it, for Hugh already suspected as much.

She measured some poppy syrup into a spoon and held it out to him. He swallowed it in one gulp and licked his lips, relishing the lingering sweetness. "Don't worry about the barn," he said then. "I haven't told my aunt who was responsible."

"Thank you, my lord." Janna was truly grateful. If Dame Alice had a mind to it, Janna could be severely punished for her crime.

"Now that Mus is locked up, and my aunt and uncle have returned to their own home, it's safe for you to come back to my manor, if you wish it?"

Unable to find an excuse that might convince him, Janna kept silent.

"Does your life in the abbey really suit your needs?" Hugh's disbelief was written plain on his face.

Janna nodded.

"I thought you so wild, so free; your spirit so fierce and unbroken."

"And so it is."

"How, then, can you stand to be shut in like this? Is it fear of Robert? I assure you, my aunt has his measure in full, and watches him closely now. He will not have another chance to harm you."

Hugh waited for an answer, but none came. "Robert is no threat to you, I promise you," he said at last. "You may safely leave the abbey at any time of your choosing. You know I am willing to offer you a home on my manor, indeed I greatly desire it, but of course you may first travel on to Winchestre, if you so choose. I think you said you wanted to go there?"

"Yes, but not yet," Janna said. "I will stay to see Mus brought to justice." She remembered the message Hugh had written to the abbess on her behalf, and her hand reached for the purse secreted beneath her habit. It would be so simple, it would save so much time if she asked Hugh to read aloud her father's letter to her mother. Tempted, she was about to speak, but the memory of her mother's pride and the lengths to which she had gone to keep her lover's identity a secret, stopped her. If her mother had been a nun and her father a priest, the sin was great indeed. She was already far below Hugh in station. Let him continue to respect her and her mother for what he knew of them, rather than revealing shameful secrets from the past.

Hugh shrugged. "If you change your mind, Johanna, my offer still stands. But now we have more serious matters to discuss. I called you to my bedside for I know you to be quick-witted and observant, and I am hoping that, together, we may be able to make some sense of this attack—for it was a deliberate attack, I'm quite sure of that now."

"I believe the dagger may have been meant for me, my lord. It could have happened by mischance, like this." Janna showed him how she'd stumbled, and how a dagger aimed at her back might well have pierced his side instead.

"But you are safe now," Hugh insisted. "The dagger was meant to harm me, and I think I know why, although I have scratched my brains to ribbons trying to find some other answer. Tell me, did you notice a young man wearing a red cloak amid the throng following the musicians? Dark hair, slightly taller than me?"

Janna wrinkled her nose as she visualized the colorful scene, the piping music, the shouting children and barking dogs. "I can't say, my lord," she admitted. "The fairground was crowded with so many people, villein and highborn alike, I would be hard put to single out anyone in particular." She looked down at him. "Who is the young man in the red cloak, and why would you think he'd attack you?" she asked, giving way to the impulse that always wanted to know more, even though she knew it was not her place to be so inquisitive.

"His name is Anselm, and he has a sister. A beautiful sister." Hugh looked somewhat discomfited.

"Ah." Janna was beginning to understand, but she couldn't prevent a pang of jealousy as Hugh's implication became clear.

"My aunt owes knight service to the king in return for her lands," Hugh explained. "I am one of those knights, as is Robert of Babestoche." His mouth pulled down in distaste at the reminder of their link by marriage.

"And Anselm?" Janna prompted, determined to hear the rest of the story if he was prepared to tell it.

"Is squire to another knight in the king's service on an estate some distance away."

"And he has a pretty sister?"

"Indeed." Hugh was thoughtful for a moment. "We grew up together on my aunt's manor, and it was always assumed that when Emma and I were old enough, we would wed."

Beautiful, and having almost the same status as Hugh. Janna was prepared to thoroughly dislike this Emma. "You are more than old enough to wed now, sire." It almost choked her to say the words.

Hugh nodded. "But Emma has only a very small dowry, while I have my way to make in the world."

"Do you love her? And does she love you?" Janna asked in a small voice.

He smiled. "No, and no. All this I tried to tell Anselm when he accosted me at the fair and demanded to know my intentions toward his sister. But he would not listen, and instead berated me for what he called my cold heart, my avaricious nature and, most especially, my faithlessness. I suggested he talk to Emma herself if he wanted the truth of the matter, but he was too angry to listen. He stamped off, muttering about the honor of the family being at stake. And I am sorry, for he was a good friend, and his sister too."

"And you think he might have worried his anger to such a pitch that he came back and attacked you?"

Hugh gave a reluctant nod. "I admit I did not notice him among the throng, nor can I believe he would ever do such a thing. But I can't think of anyone else who might wish me dead."

"Begging your pardon, my lord, but that doesn't make sense! If you were dead, you couldn't marry Emma. She wouldn't get what she wants, and nor would her brother, if his intention is to make you marry her."

Hugh shrugged. "But honor would have been satisfied, if that is his thinking."

Emma. The name stuck in Janna's mind like a small, scratchy burr. If she was the young woman in the market-place, she was indeed a beauty. If Hugh would not marry Emma, who was not only beautiful but highborn and with a dowry, albeit a small one, he would certainly never contemplate marrying anyone so far beneath him as herself. She caught his glance, and looked quickly away. Could he know that she was thinking how sweet it would be to love him, that if he only asked she could be tempted to throw caution to the winds but for the fact she was determined never to be caught in shame, and abandoned and disgraced like her mother. Not even for Hugh would she risk that.

Hugh had said he didn't love Emma, and nor did she love him. Was that what stopped them from plighting their troth, rather than Emma's too-small dowry? Involuntarily, her eyes strayed back to his face. The laughter had been replaced by a straightforward regard, a warmth and recognition that had not been there before. "You look so different," he murmured.

"And so do you, my lord." She strove for a light tone.

"Ah, yes." He glanced down at his bandages and at the bed he lay on. "I can hardly act like a heroic warrior while I'm lying here at your mercy, can I?"

"Is that how you see yourself, sire?" Janna asked demurely, and turned with relief to Sister Anne, who had entered the cubicle.

Chapter 8

Janna passed a restless night on her pallet in the infirmary. She had moved her bed as far from Hugh's cubicle as was possible, but even so she was acutely conscious of how close he was, and how vulnerable. She still worried that she might be responsible for his injury. She worried that the wound might be deeper than she'd thought, and that some vital organ might have been penetrated. She worried about the possibility of infection, the sort of infection that could lead to his death. She worried, too, about Emma, and Gytha, and Cecily, and any other pretty woman who might catch his eye. Her thoughts, her feelings for him, were in total confusion. He was handsome and kind, noble in every sense of the word. He had status and power, more so than any other man she'd ever met. Was that what had turned her head, or was she falling in love with him? She wondered if he was attracted to her, felt sure she hadn't misread the admiration in his eyes even while she heeded the warning implicit in his words about Emma. If he spoke true about Emma's lack of a substantial dowry, then he wouldn't look twice at Gytha, or Cecily either. Nor would he look at her, other than as a bedmate to pass the time.

Janna squeezed her eyes tight shut, trying to block out all thoughts of herself as Hugh's bedmate. Her hand touched her breast, felt its new weight, felt her nipple spring to life under her fingers. She groaned, and rolled over onto her stomach, and prayed for the dawn to come, even though it was not the dawn but Hugh she wanted. Truly she was of an age to wed, and to bear children. But first must come the pleasures of the bedchamber, and oh, she wanted them so badly.

She wrenched her thoughts away from Hugh, and instead soberly contemplated the mischief she had caused between Will and Agnes. She wished she could see Agnes, talk to her, and apologize for her stupid remark. She was concerned that what had happened in the marketplace might prejudice her friend against the bailiff's pledge, and she deeply regretted her part in it. She spent her last waking moments rehearsing what she might say to Agnes on Will's behalf, and how she might put her friend in the best frame of mind to hear her argument.

On rising, she found Sister Anne already in the infirmary, tending to Hugh's needs. He gave her a quick wink. Janna prayed that the infirmarian hadn't seen it, and that she would not notice the rising tide of red that heated her face.

"Go on," the sister shooed her away. "Go to Prime and break your fast. You may stay on to say the Mass and attend chapter afterward, where you will give a report on our patients. Then come back to the infirmary, for I need you to stay here while I go out to the fair."

Mindful that the nun was placing great trust in her, Janna nodded and slipped away. Her mind was so full of questions she hardly paid attention to what she was eating or what was happening during the celebration of the Mass. She looked for Agnes when the lay sisters filed into chapter, but knew she would have no chance to speak to her until it was over.

There was a collective gasp when the nuns learned that there was a man in the infirmary, but Janna gave a conscientious and clear report of his progress as well as the progress of their other patients, and her recital passed without comment other than a quick, "See to it that the lord is well cared for," from the abbess. Janna knew what motivated her instruction and bent her head to hide her amusement.

But there was more to come. "I saw Sister Johanna enter the convent yesterday. She was running, and her head was bare. She wasn't wearing her wimple or a veil." Janna didn't have to look up to recognize the whine.

"May I answer the charge, Mother?" she asked. The abbess nodded wearily. Janna wondered why she didn't reprimand Sister Martha for the Sin of Always Complaining. She launched into an explanation of Hugh's injury and her makeshift bandage to staunch the flow of blood, and was rewarded with everyone's undivided attention. Janna was willing to wager that nothing so exciting had happened at the abbey since the Danes had burned it down. She waited with bowed head for the abbess to deliver her punishment.

"I see you are correctly attired this morning," the abbess observed. "Make sure that the bloodied linen is properly laundered and made fit for wear once more. Attend to it personally. That is your penance."

"Yes, Mother. Thank you, Mother." It felt strange to address someone other than Eadgyth as "mother," and yet Janna recognized the role played by the abbess in the convent. Abbess Hawise might not fill the role to perfection but anyone else in her position might indeed make a kind, loving and wise substitute for a parent.

"M-may I...may I s-say s-something, M-Mother Abbess?"

So the missing pages were not yet found. Janna felt desperately sorry for Sister Ursel as she stammered her way through her confession of the Sin of Carelessness.

"How do you account for the pages going missing?" the abbess asked.

"I-I was w-working in a c-carrel off the...the c-c-cloisters. I w-wondered if...if the w-wind might have b-blown them away?"

"Was it windy while you were working there?"

"N-no, Mother."

"Do you leave your work unattended at any time?"

"Yes, s-sometimes. But at...at the end of...of the day I-I t-take it b-back to the s-sc-sc—"

"Scriptorium." The abbess faced the convent with a stern countenance. "Does anyone know anything of these missing pages? If so, I want to hear about it now!" When no reply seemed forthcoming, she added on a softer note, "Our good sister labors long and diligently over this illuminated life of our beloved saint, and any lost page is a betrayal not only of our own St Edith, but also our Lord, for this toil for His greater glory will have been in vain unless the pages are found."

This was worse than Janna had imagined. She waited for lightning to strike the hapless Sister Ursel, or Christ and His avenging angels to mark her for her sin. Everyone waited for the abbess's verdict. Sister Ursel had gone so pale, Janna wondered if she might swoon.

"I know how careful, how meticulous you are about scribing and illuminating this manuscript, Sister Ursel, and how much the life of St Edith means to you." Abbess Hawise sounded genuinely sorry for the nun. "To lose so many hours of your work is penance enough, for I feel sure that you have already searched diligently." Her gaze hardened as she surveyed the assembled convent. "I want you all to search for the missing pages. If you find them, you must bring them to me. And if any one of you knows something of this matter, do not let it sit on your conscience. Come and see me at once." She looked about the room, fixing everyone with a fierce stare, before bowing her head to utter a closing prayer and benediction.

After chapter, although anxious to get back to the infirmary, Janna waited for the lay sisters to file out. She wasted no time in finding Agnes among them, and drew her aside. "I was so sorry you didn't stay to enjoy the fair yesterday. Were you really not feeling well?" she whispered anxiously.

"I did feel sick—with fright." Agnes pressed her lips together in a rueful expression. "I lost my nerve and I am sorry for it, especially when you went to so much trouble to arrange for me to come with you."

Janna hesitated, wondering if she was going to regret what she said next. "Master Will was sorry too," she said at last. "He told me he looked for you, but—"

"I don't like people looking at me!"

"He wasn't looking at you, he was looking *for* you."

"Why?" Agnes pulled at her wimple in an unconscious effort to hide her scars.

"Because he cares for you, Agnes. He asked me to speak on his behalf. He—"

"No!" Still hiding her scarred cheek, Agnes backed away from Janna. "My place is here, in the abbey. I have work to do here, the Lord's work."

"Surely all our work is for the Lord, no matter where we may be, or what we do, or even how we go about it?" Janna protested.

"I am here because I love the Lord!" Agnes's voice rang out in sudden, strident affirmation. "As soon as I was old enough, I took a vow to be obedient, to live chastely and in poverty. I cannot break my vow."

"Is that your answer to Master Will, then?"

"It is!" Flushed and defiant, Agnes stared at Janna as if daring her to speak against her decision.

"I beg you to reconsider, Agnes. Master Will loves you. He has hopes that you might wed."

"I will never wed. I will never leave the abbey again!"

If she hadn't persuaded Agnes to come to the fair and then teased her about Will, perhaps Agnes's decision might have been different. Janna wondered if she might be able to persuade Will to wait, to ask Agnes again during hay-making, or at the next harvest, when they could be alone together in the fields while still being within the protection of the abbey. It comforted her slightly to think that it might not be too late, although in her heart she was sure that the damage was already done. And it was all her fault for not understanding Agnes's fear, and choosing a more opportune time to introduce her to the outside world.

Janna sighed. There was no point in arguing further, given Agnes's current frame of mind. "Just so long as you're happy," she said quietly.

"Happy? With this?" Agnes touched her scarred face. She looked angry, almost desperate, and Janna hastened to soothe her.

"Those who know you, love you. You don't have to face any more strangers if you don't want to."

"I know." Agnes managed a small smile. "Don't mind me, Janna. I woke up cross as a bear this morning. Angry with myself, angry with the world. I'm no good to anyone right now."

Janna remembered her gift from the fair. "Maybe this will help to cheer you," she said, and lifted her sleeve to reveal the golden ribbon beneath. She untied it, and handed it to Agnes, who stared at it as if she couldn't believe her eyes.

"It's beautiful," she breathed. "No-one has ever given me anything before. Thank you, Janna, this is more than I deserve when you have already done so much for me."

"You'd best keep it hidden," Janna advised, and Agnes quickly whipped the ribbon out of sight. "I will treasure it always," she promised. She leaned forward and touched Janna's arm. "Actually, I wish I had stayed at the fair, for I missed all the excitement. Was it an accident, do you think, or did someone mean to harm the lord?"

"I wish I knew." Janna shook her head. "But I know him already," she added on impulse. "I stayed on his manor farm before I came to the abbey." Her mouth quirked into a dreamy smile. "He is young, and very handsome."

"Is he your beau?" Agnes asked eagerly.

Janna laughed. "He is a lord. I am lowborn, remember, and the daughter of a *wortwyf*. I am nothing and nobody."

"But if he loves you?"

"He does not." Janna thought of Gytha, of Cecily, of Emma. Was Hugh as innocent with women as he seemed? She wasn't sure what to believe: that she was the intended target, or that the attack was indeed meant to punish Hugh for not honoring his pledge to the delectable Emma.

"I must go," she said now. "Sister Anne and the lord Hugh both need me. But I haven't forgotten my promise to you, Agnes. If I can persuade Sister Anne to it, do you still want to come and help in the infirmary?"

"More than anything!" Agnes's smile glimmered like sunshine after rain.

Janna hurried off, feeling regret on Master Will's behalf yet relieved that Agnes didn't blame her for what had happened, and that she seemed to have recovered her usual high spirits. On her way to the physic garden, she lingered for a moment at the abbey's cemetery. It was a quiet, peaceful spot, sheltered in part by yew trees although several headstones lay in a patch of sunlight, recording the passing of nuns long gone and probably mostly forgotten. Janna wondered who they were, and if the sunshine warmed their tired old bones and gave them ease. She hoped that they rested in peace after a lifetime of service to God.

The sun would also be shining on her own mother's grave, set in the wasteland of unconsecrated ground beyond the chapel at Berford. Janna hoped that the grave was safe, undisturbed; that it had not been vandalized by superstitious villagers. "Rest in peace," she whispered. "I will avenge your death, I promise you."

She walked on through the kitchen garden and into the herbarium. She had come to know it well, including those rare plants that had come from far-off lands, for Sister Anne had schooled her in their healing properties. She looked about with a critical eye as she leaned over to pick the flowers, leaves and roots she needed. Too many plants were being choked by a rank growth of useless weeds. Some of the herbs had finished flowering, and their dead heads needed cutting off and the seeds preserving. Leaves also needed to be cut and dried before they shriveled in the autumn chill, while roots must be taken before winter snow drove living shoots under the earth to wait for spring. She would ask leave to work in the garden now that she no longer had to prepare goods for sale at the fair. She would ask if Agnes might join her, so that when it came to the big question of Agnes's future, she would be able to say in all truth that the lay sister knew everything she could teach her.

As Janna sniffed the pungent aromas of the plucked herbs, she smiled at the memories of her childhood that they evoked. Suddenly mindful of the patient who awaited her, she hurriedly sought out the last of the plants she needed then went indoors to the infirmary to make up some new medicaments.

To her surprise, she found a number of people gathered around Hugh's bed. There seemed to be quite a party going on under the indulgent eye of Sister Anne who, as Janna entered, was making a vain attempt to shush their exuberance.

"Johanna!" Hugh saw her first, and called out a greeting. Godric gave her a smile, as did Cecily, while Hamo, Hugh's nephew and Cecily's young charge, took one delighted glance at her then cast himself into her arms. Janna hugged him hard, while looking over his shoulder at the fifth member of the group. She tried to suppress her amusement as she noted a look of recognition, followed by embarrassment and dismay, flit across Gytha's face. "John!" Gytha said the name like an accusation. Which it was, Janna realized, as the girl continued furiously: "You let us believe you were a youth! How could you trick us like that! I would never have confided in you had I known you were a—a nun!"

Janna had to try even harder not to smile. "I beg your forgiveness," she said gravely. "I was in hiding, and being a youth was part of my disguise. I did not mean to shame or embarrass you, mistress, and I assure you that your secrets are safe with me."

Gytha slid a sideways glance at Hugh, then looked hurriedly away. Both remembered well her stated intention to wed Hugh and her determination to let nothing stand in her path. "But I've taken no vows," Janna said, trying to smooth the awkward moment. "I sought shelter here and, as you see, I help to look after such patients as come to the abbey."

"I, too, have my lord's best interests at heart," Gytha said importantly, feeling herself now on safer ground. She proffered a basket to Janna. "I have brought some delicacies from the manor's kitchen to sustain him while he recovers from his wound. Please see to it that he receives this good food from now on."

"There is naught wrong with the food we eat here at the abbey." Sister Anne's patience had finally snapped. She bustled forward and snatched the basket from Gytha. "Rest assured, the lord Hugh will not go hungry, nor will he lack meat for it is allowed here in the misericord." She looked at Janna. "I shall take this to our kitchen and, while I am there, I shall make up some new medicaments with the herbs you have gathered. After that, I shall go on to the fair. There is no need to change the dressing on the wound for now; you may do it later when the lord's guests have gone. In the meantime, please keep watch over the other patients—and I mean all the patients, not just this one—while I am gone."

"Yes, Sister." Janna set Hamo aside and stepped out of Sister Anne's way. She was delighted to see the little boy. She was afraid that his abduction might have changed his bright and trusting nature forever, for he had suffered cruelly at the time. But his affectionate hug had done much to reassure her.

"How are you doing, my young lord?" she asked.

He smiled up at her. "I am quite well now," he said.

"But he has nightmares sometimes," Cecily piped up. Hamo looked embarrassed.

"I would have nightmares too, if I'd been abducted like you were, Hamo," Hugh said quickly, and was rewarded by the boy's relieved grin.

It was clear that Hamo worshipped his cousin, and took comfort from the fact that someone as big and brave as Hugh might also have nightmares. His glance switched to Janna. "Are you a nun now?" he asked.

Janna smiled. "Not exactly," she said. She was sorry the boy was having nightmares, and wondered if it might be possible to divert him by giving him something else to think about. "Tell me, Hamo," she said, "do you know your letters and numbers?"

"No," Hugh answered. "It is my duty to teach Hamo the arts of war and of polite society, to fit him for his eventual role as lord of the manor. While I, myself, have acquired some knowledge of reading and of writing, there is no need for Hamo to learn such things, for he will have a scribe at his disposal."

"There are some children who come here to learn their letters with Sister Grace and Sister Maria," Janna said, ignoring the disdain implicit in Hugh's words. She couldn't believe anyone would choose not to learn if given the opportunity.

"It might be something to think about, my lord?" Cecily spoke up, anxious for anything that might help Hamo forget his ordeal.

Hugh inclined his head. "Perhaps when he is older. If Dame Alice thinks it necessary." He heaved himself up into a sitting position, wincing at the pain of it.

"How are you today, my lord?" Janna asked hastily, thinking she should focus on her duty of care rather than advising their newest patient on how his young cousin should be raised.

"Sore," Hugh answered with a smile. He now wore a nightshirt, and Janna was glad of it. She wondered where Sister Anne had found such a garment.

"Do you want to tend my wound?" He plucked at the fabric, ready to raise his shirt, and Janna panicked.

"No!" She read the amusement on his face at her sharp rejection. "I can look at it later," she amended. She felt the prickle of perspiration as she recollected Hugh's hairy chest.

Gytha shot her a hostile glance. "So you really are a healer, even if everything else you told us was a lie?"

"There was a good reason for Sister Johanna to hide her true identity, but it doesn't concern you, Gytha," Hugh reprimanded her.

Gytha flushed, looking resentful.

"But I do regret having to deceive you all," Janna said kindly. She glanced at Cecily. "I regret all the lies I've had to tell."

As Cecily bent her head to hide the stain of guilt coloring her face, Janna turned back to Hugh. She laid her wrist against his forehead. Touching him threw her into such confusion, she couldn't tell if he was feverish or if it was her own burning emotions that scorched her skin.

"Do you feel hot, my lord?" she asked anxiously. If the wound became infected, Janna knew that fever would follow as the infection spread.

"No, I'm just uncomfortable. Of course, being attended by a beautiful woman—" Hugh's gaze raked the small cubicle. "By so many beautiful women—would heat any man's blood!"

"I'm sure Sister Anne will give you something to make you feel easier as soon as she returns." Janna moved to the entrance of the cubicle, anxious to escape Gytha's hostility, Cecily's discomfort, and Hugh's awkward compliments. "I must see to my other patients," she said.

Godric's voice stopped her. "Before you go, Janna. How long do you think my lord will need to stay here?"

"He should not leave until his wound has knitted together. It's quite deep, so it may take some time to heal. But it's not my place to say how long his recovery will take. You must ask Sister Anne."

"Shall I then stay here with you, my lord?" Godric offered eagerly.

"No, indeed, Godric. I thank you, but I would rather you kept an eye on our sales at the fair and on what is happening at my manor. I shall send for you if I need anything."

Godric's face fell. Janna suspected that she was part of the reason he wanted to stay, although she did not doubt he wanted also to do his very best for Hugh. She caught Cecily's eye and inclined her head toward the curtain, hoping the young woman would take the hint and come outside. As she left the room, she heard Hamo say, in a loud, clear voice, "If Janna's not really a nun, you and she could be wed, cousin Hugh. I'd like that, I really would."

She lingered just long enough to listen to Hugh's answer. To her disappointment, he gave only a light laugh. Any reply he might have made was blocked by Gytha's hasty questions: "Shall I bring you a change of clothes tomorrow, my lord? And I know how much you like my mutton pies. Shall I bring you one at the same time?"

So Gytha was still intent on her pursuit of Hugh. Janna wondered if she knew of Emma's existence, but suspected she did not. As the cook's daughter, she would have been born and raised on the manor farm that Hugh had later come to manage, whereas Hugh had told her he, and Anselm and Emma, had spent their childhood at Dame Alice's manor.

"Did you want to speak to me, Janna?" Cecily asked.

"I wanted to warn you." Janna drew Dame Alice's tiring woman away from the cubicle so they could not be overheard. "You can see, from what has happened to me, just how determined Robert of Babestoche is to keep the real cause of my mother's death a secret. You are already a threat to his safety and his conscience. I know you are careful when you are with him, but I worry that it won't be enough to protect you, Cecily."

"Robert doesn't suspect that I know anything beyond that your mother helped me..." Cecily's voice wobbled uncertainly. She drew in a breath. "Helped me when I was in trouble," she finished in a rush. "He believes himself safe, for he has told me that my lady would dismiss me if she knew of my 'disgrace.' That's what he calls it, although he was the seducer, not me." Indignation flushed Cecily's cheeks. She took hold of Janna's hand. "I am a coward, I know, not to tell Dame Alice about him, or about his responsibility for your mother's death, but in all conscience, Janna, my lady has been so distressed over the death of her babe I cannot add to her grief by telling her the truth about her husband."

Janna nodded. Cecily wasn't telling her anything she hadn't already suspected. "I just want you to be careful, that's all," she said. "And keep your mouth shut about what you know."

"I will. I am frightened too. I don't have your courage or the skill to protect myself from Robert or his assassin. That was why I was so glad when my lady asked me to take Hamo to stay at Hugh's manor. In truth, when she and Robert came to stay there after Hamo went missing, I asked my lady to release me from her service. But she will not hear of it, nor have I pressed her, for I have been with her since I was a child and I know not where I would go if I was to leave her manor." Cecily's face crumpled. She pressed Janna's hand. "Never was anyone so wrong about a man, and so wrong about the nature of love as I," she said wretchedly.

"You are in good company," Janna comforted her. "Remember, Dame Alice made the same mistake about Robert as you did."

Cecily's confession over the nature of love, the unknown Emma, and the consequences of a broken vow all jostled for space in Janna's mind as she moved from bed to bed, here dispensing a soothing syrup for a troublesome cough, there medicating an ulcerous sore, or bringing ease to ancient limbs with a liniment rubbed in with strong and careful hands. But even Hamo's unexpected question and Hugh's laughter took second place behind the most pressing question of all: Who had wounded Hugh—and why?

She was no nearer to answering that riddle when she returned to Hugh's bedside late in the afternoon, and found him entertaining a new visitor. She recognized the girl instantly as Emma, and was about to withdraw and leave them alone when Hugh's voice stopped her.

"Johanna," he said. "Stay a few moments to hear this, will you? I know you to be a shrewd observer, and we have need of your counsel."

"But—" Emma half rose from the stool on which she was sitting. Hugh reached over and placed a hand on her knee to stay her. Janna noted the intimate gesture, and felt hugely uncomfortable. Yet her curiosity was piqued, and so she ventured further into the small room.

"Johanna once solved a serious crime that took place on my manor," Hugh told Emma. "You may speak freely in front of her." Unobserved by Emma, he winked at Janna. "Besides, having taken the veil, Johanna is bound by the vow of silence, as are all the nuns under the Rule of St Benedict." He sounded solemn enough, but Janna knew he didn't believe a word of it. Nevertheless, she was grateful for his public expression of confidence and so she stood quietly, and waited to learn what troubled the young woman.

"It's Anselm," Emma confessed. "After I spoke to you yesterday, Hugh, I went in search of him, for I was much distressed by this quarrel between you. It is all so unnecessary. If only he would see reason!" Her voice was raw with emotion. "He's angry with me, but he's taking it out on you, Hugh. And it's just not fair!" She took a couple of breaths in an effort to regain her composure.

"He's taking what out on me?" Hugh prompted. "Is there trouble between you two?"

"Yes." Now Emma looked defiant. "The fact is—I have fallen in love."

Hugh looked a little taken aback, while Janna was filled with foreboding. She would have left the cubicle there and then, but didn't want to draw attention to her obvious dismay.

"And that is why Anselm was so insistent that we should wed when I spoke to him yesterday?" Hugh asked warily.

"Yes! That's what he wants: a good marriage for me. A safe match with someone we've both known and loved since childhood. He wants a brother-in-law he can look up to, someone he can trust."

"But I have nothing to offer you, Emma. You know that. You have always known that my aunt owns my manor, and that Hamo is her heir. Anselm knows that too."

"Yes, yes, of course I know your circumstances." Emma spoke impatiently.

"Then you can have no quarrel with your brother, for I am the cause of his anger, not you. But in truth, Emma, if you love me and are so sure you want this match, I would agree to it if only for the sake of—"

"No, Hugh, no! You misunderstand me. I'm not in love with you! Don't think that for one moment." Embarrassed by her hasty words, she rushed to explain. "I don't mean any disrespect, please don't think that. You know I love you as a sister. I always will. No, the trouble lies with the fact that the man who has won my heart is just not good enough for Anselm."

Janna risked a glance at Hugh, and was amused to see the look of relief on his face. She was sure it was mirrored on her own. She hastily bent her head so that he could not read her expression, and subjected the rushes covering the floor to an intense scrutiny.

"So who is he, this man who has won your heart?"

"He is called Peter Thatcher, for that is what he is and what he does. And you won't find as good or careful a craftsman for many miles about." This was said defiantly. It was clear Emma had become used to defending her beloved.

"A thatcher? A free man?"

"No. But we are both happy and content to live at the manor under his lord. Peter is a good man, Hugh, you must believe that. He is kind, and gentle, and he makes me laugh!" In her desperation to be understood, Emma had grasped Hugh's hands in her own, and now she squeezed them hard and released them. "I love him," she said softly. "I love him with all my heart. I want to live my life with him, have children with him, and grow old with him." Janna felt a moment of pure envy that the girl seemed so sure of her love and her happiness. But the reality of the situation cooled her wits sufficiently to listen carefully to what followed.

"Why is Anselm so against the match?" Hugh asked.

"He says that, as I have a small dowry, I should make a better match than Peter. Indeed, he told me that he was taking steps to increase the amount of my dowry, and I could then have anyone of my choosing, any free man, that is. He talks of family honor yet, in truth, our family is not so noble or high that I can be proud in my choosing. But I know who he really wants me to wed. *You*." Emma's smile was rueful.

"And that was why he was so insistent yesterday that I honor my pledge to marry you? Although I have to say, I do not recollect any such pledge between us."

"No, there never was. I think it was Dame Alice's fond hope that the two of us might make a match, but you have nothing to reproach yourself with, Hugh. Anselm is trying to build a castle out of straw when he says there is an understanding between us."

"Do you want me to try to talk to Anselm, and put in a good word for your thatcher?"

"It's too late for that!" Now there was real distress in Emma's voice. She looked up at Hugh. "Don't you see? After you told me of your quarrel with Anselm, I went to plead with him. But he would not listen, he pushed me away. I fear that he has fallen in with bad company, for I found him at the cockfighting pit, making wagers, spending coins we cannot afford. I swear he had been drinking, for he was unsteady on his feet, and seemed to be paying more attention to a pair of half-dead birds than to me. But he must have been listening to me after all and taken great insult from it, for this is the result!" There were tears in her eyes. She blinked them away. "I came as soon as I heard what had happened. Oh, Hugh, I am so sorry for this, and I am sure Anselm will be too, once he is sober, once he's had time to reflect on his actions. I'm just so grateful he didn't manage to kill you!"

"So am I!" Hugh laughed, but with little amusement. "But I think you're wrong about Anselm, truly I do. I didn't see who attacked me, but I didn't notice him among the crowd around us, and neither did Johanna. In fact, they were mostly women and children."

A brief flash of hope lit Emma's face. Then she frowned. "Perhaps he hid himself until the last moment?" she fretted. "Be sure I'll ask him. I'll find out the truth of the matter."

"In the meantime, tell me what I can do to help you in your troubles."

"I don't know." Now Emma looked worried. "You must stay out of Anselm's way, for the first part. For the second, I wanted to see how you are, and to apologize for Anselm. I can't believe he would do such a thing! And for the third, I also wanted to make sure that someone was taking good care of you." She flashed a grateful smile at Janna. Her forehead creased into a frown once more as she faced Hugh. "I confess I can't see any way out of this coil of trouble other than to give up my attachment to Peter, and that I will not do. My brother has no right to keep me from the man I love."

"If you suspect that Anselm is drinking and gambling, perhaps you should stay away from him for the while, just until he returns to his senses?" Hugh suggested. "Take courage, Emma, for the fair will soon be over and you'll return to your manor. Will Anselm go with you? Does he live there with you still?"

Emma nodded. "I wish he did not," she said bitterly. "Then he would not be able to interfere with my life as he does now."

"Have you spoken to your lord regarding your match with Peter? If he sanctions it, then surely your brother will have to agree?"

"We haven't asked my lord, but what you say is true." Emma looked somewhat happier. "I shall speak to Peter about it."

"He does want to marry you?"

"Oh, yes." A sudden smile smoothed the worry from Emma's face. "It's what we both want more than anything," she said. "See what he has given me as a token of his love?" She pointed proudly at the ring she wore on her right hand.

Both Hugh and Janna leaned in for a closer look. It was a broad band of gold chased with lilies, so carefully enameled that the drooping white trumpets and interlinking foliage looked like miniatures of the real thing. Janna wondered how a humble thatcher could afford to purchase anything so fine, and had her question answered almost immediately.

"I admired it yesterday at the fair," Emma said, adding somewhat defensively, "Peter tried to buy it for me as a betrothal gift, but he didn't have enough coins and so we bought it together. I shouldn't really wear it until we are wed, but it is so pretty I cannot resist it. Besides, it is safer on my finger than off."

"Peter is here, at the fair?" Hugh was startled. "Is that wise?"

"Never fear, he is keeping out of Anselm's way." Emma bent to kiss Hugh goodbye, then cast a curious glance at Janna. "I'll leave you in the good care of Sister Johanna," she said, and walked out.

"Do you believe that Anselm was behind the attack on you, my lord?" Janna asked, as soon as Emma was out of hearing.

Hugh frowned. "I can't be sure," he said slowly. "I know him well, and I would have said such an action was not in his character. Yes, I have seen him angry before now. He has a quick temper, but I have never known him attack a defenseless man without provocation. Certes I did not recognize him in the crowd coming toward us just before I was attacked, and yet whoever did the deed must have been there among them."

"If not Anselm, then who?" Janna asked, coming back to the question that worried her most. "Was anyone in the crowd from your aunt's manor at Babestoche, my lord, any-one at all?"

"No." Hugh thought about it. "No," he said again. "You're still worried about Robert, aren't you?"

Janna nodded. She picked up the salve left by Sister Anne, and turned back to the bed. "Could you please lift your shirt, my lord?" She tried to ignore the heat coursing through her body as, with a grin, he obeyed her instruction.

She carefully unwrapped the cloth that bound the wound. "It is quite clean and is healing well," she told him, as she smoothed the cool paste over the ugly gash in his side. She felt him shrink from her touch and knew that she hurt him, but he kept silent. "You are lucky, my lord," she reassured him. "The dagger could have gone deeper, or at an angle, and done a lot more damage than it has."

"A glancing blow, one meant to warn rather than kill, think you?"

"Or a blow meant to silence me and, perhaps, checked when the assailant realized he had the wrong mark?"

"I wish you would put that thought out of your mind, Johanna. I feel sure that I was the target and, whatever Emma says, I must see Anselm again and talk to him about it." Hugh shifted restlessly. "I shall visit him just as soon as you let me out of here."

"Is that wise, my lord?"

Hugh gave a small huff of amusement. "Better perhaps to visit him later, at his manor, after he has had a chance to cool down and sober up?"

Janna hesitated. It was not her place to advise him, and yet he had asked her to stay and hear Emma's story, so presumably he placed some value on her opinion. "Is this not something best left for brother and sister to work through?" she asked diffidently. "It would be a pity to heat things up again, perhaps make matters worse by your interference, especially as you have all been friends from childhood."

Hugh looked thoughtful. "You may well be right," he admitted, "but I can't stay away and do nothing to help, not when Emma's happiness is at stake."

"You risk your life by interfering," Janna reminded him.

"I doubt Anselm will try anything like that again—if in truth he was behind this attack." In spite of his reassuring words, Hugh sounded troubled.

"He must care deeply for his sister to go to these lengths to secure her future."

"Unless drink has addled his brain he must know that killing me isn't the way to go about it! And I hope that once he is away from the temptations of the fair, he will listen to what I have to say regarding Emma and her betrothed."

Janna saw that Hugh was bound to his course, and that nothing she could say would dissuade him from it. "Then I wish you every success in helping Mistress Emma find happiness with the man she loves, my lord." She finished spreading the last of the cream, and bound the wound tight with a clean linen bandage.

"I suppose a goodnight kiss is out of the question?" Hugh asked, with a twinkle in his eye. A quiet rustle behind Janna alerted her to the fact that they were no longer alone.

"I don't believe that's part of your treatment, but you could ask Sister Anne to oblige, if you feel a kiss might help your recovery." With flushed cheeks and bright eyes, she pushed past the infirmarian and fled.

Chapter 9

At Sister Anne's insistence, Janna stayed behind again the following day. "We cannot both go to the fair; someone must stay here to attend our new patient," the infirmarian said. "I would send you, Sister Johanna, but I fear you might not be safe on your own. Yet I worry that it might not be safe for you here, either, as the lord Hugh is apparently unaware of proper decorum here in our abbey. You would be well advised to keep someone with you when you tend him. There can be no future in a liaison with him, you know that, don't you?" She bustled off without giving Janna a chance to reply.

Janna knew that the nun's advice was sound; nevertheless, she was content to stay behind, the presence of Hugh being more than enough compensation for missing the delights of the fair. The thought of the bailiff, anxiously awaiting news of Agnes, sat heavy on her mind, but there was little she could do about it. To send a message with Sister Anne was out of the question. Besides, Janna reasoned, Agnes had seemed to like the man in spite of her fear of the unknown. With further thought, she might well repent her hasty decision. Better to leave it alone for the moment, and see if time wrought any change to her feelings.

As a lay sister, and with work to do in the infirmary, Janna had been excused from attending most of the offices that the nuns observed through the day and night. Nevertheless, she was expected to attend Mass every morning, and so she did, going on afterward to the chapter house to make her report. She sat patiently while the business of the abbey was discussed and waited, with some curiosity, to hear details of the latest sins. For once, Sister Martha was silent. They were about to file out of chapter when a scared voice piped up from the back of the room.

"I have found the missing pages from Sister Ursel's manuscript."

A hush fell over the convent, broken only by a gasp of relief, quickly suppressed, from Sister Ursel. Every eye turned on the hapless novice who had spoken up. She slowly withdrew from her sleeve two sheets of vellum. Even standing some distance away, Janna could see clearly the glowing illuminations that bordered the script: gold, blue, red and green birds and flowers, all minutely observed and exquisitely drawn. She echoed the scribe's sigh as she realized that, although somewhat crumpled, the pages were undamaged.

"For what reason did you take these pages?" The abbess's voice was awful in its thunderous judgment.

"But...but I d-didn't." In her fright, the novice stammered almost as badly as Sister Ursel. Desperate to avoid blame, she rushed into explanation. "I-I found them lying under a bush in the cloister garth. I was just walking past on my way to chapter, and...and the pale color of the parchment and the gleaming gold and colors of the illuminations caught my eye. I-I must confess to the Sin of Curiosity, but I stepped aside to see what it could be." She hastened forward, holding out the sheets to the abbess. "See, Reverend Mother," she cried. "The pages are still slightly damp from the dew. In Christ's holy name, I do not know how they got under the bush for I did not take them, but I give thanks that they are found undamaged."

"I-I s-searched the c-cloister garth, M-Mother, when the p-p-pages went m-missing. They were n-not th-there when...when I l-looked b-before."

The abbess nodded thoughtfully. She gestured to the novice to return the missing pages to Sister Ursel. "I will speak to you in my rooms," she told her sternly, and turned to survey the silent nuns. "This is not the end of the matter. Be sure I shall be asking questions of you all."

"Someone must have taken those pages and hidden them," Agnes said, when she and Janna came together after chapter. "Who do you think it could be? Who could want to do such a dreadful thing?"

"I don't know." Janna shook her head in wonder. "Did you see Sister Ursel's work? It's so beautiful, I can't believe anyone would risk damaging it by taking the pages." She mused silently for a moment. "It's an act of great cruelty," she said. "Sister Ursel has enough affliction to bear, without taking away her peace of mind."

"Ah yes, her peace of mind." Surprised by the echo of bitterness in Agnes's voice, Janna raised her eyebrows in an unspoken question.

"Have you noticed, Janna, that although we all profess to love the Lord and are happy in His work, our small jealousies and tempers, our wishes and desires still manage to disturb the peace of the abbey as well as our own serenity?"

Janna scrutinized Agnes. She wondered if this was a general observation or if there was something more particular on her mind. "Are you talking about Master Will's offer of marriage?" she ventured.

"No!" Agnes gave her a smile that didn't quite reach her eyes. "No, I wondered if someone had a particular grudge against Sister Ursel, that's all."

"The nun with the barking dog?" Janna struggled to remember her name.

"Sister Catherine? She hates everyone—and so does her dog. And I have to say, they are not well regarded in return. In fact, you'd be hard put to find anyone with a kind word for her, or her dog. You see, Janna, that's exactly my point. I don't know why she stays here when she takes so little pleasure in what we do and how we live, and takes out her dissatisfaction on us all."

Janna was more interested in Agnes than in Sister Catherine. "What about you?" she asked. "Are you happy?"

"I already told you, I am here because I love the Lord," Agnes said defensively.

"Yes, but are you happy?"

"I am content. That's enough." Agnes turned and walked away. Janna stared after her, wishing she knew what to do or say that might lift her friend's spirits. But perhaps it was no more than that Agnes was in pain. "Come to the infirmary," she called after her. "If you'll pick some violets for me, I'll make up a new salve for you to try." She thought of something. "I'll even introduce you to our new patient if you like!"

"Your handsome beau?" Agnes gave her a broad grin. The mischief on her face told Janna that this time, her smile was genuine.

A repentant Hugh awaited Janna in the cubicle off the infirmary. "I owe you an apology," he said, as soon as she entered. "Sister Anne reprimanded me last night for teasing you. But I meant no disrespect by my remarks. In truth, Johanna..." He stretched out a hand to her. Janna's first instinct was to grab hold and not let go. She set down the bowl of water she carried and, with a huge effort of will, placed her hands behind her back, clasping them tight to keep her firm in her purpose.

"You are lonely and in pain, my lord," she said. "'Tis no more than that."

Hugh looked a little abashed, and she was sorry that her words may have hurt his feelings. Or his pride. "Please take off your shirt," she said, hoping to ease the awkward moment by keeping busy. She brought the basin to his bedside, added some soapwort leaves to the water and frothed them up. She was about to remove Hugh's bandage when she heard a throat being cleared, and then a quiet cough. Agnes stood half hidden behind the curtained entrance to the cubicle, clutching a handful of fragrant violets. Hugh stirred, and Janna knew that he'd seen the lay sister and the scar that marred her face. She wished now that she had warned him about Agnes. She couldn't bear it if her friend's self-esteem sank even lower because of Hugh's reaction.

"Agnes!"

"I-I've brought the flowers you wanted." Agnes had edged right behind the curtain, out of Hugh's sight.

"Come in, please do," he called. "I'm quite safe even though I don't have a shirt on."

Hiding a grin, Janna stepped aside so that Agnes could see his welcoming smile for herself. She noted how the lay sister automatically pulled up the side of her wimple as she ventured into the cubicle.

"Another healer come to visit," Hugh said lightly. "I am indeed honored to receive so much attention!"

"Agnes is my friend," Janna said, proud to make the claim, for in truth her life had been somewhat short of friends until now.

"Sister Johanna is teaching me about herbs and their healing properties," Agnes said quietly. She ventured no closer to Hugh, but she didn't run away either.

"You couldn't have a better teacher," Hugh said. "She and her mother were known at my aunt's manor and beyond, and their skills were highly valued by all who came under their care."

Agnes shot a surprised glance at Janna, then bobbed a quick curtsy to Hugh. "I must go," she said.

Janna put out a hand to stop her friend's departure. "My lord, would you mind if I showed Agnes your wound? While I hope she won't have any more dagger wounds to tend here in the abbey, there might still be accidents with scythes, or knives, or pitchforks."

Hugh smiled. "Come and have a look," he invited. "I won't bite—so long as you promise not to hurt me!"

A reluctant grin twitched the corner of Agnes's mouth. Her eyes widened as she noted the hairy chest bared in front of her, but then she peered closely at the wound while Janna showed her first how to wash it clean and then how to medicate it. Janna proffered the last of the paste that she'd used to spread on the wound. As she detailed what was in it, Agnes took a good sniff of the aromatic salve.

"I wish you'd come back to my manor, Johanna," Hugh said wistfully. "In truth, you have far more skill than Mistress Tova and her daughter."

Gytha and her mother would not like to hear such a judgment from Hugh, Janna thought. "It's as well that I'm here to care for you now, my lord," she said, and proceeded to bind his wound under the watchful gaze of Agnes.

She was just finishing when the sound of voices alerted her to the fact that they would shortly have company. "I must see to the other patients now, my lord," she said quickly, and left the cubicle, drawing Agnes after her.

"He's nice! And you're right, Janna. He's very handsome." Agnes quickly averted her face as she passed Godric and Gytha. Janna stopped to greet them, hoping for an opportunity to talk to Godric on his own for once. But Gytha lingered beside him, clutching a laden basket. Her curious glance flicked from Godric to Janna, and back again. With a sigh, Janna excused herself and hurried on after Agnes.

"The lord Hugh was kind to me," Agnes continued, as Janna fell into step beside her once more. "I don't have any experience with men, but he seemed like a real gentleman."

"He is a gentleman. He's a highborn Norman—but landless, alas." Janna stopped beside Sister Angelica. "Would you like me to rub your back for you today, Sister?" she asked, motioning Agnes to stay with her. It was a good opportunity for her friend to find her way around the infirmary, and learn what would be required of her, Janna reasoned.

"Yes, indeed I would." Without being asked, Sister Angelica retreated into her cubicle and unfastened her habit.

"He also has a lovely, hairy chest," Agnes said, as she surveyed Sister Angelica's bare, wrinkly old back.

"Who?" the old nun demanded, in a scandalized voice.

Agnes giggled. "Janna's beau," she said saucily.

"He is not!" Janna glared at her.

"I don't know about that." Agnes still sounded amused. "I saw how he looked at you, Janna. He...values you, I think."

"Value isn't love," Janna said tartly, thinking of Hugh's laughter when he heard Hamo's question.

"It's a good start," Agnes said seriously.

Janna remembered Hugh's request for a goodnight kiss. Her face began to burn. She didn't want to think about Hugh as a beau. She didn't want to think about Hugh at all!

"Master Will values you too, Agnes." Janna carefully began to massage the old nun's back. "He loves you, you know."

"Shh!" Agnes put a finger to her lips, then pointed at the nun lying supine on the bed in front of them.

"I might be old, but I'm not blind and deaf," the old nun snapped. "And if you think I'm going to tell tales about you, you are wrong. There are enough sisters stirring up trouble as it is, without my adding a whole lot of rumors and lies to the stew."

"I beg your pardon, Sister Angelica." Agnes's tone was meek, but her eyes danced with amusement as her gaze met Janna's.

"Besides," the old nun continued, "it's hard living without a man. I should know, for I was once wed." Her voice was ineffably sad. "My husband died young. In my grief I sought refuge here and took my vows. And lived to regret it, I might say, when I realized what I'd done," she added, her tone now sharp as a wasp's sting. "I'd thought life would be peaceful, here in the abbey. I little knew that I would live out my days surrounded by gossiping women, some of whom would do better service to the Lord if they held their tongues and paid more attention to the love and charity they profess but don't often practice!"

Janna and Agnes exchanged glances. Agnes was the first to speak. "Why did you not leave the abbey when you realized your mistake?"

"Because I had taken my vows, child. Not for anything would I break a vow freely given to our Lord Jesus Christ."

"Oh." Agnes bent her head. But Janna had seen the light die in her eyes, and reckoned she knew the cause of it. Her heart felt heavy for her friend. In spite of the bailiff's high hopes and easy dismissal of any potential problems, she knew that Agnes, too, would honor the vows she had made, even if it was at the expense of her own happiness.

*

Once Janna had finished ministering to all the patients in the infirmary, Agnes slipped away and Janna returned to Hugh. She could hear his voice as she approached. He was giving instructions to Godric who, she saw as she entered the cubicle, was nodding seriously in return. Gytha stood beside the bed, dangling her basket, which was now empty. There was a pie set on a small table beside Hugh, and some fruit pastries and honey wafers.

"You may take these to your kitchen," she said graciously, when she saw Janna. "These are for my lord, whensoever he requests them."

"It's kind of you to bring them in, Gytha, but truly, I do not need you to bring me any extra food. The good sisters are feeding me very well." Hugh sounded weary as he broke off speaking to Godric to address her.

"Nevertheless, my lord, you must keep up your strength, for we all want you recovered and home again just as soon as may be," the girl answered pertly. "We miss your presence at the manor." She lowered her lashes and blinked flirtatiously. But her gesture was wasted on Hugh, who had turned to Godric once more. Godric continued to listen attentively, although he'd given Janna a beaming smile as she entered. She stood quietly while Hugh detailed further chores he wanted done.

Once he'd finished speaking, Janna addressed Godric directly. "Do you go to the fair at all?"

"Not today." He shook his head. "Morcar, our new reeve, is proving conscientious and capable enough in selling our goods. It's better for me to keep watch over the manor while my lord is here."

Janna hesitated. She cast a quick glance of appeal at Hugh. "Godric, you know all those who work at my lord's manor, and also those who are employed at Babestoche Manor by Dame Alice. Whoever is responsible for the attack on my lord may well have fled the fair. Nevertheless—"

"That's a good idea," Hugh cut in swiftly, anticipating Janna's thoughts.

"Spend some time looking around, Godric, and then report back to me if you will. I would like to know who is here, all those you recognize, anyone at all." "I'll come with you, Godric." Gytha favored him with another flirtatious glance. Janna hid a smile. It seemed the cook's daughter couldn't help herself; any man was grist to her mill. Unless…Janna's next thought wiped away any trace of humor. Unless Gytha was beginning to realize her efforts were wasted on Hugh, and was now planning to woo Godric instead?

*

Janna was thoughtful as she went about her chores that afternoon. Hugh's presence at the abbey was a great talking point, although the hum of speculation was mostly conducted in illicit whispers. As someone who was in direct contact with him, and who could provide up-to-date reports as to his welfare as well as an eye-witness account of the attack, she suddenly found she was extremely popular. She, in turn, made the most of the opportunity to question all who approached her to find out if any of them knew aught of her mother.

In this, she drew a disappointing blank. Most knew her mother's name because of the Mass that, at Hugh's instiga- tion, had been said for her soul. Some had heard of Eadgyth's plight when first she'd come to the abbey, but they had not set eyes on her, nor did they know where she'd come from. Janna hadn't had a chance to question the abbess, but she talked to Sister Brigid, believing that the porteress might well have spoken at length to her mother when first she'd called at Wiltune to beg for help. Brigid was a great gossip, and prided herself on knowing everything about everyone, but even she knew nothing that might further Janna's quest.

Janna found it hard to imagine her proud mother begging anything from anyone, most especially not the haughty, grasping abbess; she must indeed have been desperate. Now that she herself was experiencing life in an abbey, Janna was beginning to understand something of her mother's past. She was quite sure that Eadgyth must have come from an abbey somewhere, although she was less sure of her mother's position there. Everything seemed to point to the fact that Eadgyth had taken her vows and perhaps even risen to a position of some prominence as the abbey's infirmarian. Yet she'd always called herself a *wortwyf*. She certainly hadn't the same knowledge as Sister Anne or she would have passed it on to Janna, just as she'd passed on everything else she knew about the healing arts. The only part of the mystery Janna really understood was her mother's attitude toward the church. Betrayed and deserted by the man she loved, as well as by the nuns with whom she'd previously found a home, growing great with child and forced to beg for bread and shelter, it was small wonder that Eadgyth had turned her back on Christ, and grown so hard, so independent and distrustful, so determined never to be in anyone's debt ever again. Janna was proud of her mother's indomitable spirit, and for what she had achieved; she just wished Eadgyth had been more honest and open with her daughter. She touched the purse under her habit wherein the letter was sealed. Her father had a lot to answer for and, by God, she would demand a full accounting when they finally met!

It was approaching dusk when Godric returned, this time without Gytha, to report on whom he'd seen at the fair. Several names were familiar to Janna: villagers who'd consulted her mother in the past, including the miller and his wife, as well as Aldith the midwife, the priest from Berford, and Fulk the apothecary. She was sorry not to have seen Aldith, but she was happy she'd missed the rest of them.

The two men discussed them all, but could come up with no reason why any should wish to harm Hugh. But mention of their names troubled Janna anew. "They are some of the villagers who once set fire to my cottage," she ventured. "If they know I'm alive, any one of them would wish to ensure my silence about what really happened that night. I can't help but believe I was the intended target and not you, my lord."

She looked at Hugh. This time he did not hasten to reassure her that she was wrong. "And I am so sorry that you were injured instead," she added.

"If I have saved your life, I am glad of it," Hugh said. "But if this is really the truth of the matter, you must give me your assurance, Johanna, that you will stay safely inside the abbey until we can establish who was responsible."

Janna sighed. "I will," she agreed reluctantly. "But if possible, can you keep my name out of your enquiries?"

Hugh nodded. "Godric and I will question the villagers, and see what we can learn. I promise you, we will not rest until we have found out who was behind this cowardly attack, and also the reason for it."

Chapter 10

Janna passed a restless night in the infirmary. Although she was comforted by Hugh's promise to continue enquiries, and although she was where she'd planned to be, she couldn't shake off the sense that she was trapped, and with no prospect of release. Several times she rose and flitted quietly between beds to check on the patients. Once, she crept into the cubicle that housed Hugh. She looked down at his sleeping form, and had to fight the urge to touch his cheek, to kiss his lips. After that, she stayed away, but when she finally slept, he was with her in her dreams.

With the new dawn came the realization that the fair was now over. The bustle in the forecourt suggested that most of the merchants and traders who'd been housed at the abbey would depart just as soon as Mass was over. Janna had enjoyed all the excitement, and was sorry to see them go. It seemed to her as if, stone by stone, the walls were closing in on her once more.

What further depressed her spirits was the fact that Hugh too would soon depart whereas she could not, at least not until she'd accomplished her ambition to find out more about her mother, as well as learning the skills to enable her to read her father's letter. But these goals seemed to have slipped forever from her grasp. Yet she could think of no other place to go, for even Winchestre had become an impossible dream now.

Janna had taken every opportunity to listen to the chatter of merchants and pilgrims alike, for they traveled about the country and spoke to people, and so she knew all that was happening in the tug of war for the crown. She'd learned that the earlier peace talks between King Stephen's queen and the Empress Matilda's half-brother, Earl Robert of Gloucestre, had come to naught, and that Bishop Henry of Winchestre, the king's brother, had traveled to France to ask the French king to mediate in their quarrel.

Meanwhile England was still in turmoil, with the king rushing from place to place, trying to buy support by promising to give land and castles to the barons while they, ambitious and greedy as ever, spent their time capturing castles from each other, from the empress's supporters, and even from the king, changing their allegiance whenever it suited their purpose. Under the circumstances, Janna had begun to realize that the chance of finding her father in Winchestre was almost nil. While the king's cause was in the ascendant, bolstered by the presence of a large army of Flemish mercenaries, a number of disaffected barons had defected to the Empress Matilda, creating a further problem for Janna: If her father was a nobleman, she had no way of telling to whom he owed knight service, or which side his overlord might support.

And if he was a priest? Janna sighed at the thought of how difficult it would be to find him. All her hopes were pinned on reading the answers in his letter, but how could she persuade Sister Anne to allow her to skip her duties and instead sit with Sister Grace and the chantress's pupils in the cloister and learn, in charity, something for which they had paid a fee?

It was with a heavy heart that Janna made her morning visit to Hugh. Soon he would be well enough to leave the abbey and she would miss him, both for his company and as a link with the world outside.

"Why such a long face, Sister?" he greeted her when she walked into his cubicle.

"It is because you are healing so fast, my lord." It was safe to tell the truth for Sister Anne was nowhere in sight. Even so, as soon as she'd spoken, Janna regretted making her feelings so obvious.

He looked a little puzzled. "Does this mean I may return to my manor?" he ventured.

"Only when the infirmarian says it is safe for you to make the journey."

Hugh was silent for a moment. "If you're so unhappy here, why not come home with me?" he suggested. "My manor is far enough from your old home that you may hide there in safety."

Janna closed her eyes against a sudden flood of emotion. To go home with Hugh would give her more happiness than she'd ever known. But she was afraid of where it might lead, this invitation that was kindly meant and that sounded so innocent. Her resolve hardened. She would never put herself in her mother's position. Never!

She opened her eyes. "I thank you, sire, but I cannot," she said steadily.

"And I am sorry for it. Being here, watching you..." The admiration in his eyes was unmistakable.

Janna swallowed hard. She was trying to think of some light rejoinder when the heavy curtain of the cubicle was pushed aside. Emma raced in and cast herself, sobbing, into Hugh's arms.

"Hugh!" she choked, too distraught to say anything other than his name.

"Hush, Emma. What is it?" He held her tight, and patted her back in a vain attempt to calm her. Janna debated whether she should run to find some soothing mixture for the young woman, and was just about to leave when she caught Hugh's imploring expression, which told her he was out of his depth and didn't know what to do. She pointed her finger toward the entrance, indicating that she should go, but he shook his head in an emphatic "no." His shoulders lifted in mute appeal. Janna patted her hand in the air, miming that he should keep on gentling the girl, and let her cry her worries into silence. He nodded.

When Emma had calmed somewhat, he tried again.

"What grieves you so? Tell me, and I'll do what I may to help you."

Emma began to cry once more, sounding utterly lost, beyond consolation. Hugh waited patiently. Finally she managed to choke out a word, her voice muffled against Hugh's chest.

"Anselm? What has happened to him?" Hugh's voice was sharp with tension. "He is dead." Emma broke into another storm of weeping. While they waited for her to compose herself sufficiently to tell them how he had died, Janna mused that, no matter how fond Emma was of her brother, this would answer the girl's difficulties so far as her marriage to the thatcher was concerned. And then she discerned a further possible cause for the girl's distress. This was confirmed when Emma was finally able to speak.

"I am so afraid for Peter," she quavered. "You see, we weren't careful enough to stay hidden. Anselm saw him at the fair with me and, before I could say aught, he charged up to us like a war horse at full gallop. He noticed my lily ring and asked about it. Knowing how angry he would be, I tried to pass it off as a trifle, but Peter faced up to him and said it was a gift of love, to mark our betrothal."

Emma scrubbed at the new tears leaking from her eyes. "My brother had taken too much ale and was wild with it. He started to shout at Peter, calling him all sorts of foul names. He said he was lowborn, good for nothing; he berated him for taking advantage of me. Finally, Peter couldn't take it any longer, and he turned on Anselm. He gave him a bloody nose. It was only that I shrieked and came between them that the fight was stopped. But there were witnesses, and the hue and cry has now gone out for Peter."

"But he has not been taken?"

"No. At least, not as far as I know."

"Do you know where he is?"

"No." Even Janna, who did not know her, could see that she lied.

Emma began to cry again. "Don't think my tears and my concern are all for Peter," she said. "I mourn my brother; oh, I weep for him! I know we've had our differences, but he is everything to me, he is my only family, he was the greatest part of my life!"

Janna could see that Hugh, too, was struggling to contain his emotion. "I am full of remorse that we parted on bad terms," he said now. "I should have gone after him, tried to talk some sense into him!"

Janna thought Hugh was missing the point, but forgave him for it.

Nevertheless, she knew the question had to be asked. "Do you believe that Peter is responsible for Anselm's death?"

"No!" Emma's denial came without thought. She paused. "No, I do not believe he could ever do such a thing," she said more slowly. "True, he was upset and very annoyed, but we talked it through and decided we would go to our lord and ask for his support, as Hugh suggested we should. I'm sure Peter believed, as I did, that there was still a chance we might persuade Anselm to accept our betrothal. Besides, Peter is a

159

villein, and tied to our lord. He knows the penalty for killing, or even injuring, a free man, a Norman. He would pay with his life." Emma gave a sudden shiver. "He is not guilty of this, I swear it!"

"How did your brother die?" Janna cast a quick glance at Hugh, worried that she was overstepping the bounds of propriety. He gave her a nod of encouragement. They waited for Emma to answer.

"He...he was slaughtered like an animal!" She gave a hiccupping sob of outrage. "His throat was cut, and he was left to bleed to death in a ditch."

"Where? What ditch?"

Emma looked a little bewildered by the question. "It was—it runs on one side of the marketmede," she said slowly. "It's near the cockfighting pit."

"Did you see your brother actually lying there, in the ditch? Did you notice anything unusual at the scene?" Janna knew she must sound unsympathetic, but the question was important. When first her mother and then her pet cat had been killed, she'd worked out the truth of their deaths from blood stains, confusing at first the stains of red wine with the blood pooled beneath the animal.

Emma stared at her with an expression of outrage. Fortunately, Hugh understood the reasoning behind the questions. "We need to know as much as you can tell us so we can help you find out the truth," he said.

Janna felt encouraged by his use of the word "we." It prompted her to explain further. "Forgive my questions, mistress, but it's important to find out just where he was murdered, and if his body was moved afterward," she said. "It could give us some insight into his killer's movements, and maybe even tell us who the killer might be."

Emma blinked. "Yes, I saw Anselm's body," she said slowly. She put her hands to her eyes as if to ward off the sight of her dead brother. "There was…there was so much blood. So much! His clothes were soaked scarlet with it."

"Was there any blood on the ground outside the ditch? Any drag marks, or anything else to indicate he may have been killed elsewhere and his body taken there and dumped?"

Emma shuddered. "I don't know," she whispered. "I didn't think to look."

"I'll go and have a look around as soon as I can leave here," Hugh promised.

Janna nodded. "What happened after you saw your brother, after you identified him?" she asked.

"A priest was with him; he'd been called to say the last rites, to anoint Anselm and give him absolution. But he was too late. My brother died unshriven." Tears streamed freely down Emma's face. "The priest asked one of the guards to summon the steward. There were no witnesses to what had happened, but the steward has questioned the man who raised the hue and cry after Peter. The man is from our manor, he knows us all, and that is why the guard came to find me." Emma wiped her eyes and nose on the sleeve of her gown, and swallowed hard. "I wish we'd never come to the fair!" she wailed. "I was so looking forward to it, it was such a treat. If only we'd known what awaited us here!" She broke into despairing sobs once more.

Janna exchanged glances with Hugh. "I'll go and talk to the steward," he said. Setting Emma gently to one side, he swung his legs out of the bed, ready to put his thoughts into action. "I'll also talk to the witness, and to Peter—*if* you can find him, Emma?" His slight emphasis on the word brought a blush to her face. She gave a reluctant nod. "And perhaps I should also have a look at Anselm, in case there's anything about his injuries that might tell us something about his assassin?"

"You need not look far for that, my lord." Emma's voice was thick, choked with tears. "He has been brought here, to the abbey. The porteress told me that Anselm will be kept in the mortuary chapel until such time as the steward has finished his enquiries and allows us to take him back to our manor for burial."

"You should not leave your bed yet, my lord, not until your wound is quite healed," Janna said firmly. "I'll go to the chapel. I can tell you everything I find out." Something Emma had said on her previous visit came into Janna's mind. She wondered if it had any bearing on what had just happened. "Mistress, one more question, if I may?" she asked. "You mentioned before that Anselm had promised you a larger dowry. Where was that to come from, do you know?"

"No, I do not."

"From a win at gambling, perhaps?" Janna suggested.

Emma jerked upright, looking both startled and dismayed.

Janna turned to Hugh. "He may have thought, if he increased Mistress Emma's dowry, that you might be more willing to wed his sister, my lord." Hugh groaned aloud. "Are you saying both Emma and I are responsible for what has happened to Anselm?"

Janna realized she was in deeper waters than she'd expected; certainly much further than she'd intended to go. Nevertheless, she felt it important to continue. "I am saying, my lord, that if Anselm meant to buy your favor, he would not have attacked you."

Hugh nodded thoughtfully. "So the attack on me and the death of Anselm are definitely not related?"

"It would seem so. The fact that Anselm was probably murdered close to the cockfighting ring indicates that his death might well have been related to his ill-fortune at gambling."

"None of this helps to exonerate Peter from this crime!" Emma said impatiently, her concern not only with justice for her brother, but also for her lover.

"Both Anselm and I were attacked with a knife or a dagger," Hugh mused. "Doesn't that make some sort of connection?"

"Every man I know, whether freeborn or villein, owns a knife or a dagger, or both," Janna pointed out.

"Peter owns a knife, a dagger, and other cutting implements besides. It is his trade," Emma said bleakly.

"Then let us see what else we can find out." Hugh now had hold of his clothes, which had been laundered while he was lying abed.

"My lord," Janna protested. He grinned at her, and mimed lifting his shirt. Recognizing defeat, Janna took Emma's arm and led her from the cubicle so Hugh could dress. "Would you like me to make up a potion to soothe you?" she asked.

"No!" Emma shrugged her off. "No, I thank you," she continued more calmly. "I beg your pardon for answering sharply, mistress—Sister." She cast a quick, bemused glance at Janna's habit. "I'm not myself at present. But I will come with you to see Anselm, to...to pay my respects. I hardly had a chance to look at him before I fled from the ditch to be sick." She shuddered, the horror still fresh in her mind. "After that, my only thought was to find Peter. I knew the steward would raise the hue and cry once he learned about the fight."

"You told him to hide himself?"

Emma nodded. Her eyes were bleak as a storm-filled sky as she said, "I suggested he leave Wiltune immediately, flee back to our manor and hide in a—a tumbledown barn where we used to meet...privately. I told him I'd talk to someone who might be able to help us, and that I'd come back to find him as soon as it was safe, once the man responsible for my brother's death was safely locked away. And then I came straight here to find Hugh." She straightened her rumpled kirtle, then raised trembling hands to her veil, which was also much awry. "I must look a fright," she whispered, as she adjusted its folds.

"Not a fright, just very distressed. But you may be sure, mistress, that my lord will do all in his power to help you, as will I," Janna comforted her.

*

As they entered the mortuary chapel, Janna steeled herself for her first sight of Anselm. She remembered, only too vividly, the death of her cat, what it had looked like after its throat had been cut. A shiver of distress ran through her at the memory.

Sister Anne was already there, bent over the dead youth. By the look of the cloth she wielded and the basin of stained water beside her, she was doing what she could to clean away the blood and muck from the ditch and make the body more presentable. She glanced up as they approached.

"Come and help me, Johanna," she said, then straightened slowly as she noticed who else was present. "My lord, you should not be up and walking about."

"I had to come, Sister." Hugh gestured at Anselm. "My dearest friend lies here and I have sworn to do what I may to avenge his death."

Sister Anne looked thoughtful. Then she beckoned him closer. Janna and Emma followed Hugh, and all bent over to inspect Anselm. Janna drew a breath of surprise as she recognized his face. This was the desperate youth she'd seen at the cockfight. She'd wondered if he would wager his soul, and now it seemed that he had. Pity washed through her at the terrible waste of his life, and the havoc his death might yet wreak on the innocent.

There was a jagged gash across his throat, while his nose was bruised and swollen from its earlier contact with Peter's fist. Signs of a fight were unmistakable on Anselm's face, but had he suffered any other wounds? Janna raised the sheet that covered Anselm and peered at his naked body beneath.

"Sister Johanna!" Sister Anne looked absolutely scandalized. Janna quickly dropped the sheet.

"I'm looking for scratches or bruises, or any signs that he might have tried to defend himself. If he did, his assailant might bear the marks of it," she explained hurriedly.

"There's nothing to see. I would have noticed while I was washing him," Sister Anne said stiffly.

Janna inspected Anselm's arms, then picked up his hands, one by one, paying special attention to his nails. "I can't see any skin fragments, or blood, or bruising on his arms. It seems he made no effort to defend himself. Either he was taken by surprise, or he knew his assailant." She looked at Emma.

"It wasn't Peter. And it wasn't me, either!"

"No! No, of course not. But you mentioned someone who raised the hue and cry, someone who knows you all. Could he have any reason to…?"

Emma thought about it. "No. I can't think why Odo would want Anselm dead."

"Do you know him well enough to be sure?"

"I know him as well as anyone else on the manor. He's been there as long as I have, probably longer in fact, for I think he was born there. He is but a villein, but I believe he is liked and trusted by all."

"Is anyone else here from your manor?" Hugh asked.

Emma shook her head. "I haven't seen anyone I recognize, but there was such a crowd at the fair that anyone could hide if he didn't want to be seen."

"Can you think of anyone, anyone at all, who might wish Anselm harm?"

"No. No, I cannot. You know what he was like, Hugh." Emma gazed at him with tear-filled eyes. "Everyone loved him."

Except Peter Thatcher, Janna added silently.

"You yourself said that he'd got into bad company, and that he was drinking too much," Hugh reminded her. "Could it be that a drunken fight got out of hand?"

Emma shrugged sadly, but didn't reply.

"I noticed him at the cockfighting pit on the first day of the fair," Janna said, thinking it was time to reveal what she'd seen. "I think he'd just lost a wager, for he seemed in great distress."

"Could he have owed money to someone?" Emma asked, ready to clutch at any straw that might be offered. "Could this be a money-lender's revenge?" "No, no, it's nothing like that." Sister Anne was bursting to tell what she knew. "I heard that he got in a fight over a young woman. The steward seeks his assailant even now. 'Tis said the woman is very beautiful. The pity of it is that such beauty would so inflame men's passions as to lead them to—Why are you pulling such faces at me, Johanna? I beg you to remember that you are in the house of God."

Janna was sorry she'd called attention to herself, yet was relieved that she had, at least, succeeded in stopping the nun's prattle. She couldn't help feeling amused by the revelation that Sister Anne, too, was not averse to listening to gossip, yet she was sorry that Emma was there to hear it.

"She's pulling faces because this is the young man's sister." Hugh indicated Emma standing silently beside him. "The fight was between her brother and...and her betrothed."

"Oh, mistress, I do beg your pardon!" Sister Anne clasped her hands together, unconsciously praying for forgiveness.

"Where are Master Anselm's clothes?" Janna asked, feeling sympathy for the infirmarian's embarrassment and seeking to divert attention from it. "Maybe they can tell us something."

Sister Anne drew herself upright, her body rigid with disapproval. "'Tis the steward's task to investigate this terrible crime," she said frostily.

166

"Please, Sister, allow Johanna to do whatever she may to help us understand what has happened this day. I know, from past experience, that she has a keen eye and a quick mind, and she may well see something that the steward has missed."

Janna flashed Hugh a grateful glance; the glow of his approval heated her cheeks.

Sister Anne studied her thoughtfully while she made up her mind. "Over there," she said at last, and pointed at a pile of bloodstained garments on a nearby bench.

"May I?" But Janna didn't wait for Emma's nod of acceptance. She picked up Anselm's soiled tunic, inspected it carefully and then turned her attention to his hose. She learned nothing from the garments, and looked around for his belt. A blood-stained sheath hung from it, and Janna drew out the dagger safely concealed within. It looked clean enough. Janna sheathed it and glanced about for a purse or scrip, for Anselm would surely have had some sort of pouch to carry his money and possessions. But there was only a cut string. Janna remembered the cutpurse she'd seen on the first day of the fair, and wondered if the youth had grown more desperate as the days progressed. If so, he would have to answer to a crime far worse than theft.

"My lord," she called to Hugh. Emma followed him over, and Janna showed them what she'd found. "Did you see any sign of a purse when you undressed Master Anselm, Sister Anne?"

"No, I did not. I wondered about it at the time, but I'm afraid it went out of my head once I saw the state of this poor young man." Sister Anne fussed with the sheet, rearranging it carefully around Anselm's shoulders and tucking it in to make sure no-one else would be tempted to take a peek underneath.

Janna told Hugh and Emma about the cutpurse she'd seen. "My guess is that your brother won some money at the cock-fights after all," she told Emma. "No-one would bother to steal his purse else."

"But why didn't the robber just cut his purse and run away? Why kill him?" Emma wailed.

Janna could think of one very good reason, but she didn't say it out loud, not in front of Sister Anne. She waited while Hugh and Emma bowed their heads and said a prayer for the dead man. She would talk to them later, and see if they agreed with her opinion. Meanwhile she needed to come up with an argument convincing enough to gain permission to leave the abbey. When Hugh and Emma left to pursue the killer, she would accompany them.

*

"I've had some thoughts about who may be responsible for Anselm's death," Janna said, once she and Emma had escorted Hugh back to the infirmary. She'd hurriedly mixed up a potion to give him, for he was pale and drawn, the effort of going down to the chapel having taken a toll on his resilience. She handed him the mug, and he drank the potion down.

"Thank you." He handed it back, and closed his eyes with a grateful sigh. "Tell me what's on your mind?" he said, as he stretched out to make himself comfortable.

"I think Anselm was killed because he knew the thief who cut his purse. I believe the thief may have been Odo."

"Odo?" Hugh opened his eyes again.

"Odo?" Emma echoed.

Janna nodded, and turned to her. "Your brother must have had coins in his purse for it to have been taken."

"But why blame Odo for that?" Emma objected. "It may be that Anselm saw the thief cut his purse and chased after him—and was murdered for it. It could have been anyone."

"I don't think so. If Anselm saw the thief and chased after him, he would have drawn his dagger, he would have been armed and on his guard. There would have been a fight, and he would likely have received other cuts as well as the one that killed him." Janna paused to order her argument. "No, I think Anselm knew the thief and that was why he had to be silenced. I also believe he was taken by surprise, and by someone he trusted, and that was why he had no time to arm and defend himself before his throat was cut."

But had that assailant been Odo—or Peter Thatcher? Janna recognized that her comments could apply to either man, but she knew Emma would hear nothing against her beloved. That possibility was something she must discuss later with Hugh, when they were alone.

"It could be that Anselm met Odo, either by chance or arrangement, near the ditch where his body was found," she hurried on. "He would have had no cause for concern, no reason to fear a man he knew well. The attack, when it came, must have been sudden and completely unexpected. Odo had to kill your brother before he could take his purse, for he could not leave him alive to bear witness. I suspect he cut the purse off afterward, to make us believe it was the work of a common thief."

"If that is so, the purse will be stained with Anselm's blood!" Forgetting his wound in the excitement of the chase, Hugh jerked upright. He subsided with a groan. Sweat broke out across his forehead. Janna hoped the sudden movement hadn't torn apart the newly healing skin.

"We must go after Odo," Emma said with determination. "Hugh…" Her voice trailed away as she noticed his pallor.

"I'll come with you," Janna said quickly. "The fair is over and people are already leaving Wiltune. We must make haste."

"It's not safe for you to go alone. I'm coming with you." Hugh swept aside the blanket that covered him, revealing a shirt stained with fresh blood.

"No, my lord, you are not." Sister Anne had entered the cubicle and taken in the situation with one glance. "Look at the damage you have caused by rising from your bed too soon! You must rest and give that wound a chance to heal or I will not answer for the consequences."

"I can go in the lord's place," Janna said quickly, adding, "if you will give me permission to leave the abbey, Sister?" The infirmarian looked somewhat doubtful.

"Please!" Emma was anxious to be gone, but fearful of carrying out her task alone.

"You have taken no vows, you have merely sought safety here in the abbey?" Sister Anne questioned.

"Yes, indeed."

"Then you are free to leave whenever you will. But..." Sister Anne checked Janna's rush to the door. "But if you leave, you may not find it quite so easy to return."

"Why not?" Hugh demanded, before Janna could say anything. "Surely the pursuit of truth and justice is all part of carrying out God's work?"

Sister Anne nodded thoughtfully. "There is some merit in what you say," she conceded.

"Then let Sister Johanna accompany Mistress Emma, I beg you, for there are questions to be asked of those who may already be making preparations to leave Wiltune. There is no time to lose." Hugh cast an uncertain glance at Janna. "But please be careful," he said. "Both of you. And especially you, Johanna. Don't take any chances, please."

Chapter 11

Janna felt an exhilarating sense of freedom as they left the abbey. Nevertheless, she couldn't resist a nervous glance over her shoulder as they came to the site of the fair. There were still a number of people about, those who were busy demolishing booths and stalls, plus some of the traders who'd occupied them and were now busy packing away their goods and loading them onto sumpter horses or stacking them onto carts.

"I don't know where to start looking," Emma said dismally. "What if Odo ran away from Wiltune straight after he attacked Anselm?"

"He stayed to identify your brother and raise the hue and cry for Peter," Janna reminded her. "Besides, why would he run away and thus arouse suspicion, when he can bear witness to the quarrel with Peter, knowing that your lover will wear the blame for Anselm's death?" Taking advantage of Emma's silence, Janna continued. "He probably has a purse full of coins now. I think he might be tempted to stay on to enjoy his ill-gotten gains, for he won't be able to spend them once he returns to your manor."

Emma nodded, looking slightly more confident. "We came together, Odo, Anselm and I," she said. "Perhaps he would not leave without me, for that too might look suspicious?"

"Yes, indeed. And was no-one else here from your manor?"

"Only Peter," said Emma, thoroughly downcast once more. "Anselm and I wanted to come to the fair. Odo and Peter were both given leave to come, but Peter thought it wise not to travel with Anselm, so he came alone."

"Let's try the cockfighting pit first then," Janna suggested. "If Odo saw your brother winning there, and if there are still fights going on and wagers being made, a full purse might tempt him to try his own luck."

They turned toward the pit, and the ditch that ran beside it. The fairground was filthy with discarded produce, rotten and trampled underfoot, along with the excrement of the birds and animals that had been brought and traded, and had left their mark. Janna wrinkled her nose at the smell. She lifted the hem of her habit, and trod carefully through the refuse.

The cockpit was deserted now, and there were no signs of men making wagers over dice or any other means whereby a quick profit might be turned. Janna scanned the scene, then walked over to the ditch. Discarded bits of bread, rotting meat, fish bones and other uninviting objects lay half-submerged in the scummy water. She shuddered. "Where did they find your brother?" she asked, feeling sorry that she'd asked Emma to revisit this sad, dreadful place.

"Not here. Further along, near those trees." Emma waved a hand to show where she meant. Janna set off to see for herself.

"The trees make a good screen," Emma said thoughtfully, as she showed Janna the exact spot where she'd found her brother.

"Yes. Odo may have asked your brother to meet him here, for there's no reason for him to be here else. Unless he came over to relieve himself?" Janna had detected the stink of stale urine in the air. This patch of trees had obviously formed a handy latrine for fairgoers. As such, Odo might have been taking a bigger risk than he realized if he had made such an arrangement. Someone answering the call of nature might easily have surprised them. But it seemed more likely that the attack had come about by chance, an impulse born of propitious circumstances.

She shrugged. It made no matter how or why they'd met but what had happened once they did. She looked at the stained and stagnant water in the ditch and the bloody marks on the ground where Anselm's body must have rested after they lifted him out. Emma had gone pale. Janna hoped the young woman wasn't going to be sick again. She moved away to inspect the ground nearby, drawing Emma away from the stinking ditch as she did so. She could find no other stains, nor any scuff marks to indicate that a body had been dragged from somewhere else.

She straightened. "Let's see if we can find Odo," she said, and began to pick her way back through the filthy fairground once more.

"I wish I could be sure Anselm wasn't behind the attack on Hugh," Emma said, as she followed Janna back to the marketplace.

"I don't think you need to worry about that." Janna spoke over her shoulder.

"It's possible I was the intended target."

"But why?"

"It's too long a story to tell you now. In the meantime you must try not to think badly of your brother. Really, there was no reason for him to attack Hugh."

"My brother is usually open to reason, but he was very angry with Hugh when I spoke to him, angry enough, I think, to take action against even a once-beloved brother-in-arms.

He talked about how Hugh had dishonored our friendship and brought shame to our family. I tried to calm him down, but he wouldn't listen to me."

"I expect it was the drink talking. He must have known that attacking Hugh wouldn't serve his cause at all, or yours. We can only hope that he came to his senses in time." Emma's confession made Janna feel a little more confident about her own safety. "You said Anselm was watching the cockfighting. Was he winning or losing then, do you think?"

"Losing, I am sure. He looked quite desperate."

"Yes, I thought so too, when I saw him. But his luck might have turned later, perhaps shortly before he died?"

"I don't know." Emma looked wretched. "After the fight between Anselm and Peter, I wanted no more to do with my brother and so I stayed away from him as much as I could. He was so angry with me—and with Hugh." Emma gave a half-strangled sob. "And so my brother died alone like a pig in a ditch, victim of an unknown hand, but after quarreling with those who loved him best. I'd give anything in the world to have him alive again so I could tell him..." Her voice trailed off into silence.

"That you would give up Peter?"

"No!" Emma's voice was low, but fierce. "There's no need! It was only Anselm's stiff-necked pride that made a problem of my love for Peter."

Janna nodded in sympathetic agreement. She hurriedly picked her way across the marketplace toward the bush tied to a pole that marked the site of an alehouse. It stood close beside the shop of Fulk, the apothecary. The fair being over, both were now open for business, but the alehouse was by far the more crowded. She pushed through a group of men who, with full mugs of ale in hand, stood blocking the door.

"We can't go in there!" Emma sounded scandalized. Janna glanced behind, and gestured impatiently for her to follow. "If

Odo's not in here, I wager we'll find him in one of the other alehouses," she said, and marched inside. She wondered if the alewife would recognize her, for she'd been there before, but her habit turned out to be an effective disguise. In fact, the alewife looked even more scandalized than Emma when she noticed a lay sister on her premises.

"You'll be putting my customers off their drink," she muttered angrily.

"We're looking for someone, mistress," Janna explained. The alewife flounced off and left them alone. "If you see Odo, don't let him know your suspicions, don't accuse him of anything," Janna warned. "Pretend you're glad to see him. Say you feel faint, and ask him to buy you a mug of ale. See if he takes the money to pay for it from Anselm's purse."

Emma hesitated, looking nervous. "Go." Janna gave her a nudge to get her moving. "Don't worry, I'll be right here if there's any trouble." She stayed beside the door, watching as Emma began to circle the crowded room. She was the butt of several ribald comments, for women did not frequent alehouses alone unless there was a purpose for their presence. With head held high, Emma ignored the lewd suggestions, but Janna could see the angry flush coloring her face as she tried to avoid a groping hand only to encounter another. Taking pity on her plight, Janna hurried over to join her, for she knew the alewife was right: her presence would inhibit the drinkers in more ways than one.

"He's not here," Emma said, once the circle of the room was complete.

"Then we'll try another, and another, until we find him." To Janna's surprise, Emma nodded in agreement. She was glad not to have to argue her case, but her spirits sank low as they visited one alehouse after another without success.

"He's already gone, hasn't he?" Emma sighed.

"There's one more to try." Janna led her to a rundown establishment tucked away in a small lane off the marketplace. It was frequented by a bunch of rogues and lay-abouts, judging by a few patrons who were openly relieving themselves at a side fence when Janna and Emma entered the yard. They averted their faces and pressed on into the crowded alehouse.

"He's here!" Emma hissed out of the side of her mouth.

"Lean on me." Janna took her arm. "Say you want to go home; tell him I've been helping you look for him. And don't forget to ask him to buy you something to drink."

Emma sagged slightly, and allowed Janna to support her over to a table where two men were busy at a game of dice. Judging from the coins on the table, and the raised voices, the loser wasn't happy about the sizeable gains being amassed by the winner. At sight of Emma, the loser sprang up and made a sketchy bow. "You should not be here, mistress," he said.

"No, I should not," Emma said tartly, "but I have been looking for you, Odo. I wish to go home now to...to..." Her voice faltered.

"To tell your lord what has happened here," Janna said firmly. She patted Emma's shoulder to comfort her and let her know she was not alone.

"I'll come at once." The man scowled at his associate, who sat back on his stool with a smug expression and began to count the pile of coins set in front of him.

"I-I feel faint. I need to sit down. Mayhap a drink of wine or ale will help to revive me?" Emma said quickly.

"This is no place for you, nor for you, Sister." Odo's mouth turned down in a thin line of disapproval as he surveyed Janna. Not giving Emma any chance to argue, he took her arm and led her outside. Janna made haste to follow the pair. She said nothing until they'd left the laneway and were back in the marketplace. As soon as there were people about and it was safe to stop, she called out, "I beg you, mistress, for the sake of your health, take some refreshment before you set out for home."

"Oh, yes." An expression of relief illuminated Emma's face. "But I've spent all my money at the fair." She turned to Odo in appeal. "Would you have a coin to spare for a drink and perhaps a pie from the cookshop, Odo?"

"Yes, of course, mistress." Odo's hand went to his purse. He hesitated. "I, myself, had a lucky wager on a cockfight," he mumbled, as he opened it to extract a coin. The purse was new, and made of fine leather. Bought with Anselm's winnings, Janna felt sure of it, just as she felt sure that Anselm's purse was now safely at the bottom of the ditch, or buried in a bush perhaps. How could they trap the rogue into admitting his foul deed when there was no evidence of it save a purchase he might well claim to have bought out of his own coin?

She gazed at the purse, and then at his tunic, noting how clean it was in front compared to his sleeves, which were dirty and travel-stained. Her gaze narrowed. A fierce exhilaration pulsed through her body.

"Pray fetch some refreshment for Mistress Emma," Janna ordered, thinking to set his arrest in train while he was out of hearing.

Odo nodded and set off for the cookshop, moving with alacrity. Janna guessed he was relieved not to be questioned about his newfound wealth. But his turn would come, she promised herself.

"I didn't recognize Anselm's purse," Emma said forlornly.

"It's new, that's why." She looked around the marketplace, hoping to see the steward or one of the abbey guards, anyone with the authority to apprehend the villein on his return. Her spirits rose when she spied Godric in the distance.

"Godric!" she shouted, waving energetically to attract his attention.

He hurried over. "My lord Hugh asked me to come looking for you. He's worried about you. And there is news." He turned to Emma. "Word has come from the steward that the man who murdered your brother has been arrested, mistress."

"Odo?" Not understanding, Emma looked about for the villein. He was walking toward them, balancing a pie and a mug of ale and looking very pleased with himself.

"Not Odo. Peter Thatcher."

"No!" As understanding came, Emma's eyes filled with tears. "But I told him to hide!"

"And it counted against him when he was caught fleeing from here."

"But he's innocent!"

"If that is so, he will be let free." But Godric looked as if he didn't believe it for a moment.

"He is innocent," Janna affirmed. She felt great sympathy for Emma, and a seething sense of injustice on behalf of the hapless thatcher. "Where is the steward now?"

"At the abbey," Godric answered. "The thatcher has been brought there to await trial at the abbess's court. But his own lord will have to be summoned, before the case can be heard."

"Where are the guards?" Janna looked about for anyone with some authority.

"Have you seen any of them about?"

"I just walked past one of them. He's over there."

Janna looked where Godric pointed, and felt her spirits lift with relief. "Ho there!" she shouted, and beckoned the guard to come to them.

"Did I hear mention that the thatcher has been arrested for the murder of your brother, my lady?" There was a definite air of self-satisfaction about Odo as he handed the pie and ale to Emma.

"Yes, Odo; the thatcher has been taken into custody," Janna answered for Emma. "But the wrong man stands accused. Hold onto Odo, Godric. Hold him tight!"

To her relief, Godric asked no questions but immediately made a grab for the startled villein. He had no chance to defend himself before Janna took a firm grip of his other arm, and called out to the guard: "This is the man responsible for the murder of the man found in the ditch!"

"We already hold the culprit." The guard ambled over at a leisurely pace. He made no move to relieve Janna and Godric of their struggling captive.

"This man is guilty—and I can prove it!"

Odo strained against their grasp. "You are mistaken. Let me go!"

"See the blood on his tunic?"

"But I washed—"

"Not carefully enough," Janna assured him. "There is a spray of blood spotting his sleeve. Can you see it, guard?" The guard took a reluctant step closer and bent to inspect the marks. Odo's struggles increased. Fear had given him added strength and Janna wondered how long they'd be able to hold him if the guard wouldn't assist them.

"The steward asked me to identify Anselm," Odo blustered. "I had to come close to make sure it was him. There was so much blood staining his face and clothes, small wonder if I bear the marks."

"That might account for stains down the front of your tunic, although you were quick to wash away signs of your guilt. But how did Anselm's blood spatter onto your sleeve?"

Odo was silent. All his energy was now focused on his frantic struggles to escape. A crowd had gathered around them. There were mutters of sympathy as news of Emma's identity was passed around. Making up his mind, the guard reached out to take Odo into custody. Janna instinctively relaxed.

At once Odo lunged sideways, catching Godric off-balance. He tore himself from Godric's grasp and charged into the crowd like a rampaging bull. But the onlookers had heard enough to know where their sympathies lay, and they closed around him, hemming him in until the guard came close enough to grasp him. A stout rope was hastily fetched from a nearby trader, who was busy packing the remainder of his goods onto a cart.

"Do you believe this man murdered your brother, mistress?" the guard asked Emma, once the villein was safely bound. "You need proof for this accusation, for I must tell you we already have a number of witnesses to a fist fight between the thatcher and your brother. There's reason enough to suspect that the grievance between them did not end when the fight was broken up."

"What about the spatters of blood on Odo's sleeve?" Emma asked quickly.

"And his purse is new—and still bulging with coin, even though he's been losing at dice," Janna added.

Odo scowled at her. "A lucky win at a cockfight. More, there was no reason for me to kill a man whom I hold in high regard, but there was every reason for the thatcher to kill the man who came between him and his betrothed." Odo's struggles had ceased in the face of the guard's skepticism. Janna suspected he was going to try and brazen it out. She was equally determined that he would not succeed.

"What knowledge do you have of this matter, Sister?" The guard's tone was respectful, as befitted Janna's habit.

"She solved the crime, and she also helped me find Odo," Emma said, earning Janna a furious glare from the villein.

The guard nodded thoughtfully. "Do you know the accused? Or the man we already have locked away? Can you speak to the good character of either of them, Sister?" Reluctantly, Janna shook her head.

"I know them, both of them—and I know the thatcher isn't guilty of this crime," Emma insisted.

"You say that because you are in love with him!" Odo growled. "But I know your brother opposed the match. I, myself, witnessed their fight over you, as well as the argument you had with your brother."

"So you were at the cockfights with Anselm?" Janna interposed.

"Yes. I won some money there. I already told you that." Odo's confidence was increasing by the minute. He turned to the guard, who was looking uncertain. "Perhaps you should start your enquiries by interrogating Mistress Emma here. She is the dead man's sister, and she also had a reason for wishing him harm."

"Oh! Oh, you—" Emma's hands clenched in impotent rage. "I'll see you hang for this," she hissed.

The unhappy guard turned to Godric. "Do you know this man? Or the dead man, or the man they call Peter Thatcher?" he asked hopefully.

"No. But this is the man responsible for the killing, I'd be willing to wager my life on it," Godric said, loyal to Janna as always.

"Take him to the steward," Janna suggested. "Let him tell his story, and see who the steward believes."

Glad to have a face-saving way out of the bother, the guard nodded and led Odo away.

"You're quite sure of Odo's guilt, are you, Janna?" Godric fell into step beside her as she followed the guard with his prisoner.

"He wears his guilt on his sleeve." Janna felt a twinge of pity. If found guilty, Odo would be tried and then hanged for his deed, but Anselm's murder might have been just a moment of madness. A chance meeting at the makeshift latrine perhaps, and a boast of a wager that had paid off handsomely. She looked at Emma then, and her pity died. It was true that Anselm's death had opened the door to her future happiness, but Janna was sure that the price paid was far too high. Anselm's unreasonable hopes for his sister surely reflected his love and regard for her. Sooner or later he would have come to realize that he could not rely on Hugh to make her happy, and would have accepted Peter into the family.

"Try not to worry," she told Emma, who had hurried to join them. "The truth must come out and then Peter will be let free."

"But the guard doesn't believe us." A tear rolled down Emma's cheek. She looked thoroughly cast down.

"Then we must talk to the steward when we get back to the abbey, and see if we can convince him instead." In spite of her words, Janna felt her confidence ebbing. Odo's guilt hinged entirely on her word—but what if the steward didn't believe her, and let Odo go free?

"We're all with you, we'll all be saying the same thing," Godric reassured her. "My lord Hugh, Mistress Emma, you and me—the steward will have to pay attention to what we say."

Janna flashed him a grateful smile. He took her arm, and pressed it to his side. Together they walked on, while Janna thought through the evidence and wondered if it would be enough to convince the steward. She had an idea. "Tell me, mistress, is there anything missing other than your brother's purse? Did he perhaps wear a token around his neck, or carry some lucky object about his person? Is there anything that might help to connect him to Odo?" Emma gave a forlorn sniff. "No, he wasn't one for trinkets, he wore nothing like that. Except—" Her face brightened somewhat.

"Except?"

"He found a pebble once, in the stream near where we lived. We were just children at the time. He showed it to me.

It was very pretty, with golden streaks through it. He told me they were real gold and that the pebble was worth a king's ransom. Oh, I so wanted that pebble and I begged him to give it to me, but he wouldn't—I think only because I wanted it so badly. He kept it in his purse, and sometimes he'd bring it out to tease me. Later, when I was older and had stopped coveting it, I noticed that he still had it and I questioned him. 'Is that really gold?' I asked him, and he said no, but that he kept it now for luck. 'It's my lucky pebble,' he said—but it didn't bring him any luck at the end, did it?"

"No. But it may well bring luck to your thatcher," Janna comforted her, hoping that if Emma mistook the streaks for gold, so, too, might Odo. "The lord Hugh will want to know what's happened," she continued. "He'll speak up for Peter, once he's seen for himself the blood splattered on Odo's sleeve, and the new and bulging purse at his waist. A lucky wager indeed!" She gave a snort of disbelief, earning a fleeting smile from the tearful Emma.

"Why don't you move from your lodgings and stay in the abbey's guesthouse for the while, so you can be close to your brother, and to the steward, if he wants to question you further?" Janna suggested, returning to more practical matters. "I'm sure that, even if he's not well enough to come himself, the lord Hugh will arrange for an escort to take you home, and your brother's body too, once it's released for burial."

Emma nodded, grateful for the suggestion. "Thank you, Johanna," she said. "Thank you so much for helping me find Odo, and also for finding the proof to incriminate him."

"We just have to hope it's enough to convince the steward." Taking comfort from Godric's support, Janna followed the guard and Odo toward the abbey gate. She was preoccupied, now, with a new problem, one that sent ripples of unease through her mind. Anselm's death had left one question that might never be answered: Was he responsible for the attack on Hugh, or had she been the intended victim all along?

She cast an involuntary glance over her shoulder, discouraged to realize that, unless the culprit could be identified beyond doubt, she would always walk with danger at her back.

Chapter 12

Sister Brigid barred their way at the gate, but reluctantly stepped aside when the guard dragged forward the new prisoner. "The steward has gone to see the abbess," she told them, as she produced the key for the holding cell. "Please send for him," said Emma. "We need him to hear the evidence against this wretch." She insisted on accompanying the guard and Odo to the cell so that she could comfort her beloved while they waited for the steward to arrive. Janna watched them mount the stairs beside the small wayfarers' chapel above the gate before she and Godric hurried to Hugh's bedside. He was waiting impatiently, anxious for news. An expression of great relief crossed his face when he saw they'd returned unharmed.

Janna quickly told him about their search for Odo, and his capture. "But Godric tells me Peter has been apprehended and brought back here," she said. "You must excuse us, my lord, for we must go and speak on his behalf and against Odo. I believe we have evidence enough to hang him for this deed."

"Then I shall come too, and lend my weight to your argument." Hugh threw back the bedclothes.

"My lord, you really shouldn't move from your bed," Janna protested.

"I wish to confront Odo," Hugh said firmly. "I intend to make sure that he is punished in full for ending the life of my friend. He will not escape the hangman. Nor will an innocent man hang in his place."

Janna gave a grudging nod, but insisted on checking that his wound was tightly bandaged before she allowed him out of the cubicle. By rights, she should have guided lay visitors out of the infirmary and into open meadowland where stood various barns, a pigsty, byre, stables, the fish pool and a dovecote. The path circled the meadow in a wide loop, leading back into a smaller courtyard where could be found the kitchen, smithy, brewhouse, bakehouse and carpenter's shop. A moment's reflection convinced Janna that Hugh was in no condition to go on such a long detour and so she and Godric supported him through the inner passage to the parlor and out through the cloister. She had lost track of time, but realized that the dinner hour must have come and gone when she saw several nuns promenading on the grass. There was a scandalized hiss of indrawn breath. Strangers in the cloister garth, and men at that!

"Custody of the eyes, Sisters," the prioress said quickly, following her words with a glare in their direction while the rest of the nuns reluctantly averted their gaze.

"You'll have to leave the abbey with me now," Hugh told Janna, struggling to restrain his laughter as he added, "I fear your reputation is irrevocably ruined."

"Do not make it worse by laughing at them." Janna was all too aware of the presence of Godric, who had hold of Hugh's other arm and doubtless was interpreting Hugh's comments to make more of them than he should.

"I suspect that, regardless of my demeanor, the good sisters will draw their own conclusions, but let me do what I can to salvage your good name." Hugh shifted his weight to lean more heavily on Godric. "You can leave hold of me now," he told Janna.

She dropped his arm, and stepped back to walk behind the pair. At the same time, she began to marshal the argument she would need to defend herself in chapter, for there was sure to be much malicious speculation resulting from her actions this day.

They passed the carrel where Sister Ursel worked. A couple of sisters stood beside her, looking over her shoulder to admire the page she was illuminating. Another nun worked in the carrel beside her. A quick glance confirmed that Sister Ursel's work was far superior. There was a red blotch on Sister Philippa's sheet of parchment. It had been clumsily scraped, but the blotch still showed quite clearly. Even Janna, who did not know her letters, could see the difference between the fine strokes made by Sister Ursel and the thick, uneven letters formed by Sister Philippa. She wondered if the nun resented the comparison and sought daily to improve, or if she simply carried out her task to the best of her ability.

Janna took a deep breath, enjoying the kiss of the sun on her face. Mindful of the urgency of their mission, still she envied these nuns their leisure to pull weeds and snip dead flower heads, and sniff the perfume of the last late-blooming roses. She saw that several of the sisters were using this opportunity to give their pets a little fresh air and exercise. As she walked past, she noticed a small dog squat on the grass to relieve itself. Its owner gave a furtive look around, then bent and scooped up the steaming pile between two sticks, hastily gathered for the purpose. The young novice deposited her burden under a rose bush, poking the excrement into the earth with the sharp end of one stick. While the abbess and obedientiaries turned a blind eye to the issue of pet-keeping, it was accepted, if not openly acknowledged, that the animals' waste must be put to good use. Consequently, the rose bushes thrived, as did all the shrubs planted within the cloister.

A sudden cry set Janna's head swiveling to find its source. "Filthy beast!" One of the sisters hopped about, her foot in the air as she attempted to undo her sandal. "I stepped right into it! Who did not clean up after her animal?" She looked around, fired with righteous indignation.

Silence met her question. Several of the nuns lifted the skirts of their habits and dropped them over their pets, concealing the animals from sight. The offended nun looked from one to the other. "Who was it?" she demanded, but no-one replied. With an outraged snort, she tried to scrape her soiled shoe clean on the grass. Janna wrinkled her nose. The smell was no worse—in fact, it was a great deal less offensive—than the stink of the fair, yet it seemed somehow more malodorous here in this quiet garth with its cool, splashing fountain.

Janna led her companions to the cell above the gatehouse. She stood back as the guard unlocked the door and gave them entrance into the small room. At their appearance, Odo sprang to his feet. "I tell you, I am innocent of all—"

His protestations died as he glanced from Janna to Hugh. His eyes flared open in momentary alarm, and he shrank back against the wall and hung his head as if trying to become invisible. Janna studied Odo closely, wondering at the sudden change in his demeanor. He'd been ready to shout his innocence aloud when he thought he faced the steward; why had his guts suddenly turned to water?

Emma stepped forward and touched Hugh's arm. "This is Peter." She indicated a hunched figure sitting on the floor. He struggled to rise, but Emma pushed him back down. She sat next to him, and took hold of his hand. "They've chained him up!" she said indignantly.

Janna could see the heavy fetters that bound Peter's hands and feet and kept him seated.

He shifted uncomfortably under their gaze. "I swear I am innocent of this crime," he told Hugh.

"And we're going to prove it," Janna said, earning a sneer from Odo.

The door was unlocked once more, and this time the steward followed the guard into the small cell. "I have already interrogated the prisoner, and I am satisfied that he is guilty of the crime of murder," he said, addressing his remarks to Hugh, correctly assessing him as being the most important of their company.

"But there are some things you don't know about this man." Hugh indicated Odo. "Tell him, Sister Johanna."

Determined to do her best for Peter Thatcher, Janna launched into an explanation, pointing out to the steward the significance of the purse missing from the dead man's effects and why the murderer must have taken Anselm by surprise and slit his throat before he could put up any resistance. "I believe the purse was taken after the murder, so it would have been stained with the dead man's blood," Janna continued. "Odo kept the money, but he had to throw the purse away and buy a new one." She pointed at the evidence hanging from Odo's belt. "Ask your men to search the ditch and the grounds of the copse where Master Anselm's body was found. The blood-stained purse might still be lying there—unless you'd care to tell us where you left it, Odo, and save the men a search?"

Odo turned his face away and did not answer.

"There is no point denying your role in Anselm's death," Janna said. "See, my lord, the spray of blood on his sleeve? I have seen animals slaughtered and I know that such a spray occurs only as their throats are cut, and not after death, as this rogue claims."

Hugh stepped over to the cowering man. "Look at me, damn you!" He prodded him in the chest. Odo slowly raised his eyes to Hugh's face. Hugh glared at him. "You wear the blood of my friend, and I'll see you hang for it." He gave Odo a shove, sending him crashing back against the wall.

It occurred to Janna that, in spite of Hugh's threats, Odo seemed to be recovering some of his defiance. He straightened, brushed himself down and faced them. "Master Anselm was my friend too," he said. "The blood on my tunic came after his death. I washed most of it off for it was unsightly, and I reeked of it. I didn't reckon that a few drops of blood on my sleeve would make much difference."

"More than a few drops of blood. You wear the spray of death on your sleeve—and a new purse of ill-gotten coins at your waist." Janna turned to the steward. "There must have been even more money at the start, for we found this rogue in the alehouse, losing a pile of coins at dice."

"I won it! I won it all in a wager!"

Hugh raised an eyebrow in disbelief. "And where would a lowborn cur like you find spare coins for such a wager?"

"It was my last coin on a lucky guess, my lord."

It seemed to Janna that for the first time, there was a ring of truth to Odo's words. Her doubts returned as she wondered if, after all, she might have misread the signs of his guilt.

It seemed Hugh did not share her misgivings. "There is no point in denying your role in this, for the evidence against you proves that you are lying. You killed a man to get at his purse; do not attempt to lay the blame elsewhere." The steward scrutinized the faces of the men in front of him, as if trying to divine their guilt. He was clearly not convinced by their arguments. There was one last thing Janna could try, but she had no way of knowing if it would pay off.

"May I suggest that you search through the contents of this man's purse?" she said, trying not to betray her fear.

"You'll find the coins I won through a lucky wager at the cockfighting," Odo insisted. "There's nothing else to find."

Janna ignored him. She was staking a man's life on a guess. If she was wrong, Peter might well hang instead of Odo. She wiped her sweating palms down her habit, and turned to Emma. "Before the purse is emptied, will you tell the steward about your brother's lucky pebble?"

"It's small, round and dark brown, with gold threads running through it."

Odo stiffened. He backed away until he fetched up tight against the wall and could go no further. He struggled to speak, moistened his lips with his tongue, but seemingly could utter no sound. His hands clamped tight around his purse. Janna watched, hardly daring to breathe.

The steward held out his hand. "Give it to me or I'll cut it off your belt. And your hand too, if it gets in the way."

Reluctantly, Odo did as he was bid. The steward opened the purse and spilled its contents onto a small table.

"There!" Emma swooped down and picked up the pebble, holding it aloft for all to see. The steward nodded thoughtfully.

"You don't understand. I only took what was rightfully mine, what I was owed," Odo blustered.

"*What?*"

Hugh's roar of disbelief was answered by a sullen mutter. "That's *my* money."

"You expect us to believe you won all this money at the cockfights?" The steward took up the interrogation with somewhat more enthusiasm. Odo was silent. "Speak up, man, and tell me the truth, for you can be sure that if you won such a large amount, people will have seen and noted it. And I shall certainly be asking around to find witnesses to your good fortune."

"I didn't win the money, Master Anselm did," Odo admitted sullenly. A note of aggrieved bravado crept into his voice. "But it was my money to start off with. Mine!"

"Explain yourself!"

Odo hesitated. But there was too much evidence against him now to pretend innocence. Nevertheless, he did his best to portray his actions in the best possible light. "I was with Master Anselm at the cockfighting," he said, addressing his remarks to Emma. "I was only watching, but Master Anselm was making wagers on the fights. He told me he was determined to increase the amount of your dowry." Odo's glance flicked to Hugh, then returned to Emma. "He wagered his last coin, and lost. He lost everything he owned."

"Yet you say that Anselm owed you money," Hugh cut in quickly. "How did that happen? Did he borrow from you?"

"He took all I had. As a loan, he said." Odo sounded resentful now. "It was my coin, but he wagered it on a fight, and won. And from there on, he kept on winning. But it was *my* money he wagered, and therefore I should have had his winnings. But he would not give them to me, he would not even share a half, but offered me only the coin I had given him and no thanks for anything."

"Which is fair enough," Emma said quickly. "He was the one with the skill to increase the original stake, not you."

Odo's eyes narrowed; his face mirrored his rejection of her words. "I, too, have a lass I would wed," he said bitterly. "I, too, wanted something to offer her, an incentive to share my life and my bed, for she has shown as unwilling as your own suitor, mistress." His glance flicked once more to Hugh, then away again.

Janna watched him. She felt uneasy. Something was not quite right; something had been said, or not said, something important. She was sure the rogue had given away more than he knew, perhaps more than they all realized, if only she could work out what it was. What had she missed during this exchange?

While the steward began to interrogate Odo more carefully, Janna closed her eyes, allowing her mind to go back to the start of the interview. What Odo had said. How he'd reacted. His unexpected change in demeanor after Hugh cornered him. He'd recognized Hugh, and obviously knew Anselm's plans for his sister to wed Hugh, yet Hugh did not seem to know him. Was that why Odo had begun to relax his guard? Was there some connection between him and Hugh, and if so, what was it? And why did Odo expect Anselm's gratitude? Was it only for the loan, or was it for something else as well? Her thoughts spun faster than a child's toy as she began to put the pieces of the puzzle together in the hope of understanding the whole.

"You know the lord Hugh, don't you?" she interrupted at last, realizing that she must proceed cautiously if she wished to trap Odo into admitting something that might damage him.

Sudden alarm twisted Odo's face. "Master Anselm pointed him out to me as the man he wished his sister to wed," he said, after a long pause.

"Why? For what purpose?"

Odo moistened his lips with his tongue, as if hoping to coax a convincing explanation from his mouth.

"It was you who knifed my lord Hugh, wasn't it, Odo?" Janna accused. She took a breath, and crossed her fingers behind her back. "I remember you now. You were hiding in the group surrounding the musicians, but you were conspicuous because you were one man among many women and children." She stared at Odo, daring him to deny it.

Speechless, Odo looked down at his boots.

"Show me your knife!" Hugh demanded, while Janna eased a small sigh of relief that her bluff seemed to have paid off. When Odo made no effort to unsheathe the weapon, Hugh stepped forward and stood over him. "Show me!" he demanded.

Reluctantly, Odo drew out the knife. Perhaps fearing a sudden attack, the steward grabbed it out of his hand and held it out of range. Janna moved to his side, followed by Hugh. They examined it carefully. The blade was unnaturally clean. Although it had obviously been washed recently, dark stains in cracks in the hilt revealed the telltale traces of blood.

Janna knew there was no way of telling whether the blood was animal or human, but thought it worth trying a further bluff if it resulted in the truth.

"There is blood on this knife, my lord," she said, pointing out the stains to the steward. "I'll make a wager of my own: that you'll find it's the lord Hugh's blood staining the hilt, as well as Master Anselm's. I know you have ways of ensuring that truth will prevail—very painful ways so I am told."

Odo gave a whimper of fright. Janna turned to him. "If you were to speak up, to freely confess the full extent of your misdeeds..." Janna left the suggestion hanging in the air.

The steward looked somewhat bemused. He gave a grunt that could have meant just about anything at all. Hugh jumped in quickly. "There is no doubt you will hang for the murder of Anselm," he told the cowering man. "As you cannot die twice, you may as well save yourself from being tortured until you confess the rest of your crimes. For my part, I am sure that you are also responsible for the attack on me. Now that I look at you more carefully, I realize that your face is indeed familiar."

Looking thoroughly frightened and miserable now, Odo nodded. "I was only following orders," he said sullenly.

"But...but why?" Emma cried. "Why would you attack Hugh? And on whose orders? What nonsense is this?"

"I acted for your brother," Odo said bitterly. "All along, I did what I was told, and see what harm has come to me!"

"You weren't told to slit Anselm's throat." Emma's eyes flashed with indignation. "And Anselm would never have told you to try to kill Hugh either!"

"Not kill. Wound."

"Wound? But why?"

Odo didn't answer Emma's question, but his confession confirmed what Janna had guessed. She marveled that a brother's love could have unraveled so badly, and with such devastating consequences. And yet it must have seemed a simple scheme at its inception. Emma still waited for Odo to explain himself, but he remained silent, fully aware at last of the awful fate that awaited him.

"I think I know how it might all have come about." Janna paused, for her words would upset Hugh and destroy Emma's faith in her brother. But for her own peace of mind regarding her safety, she needed to know the truth.

"I believe Master Anselm's prime mission here at the fair was to speak to you about his sister, my lord, and beg you to marry her. That didn't work, and so he made another plan: to win money at the cockfights, in the hope that increasing Mistress Emma's dowry might change your mind. But he didn't win, he lost instead. So says Odo, and I have no reason to doubt his word, for I saw Master Anselm at the cockfights myself, and so did his sister. It was apparent that, at the time, things were going badly for him." Janna paused as she tried to work out how best to word her argument so as to cause the least possible pain to both Emma and Hugh.

"I believe that, at this point, Anselm formed yet another plan to bring his mission to a successful conclusion. I believe he pointed you out to Odo, my lord, and told him to take cover within the crowd around the musicians, and wound you if he could."

"No! Anselm would never ask a thing like that of anyone. Never!" Emma cried.

"He couldn't do it himself, for the lord Hugh would have recognized him," Janna pointed out.

"But why should Anselm want Odo to wound Hugh? The whole idea is preposterous!"

"I don't think he meant Odo to wound my lord quite as badly as he did. I think his idea was that, with my lord in pain, he would need care and attention and that you might provide it, mistress." Now Janna looked at Emma. "I think your brother hoped that being in such close proximity with the lord would kindle your affection for each other and become something much more lasting. But that plan also went awry for, instead of you taking him home to recuperate, he was brought here to the abbey and thus put out of your reach."

"Is this true?" Hugh's incredulous glance went from Janna to Odo. "Is that how it came about?"

Odo shrugged his shoulders, seemingly resigned to the fact that he could do nothing now to prevent his fate.

"Oh!" Emma's hand went to her throat. Her face had lost all color; she looked about to swoon. Janna took a quick step to her side, and put her arm around the young woman to steady her.

"Borrowing money from Odo to gamble on the cockfights was your brother's last chance to buy your happiness," she said, hoping to comfort Emma. "It was you he thought of, mistress, not himself."

"If he thought of me, he would have given me his blessing to marry Peter!"

"Are you sure about all this?" Hugh asked Janna. His eyes were troubled, but the fact that he'd lied about recognizing Odo told Janna that he already knew the answer to his question. Before she could say anything, he reached out and grabbed the front of Odo's tunic. "Tell me," he demanded. "Is this true?" "True enough," the villein muttered sullenly. "I did as Master Anselm ordered. I'd intended to give you only a small flesh wound but you, Sister, you stumbled against my lord and pushed him onto my knife." He glared at Janna as if it was all her fault that his knife was open and ready to slice into Hugh.

But his grievances were not yet at an end. "Master Anselm owed me a reward, after all I'd done for him. But when I asked him for my share of his winnings, he refused. When

I demanded it as my right, he told me that if I continued to threaten him, he would inform the steward of my part in wounding you, my lord. He said the steward wouldn't believe me if I told him I was acting under his orders, for you were all friends from childhood and Master Anselm had no reason to want you harmed."

"Oh!" Faced with this final evidence of her brother's dishonor, Emma began to weep. She slumped down beside Peter, who tried in vain to loosen his shackles enough to comfort her. Seeing his struggles, the steward gestured at the guard to free him, and to put the fetters on Odo instead.

The purse was refilled and given to Emma. "No compensation for the loss of your brother, but the money was his and now it is yours," the steward said awkwardly.

"No matter how misguided his reasons, he did what he thought was best for you, Emma," Hugh said, when she made no move to take the purse. "He would have wanted you to have it."

"It's tainted with his blood!"

"Take it. If you don't wish to use it for yourself, put it to a good cause."

Emma stretched out a reluctant hand for the purse then turned to Peter. He wrapped his arms around her to comfort her. She clung to him, her desolation evident for all to see.

Janna looked at Odo. She could understand the rage and the feeling of helplessness that must have possessed him when faced with Anselm's double-dealing. She, too, knew the rage and frustration of being powerless when faced with an injustice, although she hoped it would never lead her to murder. But Anselm's behavior had been worse than Janna had realized. While she didn't regret bringing the truth to light, and setting her own fears to rest, she was sorry to have blighted his memory in the eyes of his sister and his best friend.

Feeling suddenly alone and unsure of herself, she looked about for Godric. He was standing beside the door, and she beckoned him over. He nodded at her. His smile brought her some comfort as they each hooked an arm to support Hugh back to the infirmary, for Hugh looked stricken and sick at heart.

If Peter's life hadn't been at stake, Janna knew that all of them would have preferred to remain ignorant of the truth of Anselm's last day on earth. She only wished there could have been a better outcome, for all their sakes.

Chapter 13

The attack on Hugh, the death of Anselm, and the arrest of first Peter and then Odo, had sent ripples of shocked speculation throughout the close abbey community. While Janna remained silent over her part in what had happened, tongues continued to wag long after it was all over and the principals had departed. Hugh, now healed, had accompanied Emma and Peter back to their own manor for Anselm's burial, leaving Godric to keep watch over Hugh's manor. Odo was still shut away, awaiting such time as his lord could come to the abbey, bringing witnesses for his trial. To all intents and purposes, life at the abbey had returned to normal, but Janna missed the flurry and excitement of the fair, and the presence of merchants and pilgrims in the abbey's guesthouse. Most of all, she missed Hugh and Godric.

The days grew shorter. Leaves of red and gold floated downward, forming mushy piles underfoot in a mean, drizzling rain that seemed as if it might last forever. Janna was glad she had shelter, for the nights were long, and bitter with cold. Frost sparkled in the garden in the mornings, and her breath puffed out in misty clouds when she went outside. She was grateful that Sister Anne had insisted that she stay on to help in the infirmary, and she took comfort from the fact that while she was at the abbey she continued to learn for, true to her promise, Sister Anne had initiated her into the mysteries of bodily humors and the remedies to keep them in balance. Janna now knew how to feel a pulse and what to look for when checking urine, as well as acquiring such techniques as cupping, purging and bloodletting. She was also learning the prayers and chants that accompanied some of the cures, and the healing properties of precious stones. Sister Anne had also mentioned astrological charts, but she hadn't shown Janna how to calculate and draw them. Janna was under the impression that the nun didn't entirely approve of such things. But she had allowed Janna to splint a broken arm after one of the young oblates was surprised climbing a tree and fell out of it in her haste to obey Sister Grace's command to "come down at once!" She had even stitched an open wound together, after draining it of pus. And with the cold weather came such an outbreak of ague and aches, colics and colds, she and Sister Anne were kept ever busier ministering to the sick and the elderly.

With her growing skills and experience came confidence, but underneath it all, Janna was seized with a wild impatience. Her quest to learn to read and write was still beyond her reach, while her search for information about her mother had come to a dead end. The company of women, the sense of being continually watched, and judged, further chafed her spirits.

She had done her best to put a convincing argument both to Sister Grace, and to the chantress, but had been refused. Sister Grace had tried to soften their rejection. "As a lay sister, you have no need for this sort of knowledge," she said. "Unfortunately you have no dowry, but you do have special skills that could benefit the abbey. Perhaps if I spoke to our abbess about you? Perhaps if you took your vows?"

Janna knew that she couldn't. She'd spent long enough in the abbey to respect the belief that had prompted the nuns to give up their temporal lives in the service of God, but she did not share that unquestioning belief, and could not make such a sacred vow without it. She looked to Agnes to cheer her low spirits, but the lay sister's ready wit and sense of humor seemed also to have deserted her. Janna thought she knew the cause, but when she ventured to put in a good word for the bailiff, Agnes snapped at her and walked away. Thereafter she seemed even more morose, lacking even the will to continue her education in the healing properties of plants. Try as she might, Janna had been unable to lift her friend's depression. She was sorry for it, and felt sorry too, for Master Will.

Mindful that she'd never gone back to the fair to give him Agnes's answer, she manufactured a reason to visit the apothecary in the hope that she might encounter the bailiff on her journey. Sister Anne was dubious at first, but Janna insisted that she needed some special oils that only an apothecary could provide to mix with the herbs she'd cut and dried, for the two of them were laying in a store of medicaments to last through the cold, dead months of winter.

"And we also need a new supply of galangal," she said persuasively. "It's so good for Sister Angelica's heart. She says it's hot enough to waken the dead!"

Sister Anne nodded in grudging agreement. "But you cannot go alone, I will come with you," she said, adding, "and we shall see if Master Fulk can also provide us with a cooling jasper stone. That, too, is helpful for alleviating heart pain."

Fulk. Janna and her mother had fallen foul of the posturing apothecary when he'd attempted, and failed, to care for Dame Alice and her newborn babe. Janna knew he would not welcome her into his shop, but her circumstances, now, were different. Fulk would not dare to be uncivil to her while Sister

Anne was present. And so, accompanied by the infirmarian, Janna marched into the apothecary's shop, made confident by the knowledge that there were coins to spend and that her habit would protect her good name and reputation.

Fulk didn't recognize her at first, and behaved with equal obsequiousness to both of them. A dawning awareness brought a frown to his face, but whatever he might have said was instantly repressed as he met the stern eye of Sister Anne. He and Janna both went along with the pretense that they'd had no previous dealings with each other, and so their transaction was conducted with courtesy on Fulk's part, and secret glee on Janna's.

Master Will waylaid them on their way back to the abbey. "May I have a quick word with your young apprentice, Sister?" he asked Sister Anne, who nodded and walked on. But Janna noted that the elderly nun kept close enough to overhear their conversation.

"Have you spoken to Sister Agnes?" he asked eagerly. Janna put a warning finger to her lips, and glanced at Sister Anne. "Does she look favorably on me and on my request?" he asked, in a lower tone.

Janna was at a loss to reply. *Yes, she looks favorably on you, but no, she won't think about marrying you, even though she wants to and it's tearing her heart out?* It was the truth, but it offered no answer and no comfort to the bailiff. "Yes, I have spoken to her," she admitted at last.

Master Will's eyes lit with hope. "And?" he asked eagerly.

"She is afraid, Master Will, afraid to leave the abbey. You must give her time." Janna hoped she wasn't raising his hopes unnecessarily.

"But I can't see her! I can't speak to her! How can I state my case, how can I woo her while she hides in the abbey?"

Janna shook her head. "Have patience," she urged. "Perhaps if you seek her out at haymaking, or the next harvest?"

She hurried to catch up with Sister Anne. Together, they passed through the gate, which clanged shut behind them, closing out the world, closing them in. She wondered if Sister Anne would refer to the conversation she must have overheard, but the infirmarian said nothing, although she looked thoughtful when next she encountered Agnes.

They were working in the garden when Janna told Agnes of her meeting with Will. They were busy, for there was always much to do. Fruits and berries had been picked and laid up in store or preserved in syrup. With the days short and the weather growing ever more frosty, seeds had been collected and cuttings taken. It was time, now, to dig the ground over and make it ready for planting once spring warmed the earth once more.

Janna spoke low to Agnes so that others might not hear what she had to say. Agnes averted her face as she listened to Janna's account. "It makes no matter what his wishes might be," she said, although her voice trembled slightly, giving the lie to her words. "I will not renounce my vows, I will not leave the abbey."

Janna sat back on her heels. She wondered what she could say that might change Agnes's mind. Then she remembered something. After glancing around to check that no-one was watching, she raised the hem of her habit and groped underneath for her purse. "Look what I found in the forest one day," she said, and drew out the small statue of the mother and her child. She handed it to Agnes.

Agnes's expression softened as she cradled the figurine in the palm of her hand. "She looks so loving," she murmured, as she gently traced the mother's face with a grubby finger.

"You, too, could have a child of your own to love. And you told me yourself that the bailiff's youngest has great need of a mother."

"Don't talk nonsense!" Agnes thrust the figurine into Janna's hands. She surged to her feet and stamped off.

"I saw you with those children at harvest," Janna called after her retreating back. "You have so much love to give, Agnes. Don't waste it!"

Agnes made no reply, but hurried on. Janna sighed, conscious that she'd done her best but that her best wasn't good enough. She picked up the sharp knife she'd brought out with her, and set about pruning some rose bushes, cutting their bare branches right back so that they looked like small brown skeletons. It calmed her to work in the garden. Being outdoors gave her an illusion of freedom, and she reveled in the hard labor that ensured she slept well at night. She felt as if she was part of the rhythm of nature, almost as if she was one of the shrubs she was pruning. Their stark, bare branches looked dead, belying the promise of the life within that, come spring, would burst forth into exuberant growth once more. Like the shrubs, she, too, was biding her time. For Janna was resigned, now, to staying at the abbey through the winter. She knew she would perish if she left, if she tried to survive in the forest on her own.

*

The arrival of Odo's lord along with a handful of witnesses was the first sign that the abbess had convened a special court to bring Odo to trial for the death of Anselm. Odo was still held captive at the abbey; it was said that the abbess resented paying for his upkeep and wanted the matter dealt with as quickly as possible.

To Janna's dismay, these first visitors were quickly followed by another party: Dame Alice and her husband, Robert of Babestoche, along with Mus and several other villeins. None of them looked happy about being there. Her heart felt heavy, for she took no pleasure in seeing either Odo or Mus again, nor did she relish having to face them in court knowing that, even if she was allowed to speak, it would be her word against theirs. But her spirits lifted when Hugh and Godric arrived shortly afterward, accompanied by Cecily. She would not be short of friends if it came to speaking out against the pair.

The cases against the accused were heard within the confines of the abbey itself, in the chapter house, which was more used to hearing the tittle-tattle of the abbey than the serious crimes now being aired. Mus was brought in first, attended by Robert of Babestoche along with those others from his manor who had come to testify on his behalf. Looking them over, Janna wondered how many coins the witnesses had been paid to speak of the mouse's good character, for she had no doubt they had all been handpicked with care by Robert and rewarded accordingly. She quaked as she met Robert's malevolent stare. It was her word against his and that of his men.

To Janna's dismay, the abbess was nowhere to be seen; the steward presided over the court. A roomful of men would not, perhaps, be sympathetic to a woman's plight—particularly, Janna thought, when they heard how she'd managed to defend her honor! She needed a woman to speak up for her, someone highborn, whose opinion would be listened to and respected. Someone like the abbess—or Dame Alice. But the dame sat quietly on her own at one side of the chamber, looking as if she wanted no part in the proceedings. At least she was present, and would hear what Janna had to say. And, although she was bound by Cecily's secret and could not give good reasons for Mus's actions, nevertheless he would be judged accordingly.

Janna's was encouraged by the presence of Will, the bailiff. She recognized several of the people with him, and realized they too would be called on to bear witness as to what had happened on that day. The bailiff knew the truth of the matter, and so did they. They would corroborate what she said, while the bailiff could also give evidence of his own: finding the length of cord in Mus's scrip, ready to form a noose for her own neck.

Casting her glance further, Janna saw Hugh and Godric in the crowd. Cecily was with them. She looked serene, even happy. Janna was pleased that the tiring woman seemed to be over her disastrous relationship with Robert. They were looking her way, and she raised her hand to them and smiled, pretending a confidence she could not feel. Her heart hammered painfully; her breath came short. She longed for the ordeal to be over.

Although Robert and his villeins spoke in glowing terms of Mus's character, to Janna's great relief, Mus's appeal met with little sympathy from the steward. Then it was Janna's turn to bear witness. She defended her honor with vigor, backed by the word of the bailiff and his men, who produced damning evidence that Mus had asked after "the new sister called Johanna" as soon as he arrived, even before he'd met her out in the fields. Several pairs of sharp eyes had noticed how quickly he'd taken up position beside her while they were working, and Master Will's description of the cord found in his scrip set the final seal on his guilt.

Janna stole a glance at Dame Alice. She was sitting back, looking thoughtful. The abbess had come in, and had taken a seat beside the dame, both of them onlookers of the unfolding drama. But when Robert offered to pay amercement for Mus's release, Dame Alice spoke up at last.

"I will not have that man in my employ any longer," she said firmly, "and I will not have him set free to prey on this unfortunate young woman or, indeed, on any other. Take him to the castle at Sarisberie. He can stay in the dungeon until such time as he ceases to be a menace to our community."

From the dame's tone, it was clear that she believed that the time would come only when Mus was dead. Janna was jubilant, until it occurred to her that Robert might well find some way to pay the money for Mus's release without Dame Alice being aware of it. She reminded herself to stay on guard and her fear increased for, as Mus was dragged out of the chapter house by the guards, he spoke to her.

"No matter how long it takes, I'll find you when I get out," he hissed. A finger sliced across his throat accompanied his words.

Janna shuddered. She thought of reporting the incident to the steward, but he was already engaged in summoning those involved in the case against Odo. She met the cold stare of Robert of Babestoche, and shuddered anew. While she stayed within the abbey confines she was safe, but she would always be a threat to him. She must never forget that.

As it turned out, Janna played only a small part in giving evidence in the case against Odo. His lord, as well as villeins from his manor, spoke on his behalf, seeming at a loss to understand why someone who had shown no signs of violent behavior in the past should have been driven to commit such a desperate deed. Emma was called next, to tell what she knew. So were Peter Thatcher and Hugh. Although all were careful not to raise the fact that Hugh had been wounded by Odo, albeit on Anselm's instructions, the matter came to light as further damning evidence against the villein.

Finally, Janna was called. She found it difficult to look at Odo as she answered the steward's questions. She knew the villein was headed for the gallows and that nothing she said or withheld could make any difference to the sentence that would be passed on him, yet she had never seen a man condemned to death before, and it troubled her greatly. She was almost sure Odo had not plotted to murder Anselm, that the act had been a momentary madness, an angry reaction to being cheated out of what he considered to be rightfully his. In truth, Janna believed that Anselm's behavior had contributed in large part to his death—but the steward did not see it that way and Odo was duly sentenced to be hanged.

Janna's spirits were leaden as she watched the villein being dragged away. Before she had a chance to escape back to the infirmary, Hugh walked over to her, flanked by Emma and Peter. Emma pressed a small purse, bulging with coins, into Janna's hands.

"We wanted to thank you again."

Startled, Janna looked down at the purse. It was drawn tight with a string, and smelled of new leather.

"It's the money won by Anselm at the cockfights," Emma whispered. "I want you to have it. If not for you, Peter could have been standing there, facing the death sentence." She looked white and strained. Her brother's death and Odo's trial had taken their toll.

Peter stepped up and put his arm around Emma to give her strength. "My thanks to you too, mistress, er...Sister Johanna," he hastily corrected himself.

"That was well done, Johanna, and you are safe now." Hugh looked her straight in the eye. "Tell me, have you tired of holy orders yet? Are you ready to come home with me?"

Janna heard an exclamation, quickly choked off. Godric had joined them, along with Cecily. What was he thinking? What was *Hugh* thinking? She could feel the heat mount in a wave through her body; she was sure her face had turned scarlet.

"No, my lord, but I thank you for your offer," she murmured, and tucked the purse deep into the sleeve of her habit.

"Be sure you will always have a home at my manor. You may come whenever you wish." Hugh's reassurance settled Janna's doubts about his intentions, but left her spirits even lower. A home, no more than that, was on offer. And a home was something she valued, almost above everything—but preferably a home of her own, living with a man whom she loved. Nevertheless, she would not close off her options for the sake of misplaced pride, for she had no knowledge of what the future might hold for her.

"Thank you, my lord, but I am content to remain here for the moment." She stole a glance at Godric. Was that disappointment she could read on his face? Or was he not thinking of her at all, standing as he was with Cecily by his side? The tiring woman was smiling; she seemed content. And why not, with someone as strong and steady as Godric in her life?

Janna hastily pushed the thought aside and turned to Emma. "Thank you," she said, indicating the purse in her sleeve. "Be sure I shall put the coins to good use."

Emma smiled, seeming pleased that the ordeal was over, and all debts paid. "We have a long journey home, and it is too late to leave now," she said. "Do you think the abbey can provide us with accommodation for the night?"

"I'll take you to the guest house." Anxious to break the tension of their meeting and her disquieting speculation about Godric and Cecily, Janna beckoned the group to follow her to the outer courtyard. Having shown them where the guest house was situated, she sketched a hasty farewell and hurried off to find the guest mistress to deal with their needs. With that task accomplished, she was desperate to find a quiet place where she might gain some privacy; she needed time to come to terms with Mus's threat and Odo's fate, and to sort through her own muddled emotions regarding Hugh and Godric. She made straight for the herbarium, conscious that she was running away, but thinking it the wisest thing to do.

"*God's great cathedral*," her mother had said of nature, and that was where she needed to be right now. But her trial was not quite over.

"Sister Johanna!" The abbess's voice halted Janna's footsteps. Reluctantly, she turned, and was surprised to see Dame Alice by the abbess's side.

"Mother Abbess. Dame Alice." She bobbed her knee in reverence.

"I am troubled, Johanna," Dame Alice said, "for I am at a loss to understand why my husband seems so set against you now. After what I heard today, I feel sure that the man they call Mus was acting on his instructions. Is—or was—there some liaison between the two of you that I should know about?" "No, my lady." Janna was horrified that the dame should think such a thing of her. Yet she could not speak the truth, could not betray Cecily's secret. She wished Cecily was here to speak for herself, but knew that the tiring woman would never find the courage to confess her liaison with Robert, or its dreadful outcome. She faced Dame Alice and the abbess, and read the doubt and distrust in their expressions. "Perhaps if you asked Lord Robert for an explanation? Perhaps he...?"

The dame's lips compressed into a thin line, telling Janna that she'd probably already tried that, and had got nowhere. Janna knew she stood condemned, both by her own silence as well as Robert's. She bitterly resented their judgment, but knew she was powerless to reclaim her good name without blackening another. Her anguish was slightly eased by the thought that, in the face of her and Cecily's continuing silence about his responsibility for the death of her mother, Robert must surely believe himself safe at last. Which must mean that Janna herself was safe.

"You may go about your work." The abbess's cold tone dismissed Janna from their presence. With downcast eyes, she bobbed her head and fled. But it was quite some time before the memory of the trial, and the hurtful condemnation that followed it, began to fade.

Chapter 14

Over the following weeks Janna found ease working in the garden, and in the round of daily chores that were in her care. In addition, she had come to enter fully into the life of the convent, attending Masses as well as the regular offices that divided the nuns' days and nights. She appreciated the grandeur of the church and had grown to love the musical chants. Although her life was regulated by the constant pealing of bells, she had become used to them. She enjoyed the calm, unhurried pace of the abbey and the comfort of her surroundings, especially when she compared her life now to what she'd once known.

Resigned to living within the abbey confines for the while, she envied the nuns their acceptance of God's presence in their lives, their certainty about themselves and the vows they had taken, although she could not share their faith. Nor could she accept wholeheartedly all that she was told. But she found some of her questions were frowned upon and so instead, she searched her own heart for the truth.

She celebrated the Christ Mass and all the festivities with a glad heart, for she loved the story of how Joseph and Mary had trudged to Bethlehem while Mary was great with child, and how the baby Jesus was born in a manger. And if she compared the story to her own mother's travels, and the abbess's grudging provision of a safe haven, she was wise enough to keep her thoughts to herself.

Those days were joyous indeed, with extra provisions and delicacies in the refectory, and extra leisure time to talk, read and even to play games of skittles in the cloister garth while making the most of the few hours of pale wintry sun. With shorter days and long cold nights, the nuns and lay sisters were kept busy indoors, spinning wool and weaving homespun cloth to make the habits and tunics they wore, or stitching and mending garments in need of repair. Every evening the convent gathered in the calefactorium, where a fire was kept burning constantly throughout the winter and the nuns were allowed to talk. It was their last chance to warm themselves before going up to bed in their freezing dorter.

Janna often slipped away from the infirmary to join them, for it was an opportunity to talk, to question the sisters about the scenes painted on the walls of the church. They were shocked at her ignorance, but for the most part they delighted in recounting the stories of Jesus, Mary and the saints. And Janna enjoyed hearing them, for she knew little of stories, especially the ones from the Bible. She reveled in the drama of Jesus' life. Some of it she already knew, but now she heard about His temptation by Satan in the desert, His confrontation with the moneylenders in the temple, His encounters with the Romans and the Pharisees. She loved to hear of His friendship with the disciples and how they had forsaken all they knew to follow Him, although she couldn't help feeling sorry for the families they left behind. She marveled at the miracles, although she couldn't help doubting some of them. She wept over the account of His betrayal in the Garden of Gethsemane, His trial and cruel death by crucifixion.

She began to look about the church with new eyes, understanding at last what she was seeing. Yet at the same time she couldn't help remembering how Eadgyth had dragged her out of the small church at Berford. She could still hear her mother's impassioned cry: "*You don't need to go to church when God's great cathedral is all around you,*" she'd said, as she pointed at the beauty that surrounded them: the bright flowers in their garden, the dancing butterflies and bumblebees, and the green forest beyond.

Who was right? Her mother, or this convent of women who believed so implicitly in Christ, in the Bible, and in their vocation? Yet her mother had once been a nun herself; Janna was as sure of that as she was sure that winter would eventually give way to spring, and then to summer. She ached to find out more about her family, but resigned herself to patience, for she could not leave the abbey until winter was over. She'd thought the abbey would provide the answers she sought. Now, Janna knew that she would have to look elsewhere. She had no idea where to begin, but decided that the new year should mark the time for a new beginning and a new plan.

*

"...m-my m-manuscript, M-Mother Abbess." The stutter, the distress in the voice, told Janna who was speaking. She looked up at Sister Ursel, feeling desperately sorry for the nun and, at the same time, curious as to what lay behind this seeming run of bad luck. She listened as the nun stammered her way through an explanation of the latest calamity: another sheet of her manuscript had gone missing.

It had happened too often to be chance, Janna thought, as she recalled other instances related by the unfortunate sister. The first, she remembered, was when two pages had gone missing, only to be found later under a bush, supposedly blown by the wind into the cloister garth. It hadn't seemed likely at the time. It seemed even less likely now, especially in the light of what had happened since. Another page had gone missing. It had also been found, but this time it was torn into several pieces. It was too damaged to be repaired, and Sister Ursel had carefully lettered and illuminated the page all over again. The pieces of parchment had been kept and scraped back so that they might be reused for practice by one or other of Sister Maria's students, but Janna had seen the page when it was whole, and could imagine Sister Ursel's grief and rage at having her beautiful work destroyed in such a way.

The next occurrence was even worse. This time the missing page had turned up crumpled, torn and smeared with dog feces. The bishop had been visiting at the time, to celebrate the Mass of the birth of the Christ Child. He had stayed on as a guest at the abbey until after the new year, but his visit had been marred by several incidents involving the sisters' pets that had invoked his wrath and called down his censure.

While most of the nuns had ignored his instructions to get rid of their animals forthwith, nevertheless they kept close watch on their pets and made sure that all animals were kept from the bishop's sight. Because of the need for secrecy, little was said about the missing page, but the consensus was that one of the animals must have got hold of it, must have worried and played with the piece of parchment until it was torn and spoiled. It seemed an obvious conclusion, but Janna had looked at the sheet of parchment, had flinched on Sister Ursel's behalf, and had also noted that there were no teeth marks to be seen. But she had held her tongue in face of Sister Ursel's distress for this, more than anything, expressed such contempt for the beautiful work that it was beyond Janna's powers to imagine anyone spiteful enough to do such a thing.

Now it seemed that yet another page had gone missing. Before the abbess could respond to Sister Ursel's confession, Sister Philippa stood up.

Janna wondered what she had to say about the matter. She had come to know the nuns quite well by now, and knew that, as a scribe, Sister Philippa stood very much in the shadow of Sister Ursel. While Sister Ursel had been entrusted with the sacred task of writing and illuminating the life of St Edith, Sister Philippa and several other nuns had been set to copying, as best they may, some of the manuscripts held by the abbey. These were kept under the fierce guardianship of Sister Maria, the chantress, who was also in charge of the abbey's library.

"It seems to me that we can no longer entrust Sister Ursel with the sacred task of recording the life of our dear and revered St Edith," Sister Philippa began. Before the abbess could voice a protest, the nun went on to detail, as Janna had just done in her own mind, the various calamities that had occurred. "It shows a lack of care on the part of Sister Ursel," Sister Philippa concluded. "All the manuscripts are locked away every night. Only Sister Maria has the key, and I am sure she would have confessed its loss if it had gone missing at any time?"

All eyes turned to the chantress, who shook her head and jingled the bunch of keys hanging from her girdle in proof that she had them still.

"So the pages must have gone missing at some time during the day, while the work was under the care of Sister Ursel," the scribe persisted.

"But I h-have to leave it sometimes to...to attend services. I-I cannot move the pages while the inks are wet."

Janna was intrigued to notice that the nun's stutter was not nearly so bad while she defended herself. Was it indignation that freed her tongue, or did she only stutter while she was reading the words of God or St Benedict, or addressing her superiors in the abbey? She listened intently as the argument raged about her.

"Are you sure it is not mere laziness, a carelessness for your work that you don't keep it locked away at all times when you are not actually working on the manuscript?" Sister Philippa queried.

"I must protest, Mother Abbess," the chantress cut in. Her voice was low and musical, for it was Sister Maria who guided the nuns in their singing, and who kept them on time and in tune. "If I'm not busy teaching the children and novices to read and to write, I'm either in the library or organizing the singing of the Mass. I am not always available to lock away Sister Ursel's manuscript whenever she has to leave it. Besides, she speaks true; it is best not to move the pages until the inks are dry. More than that, I know how punctilious and careful Sister Ursel is of her work, how heavily this sacred trust rests on her shoulders, and how anxious she is to honor our saint by crafting for her the most beautiful work of which she is capable. To call Sister Ursel careless and lazy is a calumny that I cannot permit."

Janna waited to hear Sister Philippa defend her remarks, but the nun said nothing, instead bowing her head in sober contemplation of the stone flagging on the floor. Her bid to take over the hagiography had failed. Janna wondered if she would try again. Was it Sister Philippa, in fact, who was stealing and destroying pages in order to create this very situation in the hope of using it to her advantage? Janna resolved to watch the nun carefully in the future.

"Once again I ask all of you to search the abbey for the missing parchment, and to search your hearts for the truth," Abbess Hawise said sternly. "This has happened too often to be mere chance. It seems that whoever is behind this will not confess her crime, but someone must know something, or have seen something out of the way. If you have, I beg you to come to me and tell me what you know. And let me warn whoever is doing this: the longer you compound your error by keeping it a secret, the worse it will be for you when the truth finally comes to light—as you can be sure it will."

Full of indignation on Sister Ursel's behalf, Janna came out of chapter into a cold, blustery wind that threw spatters of rain into her face. She shivered, and wrapped her cloak more tightly around her. She'd been given permission to leave the abbey, along with Sister Anne, to visit the market in Wiltune. Their mission was to purchase an array of spices imported from warmer climes across the sea from the spice merchants. They were needed by the infirmarian for her various medicaments, and by the cook to season the meat that had been salted and preserved after the late autumn slaying of the beasts, as well as to flavor the fish and vegetables that were their usual fare. Instead of having a spice merchant call at the abbey, Janna had persuaded Sister Anne to visit the marketplace. "We'll find a wider variety there, and a better choice," she'd said. "It'll also give us a chance to bargain over prices as well as seeing if there's anything new, or if we've forgotten something," she'd added, smiling openly at Sister Anne's reproving frown.

Janna noticed Agnes and hurried over to have a word with her friend. "Will you come with us to market?" she urged. As Agnes began to protest, she interrupted. "No, hear me out. It will be very different from the fair. No travelers and few merchants, for at this time of the year there is little fresh produce to sell. And see how dreadful the day is!" Janna flung out a hand to illustrate her point. "No-one will venture out in this, unless they absolutely have to. Do come, Agnes. I'm sure Sister Anne won't make any objection to it." She took her friend's arm to lead her to the gate.

"No. No!" Agnes jerked away from Janna's grasp, and put both her hands behind her back.

"It's a chance to see what it's like outside the abbey. Don't you want to visit the town, Agnes?" She held her breath, hoping her friend would change her mind. It would make up, in some part, for the last disastrous outing for which Janna still felt responsible.

There was a short silence. Janna wondered what other argument she might use to persuade Agnes. "We may even see Master Will," she coaxed. "He asked after you last time I saw him, Agnes. He is very fond of you, you know. Very fond."

Agnes took another step backward. "I am happy here at the abbey," she said tightly. "I have no wish to see the town, or Master Will."

Silently, Janna berated herself. It seemed she'd come up with the worst inducement possible. "You don't have to talk to him, or even see him if you don't want to," she said hurriedly. "Just come and look at the stalls with me. There are such things to buy, Agnes, as you've never seen before or dreamed about!"

"I thought you said there'd be hardly anyone there?"

Janna sighed as she looked at the suspicion on her friend's face. Truly, Agnes had changed these past few months. It seemed also true that there was little Janna could do about it. If Agnes was to regain her sunny disposition, she would have to bring about the change herself. Still, for the bailiff's sake, she couldn't give up quite yet.

"If I should see Master Will, is there any message you would like me to give him?"

"No." Agnes turned away.

Janna was reluctant to part from her friend on bad terms. She looked about, seeking a diversion. Sister Ursel's downcast face as she trudged past provided her with a good excuse to change the subject and bring ease between them once more.

She nudged Agnes. "Do you know anything of Sister Ursel's troubles? Have you seen anything, heard anything, that might explain why sheets from her manuscript are being stolen and destroyed?"

Agnes stopped, her ready sympathy already engaged by the problem. "No, I've seen nothing," she said slowly. "Truly, Ursel has much to vex and distress her. Do you know that Chester has gone missing?"

"Gone missing? Or has the mouse been stolen, just like the sheets of her manuscript?"

Agnes's eyes widened. "I don't know. I never thought of that."

"There are quite a few dogs kept here in the abbey. Do you think one of them might have eaten Chester?"

"Oh, I hope not!" Agnes put a hand to her heart. "A mouse seems an odd pet to have, but I do believe Ursel is very fond of him. Actually, she keeps him so close always, I'm surprised he managed to escape. But you're right; he wouldn't last long if any of the dogs found him."

"Or one of the cats. You don't see so much of them, they're quite private creatures. But there are some about. In fact..." Janna paused, searching her memory. "There was a great commotion here in the cloister not so long ago, I remember. One of the dogs cornered a cat and was going to savage it, but Sister Ursel got hold of the animal and managed to drag it off its prey."

"Sister Martha told me that the abbess reprimanded the owners of both the cat and the dog. She's become very fierce about pet-keeping since the bishop's visit."

"The incident wasn't mentioned in chapter," Janna said slowly, wondering how the gnat had come to hear about it.

"The abbess is afraid the bishop will hear of it, and will know that his edict has been disobeyed," Agnes said promptly. "But she won't insist that his orders be carried out, for she knows there will be outright defiance if she tries. But Sister Martha says that the abbess has put Sister Catherine on notice: if anything like this happens again, both she and the dog will be thrown out of the abbey."

"Sister Catherine?" Janna's ears pricked up.

"It was her dog. He's the worst of them."

"But all dogs hate cats," Janna said, trying to be fair.

"True, but Sister Catherine doesn't do the right thing with her dog. I've seen her out in the cloister. When it makes a mess, she'll leave the mess lying if she thinks no-one has noticed. She's been here for so long, she seems to believe that the rules don't apply to her anymore."

Janna remembered the scene she had witnessed, the shrieking nun who had stepped into the dog's excrement. Had Sister Catherine been there with her pet? She couldn't remember.

"I stepped in some once," Agnes said. "It's disgusting. Even though I cleaned my sandals, the smell stayed on them for ages."

"You've been here longer than I have, Agnes," Janna said, anxious to get the lay sister back on the subject that most interested her. "How do Ursel and Philippa get on together?"

"I don't know." Agnes pulled a face. "We lay sisters live on the outside of the convent. You'd be the one to find that out, Janna." There was a slight edge to her voice that Janna couldn't miss. "Why do you want to know?"

"I wondered—" She had only suspicion regarding Sister Philippa's resentment of Ursel's skill, and where it might have led her. She could be wrong. The last thing she wanted was to start a rumor that might have no basis in the truth. "No reason, really," she said. With a sigh, she said goodbye to Agnes and walked on toward the gate, where Sister Anne awaited her.

"And will you be having any more tête-à-têtes with Master Will today?" Sister Anne asked Janna as they left the abbey and entered the marketplace.

Janna wasn't quite sure how to answer. Finally, she shook her head. "I don't know."

"He is fond of Agnes, is he not?"

Janna hesitated. In the months of working with Sister Anne, she'd come to like and respect the nun. She knew that Sister Anne was not easily shocked; in fact, she wondered if the nun had lived some of her early life outside the abbey, for she seemed to have more of an understanding of the world and its ways than many of the other sisters, judging by some of the complaints they raised in chapter. She decided to trust the nun with the truth, for the truth could not hurt Agnes, who had done nothing wrong, while the infirmarian might well be in more of a position than Janna to help ease the situation, if help was possible.

"He wishes to wed Agnes, but Agnes will not hear of it." Janna stepped closer to Sister Anne. The marketplace was more crowded than she'd expected, and she didn't want anyone to overhear what she was about to say. "It is my belief that fear keeps Agnes in the abbey, for I recall she once confided in me that she would like to marry, to bear children. But that was before Master Will made his intentions plain, before she had any real choice in the matter, and before she came out to the fair with us and saw for herself what life is like outside the abbey." She looked at Sister Anne. "And I do blame myself for that," she said.

"The timing was ill-judged, perhaps, but the decision to retreat was Agnes's, not yours, Johanna. You had no way of knowing how she would react. Indeed, I suspect Agnes didn't know it either until she put herself to the test."

"It's such a shame. Such a waste!"

"Serving our Lord Jesus Christ can never be said to be a waste."

Janna smarted under Sister Anne's reproof, yet memory of her mother bid her go on, even at the risk of making matters worse. "But surely it is possible to serve the Lord in other ways too? Other people can live good lives as well as nuns.

Sometimes they may do even better!" she added, thinking of how hard a life they'd lived, and how her mother had always treated the sick and helped those less fortunate whenever her skills were called upon.

"Watch your tongue lest it get you into trouble, Johanna." Sister Anne strode on, making her displeasure plain by the set of her back and the tilt of her chin.

Janna was about to follow when she noticed the bailiff in the distance. She was sure he'd seen her, but he made no sign, nor did he come toward her. Even as she debated leaving Sister Anne to go to him, he turned and hurried away. Had he given up on Agnes so soon then? Dismayed, Janna quickened her pace to catch up with the infirmarian.

The nun's disapproval abated somewhat in the face of Janna's excitement when they reached the stalls of the spice merchants. They were expected to pinch and prod, to sniff and taste before selecting their purchases, and Janna took full advantage of the opportunity. Her head swam with giddy delight as she sampled cinnamon, licorice and sweet white powder, sneezed over freshly ground pepper, and danced about in agony while spitting out a burning mouthful of ginger.

"Sister Anne? Sister Johanna?" Janna felt great relief at the sound of Master Will's voice. He carried a small parcel wrapped in a damp, muddy scrap of woven hemp. He held it out as if it was the most precious object he owned. "By your leave, Sister," he said in a low voice, as Janna took the object from him. "I have here a gift for—for the abbey."

Sister Anne inclined her head. "What is in the parcel?"

"The bulbs of white lilies. I beg you to plant them in the garden of the abbey, for I have heard it said that the flowers honor the Virgin Mother Mary, being so pure, chaste and beautiful. For that reason, I believe they are sometimes called the lilies of the Madonna."

Sister Anne pursed her lips in thoughtful contemplation. Just as Janna began to fear she'd be forced to give Will's gift back to him, the infirmarian nodded. "I thank you for your gift, Master Will," she said briskly. "We shall plant the lilies and pick the flowers to decorate the church and the shrine of St Edith on feast days."

"Thank you, Sister." Will folded his hands and stepped back. Sister Anne walked on, but Janna lingered just long enough to hear his whisper. "I know Agnes loves to work in the garden. Please tell her to remember my pledge whenever she sees these flowers, for they remind me of her and they are a living token of my love."

"I will." Janna felt her heart flood with emotion as she recalled Agnes's delight in the wild flowers growing in the fields, and her wistful comment about their perfection. Will could not have chosen a more apposite gift for Agnes—for, in spite of what he'd told the infirmarian, Janna knew quite well that this was a gift for Agnes rather than the abbey.

As the bailiff strode off, she took a long look around the marketplace. This was her last taste of freedom for a while. She smiled as she spied a happy family group in the distance, the father swinging a young boy around and around in circles, while the boy squealed his delight and his laughing mother clapped and cheered the performance. Giddy with the movement, the father set down his son and staggered a few steps. The mother rushed to take his arm to steady him. She looked up into his eyes. They exchanged fond smiles, and—

And Janna's heart stopped beating as she recognized Godric and Cecily, along with Hamo. They had not seen her. For a few long seconds, she stared at them while the world stood still.

At last the silence ended, and the market came back into focus. Once more Janna could hear the cries of the traders, sense the bustle going on around her, smell the dung of the animals mixed with the earthy scent of market produce. Life was going on all around her, but inside she felt as cold as death, and as dead as stone.

Chapter 15

To take her mind off the shock of seeing Godric and Cecily looking so happy together, Janna immediately sought out Agnes on her return to the abbey. Sister Anne had told her to plant out the lily bulbs, but Janna would not do it unless Agnes was there to witness both their burial in the earth, and to hear who had given the bulbs, and why.

She found Agnes directing a group of weary travelers to the guest house, and waited until they had gone and Agnes was free. Then she showed her the wrapped parcel and told of their meeting with Will. Agnes heard Janna out in silence. Janna thought she could detect the glint of tears in her eyes as she said, "Master Will has given a lovely gift to the abbey."

"To you." Janna wasn't about to let Agnes lie to herself, even if it was at the cost of their friendship. "Let's plant the bulbs in the cloister garth, so all the sisters can enjoy their beauty. You choose a spot and I'll go and fetch a pick to break the ground."

"Do you really think Master Will meant it when he said these flowers remind him of me?" Agnes asked, when Janna returned.

"Beyond a doubt," Janna assured her, and handed over the package. "He gave these to *you*. You must plant them yourself." She smacked the pick down into the iron-hard ground, digging deep to loosen the earth.

Agnes carefully unwrapped the bulbs and knelt down. As Janna continued to dig, Agnes scooped out little nests in the loose earth and, following Janna's instructions, set each bulb upright inside the hollows. With enough ground prepared, Janna threw down the pick and helped Agnes sprinkle soil over the bulbs.

"There'll be lilies gracing the altar of St Edith by summer," Janna assured her, as she patted earth over the last of the bulbs.

"And what shall I do then?" Agnes turned to Janna, her distress plainly written across her face. "I like Master Will, but I hardly know him. I can't even begin to think of him as a husband!"

"You could get to know him better, if you would only give him a chance." Janna kept her head bent and her hands busy. This was more of an admission from Agnes than she'd dared to hope. She didn't want to take any risks, or spoil such a promising train of thought.

"How can I come to know him when I cannot leave the abbey?" Agnes's voice was bleak with despair. "I have taken my vows. I cannot break them."

"But they are not your final vows, surely? Is it not possible to get dispensation? Can you not ask Sister Grace about it? After all, you were only a child when you came here!"

"You've heard the story of Wulfrid and the Saxon king and the founding of our abbey, Janna. You know that she was a nun, but the king forced his attentions on her and our dear saint was the result of their union. If Wulfrid was not free to marry a king, how could I ever be free to marry the bailiff? Besides, do you remember that Sister

226

Angelica told us she'd made a mistake coming here, and how much she'd come to regret it? But she would not break her vow—and neither will I, Janna. No." Agnes looked fiercely determined as she shook her head. "I won't even think about it."

In spite of Agnes's passionate avowal, Janna remained skeptical. "Are you sure your vow is all that stops you from considering Master Will's offer of marriage?" she ventured.

Agnes averted her head. She stood up, and tried to brush her hands free of dirt.

"You said you cannot leave the abbey. Is that cannot—or will not?" Janna persisted.

"Cannot! Will not! All right, I'm afraid to leave the abbey again. There, I've said it!" Agnes's voice rose. "I hate people staring at me, staring at my scars," she cried. "I hate it!"

"Shh." Janna was about to put her hand on Agnes's arm to comfort her, but saw that her fingers were stained with mud. Instead, she tried to comfort her with words. "People might stare at first, but only until they're used to you. But they would stare at you no matter what you looked like, for they would be curious to see Master Will's new wife, particularly one newly come from life in a convent! But think on this: Once their curiosity is satisfied, they will accept you as one of their own and take you for granted."

"With this to remind them always that I am grotesque?" Agnes's fingers traced the scar on her face, leaving a muddy trail down her cheek.

"Master Will called the lilies 'pure, chaste and beautiful.' He said they remind him of you. He doesn't think you are grotesque, and neither does anyone else. For certes, no-one here does, nor do they stare at you. They're so used to you, they no longer even notice you!"

"Are you accusing me of the Sin of Pride?" Agnes's lips twitched upward into a half-smile.

Janna felt a profound relief that her friend could find some humor in the situation. It meant there was still hope for her cause. "Perhaps, rather, you should ask yourself what harm it does if they do stare at you?"

Agnes was silent as she contemplated Janna's question. Then she shrugged. "I have made my vows. I cannot unmake them."

"Master Will seemed to think there might be a way around the problem—if problem it is."

"And what would a bailiff know of abbey life, and he a man at that?"

Janna had no answer, but still she wondered if Agnes was using her vows as a convenient excuse not to face her fear. She resolved to question Sister Anne about the matter.

"And what about you?" Agnes's voice broke into her thoughts.

"Me?"

"Yes, you. When you came into the courtyard with Sister Anne you looked as if you'd seen the devil himself! Did something happen in the marketplace—apart from meeting Will there?" Agnes's face and tone reflected her concern, and Janna was touched. She wasn't used to having a friend, someone close enough to care what happened to her. Although she hadn't hesitated to interfere in Agnes's life when she thought the cause was just, it was odd to have the tables turned on her in this way. Hard, too, to break a lifetime's habit of keeping her own counsel in order to confide in someone. The image of Godric and Cecily together was burned on her brain, etched there with acid. She knew they both lived at Hugh's manor and that their care of Hamo must keep them in each other's company. She'd known that in her head, but now she knew it in her heart. The knowledge brought stinging tears to her eyes. She began to describe what she'd seen to Agnes, wanting now to share her burden, wanting relief.

"But why are you so upset? I thought the lord Hugh was the one you cared for?" Agnes looked confused.

"He—No! I—yes, I suppose I do. Care for him, that is. I admire him. But Godric is my *friend*."

"Your friend? Why, then, should you mind if your friend woos Mistress Cecily?"

Why indeed? Janna had no answer for Agnes, or even for herself.

*

Darkness had fallen, and the bell was summoning the convent to Vespers by the time Janna left the physic garden. She'd taken refuge there after she and Agnes had finished planting out the lilies. Telling Agnes what she'd witnessed had stirred the emotion boiling in her heart and mind to such a pitch that the company of others had become unbearable.

She decided not to attend the office, for her hands were thoroughly muddy and needed a good scrub. On her way past the scriptorium, Janna noticed Sister Ursel hunched over her manuscript. In the faint light cast by the candle on her desk, Janna saw that there was a quill in her hand and a pot of ink at the ready, but she didn't seem to be writing anything. In view of what had happened, Janna couldn't blame her for losing heart. She walked past, treading noisily in the hope that the nun might turn around so that she could whisper something sympathetic. But Sister Ursel stayed bowed over her manuscript. Janna wondered if she was crying.

Sister Ursel and her distress haunted Janna as she walked to the lavatorium where the sisters washed their hands before and after every meal. She wished there was some way of finding out who was taking the pages. And where was she hiding them before they could be spoiled and "found?" As she plunged her hands into the basin of water, an idea came to her. She stopped to ponder it. After giving her hands a hasty scrub, she snatched up a tallow candle set in a holder, and hastened to the dorter where the nuns slept. This was surely the best place to start her search. She was greatly relieved to find the dorter deserted, for she not entitled to be there at all.

Sleeping pallets were stacked in a neat pile in the long communal room, which was shared by novices, oblates and some of the nuns. Beyond the dorter was a short corridor, with doors leading off it. The faint sound of chanting from below reassured Janna that the nuns were now busy at Vespers. Wasting no more time, she began to rifle through the wooden chests lined up on one side of the room. They contained nothing more interesting than the spare clothing and shoes of the occupants. The nuns had no private property to store, for it was against the Rule to own anything at all, and Janna hadn't really expected to find anything of interest secreted there.

Carrying the candle, she hurried on to search the small cells on either side of the corridor leading off from the dorter. The cells were closed off by curtains, and Janna pulled aside the first one she came to. A small room was revealed, containing only a truckle bed and a squat chest, with a wooden crucifix on top. There was a hook for the nun's cloak, empty now for the nun would need its warmth in church. These cells must be occupied by the obedientiaries, and perhaps those nuns who had lived in the abbey for many years or who, for one reason or another, had earned the privilege of solitude. Janna resolved to search them all, for this was the most likely place for the missing pages to be hidden. Which cell belonged to Sister Philippa? Had she been here long enough, was she important enough to have her own cell?

With her ears strained to catch the smallest sound, she began a quick search of each cell, feeling under straw mattresses and examining the small chests beside each bed.

She searched carefully, but to no avail. The favored hiding place appeared to be under the hard straw mattresses, and she'd uncovered several secrets—a blue ribbon, a folded letter, a child's embroidered cap, an enameled brooch—but nothing that resembled the missing sheet of parchment.

Janna was on her knees, with her hand under yet another mattress, when the sound of voices jerked her upright. The voices seemed still some distance away. She was tempted to make a run for it, but there was only one cell left at the end of the corridor to search.

With her heart hammering in fright, she ran into the cell, placed the candle on the chest beside the bed, and swiftly searched through its contents. Nothing. She felt under the mattress. Her fingers touched something flat and hard. She pulled out a wooden box and studied it. It bore an inscription chased onto a silver band. She shook it, and heard the faint rustle of something inside. Her conscience stirred, but she reassured herself it was all in a good cause as she snicked open the catch.

Tucked safely inside the box was a folded sheet of parchment. She hurriedly opened it, identifying it instantly as coming from the hand of Sister Ursel. Whose cell was this? Conscious of the voices coming closer, she cast about for any signs that might identify the occupant. There were none. A pair of sandals stood beneath the empty peg, discarded now for the stouter boots of winter wear. Did they belong to Sister Philippa? It was impossible to tell. Janna peered into the box in the hope of finding some means of identifying its owner. As well as the parchment, it contained a crucifix and, strangely, a couple of teeth. Not human, surely? Janna peered more closely at them, feeling almost sure they came from some animal.

She closed the box and tried to decipher the inscription on the lid. It meant nothing to her, even when she turned the box and studied the writing upside down. Exasperated, she slammed the box down onto the mattress. A thought came to her. She couldn't read the writing, but she knew who could! She opened the box, took out its contents except for the parchment, and left them lying on the chest. She tucked the box into the folds of her sleeve and, feeling like a thief, hastily skipped out of the cell just as several sisters entered the dorter with cloaks folded over their arms.

"My pardon, sisters. I needed to visit the reredorter," she said, moving quickly away before any of them could question her. She ran downstairs and went straight to the scriptorium, hoping to find Sister Ursel. The manuscript was there, but the nun wasn't.

Janna paused a moment to admire the beautiful lettering, and the delicate lines of a drawing depicting a robin perched on the hand of St Edith. Janna knew it was a robin for its breast was shaded red. She wasn't quite so sure it was St Edith she was looking at, for she could not read the writing beside the illustration. She sighed with frustration and wondered again why, when her mother was teaching her how to write her own name, she had not at the same time taught her how to read and write anything else.

Holding the candle close to the page to see more clearly, she noticed that some of the color had smudged beyond the line of the robin's breast. In fact, the work gave all the appearance of being abandoned in a hurry, for only part of the breast was colored. Janna studied the smudge. It looked as if it might have been caused by a splash of water. A fallen tear, perhaps? She had never seen a smudge on Sister Ursel's work before, and knew that something extraordinary must have happened to cause it. She wondered whether she should make some effort to protect the work, but a moment's reflection reassured her that it was probably safe enough for the present. Whoever was behind the damage to the manuscript thought she already had a sheet to destroy; she would not risk taking another quite so soon, particularly after Abbess Hawise's stern warning.

Conscious of time passing, Janna went in search of Sister Ursel. Had she gone to Vespers after all? Was she now awaiting supper in the refectory? Janna was all too aware of the box concealed within her sleeve. She was horribly afraid that someone would stop her, and that she would be searched. Anyone finding the stolen articles could easily misconstrue the reason for finding them in her possession. Even the thief could point her finger at Janna, for was not Janna carrying a box stolen from her own cell? There was no sign of Ursel in the refectory or anywhere around the cloister. Janna made a conscious effort to slow her footsteps as she went outside to search in the garden. She didn't want to attract any attention, nor did she want to add the Sin of Running to her crimes. But Ursel was not there, or in the physic garden, or the orchard beyond.

There was only one place Janna hadn't looked. She had never been into the church on her own, and was reluctant to go there now. Vespers was over and the nuns would be having their supper. She was already late for the meal; she didn't want to be held to account for the dual Sins of Lateness and Trespass.

The church door was open, inviting her in. Janna's hesitant steps took her over the threshold. The air smelled dusty and old, perfumed with stale incense. Flickering candles cast a ghostly glow, while her shadow leaped high and dark against their light. She set down the candle and walked into the choir stalls, but there was no Ursel sitting in her usual seat, nor anyone else there either. A gasping cry came to her ears, and she kept very still, turning her head to locate the direction of the sound. She thought it came from the Lady Chapel or perhaps the small chapel that housed the shrine of St Edith, and so she tiptoed quietly toward the north arm of the crucifix-shaped church. A figure lay spread-eagled on the floor in front of St Edith's shrine, racked with sobs but trying her best to stifle them. Janna could make out a few choked gasps—"N-n-not worthy, oh God, not worthy…"—followed by a cry of agony: "Oh God, h-help me! Pl-please, please g-give me the gift of faith. Help me, S-St Edith, help me!" The nun's eyes were blind with tears; her voice desolate with grief.

Janna's first impulse was to run to her, to take her in her arms and comfort her, but she knew that this was not the comfort Ursel sought. Aghast at witnessing such despair, wanting to help yet feeling powerless in the face of such anguish, she hesitated. Should she run for the abbess? The thought was dismissed almost instantly. Ursel needed more comfort than that cold and calculating heart could provide. Who, then, could she find to console Ursel and give her the ease she sought so earnestly? Sister Anne? Sister Grace? Janna touched the box inside her sleeve. Perhaps, after all, she had the means to alleviate some of Ursel's distress. Even so, she hesitated to interrupt the nun's desperate communion with the saint. She tiptoed back to the nave. When Ursel felt strong enough to rise and face her life once more, Janna would intercept her without letting her know that her misery had been witnessed.

It seemed that hours passed. Judging from the sounds of distress that Janna could hear even from a distance, Ursel was neither aware of the time, nor of how very cold it was in the church. Janna shivered, and huddled up into her habit, wishing she had thought to fetch her cloak before going in search of the scribe. Ursel's sobbing, interspersed with prayers and entreaties to St Edith, indicated a crisis of faith that Janna could not understand. She knew she would be unable to provide counsel, and wondered again if she should rather fetch someone to intervene. She cast about for anyone close to Ursel, someone who cared enough to help her through this catastrophe, but could think of no-one. In fact, she couldn't remember ever seeing Ursel talk or laugh with anyone, not even in those few periods during the day when conversation was permitted. Perhaps the nuns were too in awe of her great gift to offer friendship? But Janna thought it more likely that Ursel's stutter turned any conversation with her into a trial. Even she had not sought out Ursel when questioning the other nuns about her mother; the realization made her flinch with shame.

And she was slowly freezing to death! Janna jumped up, hugged herself and rubbed her arms, then squatted up and down to get her blood flowing freely once more. She began to run on the spot in a vain effort to warm herself. In spite of her care to tread silently, her boots clattered on the stone flagging. She became aware that the sobbing had stopped, along with the murmurs of distress. Suddenly afraid that Ursel had crept out without her noticing, she hastened to the small shrine.

Ursel was there, standing at the entrance. Her face and eyes were red and swollen with grief. "You g-gave me a fright. I-I thought I was alone." Her voice was muffled, thick with tears.

"Forgive me, Sister. I didn't mean to startle you, but I am glad to find you here." Janna was quite happy to pretend she'd only just arrived. "I've been looking for you, for I have something to show you." She drew the wooden box out of her sleeve, and proffered it to the nun.

Ursel frowned, her face hardening with suspicion. "Where...where did you get that?" she asked sternly.

"Look inside." Janna opened the box, wanting Ursel to see the contents before she answered the question. "Please," she added.

Sister Ursel did as she was told. She saw the sheet of parchment. "Oh!" she breathed. "Oh!" She snatched up the sheet and carefully unfolded it. With reverence, she smoothed the creases, then held it under the light from the cresset candles to examine it more carefully. She exhaled in relief when she saw that her work was undamaged.

She rounded on Janna. "Did you take this page? And d-did you steal this box?" she demanded angrily. Even through her dismay, Janna noted that the nun hardly stammered at all.

"No, Sister, I did not!" In spite of knowing that she'd had no choice in the matter, Janna still felt a sense of shame. "I found your missing page inside the box—and yes, I stole the box but I didn't take your parchment. Not this page, nor any others that have gone missing in the past."

Sister Ursel's eyes went round with horror. "You st-stole the box?" she said slowly. "Why are you telling me this? You should c-confess your misdeeds to our M-Mother."

"I wanted to speak to you first. Yes, I know I was wrong to go poking about in everyone's possessions, but I was sure that whoever was responsible for stealing pages of your manuscript must have hidden them somewhere until she was ready for them to be 'found' later on. I couldn't bear it if another page was defaced and spoiled as the last one was, and so I took a chance and made a search."

Ursel shot Janna a glance of pure amazement. "You c-cared enough about my work to dis-dishonor your soul?"

"No dishonor to *my* soul. The dishonor belongs to the one who has been acting against you in this way. I don't know who it is—although I have my suspicions! But I took the box because I hope the writing will tell us who the owner is." Janna tapped the inscription on the silver band. "See? I cannot read the name inscribed here, but I know you can."

"*Laudate Dominum,*" Sister Ursel read the words aloud. "That means 'Praise the L-Lord,' Sister Johanna."

"Oh." Janna felt thoroughly deflated as she faced the scribe. "I'm sorry. I took it thinking it would tell us who has been acting against you in this way."

"But it does," Sister Ursel said slowly. "This b-box belongs to Sister Catherine."

"Not Sister Philippa?"

"No." Ursel looked surprised. "Why...why would you think that?"

"Because..." But Janna was too ashamed of her suspicions to continue. "How do you know it belongs to Sister Catherine?" she asked instead.

"Because I-I once saw her showing it to s-several of our sisters. She is very p-proud of it, but...but of course she is not meant to have any p-personal p-property so she k-keeps it hidden under her mattress—or s-so she said."

"And that's where I found it, with this sheet of parchment inside."

Sister Ursel's face reflected her shock.

"Why would Sister Catherine do such a thing?" Janna asked.

"Perhaps...b-because of my mouse and her dog?" Sister Ursel cast her eyes heavenward as if seeking the answer there. "Everyone, at s-some time or another, has c-complained about Sister Catherine's dog. And for m-many different reasons, b-but I s-suspect she blames me for drawing attention to each in-incident. The d-dog used to bark whenever I came near, you s-see. It could smell Chester, but in making its p-presence known it was imp-impossible for Mother Abbess to ignore its existence. And so...so she would remonstrate with Sister Catherine. And...and I suppose that's why Catherine t-took vengeance on me and on Chester." She gazed sadly at the parchment in her hands. "I-I found his...his remains in the cloister late this afternoon," she said. "S-Sister Catherine and her dog were close by. There was b-blood on his muzzle! I-I could see the triumph in Catherine's eyes, and I realized then how much she...she h-h-hates me!" Her voice shook. Her eyes were glassy with tears. She squeezed them shut and blotted the tears away with her hand. "It is a j-judgment on me, for my lack of faith," she whispered.

Janna remembered the incident in church, and the incident in the cloisters. She wished, now, that she'd paid more attention at the time. Two nuns who both loved their pets, but only one in trouble for it. How the injustice of it must have festered in Catherine's mind to drive her to such lengths.

"This is surely nothing to do with God's judgment, and everything to do with Sister Catherine's spite," she said. "You have the parchment safe. What will you do about Sister Catherine?"

"Nothing."

"*Nothing?*" Janna couldn't believe her ears.

Ursel shook her head. Her face was creased with worry as she thought about it. "I-I'll have to give the box b-back to her. I could tell her that I-I know she took the pages from me, and was r-responsible for their d-destruction. As for...for Chester—I-I d-don't know how he managed to escape, but I am sure Catherine could have prevented her d-dog from killing him, if she'd only h-had the will to do so. But b-blaming her cannot bring Chester back to life, while the...the fact that he is gone m-means she cannot hold me responsible in the future for...for any trouble caused by her animal. S-so I think I'll j-just tell her I'll say no more ab-about it."

"You could also tell her that if any more pages are taken, you'll accuse her openly in chapter and tell the abbess what she's done," Janna said sharply. "Tell her that you have a witness to vouch for your story."

Ursel nodded. "I-I can't thank you enough for t-taking this risk on my behalf, Johanna. I...thought that G-G-God had abandoned me. This p-page...M-my w-work..."

"I know." Janna smiled at her. "I know how much it means to you."

"And if there's anything…anything I can d-do in return?"

"No, I'm glad to have been of help." Janna looked at the parchment in Ursel's hand, at the careful writing and the small illustration beside it: a line drawing of a nun on her knees, with a beautifully decorated cross in her hands and a golden halo around her head.

Here was the answer to all her prayers! Janna marveled at her stupidity, her slowness in seeing the blindingly obvious. "Actually, there is something you could do for me, Sister Ursel, if you would," she said carefully. "I cannot read, and my future depends on my learning to do so. Will you teach me?"

She held her breath, waiting for the same curt refusal she'd received from Sister Grace and the chantress. But Ursel beamed with happiness. "No-one's ever asked me to…to do anything for them before," she exclaimed. "I-I'd be happy to share my knowledge with you, Johanna."

Janna closed her eyes, and breathed out a silent "Thank you," knowing that here in this church, if nowhere else, God would be listening, and must surely give His blessing to her search for the truth.

Chapter 16

The days passed swiftly; there were barely enough daylight hours for Janna to accomplish all that she wanted to do. She'd told Sister Anne that Sister Ursel had consented to teach her how to read, and had begged time away from her duties. Sister Anne had agreed to give her a few hours off in the afternoon whenever she could be spared, but had warned Janna that she expected her help in the infirmary at all other times. With the abbey shivering through the long, hard winter, Janna was kept busy physicking coughs and colds, the aches of rheumatics, and sundry other complaints suffered by the nuns.

She knew that Sister Anne was entrusting her to do more and more, and felt a growing sense of confidence as she went about her work. But her greatest enjoyment was to spend time in company with Sister Ursel. The scribe had requested a wax tablet and a metal stylus from Sister Grace, and had told Janna she would learn to read and write through copying from a reader, the *Disticha Catonis*.

"But I don't understand Latin!" Janna cried in dismay.

Sister Ursel had looked a little taken aback. "That is how the oblates and novices are taught," she said dubiously.

together in the scriptorium during their lessons, for it was too cold to sit out in the cloister. Ursel continued her painstaking illuminations while Janna practiced writing and sounding the letters, and attempted to read the simple words that the scribe wrote on the tablet for her to decipher.

But the work progressed too slowly for Janna's patience. Although she sometimes brought out the letter and studied it when no-one was around to see her, most of the words stayed tantalizingly out of her reach. The few she could read were too scattered for her to make much sense of them other than to learn that they seemed to be written in the Saxon language after all. But she was too proud to tell Ursel that she'd changed her mind, and so, laboriously, she sounded out the letters and tried to match the words she could read with their Saxon equivalent. The one thing she was quite sure of now was that the letter had indeed come from her father.

There was something else she could ask Ursel, and one day she plucked up enough courage to show her the brooch she'd found buried under their cot in her mother's secret hiding place. "Can you read the inscription for me, please, Sister?" she asked.

"*Amor vincit omnia*," the nun obliged.

"What does that mean?"

"It's Latin. It means 'love conquers all.' It's a b-beautiful brooch, Johanna. Where did you get it?"

"It belonged to my mother."

"A gift from your f-f-f–?"

"My father?" Janna closed her eyes. "I don't know," she whispered.

Ursel's difficulty with the word "father" reminded Janna of the nun's speech impediment. She realized then that, in their conversations, Ursel hardly stuttered at all. It was mostly when she did the readings during the meals. It was when she spoke of God. God, the "father."

Janna remembered the nun's anguish at the shrine of St
Edith, how she had prayed for faith. Was a lack of faith at
the heart of her difficulty with speech? She reminded herself
that it was none of her business. Yet she heard herself asking,
"What brought you here to the abbey, Sister Ursel?"

"I wanted to serve God." The nun was absorbed in
coloring several very small flowers, and answered without
thinking. She looked up then, and flushed a deep and painful
red. "Th-the truth is, my family p-paid a d-dower for me to
be here, to be r-r-rid of me."

"Surely not!" Janna was shocked.

The nun grimaced unhappily. "My...my f-f-father died
when I was quite young, and my mother m-married again,
and had s-several more children. My half-sister was the
b-beauty of the family. My mother knew she could find a
husband for her, and my b-brothers were provided for by
my...my stepf-f-father. I d-didn't belong in the new f-family.
And so...so I decided to s-serve God instead."

"So you're here because you wanted to come?" Janna
asked gently.

"Y-Yes." Ursel raised her eyes to Janna. They were
suspiciously bright. "I...I s-saw the abbey as a p-place of
refuge, you s-see. I was...was clumsy. I f-forgot things, I
muddled everything up. My family lost patience with...with
me. They s-said I was g-good for nothing, a...a nuisance,
so they told me to...to go and be a n-nuisance at the
abbey, instead."

"But your manuscript is a great work of art! Surely they
admired your talent?" Janna was amazed at their blindness.

"They...they didn't know. S-Sister Grace and Sister Maria
t-taught me my letters and...and once I p-picked up a quill
and a brush. I knew that this was where my heart belonged!"

Janna heard the passion in Ursel's voice. "You are so
clever," she said. "You write and illustrate your work

so beautifully. Surely it is a gift from God, and a blessing that you came here."

"Do...do you think so?" Ursel's eyes grew round as she contemplated Janna's words. It seemed she'd never considered her talent in this way before.

"Of course!" Janna said emphatically.

"But I...I feel un-unworthy."

"Your work is wonderful. Surely you must know that?"

Sister Ursel bowed her head. "I do my b-best," she whispered.

"You are *not* unworthy. You are truly blessed. Your illumination of the life of St Edith will live on through the centuries, a testament to your faith, and to your great gift. It will still be here long after we're all dead and forgotten."

"I-I never thought of that!" Ursel raised shining eyes to Janna. It was the first time Janna had ever seen the nun look truly happy and at peace.

"You should never feel unworthy. Never!"

Ursel picked up her brush and dipped it into a pot of color. As she bent once more to her task, Janna heard her humming softly under her breath. She smiled, and went back to carefully copying what Ursel had written on the tablet. *Le chat va a la chasse.* She read the phrase, and tried to translate it into Saxon. The cat goes hunting? Janna smiled. She had made a start. She was on her way.

*

The thought of Agnes's unhappiness lay heavily on Janna's conscience. She'd grown even quieter, and seldom sought out Janna's company now. When they did meet, Janna still tried to interest her friend in learning about herbs and their properties, but her task was made difficult because the garden lay bare and lifeless in the bitter winter cold, and there was little to see or do there. Nor had Sister Anne consented to have Agnes working in the infirmary, so Janna couldn't show her how to make up medicaments either.

But the convent soon had much to think about and discuss, for there was startling news from the north, brought by one of the few travelers still abroad. "Earl Ranulf of Chester and his brother, William of Roumare, captured and held Lincoln castle after tricking the castellan into admitting their wives," the traveler told them. "But King Stephen mustered his army and chased up there to lay siege against them." The traveler had stopped to talk to the almoner in the outer court, but as word spread of the news he brought, a crowd began to gather around him.

"Earl Ranulf managed to escape with some of his men. He went first to Chester to muster his own vassals along with his Welsh allies, and he also called on Robert, Earl of Gloucestre to support him, promising fealty to the empress in return." The traveler rocked back on his heels to survey his rapt audience. He was greatly enjoying the attention.

"Earl Robert was delighted at the chance to make an important new ally for the empress," he explained. "As half-brother to Matilda, he gives her claim to the throne his full support. Besides, his own daughter is married to Ranulf of Chester, so everyone in his family is happy with the new alliance. The two earls joined forces, mustered their troops and chased up to Lincoln to do battle against the king. It seems that all the signs were against Stephen from the start."

The traveler lowered his voice in hushed awe. "'Tis said that before the battle, he attended a Mass on the feast of the Purification of the Blessed Virgin. He offered a candle to Bishop Alexander but, when he put it into the bishop's hands, it broke into pieces. Everyone said this served as a warning to the king that he would be crushed. But worse was to follow. In the bishop's presence, the pyx above the altar, which contained the consecrated bread, the holy Body of Christ, fell down when the chain snapped. 'Tis said this was the sign of the king's downfall, and so it came to pass, for the battle was lost.

"The king said it was a judgment from God for his arrest of the Bishops of Ely and Lincoln, and his mistreatment of Bishop Roger of Sarisberie, but he also blamed the many barons who deserted him on the battlefield. Even so, 'tis said the king showed great courage, for although everything seemed against him he still continued fighting, laying about him with a two-headed axe until it broke. Finally, he was struck down by a stone and taken captive, along with several of his followers. He was taken to Gloucestre first, but is now in Bristou, held captive by Robert, Earl of Gloucestre."

A stunned silence greeted the traveler's words. "The empress has had a meeting with the king's brother, Bishop Henry of Blois, who is the papal legate," the traveler continued with relish. "I've heard that Bishop Henry has submitted the city of Winchestre to her control, including the royal treasury. Some of the bishops have already sworn their fealty; others will follow. It seems that, for the first time ever, England will have a queen on the throne."

The traveler looked about him, pleased at the effect of his words on the nuns. They were speechless. Not so the abbess, who swooped down on him like a black crow, full of wrath that she was the last to hear such important news. After dismissing the sisters with sharp words and an admonition to remember their vow of silence, she took the traveler away, presumably to break her vow of silence with an interrogation of her own.

But that was not the last of the excitement. Word came shortly afterward that the bishops had received the empress, and had given her the title "Lady of England," which she would hold until her coronation. All had pledged their support, with one exception: Theobald, Archbishop of Canterbury. He and the empress planned to meet at Wiltune shortly before Easter, for the empress had expressed a wish to visit the abbey where her mother had spent part of her childhood.

As soon as word of the impending visit arrived, there was a great fuss and commotion. Everyone was pressed into cleaning and tidying the abbey and its grounds. Messages flew back and forth. There was no question, now, of whose side the abbey was on. Perhaps it was the memory of the empress's mother, held dear among those few nuns old enough to remember her, or perhaps it was that the cause of the king now seemed utterly defeated.

The abbess was in the mood to celebrate the honor, and with a great feast—although not everyone was invited to share in the occasion, for the feast would be held in her own quarters and with only herself, the prioress, the archbishop and empress and their entourages to be present. Nevertheless, it was clear she was spending money with unusual abandon. Notwithstanding the fact that Lent had begun, cartloads of delicacies were ordered from the abbey's home farm and beyond: swans, peacocks, partridges and barnacle geese, casks of wine and extra eggs, milk and mead, along with several different varieties of fish, plus new utensils in which to cook the food, and new dishes to serve it on. The sisters swept and scrubbed and cleaned and polished with a will, and in their spare time were kept busy making extra candles, and decorating their saint's shrine with newly embroidered cloths and wall hangings.

Janna relished the buzz of excitement in the air. She had suggested to Sister Anne that the empress might enjoy some soothing unguents, some scented oils to refresh her after her journey, and the infirmarian agreed, telling Janna to make them up for she herself had insufficient knowledge of such things, there being no demand for luxuries of this sort in a convent.

"These are some of the ingredients I used to make up the lotions and rinses we sold at the fair," Janna told the nun. She was enveloped in a sweet haze of dried lavender and rose petals, almost swooning from their heady scent. Sister Anne took an appreciative sniff. "And they fetched in a goodly sum," she observed, and thereafter kept close watch on Janna's activities, "so we can make up some more for the fair in September."

Janna felt a twinge of unease. She was growing very fond of the elderly nun, but she had no intention of staying at the abbey for so long. "Perhaps we could call in Sister Agnes to help?" she suggested, thinking it would be a good opportunity for Agnes to start making herself indispensable.

Sister Anne shot her a sharp look. "You seem determined to instruct Agnes in healing and herbs," she said. "Why? Does Agnes wish to take her vows and dedicate her life to the abbey?"

Janna hesitated, unsure how to answer.

"And what of Master Will?"

Janna looked sideways at the nun. Sister Anne laughed. "Don't look so defensive," she said. "I know the ways of the world, of men and women. I know that not everyone wants to be wedded to Christ."

"But Agnes told me she's already taken her vows."

"Not her final vows. Besides, she is a lay sister here, she has no dower to become a fully professed member of our convent."

"Agnes thinks of her vows as binding."

"Does she?" Sister Anne's hands stilled on the mortar she was using to grind some precious cloves into powder. They would be used by the infirmary cook to spice up the last of the wrinkled old apples that had been picked in the autumn and stored in the cold room. Janna inhaled the sharp fragrance. She could recognize now the spices brought by merchants from the east and sold to the abbey. The scent of ginger and cloves, cardamom, licorice and nutmeg, teased and tantalized her senses. With an effort, she brought her attention back to Sister Anne's cryptic question.

"Do Agnes's vows not bind her to the abbey?"

"She was but a child when she came here," the infirmarian answered obliquely. "Children should not have to decide their future at too early an age. In fact, the empress's own mother…" She began to wield the mortar once more, driving it into the dried black flower buds with great energy. "Her name was also Matilda. She was the daughter of the Scots king, and her mother was the great-granddaughter of our own Edmund Ironside, and so a member of the true royal family of England. It was a good political match for King Henry, but there was one small impediment. Matilda was sent here as a child to be raised by her aunt Christina, who was Abbess of Wiltune at that time. It was said that she'd been seen wearing a wimple and veil, and that she was a nun.

"But Henry would not be gainsaid and so he appealed to his archbishop, Anselm, for help. It's said the decision went against the archbishop's conscience, for he was a saintly man, but he found in the king's interests after listening to Matilda's story. She denied she was ever an oblate here, but claimed that her aunt Christina, who was a severe disciplinarian and who even resorted to the rod when disobeyed, had forced her to wear the veil 'to protect herself against the lusts of the Normans.'"

Sister Anne giggled, sounding suddenly like the young girl she must once have been. "Rumor has it that the lustful Norman in question was actually the king's brother, William Rufus!"

"But he was—"

"An ungodly lout. Yes, I know. Fortunately for Matilda, the ruse seems to have worked, for he left her alone once he'd seen her wearing the veil. However, Matilda claimed that whenever her aunt was out of sight, she would take it off and trample on it. All swore that she had never been a professed nun, and so Anselm abided by the dictum of his predecessor, Archbishop Lanfranc, who had recognized that women who fled to the monasteries 'not for the religious life but for fear of the Normans,' and who had never taken any vows, might be free to return to the world to marry. And so Anselm blessed the marriage and, shortly thereafter, crowned Matilda Queen of England. You might like to tell Agnes that story, Johanna."

"I will. But I'm not sure if it's her vows or her fear of the unknown that is keeping her here."

Sister Anne nodded. "Tell her there is a way out, if she wishes it, but she will have to make that decision for herself; no-one else can do it for her."

"You know so much of what has happened in the world," Janna ventured. "Who has the right claim to the throne, in your opinion? The king, or his cousin, the Empress Matilda?"

"Matilda." Sister Anne answered without even having to think about it. "She was her father's only legitimate heir after her brother William died in the White Ship disaster. All were drowned in that sorry affair, save one who lived to bear witness to it. Her father, King Henry, twice made the barons swear an oath of allegiance to his daughter before he died, that they would recognize her claim to the throne. In fact, Stephen was first among the barons who swore to support her."

The infirmarian paused a moment, then added, "No-one really wants a queen on the throne, especially not one married to an Angevin! In truth, Henry had many children out of wedlock, including the empress's greatest supporter, Robert of Gloucestre. It is widely thought that he would make a far better king than Stephen, who has proved himself weak, reckless and lacking in state craft. But…" She smiled cheerfully at Janna. "It seems Matilda will soon be crowned queen and, with luck, she will take her advice from her half-brother Robert rather than her husband, who anyway spends his time in Anjou and Normandy, not England."

Janna found herself in agreement with the nun's argument in favor of Matilda's claim to the throne. She wondered where her father stood on the matter, and whether divided loyalties might cause problems between them in the future—if he was still alive.

And if she could find him.

*

All was in readiness for the empress's visit and fortunately the day dawned fine. Janna and Agnes and several other lay sisters were hard at work in the kitchen garden, planting out leeks, cabbages, peas, beans, lettuces and onions. Vegetables were the mainstay of the abbey's fare, served whether it was one of the many days of abstinence when only fish was allowed on the table, or on other days when poultry, pork or beef might also be eaten.

The dark, barren earth was yielding to the promise of spring, and Janna felt a lifting of her spirits as she observed green shoots thrusting toward the pale sunlight, the golden faces of the daffodils growing wild among the trees in the orchard, and the green fuzz of new growth on the trees. She and Agnes were on their knees, pricking holes and fitting seedlings into them before carefully covering and tamping the earth around the plants to keep them secure against rain and wind. But all the sisters, Janna and Agnes among them, abandoned their chores and hastened to the courtyard as soon as they heard the first notes of the trumpeter heralding the guests' arrival.

The archbishop and his entourage arrived first, closely followed by the empress and her train. The outer courtyard was soon crowded with the dignitaries, along with their servants, who milled about, kicking up dust as they saw to the unpacking of carts and sorting of baggage. Under the watchful eye of the steward, along with Master Will, grooms unsaddled the mounts ridden by their owners, and led them away to the stables. The abbess herself had hurried out to welcome the guests and she wasted no time in taking them to her own quarters. With all the dust and movement, and situated as she was at the back of the sisters who had crowded into the courtyard to spy on the proceedings, Janna found it difficult to see the empress. She peeped over shoulders and ducked and weaved between the heads that got in her way, but caught only a glimpse of a jeweled hand, a fine gown of silken blue, a gauzy veil. She found it very frustrating.

She joined the nuns in a deep curtsy as the lady approached, keeping her knees bent as the archbishop followed. But instead of bowing in submission, she dared to raise her eyes. The empress was talking to the elderly tiring woman beside her. Her head was averted from Janna but she turned suddenly, and caught Janna staring at her. Her eyes widened.

Instantly embarrassed and ashamed of her impertinence, Janna bowed her head. She was puzzled. She knew she'd never seen the empress before in her life. She would certainly have remembered it if she had, and yet the empress seemed somehow familiar. She had long dark hair that hung in a plait bound with a silk ribbon of the same hue as her gown, which was richly embroidered at the neck and at the edges of the long sleeves. A jeweled band kept her veil in place; she wore more jewels at her throat and on her fingers. Janna had never seen anyone so fine.

The empress passed by, followed by the archbishop, who wore robes as splendid if not more so than those worn by the empress. And then they were gone and the excitement was over. The nuns were dismissed to return to their labors.

"We'd better get back to the garden." Janna tugged on Agnes's sleeve, heaving a despondent sigh as she noticed her cracked and dirty nails. Agnes, she realized, wasn't paying any attention to her. Her gaze was fixed on the bailiff. He had not seen her, but was pointing in the direction of the stables as he talked to one of the grooms.

"Go and speak to him." Janna gave Agnes a hard nudge.

"No!"

"Why not? You used to think of him as a friend."

"That was before."

"Before what?"

"Before he spoiled everything."

"Spoiled? How?" Janna couldn't hide her surprise. "He loves you; he wants you for his wife."

"How could he want me, disfigured as I am? No, what he wants is a mother for his children, no more than that." Agnes's voice was raw with grief and resentment.

"Is that what you believe?" Janna gave an incredulous snort. "Think on it, Agnes. He's the abbess's bailiff. He could probably have anyone he chooses, and it would certainly be easier for him to choose someone outside the abbey if a mother for his children was all he had in mind. But he wants you, Agnes. Surely his words and his actions prove his love for you?"

Agnes said nothing. She continued to stare at the bailiff. But when he finally noticed her, she turned abruptly and hastened toward the outer parlor, dragging Janna along with her.

"Master Will said that, if you choose the abbey, he will not continue to pester you with his attention," Janna warned, as they came to the outer parlor. "You may well have made your meaning plain to him today, Agnes."

Agnes made no reply. She kept walking, through the parlor, along the passage and out into the garden.

Now was the time to repeat her conversation with Sister Anne, Janna thought. "If it's the vow you have taken that keeps you here, there is a way out of it." She began to relate the story of King Henry and the young woman he wanted to marry, speaking to Agnes's back, for the lay sister would not stop to listen.

"She was the empress's mother." Janna raised her voice to make her point. "And she also gave birth to a son. So the marriage was consummated, there were no holds to it."

Agnes made no comment. Instead, she got down on her knees and began jabbing hard into the earth with her fingers. She shoved the small plants into the holes and pressed them down with an angry, despairing urgency.

Janna watched, frustrated by her inability to reach Agnes, and her friend's inability to question the true reason for her rejection of the bailiff. She mourned the death of her friend's hopes but suspected that Agnes's despair ran much, much deeper—so deep that it might well last for a lifetime.

Chapter 17

Janna was in the infirmary with Sister Anne when an urgent summons came from the empress. A tiring woman brought it, a young, fresh-faced girl who seemed in awe of the infirmarian and discomforted by her surroundings. Her name was Margery, she said in answer to Sister Anne's question, continuing in a rush: "My lady has such a bad headache she can scarce see from the pain of it. It has made her sick to her stomach, and she begs you for something to ease the hurting." Her gaze rested on Janna for a moment before she looked quickly away.

"What would you do to relieve my lady's pain, Johanna?" Sister Anne constantly tested Janna in this way. Janna had first thought it an underhand trick on the infirmarian's part to learn what she could, but had soon come to realize that she herself had learned far more from Sister Anne than anything she might have taught her in return. Now she answered readily.

"Saxon leechcraft would claim that my lady suffers from *aelfshot*. A leech would call forth chants and charms to bless and empower a knife or something sharp to drill a hole into the bone of the skull to release the *aelfshot* and relieve the pain." Ignoring Margery's sharp intake of breath, Janna hurried on. "Others believe that pain comes from the devil, and that drilling a hole in the skull would similarly release the devil and cure the patient. But my mother did not—would not—use a knife, for she had no skill in cutting, or so she said. Instead, she relied on herbal mixtures and remedies to cure all ills. My mother used wood betony mixed with honey and vinegar for headaches and palpitations, for she believed it was good for the soul and the body, shielding the sufferer from night visitations, visions and dreams. She warned me to pick the herb only in August, and without iron, for it is very holy. My lady may also wear a part of the plant as an amulet for further protection."

"Very good," Sister Anne said. "It is fortunate that we have it here dried and ready for use. And I will also make up a poultice of vervain with oil of roses and vinegar to help ease the pain." She turned to Margery. "Pray tell your mistress that we shall bring the medicaments to her just as soon as they are ready."

Margery's gaze rested on Janna once more before she bobbed a curtsy and left the room.

In the infirmary kitchen, Sister Anne searched out the herbs and ingredients they would need. There was silence between them as they worked companionably side by side, for Janna was used to preparing poultices and potions and was able to anticipate the infirmarian's needs. Once they were done, she was dismayed to find that Sister Anne intended to take the medicaments and minister to the empress herself; Janna was to be left behind. She was bursting with curiosity, longing to meet the woman who would become queen, the woman who had captured her imagination and respect. To strive when all seemed lost, and to win the crown as a reward! Janna took courage from the empress's boldness and certainty of purpose, for she felt that her own cause seemed an echo of the empress's struggle. She remembered, then, the scented salves and rinses she'd prepared, and reminded the infirmarian of them, hoping that this might be enough to ensure her attendance.

And so it came about that Janna followed Sister Anne into the abbess's lodge and made her obeisance to the empress. Again, she had the strange feeling that she'd seen her somewhere before, but she was unprepared for the sudden hiss of indrawn breath as the empress's gaze rested on her face.

"Who are you?" Matilda demanded, as Janna held out the rinses and lotions she'd prepared so carefully.

"Her name is Johanna. She is a lay sister here at the abbey." The abbess answered, not giving Janna a chance to say anything as she continued, "You may leave the chamber now, Sister Johanna." It was an order, not a request, and Janna hastened to obey. She was greatly disappointed, but hardly surprised that the abbess was so quick to dismiss her, daughter of the disgraced *wortwyf* as she was. Did the abbess know her mother was once a nun? A moment's reflection convinced Janna that she must have known, which made Abbess Hawise's condemnation of Eadgyth more comprehensible.

She paused outside the abbess's lodge, wondering if she would ever have the chance to question the abbess, and became aware that she was not alone. Margery, the empress's tiring woman, had followed her out. "Begging your pardon, Sister," the girl whispered, "but are you kin to the empress?"

Janna's loud gurgle of laughter was quickly stifled, but she could not contain her surprise. "No, indeed!" she said. "Why do you ask?"

"Your eyes." Margery seemed somewhat flustered by Janna's denial. "They put me in mind of the empress."

Janna hid a smile. An elusive memory teased her until she suddenly recalled St Edith's fair and how she had looked at herself in the mirror seeking some resemblance to her father, or even to her mother. Her dark brown eyes! That was why the empress had seemed familiar. But Janna knew it was only an illusion. "Nay," she said regretfully. "I am no kin to the empress. Far from it, in fact! I have no home, no family, and am entirely dependent on the abbey for food and shelter. I certainly have no land or wealth to call my own, nor do I have important relatives among the royal family." She laughed at the very thought of it. "I wish I did!"

"Perhaps your eyes catch our attention because your hair is Saxon gold, not dark like ours?" Margery observed.

Janna's hand went to her head. She realized that some hair had escaped her wimple once more, and hastily tucked it out of sight. Smiling to herself, she couldn't help dreaming a moment of how things might be if only she could claim kinship to the future queen of England!

Sister Anne bustled out. She frowned when she saw Janna still there. "You were told to return to the infirmary, Johanna," she scolded.

"'Tis my fault, Sister. I kept Sister Johanna talking." Margery turned toward the abbess's lodge. "God be with you this night," she called over her shoulder.

"It is my belief that anger and frustration are behind my lady's headache." Sister Anne relented enough to pass on the news as they made their way back to the infirmary.

"Did the talks not go well?"

"I think not. While the legation led by the king's own brother, Henry, Bishop of Winchestre, have all sworn fealty to the empress, the archbishop has put off doing so until he's visited the king in his prison and has obtained consent to act 'as the difficulties of the time require.' Which is a neat way of covering himself should the situation change."

"Can he delay everything in this way? His words must have greatly incurred the empress's wrath."

"Not to mention bringing on a headache," Sister Anne said wryly. "But yes, the archbishop is within his rights and the empress must know that. The king was recognized by the pope when he was crowned, you see. He is not dead now, merely imprisoned. While the other bishops may ignore the implications of anointing a queen while an anointed king still lives, the archbishop is cognizant that there is no precedent for this sort of thing, and that he might well be acting against the pope's wishes if he rushes to pledge fealty to the empress."

"No wonder the empress is wrathful." Janna felt some impatience with the archbishop's recalcitrance, even while acknowledging that she knew nothing of the ways of the church or of statecraft.

"Wrathful is hardly the word for it. The empress is in a black rage, for the archbishop intends to take several bishops with him to visit the king, perhaps with the intention of changing their minds."

"Perhaps some syrup of poppies?" Janna ventured.

Sister Anne smiled. "I've already thought of that. And I'll take it to the empress myself. I know not why, Johanna, but your presence seemed to disturb her. She was very sharp with the abbess after you left the room." Janna was impressed. It would take a lot of nerve, she thought, to be sharp with the abbess! "Will the empress stay long with us?" she asked, hoping there might be another chance to see her.

"I think not. The legate has summoned a church council to be held in Winchestre in a few weeks' time, and the empress means to attend and to make sure that Bishop Henry and the rest of the legation stay true to their promise of support. I heard her tell the abbess so when she asked that same question. And in truth I think the abbess feels some relief that they will be gone soon—not least about the money she will save if she doesn't have all these extra mouths to feed!" Sister Anne cast a sidelong glance at Janna. "There is something else I heard, but for the moment it's a secret."

Janna realized that the infirmarian was bursting to tell some exciting news. "I won't breathe a word," she promised, and crossed her hand over her heart. She'd seen several nuns make the gesture, and it seemed to convince Sister Anne.

"The abbey is well rewarded for the trouble and expense the empress's visit has caused." Sister Anne paused to savor her news. It would pass around the abbey like wildfire in a wood once it was out.

"How? In what way?"

Sister Anne leant closer to Janna, although there was no-one nearby to overhear her words. "The empress has brought with her a sacred relic, the hand of St James the Apostle!" She drew back with a delighted smile, anticipating Janna's expression of awe and pleasure. Instead, Janna pulled a wry face. Her experience with the pedlar at St Edith's fair had taught her to be skeptical about such things.

"I saw the reliquary myself!" Sister Anne declared, indignant that Janna should doubt such a holy object. "It was given to the empress as a marriage gift from her first husband, the emperor of Germany!"

Janna raised a disbelieving eyebrow.

"The empress brought it back to England after the emperor died. I'm not sure why she wasn't allowed to keep it for herself, but she told the abbess that her father, King Henry, gave the sacred hand to Radinges Abbey."

"And how is it that the abbey has agreed to part with such a valuable relic?" In spite of her skepticism, Janna was becoming interested. She knew that such a thing would attract pilgrims from miles around, which in turn would generate a steady income for the abbey that housed it.

"I suspect they did not part with it willingly but, as they are known to support the king's cause, I can't think the empress would be troubled by any objections they might make. I heard her tell the abbess that, although her father, the king, has been dead these past five years, the church to honor him is still under construction. She fears that the relic might not be safe there, and she wishes it housed close to the shrine of St Edith until such time as the building is completed." Sister Anne beamed with joy at the thought of having such a desirable object in their keeping.

"There's to be a Dedication Mass tomorrow," she told Janna. "Archbishop Theobald will dedicate the shrine to God in honor of St James, and the empress will attend. But I suspect that may be the last we'll see of either of them."

*

As Sister Anne had predicted, the empress left straight after the Dedication Mass, closely followed by the archbishop and his entourage. To everyone's disappointment, the delicacies also disappeared from the dinner table, to be replaced by more usual Lenten fare: platters of cod, eels and vegetables. The convent settled down into its usual routine. And once again it was Sister Ursel's turn to read at dinner.

"Today's Rule is titled: 'Whether b-brethren who leave the m-monastery should be received again,'" she began. As the full import of the message became clear, Janna wished that Agnes was present.

"'If a b-brother who through his own fault leaves the monastery should w-wish to return, let him first p-promise full reparation for his having gone away...'"

Janna listened intently, so that she could pass on St Benedict's words to Agnes. It seemed that there was no bar to her going and she could even return twice, so long as she was prepared to "make reparation and to be received in the lowest place." But Agnes was already in the lowest place, so that would make no difference. She could leave, and leave again, but if she left a third time she would not be received back into the abbey. Janna was convinced that if Agnes could only be persuaded to marry Will, she would not think of coming back, not even once—but how to get her to make that first step? After Agnes's deliberate rejection of him during the empress's visit, would Will be prepared to wait even longer?

She sought Agnes out after chapter the next day, to tell her about the reading. It struck her, as she related its import, that she'd had no difficulty in listening to Ursel, for the sister had hardly stuttered at all. In fact, Ursel had a new confidence, a lightness and spring in her step that spoke of her joy in her work at the abbey. It was interesting, Janna thought, what a difference it made if you could only believe in yourself. And Ursel was doubly blessed, for she also believed in God, and now had faith in her worthiness to worship Him.

But if Sister Ursel had sprung to life like a new shoot in spring, Agnes, by contrast, seemed to be withering into winter. Janna looked at her friend, trying to reconcile Agnes's once cheerful disposition and humorous observations with the downcast demeanor and the cloak of despair that now set her apart from the others. "It's not too late. Send Will a message somehow," she urged. "Tell him you've changed your mind."

"But I haven't." Agnes turned on her heel and hurried out to the garden.

Most of the lay sisters were busy there now, for as well as planting new herbs and vegetables there was flax to sow for the fibers that would provide linen for new habits, tow wicks for lamps and oil from the seeds. There was an extra urgency about their tasks as they took advantage of a mild spring day. Janna shrugged and decided to move on to the physic garden, for there was much work to be done there, too. There was no point in discussing the matter further, not when her friend was so blind to the truth, and so determined not to change her mind.

To her surprise, Agnes followed her and crouched beside her to help plant out some new seedlings. "Do you really think it's too late for me?" she whispered.

Janna looked at her, noticing the red eyes, the shine of tears on a hastily wiped cheek. "I don't know," she said honestly.

"If I could only be sure of the right thing to do. If only there was a sign!" Agnes clasped her hands tight together, as if unconsciously praying for the way to be shown to her.

"It's something you have to decide—not God." Janna tried to soften her words with a smile. "You surely care for Master Will, for I have seen in the past how you've talked to him and about him. He is a kind man, and he will care for you, I am sure of that. The question you really have to ask yourself is: Are you brave enough to leave the abbey and live in the out-side world, live as Will's wife and the mother of his children? You will have to share the marriage bed, which might result in a child of your own one day, or even more than one."

A rosy blush heated Agnes's face. "I would love to have a child of my own, but it's the thought of lying with a man, being intimate, that worries me," she confessed. She heaved a despairing sigh. "I'm afraid, Janna. I'm afraid of how it will be when Will sees me, sees the full extent of my injury. What if he spurns me, turns from me in utter disgust? If I leave the abbey but he won't live with me as my husband, where will I go, what will I do?"

"According to St Benedict's own Rule, you can come back to the abbey." Janna caught Agnes's hands between her own. "But that won't happen. It won't! He loves you. Despite the scarring on your face, he thinks you are as beautiful as the lilies, remember?"

Agnes glanced toward the imposing buildings that were her home, and at the walls that surrounded the convent and kept them in, and her face pinched tight. "Master Will has had my answer. He will not ask again, you said so yourself. And even if he did, how can I answer him when I'm so unsure of him, and so unsure of myself?" She jumped up, found a spade, and dug it savagely into the earth, wincing as the shock jarred her scarred shoulder. "He'll find someone else. He will not wait. 'Tis better so."

Janna took a breath, ready to argue, but then thought twice about it. She had interfered enough already, she'd done enough damage. The wheel would turn as fate decreed. The sudden image of Godric and Cecily laughing together came into her mind, accompanied by a shaft of pain so great that she doubled over, gasping for breath. That situation, too, was beyond her control. She would just have to make the best of it. She would continue with her quest; she would make a new life for herself in Winchestre or wherever else her search for her father might take her, and she would forget them. She straightened and reached out blindly for another seedling to plant. "God's bones, look at this!" Agnes had thrown down the spade and moved away. Now she beckoned Janna over to inspect some new parsley plants which had been reduced to just a few sparse stalks.

"Hares, deer, coneys from the king's warren?" Janna looked around for a possible culprit.

"Blighted creatures," Agnes grumbled.

"But just as worthy in the sight of God as rats, cockroaches and every other obnoxious little pest—including Sister Catherine's dog!"

Agnes's mouth twitched into a reluctant smile. Suddenly she dived sideways and pounced on a small, quivering ball of fur. She scooped it up and opened her hands.

"A leveret." Janna looked down at the baby hare, recalling the time in the forest when Edwin had captured just such a one and they had eaten it. She shuddered, feeling greatly relieved that she had never known so great a hunger since then. She took the hare from Agnes, and gently stroked it. It looked up at her with bright, frightened eyes.

"This isn't the work of just one baby." Janna indicated the ravaged parsley bed. "The rest of its family must have hopped off and abandoned it." She cradled the creature against her habit, and kept on stroking its soft fur.

Agnes stretched out a hand to reclaim it. "We'd better get rid of it, stick it over the wall or something. I'm not wasting my time planting things out if they're just going to be eaten."

Janna she held the leveret out to Agnes, then snatched it back again. "I know something else we can do with it," she said, and hurriedly stuffed the tiny creature down the front of her habit as the dinner bell sounded.

*

With dinner over, Janna went once more to Sister Ursel, stealing time out from the garden where she was meant to be working. The nun greeted her with a smile, which grew broader when Janna complimented her on her reading of the Rule.

"In truth, my heart feels so full of the Lord, I-I no longer think of how difficult it is to read aloud in the company of the convent," she said. "I used to dread it so, and the more anxious I-I became, the worse it got." She hesitated a moment. "For me, it became a test of faith," she confessed. "I thought that, if I loved the Lord enough, he would f-free me to speak as others do. When it did not happen, I d-doubled and redoubled my efforts, but it seemed to m-make everything worse. I just got more and more tongue-tied. I thought God had...had abandoned me. I thought it was His judgment for...for not having enough faith, for not believing in Him. And yet I do, with all my heart!"

"God didn't abandon you. You abandoned yourself." Janna remembered the heartbroken cries she'd overheard in the church. She was sure that it was Ursel's lack of faith in herself that lay at the heart of her affliction, probably stamped on her by her unhappy childhood. The theft and destruction of pages of her manuscript must have seemed like an extra sign that God had abandoned her. "You cannot think you've earned God's displeasure, that He has forsaken you, not when He's given you such a marvelous gift," she said gently. She was coming to realize how lonely Ursel's affliction had made her. If only the nun could have shared these thoughts earlier, so much could have been said and done to give her confidence in her worth and in her work.

"I have something for you." Janna put her hand down the front of her habit and withdrew the baby hare. It had been lying still, asleep against her heart, but at her touch it jerked awake and struggled in her grasp.

"Ah." Sister Ursel took the hare from Janna and looked deep into its eyes. Its struggles ceased; it seemed mesmerized by her gaze. She stroked it gently, never taking her attention away from it for one moment. Janna watched them, and smiled.

But her pleasure turned quickly to impatience and irritation as she tried to read the words Ursel had written on the slate for her to decipher. *Le renard et le loup vont a lachasse au lapin.* She tried to sound out the words. Something about a fox and a bear? Or was that a wolf? Chasing a rabbit? Learning to read was taking far longer than she'd realized, and Sister Anne grumbled about her absence from the infirmary and begrudged the time Janna spent away from her own tuition.

"You have more need to learn from me than from Sister Ursel," she had pointed out, on more than one occasion. "Your gift lies with healing, not with learning something that scribes are trained to do. Besides, you have no time to waste, for there is much to do in the garden now that spring has come." Unable to confess the real reason for wanting to learn to read, Janna had sought to placate the disgruntled infirmarian. "I am truly grateful to you for all you are teaching me," she said. It was the truth. Sister Anne's knowledge was wide-ranging. In addition, the infirmarian always encouraged Janna to administer the potions and deal with the patients herself, albeit under her watchful eye. This was the practical experience that her mother had never given her, and Janna appreciated the nun's generosity, her willingness to share and to train her new pupil. It seemed to Janna sometimes that her brain would burst with all the new things she was trying to cram into it, but at the same time her confidence in her own ability was growing and she was happy.

At least, she was happy until the memory of Godric and Cecily intruded. Then her heart would sink like a stone to the bottom of a pond; she could imagine mud and slime oozing over, covering it, burying it in a mire of her own making. Even the thought of Hugh couldn't cheer her. He was not for her; he was far too highborn to consider her as anything but a bed-mate. And that was something she would never countenance, even though the thought of lying with Hugh sent a wave of heat through her body.

Far better to turn her back on both of them, while wishing Hugh well with his pursuit of a wealthy bride, and Godric every happiness with Cecily, for it was no more than he deserved, and she would make him a worthy and loving wife.

No, there were more important things on her mind right now, like the words scratched on the slate Sister Ursel had just passed to her. As soon as she was able to read her father's letter, she would go in search of him. She began to sound out the words, struggling to make sense of the longer, more difficult ones.

Becoming impatient with her efforts, she read the piece through quickly, and recognized it as the day's Rule that Ursel had read out during dinner.

Although she could not recall the reading word for word, she found she could remember enough to guess the words that puzzled her, and so find the meaning of the text. She picked up the metal stylus and began the task of copying out what Ursel had written on the slate, saying the words quietly under her breath as she scribed them.

When Janna next looked up, the hare had vanished. She looked around the cloister, but could see no sign of it. On the other hand, there was a suspicious lump in the front of Ursel's habit, too low and too big to be mistaken for a breast—the fabric suddenly bulged out, and as quickly subsided. Just so had Janna witnessed a child kicking from within a pregnant woman's stomach, and she smiled at the sight.

Sister Ursel caught her watchful gaze, and smiled in return. "I shall call him 'Harold,'" she said, and went back to carefully smoothing a piece of vellum with a pumice stone in preparation for a new page on the life of St Edith.

Chapter 18

With the high holy time of Easter now passed, spring gave way to early summer. The green fuzz on the trees sprouted into pale leaves that darkened into a thick canopy of green. Daffodils and bluebells bloomed and died, wheat grew higher and so did the weeds in the fields. It was time to scythe the long grass in the water meadows to make hay. Janna wondered if Agnes would go out and brave a meeting with Will, but got a sharp rebuff when she suggested it.

"I can't scythe the hay. My arm gets too sore." Janna thought she could detect an expression of regret before Agnes drew her wimple closer around her cheeks and turned her face away.

"You could mind the children."

"No. It's too late for that now." Agnes hurried off without another word, not even of farewell.

With the spring sneezes over, and warmer weather to soothe old bones, the infirmary had become less crowded. Janna was quick to take advantage of a quiet hour after dinner to visit Sister Ursel in her carrel. The nun greeted her, and handed Janna the wax slate that lay always in readiness. As she chose a passage for Janna to read and copy, Janna gazed about the cloister. The lilies had grown tall and were swelling into bud. One was already in full flower.

Janna remembered Will's comment. She wondered if Agnes also remembered, but knew also that Agnes lacked the courage to act. Janna, herself, was beginning to understand how Agnes felt about leaving the abbey. She longed to be free, and yet she dreaded having to venture outside in case she met up with Godric or Hugh. She was afraid to confront them, afraid of what she might learn.

"I'm not ready to leave, not yet," she told herself. But she knew the time must soon come for, although she was still unable to read her father's letter, tantalizing glimpses into the past were gradually being revealed to her impatient gaze. Nor could she use the winter cold and rain as an excuse for delay, for it was promising to be a warm, dry summer and conditions were perfect for traveling. All too soon, she would have to leave behind the safety of the abbey and the places of her childhood, as well as everyone she knew, including Agnes, Hugh and Godric. Utterly cast down by the thought, she looked about for something to take her mind off her uncertain future. Her glance fell on Sister Ursel's manuscript, and the delicate border of white lilies that framed the text.

"See, Janna," Ursel said, when she noticed Janna's interest. "I'm likening the lilies of the field to our saint, she being as pure and holy almost as the Virgin Mother herself."

Janna thought of Agnes. "They toil not, neither do they spin," she quoted softly.

Ursel smiled. "Of all the flowers, I think lilies are the most beautiful."

"And so is your work, Sister Ursel." Janna never let a chance go by to praise the nun, and indeed the praise was justified. To her intense satisfaction, there had been no more trouble with missing pages. Ursel had reported, under Janna's questioning, that very little had needed to be said when she returned the box to Sister Catherine. The nun had realized that her acts of vindictive spite had been discovered, and was most anxious that they remain a secret. Not only did she stay away from Ursel's manuscript thereafter, she also made sure to keep her dog away from Harold.

Janna glanced about the cloister to find him. The hare was full grown now, and was contentedly munching grass where it grew long among the lilies that Janna had planted with Agnes. She looked from the bloom to Ursel's illustration, marveling how well the nun had managed to capture its grace as well as the fine detail in the glossy petals and long throat, and the furry yellow stamens at the heart of the flower.

Sister Ursel handed the passage she had chosen to Janna. "Why don't you read this aloud to me while I work?" she suggested.

Janna hated reading aloud. She got ever more flustered as she floundered among the words she couldn't recognize and couldn't read. But Ursel was always patient and kind, and Janna understood that it was better to get her help with the difficult words than keep on misreading them.

"Your reading is improving, Janna," the nun complimented her, after a more accomplished performance than usual. Janna smiled, pleased. Soon now, she promised herself; soon the secrets of her father's letter would be revealed, and the past with it.

Shadows were beginning to creep across the cloister. It was time for her to go back to the infirmary to relieve Sister Anne. But, once she'd thanked Ursel and said goodbye, a strange restlessness stayed her passage and turned her steps instead toward the church and the shrine of St Edith. It had become far more crowded now, with the hand of St James the Apostle attracting ever more pilgrims. Nevertheless, it was St Edith's presence that Janna sought, for it had not escaped her attention that the saint's name was almost the same as the name of her own mother. It seemed right, therefore, to attempt yet another reading of her father's letter to her mother in the saint's presence. To Janna's relief, the chapel was empty, for the outer gate had been closed and not even the sacristan was present to disturb her privacy. With a feeling almost of dread, she reached under her habit for her purse. She untied it, and pulled out the sheet of parchment, then sank to her knees before the reliquary.

She hadn't looked at the letter for a little while and now she peered at it, trying to decipher the unfamiliar words in the glow of candles placed around the saint's golden casket. How she wished she'd asked Ursel to teach her to read Saxon English! It would have made her task so much quicker and easier, yet she had been sure her father's letter would be written in Norman French, all of it, instead of just the opening salutation and the close. Perhaps he had written it thus on purpose, knowing English was Eadgyth's native tongue? Perhaps he thought that, although she was able to speak Norman French, she might not be able to write or read it? But the phrases he used at the beginning and end must have been familiar to her mother. Janna had managed to read them and blushed at the memory. She closed her eyes and tried to relax, for already she could feel the strain of not knowing, knew it would scrunch up her insides and shrivel her brain, and make her so anxious that reading became impossible.

She took a deep breath, and then released it. When she opened her eyes again, her gaze fell on a wall painting of the saint. Edith's hand was raised; it was clear she had just performed a miracle, for a child and his parents were gamboling around her, while a discarded crutch lay on the grass nearby.

A miracle. Janna looked down at the letter. This time, instead of straining to read the message word by word, she glanced through it, picking up the words she'd already understood before, so that she had a framework to guess the rest of them. And, as if a veil had been lifted from her eyes, the words began to hold together, to make sense, and to speak of love, and loneliness, and longing.

"*Mon amour, ma cherie.*" My love, my darling. That was easy enough to decipher. Heart thumping hard with fear and excitement, Janna continued to read.

I had hoped to return to you long before this time, but I find that my father has gone to Normandy and so I must follow him there. I cannot send a message to him for he will not understand why I need to break my betrothal to Blanche, nor will he forgive me unless I meet him face to face to explain why I am utterly unable to wed anyone but you.

He will be wroth, but I feel sure I will be able to persuade him that, in this, I know best. While he has made a worthy match for me, I know that once he meets you and witnesses our happiness together, he will fall under your spell just as I have done, and will welcome you into our family and bless you as a daughter. For certes, no-one could be more worthy than you to be my wife, or bring such grace to our family.

You have my ring, and now I send also this ring brooch to you to pledge my love. "Amor vincit omnia." It means "love conquers all"—and so it shall.

I will return as soon as possible, for I miss you more than life itself.

Je t'embrasse de tout mon coeur, de tout mon corps, ma cherie. John.

Shock kept Janna kneeling on the floor, utterly still. She looked at the words again and again, knowing that she had read enough of them to fully understand the sense of the letter, yet unable to comprehend what was in it that had forced her mother to flee, to beg the abbess for charity rather than stay to face her lover. Even if he hadn't known Eadgyth was pregnant, he'd obviously loved her so much he was prepared to break his betrothal and face his father's wrath rather than give her up. *I kiss you with all my heart and all my body, my darling*. That was what he'd said at the end of the letter, and presumably he meant it. Surely such a love would also have welcomed a child of their union? It just didn't make sense.

Janna opened her purse and drew out the silver brooch with its multi-colored gemstones. With shaking fingers, she traced the words on the back of it.

Amor vincit omnia. Love conquers all. But it hadn't. Why? Had John's father refused to let him break the betrothal? Did he have second thoughts about setting Blanche free once he'd got to Normandy?

No! Janna frowned, trying to order her thoughts, for they flew around like a swarm of bees, buzzing so loudly in her head that she could not think straight. No. John had written to Eadgyth to explain his delay in returning to her. If he had changed his mind, once he saw his father or Blanche, surely he would have written again to explain why he would not return?

Had her mother destroyed the second letter but kept the first, to remind her that she was once loved? Was it the second letter that had forced her to flee? Janna shook her head, trying to make sense of the muddle.

There was something at the back of her mind, something someone had said. She was sure it was important, if only she could remember what it was. One by one, she recalled everyone she'd spoken to about Eadgyth, thinking through what each one of them had said. The abbess had told her nothing. The sisters had tried to be helpful, but it was obvious that they were passing on rumors, not facts. Only Sister Ursel had spoken to her mother. Janna began to replay their conversation in her mind. As the scribe's words came back to her, she realized then what had troubled her.

"*As to why your mother confided in me, she c-came to ask if I could show her how to write a name. Your name, Johanna. 'In c-case I have a little girl,' she said.*"

Johanna? If Eadgyth had read this letter, and perhaps even replied to it, she would surely have known how to write "Johanna." Why, then, did she ask Ursel to show her how to write the name?

The answer came like a blast of thunder and it cracked Janna's heart wide open. She'd often wondered why her mother had never taught her how to read or write when she'd taken such pains to school her in everything else, including how to speak Norman French. Now, at last, she had the answer. Eadgyth couldn't teach her what she herself didn't know! Janna felt numb with the shock of her discovery. Her mother had never read this letter because she didn't know how to read.

She didn't know how to read.

John had taught her mother the language of the Normans, but must have believed that she could read and write in her own language and that she would understand his message. She must have been too proud to admit her ignorance. He had written and asked her to wait for him—but she, finding herself with child, had fled. She must have thought he was writing to tell her that his betrothal could not be broken, that his father would not agree to it, and that he could not return to her.

Eadgyth's bitterness, her pride and her solitude, her determination not to speak of Janna's father, began to make sense at last. Janna bowed her head and crouched low, shaken to her very soul by her discovery. She began to cry, a storm of weeping that spoke of her sorrow for a great love gone so badly awry. How different their lives might have been if Eadgyth had only swallowed her pride and asked someone to read the letter to her! How could she have had so little faith in John's good intentions? Why could she not have trusted him?

Thinking of her mother, and the hard life they'd led, and how Eadgyth had died with John's name on her lips, loving him to the end in spite of everything, Janna felt desolate with grief. She sobbed for her mother's mistaken belief in John's betrayal; she sobbed for the father she'd never known, who had loved Eadgyth so much he'd been prepared to defy his father and break an arranged betrothal to marry her. She cried for all that had been lost.

At last, when her tears finally dried, and she was able to think more clearly about the letter and what she had discovered from it, her spirits lifted slightly. John was not a priest after all, for he was expected by his own father to marry someone called Blanche. If he'd had to follow his father to Normandy, it might mean that the family had land there, or perhaps his father had been summoned there by the king? Many barons had land both in Normandy and in England and needed to keep an eye on their interests on both sides of the channel, as did the king himself.

It was clear, from the insignia on the ring, that her father's family were loyal supporters of King Henry. Janna reached into her purse and pulled out the heavy ring, looking at the inscription in the wavering light of the candles. There was a crown on one side and, on the other, a strange beast with a tail. In the center was a swan, forming the letter J. J for John. J for Johanna. Holding the ring gave Janna a feeling of warmth, of connection with her father.

England? Or should she rather seek him in Normandy? If he was there, he might well be there with Blanche, his betrothed, who would not take kindly to her husband's bastard coming to their doorstep. She would probably be sent away. Janna wept anew at the thought of losing her father all over again. It seemed that whenever a door opened for her, it was only to disclose ever more obstacles beyond.

"Please," she whispered to the saint, "please, show me where to go, what I should do next, for I am utterly, utterly lost."

She had no idea what time it was when she finally dried her tears on her sleeve. Feeling cold and stiff after kneeling on the rough stone for so long, she scrambled to her feet. She looked at the wall painting, and at the portrait of the saint that stood so close to the reliquary containing her mortal remains. Grief sat like a cold stone in the pit of her stomach. The letter had told her as much about her mother as about her father, but it had failed to give her the clues she needed to proceed. It hadn't told her where to find him; it hadn't given any hints as to his identity either. Nevertheless, Janna was conscious that she'd taken a significant step forward in her quest.

"Thank you," she whispered to the saint, making up her mind to pick some flowers when next she was in the garden, to show her gratitude. But someone had already got there before her, she realized, as she looked down at the golden casket. A single lily lay on it, fresh and newly picked. Someone had come in this very day to make obeisance to the saint.

Janna thought of the swelling buds and the single bloom in the cloister. The lily hadn't come from there, but might well have come from some other garden. The saint's shrine was open to the public. Anyone could visit it, and someone had. Inevitably, Janna's thoughts went straight to Will—and Agnes.

Chapter 19

Through the long night that followed her discovery, Janna's thoughts moved between her father's message and where it might lead her next, to the significance of the lily on the saint's shrine. Should she tell Agnes about it? Did it mean anything—or not? One moment Janna was sure it did, but almost immediately she would tell herself it was merely happenstance. Her thoughts went round and round: Tell Agnes, or not?

By morning, she was still undecided. She visited the shrine after Mass, just to see if there was any sign she might have missed, anything that might give her some direction. There was a crowd clustered around the casket in the small chapel and the sacristan kept a careful watch over the visitors, as she did whenever the chapel was open to the public. Remembering her vow, Janna had stopped to pick a rose to place on the reliquary. She had to nudge her way past pilgrims and townsfolk, several of whom were on their knees, reverently praying for favors of one sort or another. At last she reached the reliquary. The lily was still there, drooping after a night without water. Beside it was another, freshly picked. Startled, Janna swung around, paying closer attention to all who stood within. There was no sign of Will. Had he come in before Mass, or was someone else responsible for this floral tribute?

Recollecting herself, she kneeled before the saint, and reverently laid the rose beside the lilies. They made a pretty picture; Janna hoped they pleased St Edith, and prayed that the saint's blessing would follow her cause even after she'd left the abbey.

Agnes's cry sounded in Janna's ears: "*If I could only be sure of the right thing to do. If only there was a sign!*" Had her prayer been answered? Janna looked at the lilies and made up her mind. She hurried off to chapter, determined to speak to Agnes without further delay.

The chance to talk to her came later, while Agnes was laboring in the garden and Janna was plucking sunturners for a salve to soothe a nasty rash that seemed to be doing the rounds of the convent. Thanks to Janna's insistence that she continue to learn, Agnes now recognized all of the plants and herbs growing both in the garden and in the physic garden, and was coming to an understanding of their uses. Janna secretly nurtured the hope that, if Agnes didn't leave the abbey, Sister Anne might be willing to take her on as her assistant, once Janna left. She glanced sideways at her friend, thinking it possible that if she married Will, she could put her knowledge to good use among the abbey's servants at the home farm instead. She was conscious that Agnes's fate rested in her hands. She'd miscalculated more than once; she must not do so again.

Agnes had hardly spoken of Will since the fateful day when she'd turned away from him and scurried back into the safety of the abbey. Did she still mourn over chances lost; did she regret her cowardice that day? Janna studied her friend. Was Agnes happy? Or was she now resigned to her future, and making the best of it in her own resilient way?

Janna wished for a sign of her own—and found it in a graceful trumpet of white, the first among the lilies in the garden to open. She called Agnes's attention to it, adding, "The lilies we planted in the cloister are also starting to open. The lilies from Master Will. I saw one yesterday. Sister Ursel is using it to illustrate her manuscript." She tensed as she waited for Agnes's response.

Agnes said nothing for a moment. Then she walked over to the flower and cupped it gently in her hands. "It's beautiful." There was no mistaking the sadness on her face, the note of longing in her voice.

"I visited St Edith's shrine yesterday," Janna said, tentatively feeling her way. "There was a lily lying on her casket," she added quickly, lest Agnes ask the purpose of her visit.

"A lily? Why? What for?"

"What do you think?"

"A-a token in honor of our saint?"

"Maybe."

Agnes stood motionless, staring down at the lily still cupped in her hands. "A sign?" she whispered.

"Maybe."

Agnes released the flower and swung around to face Janna. "What should I do?" She seized Janna's hand, her face open and full of anguish. "Please…tell me what to do."

"I don't know." Janna was determined not to interfere. Nevertheless, she clasped her free hand over Agnes's to show her love and support. "What do you want to do?"

Agnes shrugged her shoulders and shook her head.

Janna told herself to hold her tongue. It was for Agnes to make the decision, not her. "Do you care for Master Will?" she heard herself asking. "Do you care enough for him to leave the abbey and the life that you know? Do you trust him enough to love you for yourself, and to protect you from all that you fear?"

"I don't know." Agnes's eyes filled with tears of longing and loss. "I just don't know."

"Can you honestly say that all your heart belongs to God instead?"

Agnes was silent for a long time. "No," she whispered at last.

"Then we need to make a plan." Janna thought about it for a few moments. "I noticed the lily when I visited the saint's shrine yesterday afternoon," she said. "It was lying on the reliquary, all by itself. I went again this morning, after Mass, to take a rose to St Edith. There were a lot of people there, and there was another lily on the casket, a fresh one lying beside the one from yesternoon. I looked about for any sign of Master Will, but he wasn't there. But he might have come earlier, before the Mass started. The sacristan would allow him entry, if he came alone."

Janna paused. She was so afraid of saying the wrong thing to Agnes, of either frightening her off or of raising false hopes that might well be shattered if Will had indeed given up his suit and bestowed his affections elsewhere. She wished, with all her heart, that she knew the truth behind the lilies at the shrine. All she had to guide her was Will himself, his professed love for Agnes, his words after he'd handed over the lily bulbs: "*Tell Agnes to remember my pledge whenever she sees these flowers, for they remind me of her and they are a living token of my love.*"

This was not the action of a fickle man, Janna thought. This was the action of a man who knew his own mind and was prepared to wait—at least until the lilies bloomed.

"What if we're wrong? What if someone else is leaving the lilies at the shrine?" Agnes gazed down at the flower as she put Janna's fears into words.

"If we're wrong, nothing will have changed. But isn't it better to take action, to risk everything, rather than live your life knowing that you had not the courage to follow your heart when you had the chance to find happiness?" Janna gave Agnes's hand a final squeeze and released it. It was Agnes's decision. She must make it alone.

"But how am I to act? What shall I do?" Agnes's question encouraged Janna to believe that she had indeed found the courage to follow her heart.

"Will gave the lily bulbs to you 'as a living token of his love,' he said. Now it's up to you to leave him a sign, a sign that you return his love."

"A lily?" Agnes's eyes lit with joy. "Shall I put a lily next to the lilies already on the reliquary?"

Janna shrugged. "It's up to you," she said noncommittally, although her heart sang with relief.

"And should I take the lily to the shrine before Mass starts, not after?"

"Good idea." Janna smiled at Agnes. Agnes grinned back. "Then you must come with me," she said firmly. "I'm not *that* brave, you know! And will you pick the lily for me, just in case I can't come into the cloister before Mass?"

"Isn't picking flowers in the cloister a Sin?" Janna spoke gravely, but her eyes twinkled with mischief.

"Not if the flower is for St Edith," Agnes said firmly.

"Or even for Master Will?" Janna was delighted with the way things had turned out. "I'll meet you at the shrine as soon as you've broken your fast," she promised. She bent down to pluck some more sunturners.

But with her own concerns now settled, Agnes's thoughts had moved on to a new question. "And what were you doing at St Edith's shrine?" she asked. "I didn't think you believed in saints and miracles and all that sort of thing."

Janna slowly straightened. She was reluctant to discuss her mother and what had gone before, but she'd meddled so much in Agnes's life, she felt she owed her friend something in return. She'd asked Agnes if she trusted Will. She should similarly ask herself if she trusted Agnes, for trust was not something that came readily to her. That much she had learned from Eadgyth.

"I went there to read a letter." She stopped, wondering how much of her life she could, or should, disclose. "I don't know who my father is, you see, and I'm beginning to realize I know hardly anything about my mother either. But after she died, I found a letter that she'd hidden from me. It was written by my father, but I couldn't read it. That's why I came here to the abbey: to learn how to read and write. And finally, yesterday, I was able to read what he'd written to my mother, and understand the tragedy of their lives."

Janna's eyes filled with tears as she recounted the contents of the letter, and what it had meant to her mother.

"That's why you want me to have the courage to trust Will, to follow my heart!" Agnes exclaimed.

Surprised, Janna nodded. "Yes, I suppose that's true."

"So what will you do now?"

"I have to leave the abbey. I have no reason to stay on here."

"But where will you go? What will you do?"

"I'll continue to look for my father."

Agnes frowned. "You say the letter has told you nothing about him, who he is or where he lives. How will you know where to find him?"

"I don't know. Maybe I should try to find a passage to Normandy, in case he's still there with Blanche?"

"Where was your mother when she met him, do you know? He might well have property there. He may even be there still."

"That's a wonderful idea!" Janna's face blazed bright with the excitement of hope. "Sister Ursel told me my mother was the infirmarian at Ambresberie Abbey, so that's where I'll go."

"Your mother was a *nun?*" Agnes's eyes grew round with horror.

Janna gave her friend a shaky smile. "If she can risk everything for love, when she'd already taken her vows, so can you!"

Ambresberie. Feeling stronger, more sure of herself now that she had some direction, now that the decision was made, Janna bent once more to the sunturners. They lay before her like small golden patches of sunshine, reflecting Janna's growing optimism, the sense that her path had been made clear and that she, too, could turn her face to the sun. Along with Agnes's lily, she would bring some sunturners to the saint's shrine on the morrow.

*

"I am very pleased with the way you have settled into the abbey," Sister Anne said, as Janna entered the infirmary kitchen, her basket full of flowers and herbs. "And although you already knew a great deal when you arrived here, I am also pleased by your willingness to learn new skills, new ways of thinking and doing things."

"You're a very good teacher, Sister Anne, and I am very grateful to you." Janna set the rush basket down on the kitchen table. She knew it would be hard to speak of her plans and say goodbye to the infirmarian, but realized that she must do so while the weather was still set fair for traveling. She was about to speak when Sister Anne forestalled her.

"Now is as good a time as any to talk to you about something that has been on my mind for quite a while," the infirmarian said. "I know that, at first, you found it difficult to adapt to the ways of the abbey, but now that you are used to us I believe you need to think of your future. I realize you have no dowry, but I am prepared to speak to Abbess Hawise on your behalf, to ask if she will accept you into the abbey as a novice, preparatory to taking your vows."

"But I—"

Sister Anne raised her hand and spoke over Janna. "I am getting on in years, I won't always be here to physick our sisters. That's why I've paid special attention to you, why I've made sure to tell you all I know, and given you the experience of ministering to our sisters' needs, which I know you lacked before. You are worthy—more than worthy—to follow in my footsteps, Johanna. When I go, I will go with peace of mind, secure in the knowledge that my sisters in Christ will be well cared for by you."

Janna was appalled by the infirmarian's words, and by her expectations. She didn't know what to say. Nor could she even suggest that Agnes take her place, not after what they planned to do on the morrow. It was an impossible situation!

"What do you say, Johanna?" Sister Anne looked at her expectantly.

Janna closed her eyes, praying for guidance. Not for anything would she upset the infirmarian, not after the chance the nun had taken on bringing her into the infirmary, and all the care and attention she had lavished on her tuition. And yet upset was inevitable—unless she abandoned her quest and stayed on at the abbey.

Janna was tempted to do just that. She loved the work she did here; it gave her the greatest satisfaction to care for people and to heal their hurts. And she enjoyed the respect she'd earned as Sister Anne's trusted helper and a healer in her own right. She'd become accustomed, now, to abbey life, the quiet round of devotion, the melodious chants, being cared for and protected within the confines of the abbey. She was safe from Mus here. And safe also from the temptations of her heart—from Hugh and from Godric.

No! She opened her eyes and straightened her shoulders, mentally preparing herself for what needed to be said. "I'm so sorry, Sister Anne, but I have to leave here, and soon," she said. "I sought refuge here, yes, but the threat has passed..." Janna supposed that once she left the abbey, Robert would have no way of knowing where she'd gone and thus would be unable to act against her. The notion gave her comfort, and the courage to continue. "I also wanted to learn how to read and write and, thanks to Sister Ursel, I am able to do that now." She took Sister Anne's hand, and pressed it. "You have been like a mother to me," she said, her voice husky with emotion for it was only now, at the leaving, that she was fully aware of just how much she owed the infirmarian, and how close they had become. "I am more grateful to you than I can say, but I—I have to go. I'm searching for my unknown father, you see, and I know now what the next step of my journey must be."

"And that is?" Sister Anne's voice was harsh with disappointment.

"To go to Ambresberie." Janna hesitated. "It seems my mother, Eadgyth, was once the infirmarian at the abbey there."

"The infirmarian at Ambresberie?" Sister Anne's eyes widened. "Emanuelle!" she breathed. The hard lines of her face softened into reminiscence. "You spoke of 'Eadgyth,' but your mother would have left her own name behind when she entered the abbey and took her vows. If you go there, you must ask for information about Sister Emanuelle. She was your mother, Johanna. She was also legendary as a healer, and as something of a free thinker." The infirmarian's lips twitched upward with amusement as she looked at Janna. "It certainly explains a lot!"

Sister Emanuelle! Giving her mother a new name made her past seem even more mysterious, although it was hard for Janna to think of her in any other way than as her mother. "What else do you know about her?" she asked eagerly.

"I remember hearing that the infirmarian at Ambresberie had died quite suddenly, and that the convent was without anyone to physick them for quite some time, until a *wortwyf* arrived saying that she had a gift for healing which she wished to dedicate to God. It was a long time ago, of course, but that's how I remember it."

"My mother?" breathed Janna. Sister Anne nodded briskly. "She was said to have no formal training, but she obviously taught you all she knew. Certes, you have inherited her gift, and now you have the knowledge to go with it."

"Thank you, Sister Anne," said Janna. "I'm truly grateful to you for everything you've taught me, and also for telling me about my mother. I'm sorry, so sorry, to disappoint you."

"Searching for your mother isn't going to change anything, prove anything," Sister Anne said, determined not to be thwarted in her plans. "You know now who she is. Was. And you said before that you know nothing of your father. How do you plan to find him?"

"I don't know. I can only take one step at a time," Janna answered honestly.

Sister Anne sighed in frustration. "Why not leave the past in the past, and think about your own future, Johanna? A young woman traveling the road on her own..." She clicked her tongue, tutting her disapproval. "If you take your vows, you can live here as one of us. You'll be doing something no-one else here can do. You'll have a roof over your head, a bed to lie on, and regular meals to fill your belly. You will have a home and a family. More, you will be serving God. Are you really prepared to throw all this away, your life here with us, to chase after someone who has never known or acknowledged you, and who may even be dead by now?"

It was a fair question. And Sister Anne's arguments regarding Janna's comfort were compelling, but they also pricked her conscience. She recognized her debt to the infirmarian and hated to disappoint her. She hesitated, torn between wanting to honor her debt while also staying in the safety of the abbey, or honoring her promise to her mother that her death would be avenged. She remembered, then, her words to Agnes: "*Isn't it better to take action, to risk everything, rather than live your life knowing that you had not the courage to follow your heart when you had the chance to find happiness?*"

She would do well to follow her own advice. "I would stay if I could, you know that, but I have to go," she said, adding, "And I am sorry for it, Sister Anne, for I wish I could stay to help you. I shall miss you. I shall miss everyone here at the abbey." It was not quite true. The whining gnat, and Sister Catherine and her awful dog—she certainly wouldn't miss them! But Sister Anne, and Agnes and Ursel...

"I'm sorry," she said again, wishing she was able to explain the reasons behind her decision, for she was sure the infirmarian would understand if she knew the facts.

"I'm sorry too." The infirmarian nodded, accepting that Janna's mind was made up. "One good thing about your coming here," she said, determined to look on the bright side. "I've realized how much I need a knowledgeable assistant, and I shall waste no time in finding a replacement for you, Johanna."

It was somewhat humbling to think she could be replaced so quickly and so easily! But, meeting the infirmarian's rueful glance, Janna understood the truth behind her brisk words. She wondered who her replacement would be, and hoped she would prove worthy, for Janna had come to have great respect for Sister Anne's knowledge, as well as her kind ways with her patients and her skill in dealing with their many aches and ills.

"When do you plan to leave?" The infirmarian's question broke into Janna's thoughts.

"Soon." As soon as Agnes's future was assured, Janna thought. "Quite soon," she amended.

Sister Anne gestured toward the plants Janna had gathered. "Then I must make good use of you while you're still here," she said, and set her to work.

*

Restless, unable to sleep, Janna rose early the following morning. Her heart felt leaden at the prospect of leaving the abbey, leaving behind the friends she had made there—and elsewhere, she thought, recognizing that part of her reluctance to leave was the thought of never seeing Godric or Hugh again. She would never know if Hugh had found someone worthy to marry, someone with a large dowry and land of her own. Nor would she know if Godric and Cecily had found happiness together. There was grief in her heart, but also a faint stir of excitement at the thought of the challenge ahead, and the rewards that might await her.

How would she travel on the road to Ambresberie? Janna looked down at her habit. Emma's gift had been generous; it would pay for food and lodging on the journey. But she could not travel alone, not dressed as she was. Could she reclaim her smock and breeches from Sister Grace? By now they'd probably been donated to a good cause but it was worth asking the sister for help. She would also have to take leave of the abbess. Janna's spirits sank at the prospect.

Remembering her vow, she first visited the garden to pick sunturners. Clutching a posy of bright flowers, she went through to the cloister to pick the lily, the first to unfold its petals and show off its pristine beauty. It was fitting, she thought, that Agnes should carry the first of the blooms to Will. If the lay sister hadn't lost her courage overnight. If Will came. If they hadn't entirely misread the situation and what it meant.

So afraid was Janna of missing the bailiff, she decided to forego the morning bread and ale with which the nuns broke their fast, and go straight to the shrine. Early as she was, Agnes was there before her, and she greeted Janna with a gasp of relief.

"Thank you." She took the single lily from Janna. She was about to lay it on the shrine beside the other two but changed her mind and kept on holding it instead. She waited while Janna placed the marigolds on the casket and closed her eyes to murmur a brief prayer of thanks to the saint.

"I have news for you," she whispered, once Janna had returned to her side. Although reluctant to disturb the sanctity of the saint's shrine, Agnes was eager to pass on what she'd learned. "Some pilgrims are staying here, visiting the hand as well as the shrine of our own saint on their journey home. They've come from Santiago de Compostela. I heard them speak of their pilgrimage to the shrine of Saint James, and their desire to see the missing part of the saint that is now kept here."

"So?" Janna wondered why Agnes sounded so excited. Pilgrims often lodged at the abbey. Even if these had traveled from as far away as Spain, pilgrims often made long journeys to important shrines.

"They come from Oxeneford, and that is where they are going now," Agnes said breathlessly.

"So?" Janna was still at a loss to understand.

"So, I heard them say they plan to break their journey at Ambresberie Abbey on their way home."

"Ah." Janna began to smile.

"You could travel with them," Agnes pressed on. "It would keep you safe if you had company, especially the company of pilgrims. There are women as well as men among them, so you won't need to defend your honor."

"Defend my honor against pilgrims? Surely not!"

"Never forget that they are men first, pilgrims second." Janna was amused by Agnes's cynicism, until she remembered that the lay sister had grown up in the abbey and must have observed the antics of countless pilgrims in her time. She should remember Agnes's remark, for it might well stand her in good stead in the future.

"When do they leave?" she asked.

"Today, after they've attended Mass and visited the saint's relic one last time. You must speak to them before they go." Agnes clutched Janna's hand, suddenly aware of her impending loss. "I shall miss you so much," she said. "The abbey won't be the same without you."

"You might not be here for much longer yourself." Janna hoped, with all her heart, that her words were true.

"I'm afraid. I'm so afraid."

"Have courage. If he doesn't come, you are no worse off than if you'd never taken action at all. But at least now you have the chance to find out what might be, or you'll know what might have been." Janna wasn't sure if she was being much comfort to Agnes. Beside her, Agnes tensed, and held a finger to her mouth in warning.

They could hear the click of boots on stone. Someone was walking down the nave. They glanced at each other. Agnes's grip on the lily tightened. There was the sound of a key turning in a lock, a faint creak, then the low murmur of voices.

"I'll make sure I lock the gate behind me when I leave, Sister." A man's figure came into view, silhouetted dark against the bright sunlight slanting through the window to the east. Janna squinted at the figure, almost sure it was Will. Beside her, Agnes took a frightened breath.

The man stepped into the small chapel. His face was lit now in the soft light from the candles around the saint's shrine, and they could see his features clearly. It was Will.

In his hand, he carried a single lily. His eyes widened when he noticed he was not alone. He stopped abruptly. His gaze settled on Agnes's face. He smiled, and held out the lily.

Frozen with terror, Agnes stayed where she was. Will's smile slipped a little. Janna stuck out her elbow and gave Agnes a hard shove, propelling her forward. With a small cry, she catapulted toward Will, who opened his arms to her and enfolded her tight.

Janna held her breath as she watched them, watched Agnes cling to the bailiff, shaking with fear; watched him patting her shoulder, gentling her as he would a nervous palfrey.

"I came to ask our blessed saint to intercede on my behalf, to speak to you when I could not," he murmured.

Agnes was still for a moment. Then she raised her face to gaze at him. "I heard you," she said, and held out the lily. Keeping one arm around her, Will took the lily and placed the two flowers on the reliquary, muttering a brief prayer of thanks as he did so. He turned back to Agnes. With gentle fingers, he stroked the rough scars that criss-crossed her cheek. Agnes closed her eyes and stood quiet under his touch before raising her face to his as his lips sought hers.

Knowing it was safe to go, knowing Agnes no longer needed her, Janna silently crept away, walking on tiptoes so as not to disturb the pair or remind them of her presence.

She carried on her person all that she meant to take away with her from the abbey, but she still had no answer for what to wear on her journey. A moment's reflection sent her scurrying to the refectory, where the sisters were still assembled to break their fast. She waited until they had finished before approaching Sister Grace.

"I'm leaving the abbey today, and I must return my wimple and habit before I go, but I have naught else to wear. Can you help me, please, Sister?"

Sister Grace's mouth twitched. "Do you wish to go forth as a youth once more, or are you planning another disguise?" she asked gravely.

"No!" Janna thought about it. "Yes." Even in the company of pilgrims she would be safer traveling as a youth than a girl, she decided.

The nun looked at her thoughtfully. "Your smock and breeches are gone. The wardrober gave them to the cowherd's eldest son. But there's a nice new gown that would fit you. It belonged to one of our young postulants who has decided she wishes to take the veil."

A nice new gown? Janna liked the sound of that. "If you can spare it, I would be grateful, Sister Grace," she said humbly.

"Then come along with me now." Sister Grace turned and, without ado, led the way from the refectory to the storeroom where Janna had first met her. It seemed like a lifetime ago.

Reluctant to waste a costly kirtle on a lowly lay sister, the wardrober argued with Sister Grace, trying instead to persuade her to take a ragged robe that had been left behind by the family of a dying woman. Neither knew that Janna could understand Norman French and, once she realized what was happening, she was too embarrassed to enlighten them. She was grateful to Sister Grace, who would not take the shabby garment from the wardrober but, instead, snatched up a beautiful blue kirtle and refused to give it back.

"She deserves it," Sister Grace insisted. "I heard she came here with a full purse, and our abbess took every last coin from her. At the very least, we can give her this." She held it out to Janna.

"Thank you. It's beautiful."

Sister Grace gave a pleased nod, satisfied with her successful transaction.

"May I change in the dorter?" Not for anything would Janna let them see the full purse secreted under her habit, lest the wardrober prove every bit as greedy as the abbess had been.

The wardrober gave a grudging nod. "You may as well have the slippers that go with the gown," she said, adding in French, "'Tis true she has worked hard while here. Sister Anne says she has her mother's skill with healing, and has given our convent the best of care." Janna ducked her head to hide her pleasure, and took her treasures off to the dorter.

Her transformation was completed in only a few moments. She smoothed her hand down the silky blue fabric of her gown and smiled, well content. She had never worn anything so fine in her life. Her smile grew broader as she reached up to secure the fine gauzy veil that completed the ensemble. Her hair, grown long again, fell loose around her neck. She longed for a mirror to see what she looked like, elated to think she was no longer bound by the Sin of Pride.

"You look quite the young lady now," Sister Grace laughed, as she returned with the garments she'd been wearing in the abbey. "For certes, more attractive than the ragged ruffian I first encountered!"

Janna laughed with her. "Thank you, Sister. Thank you for your kindness."

"And thank you for your kindness to us, Johanna," the nun replied. Seeing Janna's surprise, she continued, "I have watched your progress here with great interest. I have seen how lovingly you have cared for our sisters. I share Sister Anne's regret that you are leaving us. We shall all miss you, you know."

"As I shall miss you." Janna reached out and gave her an impulsive hug, remembering too late that close physical contact with another sister was a sin. She tried to pull back. "I'm sorry," she apologized.

But Grace was smiling as she returned Janna's hug. "Don't worry," she whispered. "The Rule no longer applies to you, not if you're leaving us."

The Rule. Janna felt the burden of sins, both real and imaginary, slip from her shoulders. She felt light and free—and also vulnerable. The abbey had been her home for almost a year. There was so much she would miss.

Her interview with the abbess was brief. Remembering her previous lost opportunities and determined not to waste this last one, Janna asked Abbess Hawise for information about her mother.

"She was a disgrace to her convent; that is all I know."

Janna was sure the abbess hadn't forgotten the scene with Dame Alice. Probably the abbess's condemnation of her mother now extended to Janna herself. She knew she would get nothing further from the abbess, nor would she miss her in the least.

It was a lot harder to say farewell to Sister Ursel and to Sister Anne. "Promise you'll come and visit us, if ever you pass this way again?" Ursel demanded, and Janna promised that she would. There were tears in her eyes and fear in her heart as she crossed the cloister for the last time, and walked through the outer parlor to the courtyard beyond. She would stay for Mass and speak afterwards to the pilgrims, she decided. There was no time to do it now, for the Mass was about to start.

She walked into the nave, mingling once more with the abbey's guests, the lay servants, the beggars and pilgrims, just as she had done when first she came. Ahead of her, she spied Agnes and hurried toward her friend. The lay sister was standing beside Will, their hands touching but not clasped, as befitted the solemnity of this sacred place. Neither of them held lilies now; St Edith's task was done and her deed had been honored and commemorated.

Janna smiled as she sidled into place on her friend's other side. Agnes glanced quickly at her, and then away. "Agnes!" Janna was wounded by her friend's indifference.

Agnes's head swiveled around. Her eyes widened in shocked recognition. "Jesu, it's you!" She looked Janna up and down. "Why are you wearing those clothes?"

"Because I'm leaving today, with the pilgrims. Because I'm not a lay sister any longer."

Agnes's face fell. Janna reached for her hand.

"I can't stay, you know that. But neither can you?" It was a question, rather than a statement. Janna hoped she knew the answer, and felt a great relief when Agnes nodded shyly.

"Will's asked me to be his wife, and I have agreed to it," she whispered. "We will go to see the abbess after Mass, to see if my childhood vows may be broken and to ask what needs to be done."

"Sister Anne will help you, if necessary." Janna looked from Agnes to Will. "I wish you great happiness in your life together," she said softly, and sank to her knees as the procession passed up the nave. She breathed in the spicy incense that scented the air as the young acolyte swung the censer, taking comfort from the sturdy stone walls of the great church and a ritual that dated back almost to the time of Christ. So had it always been; so would it be long after she was gone. It made her realize that, while her quest was important to her, it was the smallest stitch in the fabric of God's great plan.

Janna smiled to herself. God didn't need her help to run the world, but he would surely expect her to do what she could to help herself.

Her way had been made clear to her, and she would follow it. She would find her father and, at the same time, fulfill her vow to avenge the death of her mother by bringing the culprit to justice. She had made a good start. She resolved that she would do all in her power to make a good finish. She bent her head and joined in with the congregation as the priest began to pray.

Glossary

Aelfshot: A belief that illness or a sudden pain (like rheumatism, arthritis or a "stitch") was caused by elves who shot humans or livestock with darts.

Ague: Fever and chills.

Alewife: Ale was a common drink in the middle ages. Housewives brewed their own for domestic use, while alewives brewed the ale served in alehouses and taverns. A bush tied to a pole was the recognized symbol of an alehouse, at a time when most of the population could not read.

Amercement: A financial penalty imposed on those found guilty of a crime.

Amor vincit omnia: Love conquers all.

Apothecary: Someone who prepares and sells medicines, and perhaps spices and rare goods.

Baron: A noble of high rank, a tenant-in-chief who holds his lands from the king.

Bailiff: Appointed by the abbess (or a baron) to manage the home farm, mills, etc.

Boonwork: At busy times in the farming year (such as haymaking and harvest) villeins were required to work extra days in the lord's fields. In return, they were given food and ale.

Breeches: Trousers held up by a cord running through the hem at the waist.

Canonical hours: The medieval day was governed by sunrise and sunset, divided into seven canonical hours. Times of prayer were marked by bells rung in abbeys and monasteries beginning with Matins at midnight, followed by Lauds, Prime, Terce, Sext and Nones through the day. Vespers was at sunset, followed by Compline before going to bed.

Cellaress: Responsible for everything to do with food and supplies for the cellar, refectory, kitchen, mill, bakehouse and also the gardens, woods and farm produce.

Chantress: Responsible for the choir, for books, and for teaching singing and reading.

Chapman: Pedlar.

Cot: Small cottage.

Cresset: A primitive light made from a wick floating in a bowl of oil or animal fat.

Currency: While large sums of money could be reckoned in pounds or marks, the actual currency for trading was silver pennies. There were twelve to a shilling and twenty shillings to a pound. A penny could also be cut into half, called a "ha'penny", or a quarter, called a "farthing".

Dorter: Dormitory.

Dower/dowry: A sum of money paid for a woman, either as a marriage settlement or to secure her place in an abbey.

Feudal system: A political, social and economic system based on the relationship of lord to vassal, in which land was held on condition of homage and service. Following the Norman conquest, William I distributed land once owned by Saxon "ealdormen" (chief men) to his own barons, who in turn distributed land and manors to sub-tenants in return for fees, knight service and, in the case of the villeins, work in the fields. The Abbess of Wilton held an entire barony from the king and owed the service of five knights in return.

Hagiography: The written life of a saint.

Hayward: Manorial official in charge of haymaking and harvest, and the repair and upkeep of hedges and ditches.

Heriot: A death duty to the lord of the manor, usually comprising the best beast, and sometimes also some household goods such as metal utensils or uncut cloth. This constituted "payment" for the loss of a worker.

Hue and cry: With no practicing police force other than a town sergeant to enforce the law, anyone discovering a crime was expected to "raise a hue and cry"—shouting aloud to alert the community to the fact that a crime had been committed, after which all those within earshot must commence pursuit of the criminal.

Infirmarian: Takes care of the sick in the infirmary (abbey hospital).

Kirtle: Long dress worn over a short tunic.

Lavatorium: Washroom.

Leechcraft: A system of healing practiced during the time of the Anglo-Saxons, which included the use of herbs, plants, medicines, magical incantations and spells, charms and precious stones.

Misericord: A room in the infirmary where strict dietary rules do not apply.

Mortuary: Death duty paid by a villein to the parish priest—usually the second-best beast.

Novice: After about a year serving as a postulant, and if your vocation remains firm, you become a novice until such time as you are deemed ready to take your final vows.

Obedientiary: Holder of an office within a convent (or a monastery) eg sacristan, porteress, chantress, cellaress.

Oblate: A young child given to a monastery or abbey by its parents.

Pilgrim: Anyone who makes a journey to a sacred place.

Postulant: Anyone who enters the abbey with the intention of becoming a nun.

Pottage: A vegetable soup or stew.

Reeve: The reeve was usually appointed by the villagers, and was responsible for the management of the manor. Shire reeves (sheriffs) were appointed by the king to administer law and justice in the shires (counties).

Reredorter: Lavatory.

Rule of St Benedict: St Benedict lived circa 480–547 AD, and composed his *Regula Monachorum* (Rule for Monasteries) in 515 AD. This became the common Rule for all Western monachism, directing monks to live in religious houses, observe all the usual religious exercises and employ themselves in manual labor, teaching, copying manuscripts, etc. Seventy-three "chapters" of direction make up the Rule.

Sacristan: Looks after the sacred relics and treasures of the abbey.

Scapular: A loose, sleeveless tunic worn while doing rough work.

Scrip: A small bag.

Scriptorium: A room in a monastery (or abbey) where monks (or nuns) wrote, copied and illuminated manuscripts. In a private home it served as the office of the estate.

Steward: Appointed by a baron to manage an estate.

Tiring woman: A female attendant on a lady of high birth and importance.

Villein: Peasant or serf tied to a manor and to an overlord, and given land in return for labor and a fee—either money or produce.

Wardrober: In charge of clothing including sewing, spinning and weaving fabric, and providing animal hide for shoes, etc.

Water meadows: The land on either side of a river that floods regularly.

Wimple: Linen head cover draped over hair and around cheeks and neck.

Wortwyf: A herb wife, a wise woman and healer.

Glossary of Latin terms from the Mass:

In nomine Patris, et Filii, et Spiritu Sancti, Amen. In the name of the Father, and of the Son, and of the Holy Spirit, Amen.

Gloria Patri, et Filio, et Spiritui Sancto. Glory be to the Father, and to the Son, and to the Holy Spirit.

Sicut erat in principio, et nunc, et semper, et in saecula saeculorum, Amen. As it was in the beginning, is now, and ever shall be, world without end, Amen.

Author's Note

The Janna Chronicles are set in the 1140s, at a turbulent time in England's history. After Henry I's son, William, drowned in the *White Ship* disaster, Henry was left with only one legitimate heir, his daughter, Matilda (sometimes known as Maude). At the age of eight, she was betrothed to a much older man, Heinrich, Emperor of Germany, and she was sent to live in that country until, aged twelve, she was considered old enough to marry him. Evidently she was beloved by the Germans, who begged her to stay on after the Emperor died, but at the age of twenty-four, and childless, Matilda was summoned back to England by her father. For political reasons, and despite Matilda's vehement protests, Henry insisted that she marry Count Geoffrey of Anjou, a boy some ten years her junior. They married in 1128, and the first of their three sons, Henry (later to become Henry II of England), was born in 1133.

Henry I announced Matilda his heir and twice demanded that his barons, including her cousin, Stephen of Blois, all swear an oath of allegiance to her. This they did, but when Henry died, Matilda went to Normandy while Stephen went straight to London to gather support, and then on to Winchester, where he claimed the Treasury and was crowned King of England.

Not one to be denied her rights, Matilda gathered her own supporters, including her illegitimate half-brother, Robert of Gloucester, and in 1139 she landed at Arundel Castle in England, prepared to fight for the crown. She left her children with Geoffrey, who thereafter stayed in Anjou and in Normandy, pursuing his own interests. Civil war between Stephen and Matilda raged in England for nineteen years, creating such hardship and misery that the *Peterborough Chronicle* reported: "Never before had there been greater wretchedness in the country ... They said openly that Christ and His saints slept."

I became interested in this period of English history while researching the Shalott trilogy. As this new series began to fall into place, I realized that this time of shifting allegiances and treachery, of fierce battles and daring escapes, of great danger and cruelty, formed a perfect setting with many plot possibilities. Janna's quest to find her father brings her into the company of nobles, peasants and pilgrims, jongleurs and nuns, spies and assassins, and even King Stephen and the Empress Matilda. With England in the grip of civil war, secrets abound, loyalties change and passions run high. Janna will encounter the darkest side of human nature: the jealousy, greed, ambition, deceit and fear which so often lead to betrayal and murder. As well as solving the mystery of her past, and of her heart, Janna's mission is to find out the truth and bring the guilty to judgment. But she will need great courage, intelligence and insight to escape danger, and also to solve the many crimes she encounters along her journey.

A note about the hand of St James the Apostle. This relic was given to Matilda by her husband, on their marriage. After his death, and to the dismay of the German people, Matilda brought the relic back to England. It was given to Reading Abbey by her father, Henry I, who was also buried there. I felt some indignation on Matilda's behalf (the hand was given to her, not to her father) so I took the liberty of moving the hand to Wiltune (where her own mother had spent her childhood) on the grounds of safekeeping, for it is true that Reading Abbey took some time in the building—forty years in all—while the citizens of Reading supported the king rather than Matilda.

For those interested in learning more about the civil war between Stephen and Matilda, there are numerous biographies on both of them, while Sharon Penman's *When Christ and His Saints Slept* is an excellent account of that period. On a lighter note, I have much enjoyed the Brother Cadfael Chronicles by Ellis Peters, which are also set at that time. While Janna's loyalty lies in a different direction from Ellis Peters' characters, her skill with herbs was inspired by these wonderful stories of the herbalist at Shrewsbury Abbey.

The Janna Chronicles begin in Wiltshire, England. Janna's quest for truth and justice will take her from the forest of Gravelinges (now known as Grovely Wood) to royal Winchestre, seat of power where the Treasury was housed. I've kept to the place names listed in the *Domesday Book* compiled by William the Conqueror in 1086, but the contemporary names of some of the sites are: Berford (Barford St Martin); Babestoche (Baverstock); Bredecumbe (Burcombe); Wiltune (Wilton); Sarisberie (Sarum; later relocated and named Salisbury); Oxeneford (Oxford), and Winchestre (Winchester).

The royal forest of Gravelinges was the only forest in Wiltshire mentioned in the *Domesday Book*. While it has diminished in size since medieval time, I have experienced at first hand how easy it is to get utterly lost once you stray off the path! Wiltune was the ancient capital of Wessex. The abbey was established in Saxon times and became one of the most prosperous in England, ranked with the houses of Shaftesbury, Barking and Winchester as a nunnery of the first importance.

Following the dissolution of the monasteries during the reign of Henry VIII, ownership of the abbey's lands passed to William Herbert, lst Earl of Pembroke. Some 450 years later, the 18th Earl of Pembroke now owns this vast estate. A magnificent stately home, Wilton House, stands in place of the abbey and is open to visitors.

While writing medieval England from Australia is a difficult and hazardous enterprise, I have been fortunate in the support and encouragement I've received along the way. So many people have helped make this series possible, and in particular I'd like to thank the following: Nick and Wendy Combes of Burcombe Manor, for taking me into their family, giving me a home away from home and teaching me about life on a farm, both now and in medieval time. Ros Liddington, for showing me around Wilton House and helping me with its history. Author Sophie Masson, who provided the French translation of John's letter. Dr Gillian Polack, whose knowledge of medieval life helped shape the series and gave it veracity. Finally, my thanks to all at Momentum for their thought, care and expertise, and for enabling me to introduce the Janna Chronicles to a whole new audience.